MW00903457

Hurricane Park

KELLEY DUPUIS

authorHOUSE®

AuthorHouse™
1663 Liberty Drive
Bloomington, IN 47403
www.authorhouse.com
Phone: 1 (800) 839-8640

Published by AuthorHouse 07/13/2020

ISBN: 978-1-7283-6681-4 (sc)
ISBN: 978-1-7283-6679-1 (hc)
ISBN: 978-1-7283-6680-7 (e)

Library of Congress Control Number: 2020912164

Print information available on the last page.

This book is printed on acid-free paper.

For Kelviyn Marshall

"Over the hill and out of the woods..."

“God, who created us without our help, cannot
save us without our consent.”
– St. Augustine

1

I don't remember when I first met Cyrus. I do remember when I first met Sandy.

That's something new to me, that stumbling of memory. When I was young, people were always impressed with my memory. For years I had an uncanny ability to remember not just events, but details. When my father was alive he used to say "That goddamn Patrick could tell you what Adam and Eve had for breakfast!" No more. That comes with getting old I guess.

She sat on a bench, reading a newspaper. It was a warm afternoon in October and Sandy was sitting in the sun, on a bench under a tree in the park, reading the L.A. Times. Despite the warm weather she wore a windbreaker. She had a cigarette between two fingers of her left hand. Every now and then she would reach up and adjust her glasses, or flick away ash from the cigarette. Next to her on the sidewalk was a grocery cart. Not a shopping cart like the ones you find in supermarkets, but one of those two-wheeled things you can drag around with one hand, the kind women used to take to the grocery store in my mother's day. From the look of things Sandy kept all of her important stuff in it.

I sat down on the same bench. She shifted a bit, although I'd made sure I wasn't sitting too close to her. She didn't look at me, didn't take her eyes off the newspaper. Over her shoulder I spied a headline: "Navy Missile Test Creates Bright Light Across California Sky."

It was early afternoon and I was starting to feel hungry. I had just come out of the library, about a hundred yards from where we were sitting, and was wondering what I should do with myself next. After all, I had the rest of the day to kill and now, the night too. And the next day and the next night. I still had a few dollars in my pocket, and I thought about going over to 7-Eleven to grab a deli sandwich. Maybe a beer. But it could wait. I wasn't all that hungry just yet, although a beer sounded good. Mostly I was still feeling a little bewildered. I had only been on the street since that morning. I had gotten off a plane from overseas a day or two before and was where I was because I had no place else to go.

Sandy looked around, not at me, though. She adjusted her glasses again, put the newspaper on the bench between us, reached into her jacket pocket and took out a plastic 175 ml. flask of Popov. She took a sip, re-capped and returned the plastic bottle to her pocket and went back to reading the newspaper.

Looking at the front page while she took her quick belt, I pointed to the headline about the Navy missile test. "I'll bet some people thought that was a UFO," I said.

"What?"

"That story there, about the missile making a bright light in the sky last night." I squinted at the story's lead.

She looked where I was pointing. "Yeah," was her only reply. She puffed on her cigarette and glanced at me for a second. "I don't think I know you from around here," she said.

"I've only been homeless for...what, two days?"

"You're a newbie." She cast a glance around the park. Her hair was streaked with gray, her face No doubt the smoking had something to do with that. Her eyes were a filmy blue. Watery.

"I just came from the library. Trying to decide what to do next," I said.

"Two days on the street. Unless you have some place to go, I'd say you have all the time in the world."

I shrugged. "I don't have any place to go. I just got back from overseas, and realized about halfway between here and Istanbul that I had no place to go when I got here. But I had to leave anyway."

"You were in Istanbul? What were you doing there?"

"Teaching. So how long have you been out here?"

"About two years. My house burned down and I wasn't insured."

"Oh. That's awful. So, uh...Where do you stay?"

"Around. I'm on the waiting list for that place over there," she jerked her thumb in the direction of the Bayview Towers, clearly visible from our bench because at ten stories it was the tallest building in town. It rented to seniors. Looking at her I could tell that she was at least my age, maybe older.

"My name's Patrick." I held out my hand.

"Sandy." She shook my hand. Then she took up her newspaper and went back to reading the real estate section.

"I guess I'll go back in the library for a while," I said.

"They won't let me take my cart in there," she said. "Only the lobby. I have to leave it there. I don't know how much you have with you, but stay close to it."

"I got my backpack here," I said, hoisting it, "and a sleeping bag. It's over there strapped to my scooter."

I pointed at my orange 150cc Tao-Tao, a Chinese model parked several hundred yards away, beyond the grass, the eucalyptus trees and the few people lounging or strolling around, at the curb on Davidson Street. "The scooter's brand-new. I just bought it." I don't know why I added that detail.

She chuckled. "You really *are* a newbie. I wouldn't leave my stuff there if I were you. And your scooter better be locked."

"Oh, yeah, it locks when I park it and take the key. You can't turn the handlebars without the key."

"Keep an eye on it anyway. Around here they steal anything that ain't bolted down, and sometimes even if it is bolted down they steal it anyway."

"Thanks for the advice. Come to think of it, maybe I'll go get something to eat," I said. Then, pausing, I added, "are you hungry?" If she were homeless I thought I should at least offer to buy her some food, although a bit of quick arithmetic in my head reminded me that I would not be able to afford to do such things often, or probably even for much longer. I still had some money in the bank, but no immediate prospects for any more. I'd had a couple of beers and wanted some more.

"No, I'm fine," she said. "Thanks."

Where was I going to sleep that night, I wondered? The park was out of the question. There were signs all over the place reading, "PARK OPEN 7 A.M. TO 10 P.M." Even a newbie could figure out that if you were in the park after ten at night, the cops were going to show up to chase you away at the very least. At worst they were going to ask you nosy questions, and maybe ask if you would mind opening your bag (assuming you had one.)

Of course I would become familiar with all of this later. For the moment, I just got up from the bench, mumbled a "Nice meeting you" to Sandy, and walked back toward my scooter to get another beer from the six-pack I had tucked into its trunk earlier. She did not look up from her newspaper as I walked away.

I would see a lot of Sandy in the days, weeks and months to come. Usually in the same spot, unless it was raining, in which case she would seek shelter under the outside awning of the library just like everyone else who had nowhere else to go.

After that first meeting with Sandy, on that first day, my memory of those days, weeks and months becomes blurry, which no doubt has something to do with the beer and sometimes wine that we "parkies" generally consumed to get us through the length of an average day.

But it also has a lot to do with the monotony. I met a lot of people in the park who had done jail time and in some cases even prison time, and they seldom failed to tell me how the days of your sentence melted one into the next until the rhythm of incarceration became so synchronized with your own rhythm that you would often find yourself not knowing what day of the week it was.

The park wasn't so different. So I do remember going back into the library that afternoon, and I do remember sitting for a while in one of the cushioned library chairs reading the Wall Street Journal, and I sort of remember walking to the 7-Eleven for a sandwich.

After that, which day was which becomes indistinct. I only remember that it was October because that was the month that I came back from Turkey and wandered into the park in the first place. Yes, I was fairly clear on that, even much later. I suppose I gravitated to Aurora Park because I had known that park ever since childhood. It was in the only neighborhood that I had ever really thought of as home, although I had no home there anymore.

2

The old man had always been a problem—he went out of his way to be one. But after his wife Marjorie died he became more so, and not for the reasons most might think. He went downhill, the family agreed, not out of grief, because he felt that by dying first, she had changed the rules in a game whose rules he had laid out years before.

He didn't feel abandoned by her. He felt cheated, the way you would feel if someone sold you a car and it threw a rod two days later.

That wasn't the way it was supposed to work. He had made dying first his life's big project. He had age on his side – he was seven years older than his wife. From the day they were married, or from not long after, anyway, dying before Marjorie had been Joe Donahy's private Schlieffen Plan. Paris would be occupied and that was all that mattered. He and his wife had spent nearly fifty years making each other miserable. It was a game the old man wanted to win.

But one September afternoon, three weeks before what would have been their fiftieth anniversary, Marjorie had a stroke, then another, bigger one in the ambulance on the way to the hospital. Both had DNR instructions in their advance health care directives. The second stroke had left Majorie effectively brain-dead, and the hospital took her off life-support the following night.

He would live another five years, but the game was over and he had lost.

Patrick said to Edith one day,"What difference does it make that she died first? As far as any of us knows, he's never enjoyed anything in his life except screaming about Jews and minorities and trying to make Mom, and the rest of us, feel guilty for all the sacrifices he supposedly had to make. He's going out the way he came in. What scares the shit out of me is that we have his genes."

Edith had no argument for that. She had felt cheated by their mother's death too, but not in the same way her father did. She felt cheated because now there was a breach she had to step into, and she didn't want to. She didn't want to deal with the old man alone. But now she had no choice; there wasn't anyone else to do it. Jessie was in Oklahoma. Pat came out for the funeral but he had been living in Baltimore for several years. Edith was stuck.

It was no wonder, Patrick thought, that after their mother died Edith hid out as much as she could. Alone with the old man now, ("Like playing football without a helmet," she said) she took refuge in her room when she wasn't cooking his meals, doing his laundry, driving him to the doctor or doling out his medications. There was a granny flat behind the house that the old man had built years before to increase the value of the property and add more room for a family that had never managed very well crowded together. It was Edith's room now. She smoked and drank brandy all day, watched reruns on TV and slept a lot.

Patrick had also heard from Jessie in Oklahoma City that Edith was addicted to painkillers and was using their father's prescription to get all the Vicodin she wanted.

But a few months later Pat was back. He joined his father and sister in California after the company Maryland for which he worked in the marketing department responded to an economic downturn by laying off 44 employees, including him. Unable to find another job in Maryland and having run through his unemployment insurance, he canceled his lease, sold off most of what he owned, packed up his car with what was left and drove across the country.

He found the situation at home worse than he expected. The

wood-frame house, which had been in the family since Patrick and Edith's grandfather came to southern California from Pennsylvania in 1930, was a mess. The old man, crippled and half-blind, couldn't clean it but insisted that he could and would not allow a cleaning crew to be hired. But since he couldn't see, he couldn't see dirt, nor could he see the pee stains and hair on the rim of the toilet or the encrusted toothpaste in the bathroom sink. Edith dutifully cooked for her father, but she didn't like to clean and was usually too drunk to do it anyway. There were termites, but the old man couldn't see them, so he denied that they were there and wouldn't allow the place to be fumigated.

Patrick had been a reporter in his youth, before he went into the more-lucrative marketing field, and he landed a job as a reporter on the local weekly newspaper. It paid little but it was close to home, and the three of them, himself, Edith and their father, were mostly living off the old man's pension anyway. What he earned on the newspaper was supplemental income, which for the moment was all he needed. When cash ran low the old man would hand his ATM card to Edith. "Go get another three hundred," he would tell her.

Edith did all of the grocery shopping. She kept herself in booze that way: since food also went on the old man's ATM card, Edith would drop a jug of E&J brandy into the shopping cart along with everything else. The old man drank Scotch every evening before dinner. Patrick would join him while Edith was in the kitchen, cooking and slipping out the back door ever few minutes for another pull on the brandy jug.

One day Edith gave herself gastroenteritis, dumping brandy into an empty stomach. She vomited for sixteen hours. Patrick called Jessie and learned that this wasn't the first time.

He loaded Edith into the PT Cruiser and drove her to Kaiser Permanente. She was too sick to walk; she had to be wheeled into the building.

Not knowing how long her treatment would take, he told her to call him when she was ready to come home. He expected that she would be in the hospital overnight, and was surprised when she called for a ride four hours later.

"So what did they do to you in the hospital?" He asked in the car.

"Put me on the I.V. drip – they said I was dehydrated-- and gave me Zofran."

"That's it?

"Pretty much."

"So...they just patch you up and send you home, is that it?"

"Usually."

"How many times you been in there?"

She shrugged. "I don't know. Two or three."

Patrick gripped the steering wheel a bit tighter and said, "They don't do much for you in that place. Probably they don't do much for anybody. Looks like all they care about is getting you out of there as fast as possible. I think you need to go to rehab."

"I'm not going to rehab!"

"Edith, you're a drunk. You need help."

"Look who's talking! You're a drunk! I've seen you sucking up beer and I've seen you hitting the Scotch with Dad!"

"I've never had to go to the emergency room for it. And I never lost a job because of it."

"I never lost a job because of it."

"Jessie told me you did. Jessie told me they fired you from that veterinarian's office because you kept showing up stinking of booze, or sometimes you wouldn't show up at all because you were at home nursing a hangover."

"Those were migraines!"

"Jessie said they were hangovers. She said you've been snowing everybody with that shit about migraines."

"Fuck Jessie! She doesn't even live here anymore! She married that

Oklahoma cowboy, but she keeps sticking her fucking nose in from two thousand miles away! Why doesn't that old bitch mind her own fucking business?"

"But she was here and she saw things I didn't when I was on the east coast. You gotta do something or you're gonna die."

"I don't care if I die! I didn't expect to make it to forty. From here on out I figure it's all gravy anyway."

He drove in silence for a minute, then glanced over at her The rage had left her face, but the stubbornness wasn't going anywhere. Her lips tightened. She stared for a long moment out the windshield at the freeway traffic. "I'll quit drinking by myself," she said.

"That doesn't work. I've ... known people who tried it. They always fell off the wagon. Usually sooner than later."

"Well, that's the only way I'm gonna do it. Now leave me alone."

3

Cyrus tells me that when he first spotted me I was sitting under a tree reading a book.

It's believable enough; the park was directly behind the public library, and I do like to read. I read all the time. Some people in the park thought there was something wrong with me because I read all the time. I earned a reputation among the parkies as a bookworm. I was also the oldest guy in the park by everyone's reckoning—Cyrus was about five years my junior and he was no youngster himself—and I didn't do drugs, nor had I ever been arrested. I was just about the only person in the park who had never seen the inside of a jail. That was because I had been lucky.

No doubt Cyrus just walked up to me and started talking. That would have been like him. He would talk to almost anyone. He knew everybody's business and could mimic most of us—he used to get me laughing with his imitations of the "parkies." I'm sure he imitated me behind my back.

He always knew the best places to camp for the night so the cops would leave him and his companion Marianne alone. Cyrus had been on the street longer than anyone and that gave him some authority. He had every bus and trolley route in the Metropolitan Transit District memorized. If you needed to go to anywhere in the city, from court to a date with your probation officer to a hearing about your application for Section 8 housing, Cyrus could tell you which bus route to take and where to change to another line. And at night if anyone was making noise or doing anything else that might attract the attention of the police, Cyrus was the first one to tell them to knock it off, and usually he was obeyed.

Marianne was pregnant for the third or fourth time. Her children, three of whom had Cyrus for their father, were all in foster homes. Each time Marianne went into the hospital to have another baby they would drug-test her, and since she didn't seem able to quit using, Child Protective Services would promptly show up and take the little one away. We were expecting this next one in November. Cyrus fretted, not about becoming a father (again), but about the whole situation and what he might be able to do to improve things. He worked occasionally; he had a part-time job as fill-in cook at Denny's a few times a month until he lost it for getting into an argument with his supervisor, (so he said, anyway) and once in a while he would go off early in the morning to meet a buddy who was a contractor and he would spend a couple of days laying down carpet or sanding floors somewhere. But he didn't have any steady work and didn't seem in a big hurry to find any, which didn't stop him from telling me, over and over after a few cans of Bud Light, that he was going to get out of the park and get a place where he could be under a roof with his daughters and "be a family again." I got so used to hearing this after a while that I stopped paying much attention. Marianne didn't seem as anxious as Cyrus to change things, not that would have turned down an opportunity to get off the streets, I'm sure. But she didn't appear to find the question as pressing as he did. "All she thinks about is tweakin'," he said to me. "If she ain't asleep, she's looking for somebody who has a little meth. She don't think ahead much farther than that."

Cyrus had been a tweaker himself. He told me he'd been clean for more than a year now, although he did still like his beer with a shot or two of cinnamon whiskey. Shots were available at Empire Liquor around the corner from the park for $1.25 a pop. But he was clean of the crystal meth, or so he said.

As for weed, Cyrus didn't care for it. I didn't either. One of the parkies, Andrew, a scraggly youngster with bright brown eyes and bad teeth who always went around dressed like he'd just held up a yard sale, kept trying to persuade me to get stoned with him. "Come on Pat, smoke some weed." "No thanks." "Just a couple of puffs?" "No thanks." "It won't hurt you." "I know, but I don't want any." We could go back and forth like that for ten, fifteen minutes. He would eventually back off. He didn't want to aggravate me too much. Marijuana had just become legal in selected places, and Andrew sometimes asked me to give him a lift to the dispensary on the back of my scooter. He was also an entrepreneur: when he wanted weed and lacked ten bucks for it, he would come around and try to sell me things he'd stolen that I didn't want or need. A knife. A Bluetooth speaker. A Red Sox cap (he knew I was Red Sox fan.) Once in a while I would break down and buy something just to shut him up. In the case of the knife, this had an unfortunate consequence later on.

4

He dropped the subject. They reached home. Edith went out to the granny flat and locked herself in. Of course she still had brandy in there, but there was nothing he could do about that except make another scene, and the one they'd just had in the car had exhausted him. Enough for now. He went into the house, got a Miller out of the refrigerator and popped it open, went into the living room and found the old man asleep in his armchair, a large-print paperback western open in his lap. Edith kept him supplied with paperbacks, driving to the public library once a week to bring him home another stack of westerns. She knew what he liked, and had noticed that his eyesight was getting too weak for regular print anymore, so she began bringing him large-print books. Patrick had to admit that she was reliable in those few things anyway. She was usually drunk by three p.m., but the old man's laundry was always done, the kitchen cabinets and refrigerator stocked, his medicines current and a supply of paperback westerns readily at hand on the coffee table in the living room. And she always got him to his medical appointments on time.

An intercom was set up between the kitchen and the granny flat so the old man could rouse her from the house if he needed anything. But she and the old man clearly did not like each other's company, and once these chores were done with, Edith would slip out to her own room and stay there, drinking and watching reruns until something else needed doing. Edith kept the old man's medicines in her room. Her brother teased her about it, calling her "the Pillmeister." If the old man seemed to be in pain, Patrick would walk out to the granny flat and tell her so through the screen door. "Okay, I'll give him a couple of Vicodin," would be the usual reply, that is until the old man's doctor changed his painkiller prescription from Vicodin to Methadone. She'd been doling out their father's medications ever since their mother died. He knew the reason why she was doing it, but left the subject alone. Questions wouldn't have helped things any.

Since Edith was usually drunk by three or four p.m., she went to bed early, sometimes right after dinner. Sometimes before dinner, in which case it would fall to him to see that the old man was fed. Going to bed that early meant that she was often up in the middle of the night, at midnight or one a.m. He would hear her tiptoeing around in the wee hours, doing her own laundry or whatever. Sometimes he would hear the TV in the living room, turned down very low while her clothes were in the washer/dryer. Being up and around in the middle of the night like that often meant that she was asleep until 10 or 11 a.m., which kept her away from the brandy jug until then anyhow. But with the old man gradually growing more confused as the weeks and months went by, he felt uneasy about that two-or-three hour period each morning when he had to leave his father alone in the house while Edith was out back napping. He would settle the old man into his chair after giving him some breakfast, leave a cup of coffee and a paperback western at his elbow or turn on the TV to some morning program that might bore him into dozing off, and remind him, in a loud voice, that he would be home from the Review office for lunch.

5

Among our band of gypsies day began early. There weren't very many places where you wanted to be caught sleeping long after sunrise unless you wanted to be either rousted by the cops or chased away by the owner of who's-ever parking lot you had spent the night in. There were plenty of far-gone cases on the street who could be found snoozing on bus benches or curled up under a cardboard box next to a public toilet at all hours of the day, but none of us was that far gone, and even those of us who were nearly that far gone (Frankie, for example, and his father Terry, both of them homeless and both of them druggies) would heed Cyrus when he rolled heavily out of his bedding at six-fifteen a.m. and put out the word to get moving. When Cyrus had found a good camping spot, he didn't want anything or anyone to spoil the arrangement.

I was usually the first one up, partly because I didn't have much stuff to move and partly because I didn't want to listen to Cyrus telling me to move. Marianne never wanted to get up or sometimes even to wake up. It became as much a part of the morning as the cries of the local seagulls to hear Cyrus trying to cajole Marianne out of her sleeping bag and start moving their two shopping carts (which held enough junk to stock a Goodwill store) back to the park to be secured under a eucalyptus for the day. This was always a two-step process: shopping carts were not allowed in the park, so Cyrus and Marianne would have to unload all of their stuff around a big tree, (they had a regular one, "Cyrus and Marianne's tree") throw a tarp over it and then go stash the shopping carts at a safe place in a nearby alley. Come evening they would do the whole thing in reverse.

Usually I was awake before 6:00 a.m. The 7-Eleven didn't unlock the cooler and start selling beer until six, so, after a quick glance at my watch I would hunker back down with my book and my flashlight and wait. Cyrus usually began stirring shortly after I did. The park didn't open until seven, but early in the morning the cops usually wouldn't bother you about it being outside park hours, not unless they were very bored and needed something to do. I would get up slowly as Cyrus started gathering his and Marianne's things together and whoever else might be with us would sleep on until roused.

As I stood up, Cyrus would shoot me a glance.

"You gonna go get 'em?"

Our eye-openers. Cyrus' was a King Cobra and a shot; mine was usually a Hurricane. Frankie, Terry and some of the other parkies were also partial to Hurricane. Most supermarket beer is about 5.5 percent alcohol. Hurricane was slightly over eight percent. King Cobra was malt liquor. It didn't have quite the kick of Hurricane, Natty Daddy or Steel Reserve 211, the park's three most popular brands, but Cyrus always had a shot of hot cinnamon whiskey with it. He gave me a handful of change.

I knew things were out of whack. I didn't want to think about it too much. It wasn't so long ago that I had begun my day as most people do, with a cup or two of hot coffee. Now here I was, in the chill of an early March morning, on my way to get breakfast beer for myself and Cyrus. But the beer tasted good and besides, once it was inside you and had the chance to do what it was supposed to do, the deserted park and the empty early-morning streets seemed to move toward the back of the stage for a while, along with that pressing awareness that now you had about eleven hours to kill before sunset.

Coming back from the store, I saw Chantal making her way down the alley that ran between the backs of the businesses along McKinley Avenue, which ran north and south along one side of the park. There was no mistaking Chantal even if she were walking away from me. She was a thin black girl, twenty-seven years old. Her most distinctive feature was her hair It was reddish-black; she tinted it. Incredibly thick and curly, it fell down to her shoulders when she wasn't wearing it "up," as she usually did for convenience. What was she doing up and around this early? I'd have to ask Cyrus. Cyrus called Chantal his cousin. They weren't related, but they had known each other for years. Since she was a teenager, anyway.

It was getting lighter, 6:15 by my watch. I went into the 7-Eleven and got the beers for Cyrus and me out of the cooler. When I turned to go pay for them at the counter, Ed was standing there. He didn't see me coming. I quietly slipped in behind him.

He scanned the liquor shelves. "What happened to all the vodka?" he asked the cashier.

"You drank it," I said from behind him.

He turned around and recognized me. "Oh, hi, Pat! What're you doing up and around at this hour?"

"Same thing you're doing. Where have you been?" I hadn't seen Ed in days.

"I found some work," he said, then, turning back to the counter, he told the cashier that if they didn't have any Popov, he'd take a half-pint of Fleischmann's. A lot of drinking went on in the park, but Ed did more than his share. Today he was getting started earlier than usual, but most of the time he smelled of alcohol by nine a.m. anyway.

"Work doing what?"

"Laying carpet."

"I saw Chantal just now," I told him.

"Really? Where?"

Ed was crazy about Chantal. Unfortunately for him he was closer to my age than hers. Ed aside, half the guys in the park who were anywhere near Chantal's own age also had the hots for her. Chantal wasn't really much to look at, if you were to ask me. She wasn't ugly; she had beautiful brown eyes. But she was thin and had bad skin from using either too much makeup or the wrong kind. But in warm weather she usually ran around half-undressed, and there was that mane of hair, so thick that I once jokingly asked her if I could have some of it. Chantal's hair was her main beauty feature. She flaunted it. I had seen her holding court in the park, sitting under the eucalyptus over near Hardy Street, on the wide blanket she and her friend Yvonne shared, her hair down and three or four guys hanging around acting nonchalant, swapping "and-then-I-said-fuck-you" stories with each other and playing rap music on their Smartphones.

This ritual only went on when Yvonne was away for a few hours, hustling money to get drugs and/or food for both of them. If you asked Chantal, she would tell you that the guys were wasting their time. She only had eyes for Yvonne. Each of them referred to the other as "my wife." They fought all the time, usually at the top of their lungs, all over the park. They were known as "The Fighting Dykes" and we were all used to their shenanigans, but the neighbors had complained and Chantal and Yvonne had been warned more than once. I asked Cyrus about the situation—his theory was that this lesbian phase of Chantal's was just that: something she was going through. Well, he had known her longer than I had. And I was still, as Sandy had said not so long ago, a newbie. What the hell did I know?

"I saw her going down the alley between McKinley and Davidson," I said.

"I wonder what *she's* doing up at this hour?" Ed paid for his booze.

"They do a lot of drug deals in that alley. But she was alone. And no sign of Yvonne."

"They're probably fighting again." Ed was nonchalant, or pretending to be. "See you later, Pat." He took his vodka and went out the door. I ordered a hot cinnamon shot for Cyrus to have with his beer.

Half an hour later, Cyrus and Marianne were in the middle of the daily portage back to "their" tree. I saw them coming across the park, pushing their two shopping carts which they had loaded up, as usual, like the Joad family on its way to California. I had asked Cyrus why they hauled around all this stuff, ninety percent of which they seemed never to use. More than once he had replied, "I'm downsizin.' You watch. By the end of the week half of this shit'll be gone." But it never was. He blamed Marianne, who threw a fit at the idea of tossing out anything she considered important, and, it seemed, that was just about everything. Cyrus and Marianne had been drifting around town together for almost three years, and he had gotten to where he just didn't want to fight with her anymore. When she seized on some pretext to start yelling at him, usually when she had been unable to make a connection for a couple of days, Cyrus would just shrug, heave a big sigh and walk away. This led to her accusing him of not caring about her, and then a new fight would start. But as much as he insisted (and he did tell me again and again) that he loved Marianne, you could see that he was getting tired of all this.

I went over and helped them put the last of their load under the tree, then volunteered to push one of the two shopping carts across Davidson to their stashing-place in the alley there. I had the beers in my backpack. As soon as we had finished hiding the shopping carts, Cyrus and I sought the nearest park bench, sat down and began sipping at our breakfast.

"On my way to the store a while ago I saw Chantal. She was going down the alley over there." I pointed.

"Did you say hello?"

"No, she had her back to me. I wondered, though. You know she's never up at dawn like us. She usually sleeps until nine or ten."

"Tweakin'. That's what they do. They throw them blankets over their heads and then they stay up for two days."

"Yvonne wasn't with her."

Cyrus stretched and yawned. "They're probably fightin' again. It'll blow over."

"Do you know what they're always fighting about?"

"I have an idea."

"Give me a hint?"

"Cage."

"They're lesbians."

"Don't matter. I told you I think this is just a phase she's going through. You know I like Chantal, but she'll do just about anything for twenty dollars worth of dope."

"How do you know it's Cage, if it's anybody?"

"I don't. But I talked to Jennifer." Jennifer was Cage's mother.

"I haven't seen Jennifer for days. Cage either."

"He's in jail again. I don't where she is."

"What did he get picked up for this time?"

"Outstanding warrant. He missed an appointment with his parole officer. But keep what I just said under your hat, okay? I mean about Chantal."

Cyrus liked to be mysterious, and he liked everyone to think he was the guy with the inside dope, the one who knew all the secrets in the park.

"Even if she and Yvonne are fighting now, they'll be asleep in each other's arms again by noon. We'll see it," I said.

"Yeah, probably." He glanced over one shoulder, then the other. Cyrus liked to be aware of what was going on all the time. "Speak of the devil."

Yvonne was coming across McKinley Avenue, slowly pushing a very heavily-laden shopping cart. She and Chantal had even more junk than Cyrus and Marianne had. It took three trips to get all of their stuff from the alley to the park every morning.

I took off my backpack and Cyrus and I hid our open beers in it. I carefully stowed the pack under the bench, glancing around to make sure no one had seen me do it, neither a sticky-fingered parkie nor a cop cruising by. Cyrus and I went over together to lend Yvonne a hand.

"You got two more?" Cyrus called as we approached her.

"Yeah. You know where our spot is. Hi, guys." She smiled, glad for the help.

"Hi, Sweetie," I liked Yvonne. She put up with an awful lot. "We'll be right back."

I walked off after Cyrus. (Cyrus wasn't heard to catch up with. He had a bad knee, he was slightly bowlegged and he also hauled a beer gut—his walk was more of a rolling waddle.) We had done this job for Yvonne and Chantal before. It was a nuisance of a chore. Chantal and Yvonne's shopping carts were so overloaded that on our slow way back down the sidewalk toward the park from the alley where they usually spent the night, stuff fell on the sidewalk: a carpet, a pair of shoes, a sweater, an umbrella. Each time we had to stop and pick up the offending item.

"I wondered why you have so much shit," I said to Cyrus. "These two make you look like Francis of Assisi walking into the woods naked."

"And they keep going to Lucy's for more," Cyrus said.

St. Lucy's was the local Catholic church that distributed food and clothing to the poor and homeless on Mondays and Wednesdays between nine and eleven a.m. Sister Paula, who handed out food and chits for secondhand clothing from the parish thrift shop, was a popular figure in the neighborhood. "Going to see Sister Paula today?" was a common early-morning greeting around the park, twice a week, anyway.

Yvonne and Chantal's usual tree was at the top of a small knoll at the northeast corner of the park where Davidson Street and McKinley Avenue intersected. We only had to get the carts across McKinley and we were almost there. But then we had to push them up that little hill, over grass. We were both huffing and puffing by the time we reached the tree. Yvonne was already unpacking Cart #1. She had spread out a big blanket on the ground and was arranging things around it, settling in for the day.

"Where's Chantal?" Cyrus asked. He already had a pretty good idea. I think he just wanted to hear Yvonne's answer.

"I don't know. I haven't seen her since about midnight," Yvonne replied. "I fell asleep and when I woke up she was gone."

"She'll be along," I said.

We all knew that Chantal would be back, and soon. Yvonne knew it better than Cyrus and I did. As I said, I liked Yvonne. I also liked Chantal, but anyone could see who was doing most of the work in their little camp. Yvonne would disappear each day, returning late in the afternoon or early in the evening.

While she was gone, Chantal would mostly sit on the blanket, tinker with her makeup, fix her hair, do crossword puzzles or play Sudoku, sleep, socialize, go into the library when she needed to use the can, and, when she was hungry, either bust out the peanut butter and jelly that was left over from the day before or make the rounds of the park asking if anybody had any food. She did a lot of small-scale mooching like this: never anything big, just a bite or maybe a soda. She had hit me up for Dr. Pepper plenty of times.

Fortunately she didn't smoke. Many of the parkies did. Some of them smoked a lot. Cigarettes were a unit of currency in the park, just like in the old prison movies. A new homeless person straying into our midst could make himself or herself very unpopular very quickly by bumming too many smokes and failing to offer any back.

Chantal's only vices seemed to be crystal meth, weed and Dr. Pepper. Usually Yvonne provided all three, and food too. In short, Chantal had it pretty good and we all knew it. Chantal knew it too, which was why I didn't need to tell Yvonne that Chantal would be back shortly. Yvonne was very forbearing with Chantal. Yvonne was exclusively lesbian and Chantal swung both ways, which gave Chantal the upper hand in the relationship. To say that I felt sorry for Yvonne would be using too strong a phrase. Let's just say that Cyrus and I both watched what was going on every day under that tree and around the park, and we both occasionally got a little impatient with Chantal, to the point where sometimes her shenanigans would cause one of us to mutter something or roll his eyeballs at the other. What Yvonne and Chantal had wasn't a very equitable arrangement, but it also wasn't any of our business. We muttered to each other about it, but we had our own things to worry about.

6

It was on a Friday that he came in around noon and found his father stomping back and forth between the living room and the dining room, sputtering and cursing to himself.

"What the hell is going on?"

"It's that sister of yours," the old man nearly yelled. "Goddamn it, I can't get her attention! She doesn't answer the intercom! She was supposed to take me to the doctor this morning! I can't rely on that woman for ANYTHING! She's probably lying out there right now with a snootful!"

"Let me check."

He went out to the granny flat and knocked on the heavy wooden door. No answer. He tried the doorknob. Locked. No surprise there; she always locked the door when she took her morning naps; in warm weather like today's she slept in the nude and didn't want anyone walking in on her.

The outside light over the door was still on from the night before. Nothing unusual there either, she often turned it on after dark and forgot about it. A window air conditioner, set on fan rather than a/c, hummed away in the window beside the door.

Again, nothing unusual; she ran the fan during her daytime naps, and also at night, to mask outside noise.

He moved over to the window to try and get a look into the room. She kept the windows covered with aluminum foil to ensure darkness when she wanted daytime sleep, but a bit of daylight always got in around the edges. He got up on tiptoes and peered through the tiny sliver of window next to the air conditioner that was not covered with foil, but the light inside the room was so dim he couldn't make out anything. Might she have gone to the store? No, the family Buick was still parked in the carport, and she would not have walked to the store. She was overweight and never walked anywhere if she didn't have to. He knocked on the window. No response to that either.

Returning to the house, he tried the intercom and got no answer. No doubt the old man was right; she had probably spent part of the morning watching TV and slurping up brandy like she usually did. She was drunk and passed out, at noon. There was nothing unusual about that, but she had known about the old man's medical appointment that morning. He had heard her remind their father about it the night before. Edith's being drunk in the middle of the day was not news, but allowing herself to get too bombed to take him to the doctor was definitely not like her.

He tried to think of something that might have made her start drinking earlier than usual. She was chronically depressed. Depression ran in the family. He had experienced it himself, but with him it usually came on gradually. There were warning signs. He had seen a doctor about it and had been on Wellbutrin for several years.

Edith had never sought treatment for her depression, and her fits would come on quickly, with little or no warning. He could remember times when she had seen something on TV that upset her enough to grab the E&J bottle, take a series of deep swigs, wait a few minutes for the booze to kick in and then go off to bed, taking refuge in sleep from whatever had caused the upset. That's what chronically depressed people do, he had read somewhere. They sleep.

He decided to let her sleep.

He picked up the notepad from the kitchen counter that had important phone numbers in it and called Dr. Gonzales, his father's regular physician. He lied about what had happened, telling the receptionist that there had been a mixup and they thought his father's appointment was for the next day. He rescheduled the appointment for the following week and, snapping shut his cellphone, assured his father that either Edith or he himself would make sure he got there. He made lunch and a pot of coffee for his father and himself and went back to the newspaper office. By late afternoon Edith would have slept off her drunk and would be puttering around the property again.

He only hoped the two of them wouldn't get into it – sometimes Edith and the old man got into shouting matches, and there was that one time when she grabbed him by the arm. His skin, like that of an onion, tore and he began bleeding. Edith got the bleeding stopped and the wound bound up. This happened while Patrick was in Maryland.

The episode passed, but Jessie had told him about it on the phone, expressing her fear that if anything like this happened again, Edith could be arrested and charged with elder abuse.

The irony gave him pause. The old man had never been tall; for most of his life he had stood at five feet, eight inches. With old age he had shrunk about an inch. But before his seventies he had always had broad shoulders, pronounced biceps and a strong back. He had built the granny flat mostly with his own two hands when Patrick was a teenager. Hard physical labor had been the old man's joy; he was never happier than when he was out in the back yard, digging, planting, mowing, hauling and working up a sweat. The idea that he was now so frail that Edith could injure him in a drunken rage was something entirely new, strange. It never would have occurred to him had he not heard the story from his older sister.

At five O'clock he rode his bicycle home. He went into the house and shook his father awake, informing him that the situation since midday had not changed. Edith would not answer the intercom, nor would she pick up the cordless phone when he dialed

Together, his father walking very slowly, they went out to the granny flat. But the door was locked. What to do next? The old man suggested that they break the door down. But with what? He looked around the driveway and yard and under the carport where the Buick was parked. There was nothing that could be used for a battering ram, and even if there had been, it was just too ridiculous, the idea of himself and a ninety-year-old man trying to bash down a locked and heavy oak door.

There was nothing left to do except call the police.

When they arrived, he explained to them what was going on. The two officers then walked around the granny flat looking for another possible way inside.

They found one: he had forgotten that the screen on one of the windows on the west side of the building had been missing for years, and the lock on the sliding window had likewise been broken for a long time.

The cops climbed up to the window and slid it open. After admonishing him not to follow them, first one and then the other climbed in through the window. "Edith? Are you in here?" he heard one of them call.

He walked away. By now there was little doubt what the result of all of this was going to be, and he wanted to postpone it, even if only for another minute or two.

He walked down to the end of the long driveway and paused where it met the sidewalk. He stood looking out at the street. Then he turned and slowly walked back. By then the officers had opened the granny flat door from the inside. One of them stood in the driveway, talking to the old man. The cop had his back to Patrick. As he drew closer, he heard the policeman ask, "Where's your son?"

He himself had made the call to 911, and knew, even as he punched in the number, what he was about to be told.

7

Cyrus and I went back to our bench. My backpack was tucked right where I'd left it under the bench, and our open beers were snugly inside, still cold.

"So what are you going to do when Marianne has that baby?" I asked.

"I don't know. But things ain't gonna stay this way. I'm gonna get out of here."

"When?"

"Soon's I can make it happen. I been on the street more than two years. I've put in for Section 8, but that takes forever. Not sure I want to wait two years, maybe more. I want to have my daughters under a roof. Be a family again."

"What about Marianne?"

Cyrus kicked at the grass with his toe. "Shit. She won't quit using! I love her and we been together a long time. Two years, almost. But she won't quit using. I quit more than a year ago."

"You told me."

There was a tree in the park we referred to as "the tweaker tree." On an average day, anywhere from four to maybe ten people would gather around it, coming and going, lounging on the grass, laughing, joking, playing rap music and doing crystal meth. Marianne was often among them.

"I've tried and tried, over and over, to get her off the stuff," Cyrus said, "but she keeps going back and using again. I'm close to fed up."

"What about the baby?"

"Well, we'll see. If this time's anything like last time, they'll drug-test her when she goes into the hospital and if she comes up positive, CPS will take the baby like they did last time."

We sat in silence for a minute or two, watching the morning traffic go by. This was Wednesday and everyone was on their way to work.

"You're just going to go off and leave her here?"

"She has a place."

"She DOES?" This was news.

"When she come out of Lion's Gate last year after going through their program, they set her up in a place." Lion's Gate was a detox facility run by the county in conjunction with the Lions Club.

"Where is it?" I asked.

"Long Beach. But she don't like to go there. I seen it. It ain't much. Four other people, and they got her sharing a room that's about ten feet long and eight feet wide, and it don't even have a window. She says she'd rather be out here, sleeping under the stars."

"I imagine drugs are easier to get out here."

He looked at me without nodding or shrugging: silent acknowledgment.

The Sheriff's department bus went by. Prisoners were being transported to the main jail facility downtown. It went by every morning about this time. Often Cyrus waved at the bus, or if he was in a jovial mood, did a little dance in the hope that some of the jailbirds on board would notice him out the window. But this morning he just turned his head and watched as the bus passed the park on its way to the freeway.

"That's the loneliest ride in the world," he said. "I've taken that ride."

Cyrus had been in jail two or three times, usually for some minor thing like failure to keep an appointment with his probation officer. Once, before he quit using, he got picked up for having a small amount of drugs on him. Then Marianne had had him arrested for domestic violence once, before I knew either of them. He did some jail time for that. He almost got arrested once after a scene at the library. I wasn't there but I heard about it from Cyrus later. The cops had actually come looking for him, but no arrest was made that time. He'd been in the library charging his phone when Marianne came in and started making a scene about something; he didn't say what. When other library patrons complained about the level of their voices, they went out to the sidewalk in front of the building, where she began screaming, punching and kicking Cyrus. "She'd gone about three days without tweak," he explained. Someone in the library had called the police.

We had finished our beers and were walking back toward Cyrus and Marianne's tree, where she had already spread out one blanket, pulled another over her and was asleep again. "She only got up an hour and a half ago," I said.

"That's Marianne. Oh, look. Sandy's here."

Sandy was on her regular bench, wearing her regular black parka and Nikes, and in her regular posture: one leg crossed over the other and newspaper in her hands, cigarette burning between two fingers.

"She's here early," I said.

"She sometimes waits at the liquor store for Sam to open. She helps him sweep out the place and he lets her have the paper for free. And she gets her morning half-pint. Come on, let's go say good morning. I want to take a look at the sports page."

We both knew this routine. Sandy didn't like anyone borrowing her newspaper. She complained that they always brought it back creased and wrinkled. Cyrus sometimes asked if he could take a look at the paper, and always made an elaborate show of his request.

"Good morning, Sandy!" he said brightly as we approached her.

She gave us a glance. "Oh, hi, guys." She went back to her paper.

Cyrus fell on his knees before her bench. "Oh, dear Sandy, may I please please please look at the sports page? I promise, promise promise I won't mess it up!"

"Oh, knock it off," she chuckled. Sandy didn't often chuckle, but she liked Cyrus. "Here," she went through her paper, carefully slipped out the sports section and handed it to him. "Be careful with it."

"I'll guard it with my very life," Cyrus said as he turned the page to check the baseball scores. He made a big show of handling the paper as if it were extremely fragile. Sandy smiled at his clowning but said no more.

I sat next to Sandy and looked over at the tree where Cyrus and Marianne's belongings were stacked, my own things buried somewhere beneath. Next to it all lay the sleeping lump that was Marianne.

"Ranger Dave'll be here later," I said. "Somebody better be over there to tell him that's our stuff."

"Marianne will tell him."

"Marianne's asleep."

"I'll wake her up, don't worry. Ha, ha! My Yankees beat Baltimore! Meanwhile, *your* Red Sox lost 6-3 to Tampa Bay!" Cyrus was a rabid Yankees fan. I was a Red Sox fan. It was understood that under no circumstances would he and I ever be able to share a place, that is even if one of us managed to get one. A Yankees fan and a Red Sox fan cannot live under the same roof.

"The season just started," I told him. "Don't count your bragging rights before they're hatched."

"Yankees RULE!" he crowed.

"Yankees SUCK."

"You know why I don't like the Red Sox?" He rattled the newspaper, getting a look from Sandy. "Racism. They were the last team in baseball to integrate."

"So? Since everything with you always gets back to RACE, then by rights you should be a Dodgers fan. They brought Jackie up in forty-seven, as we all know. The goddamn Yankees didn't integrate until they brought up Elston Howard. '55. Eight. Years. Later! If baseball is nothing to you but who integrated first, you should be rooting for the Dodgers."

"The Dodgers have only won the Series what, five or six times? The

Yankees have won twenty-seven! YES!" He pumped his fist, knowing well how the gesture annoyed me.

"You are *so* chickenshit," I said. "As Bob Dylan said, 'you just want to be on the side that's winning.' And they don't ALWAYS win. Most of those twenty-seven World Series rings you're ululating about date from *before 1962*. In the rest of the twentieth century they only went to the Series seven times, and lost two of those. What have those overrated prima donnas done in THIS century? Huh?"

"Yoo-yoo-lating? What the fuck?"

"Look it up."

We had been playing this duet all through spring training. If we were both still in the park come summer, it was bound to continue. That would be fine with me; arguing about baseball was more interesting than watching the tweakers come and go. And the cops, who cruised by frequently during the day depending on how little else they had going on. Obviously our little band was not at the top of their priority list. We had no gangbangers that I knew of; seldom was there any disturbance in our park outside of Yvonne and Chantal's occasional shouting matches.

Around nine O'clock Ranger Dave's truck pulled into the library parking lot. He always showed up on Wednesdays. He wasn't really the law, although he wanted all of us to think he was. He represented the Parks and Recreation department.

One of his jobs was to keep the city parks clear of litter. He had a staff, mostly made up of people who were working off community service time, to pick up the trash. He dealt with the bigger stuff. On Tuesdays he would walk through the park, sticking solid waste removal warnings on anything left there that was too big to poke with a stick and lift into a bag, such as the piles of personal effects that the park's homeless people stacked under the trees. On any given Tuesday there were three or four such stacks around the park; he would tag them for removal the next day.

Dave really wasn't such a bad sort. If you were sitting next to your stuff to tell him it was yours, he wouldn't take it. He'd wag his finger at you, issue a warning and go on his way. But if your stuff was unattended, he and his pixies would load it on to his truck and haul it down to the old city general services lot, mostly abandoned since the city had built a new one elsewhere, but handy as a transfer station. You had forty-eight hours to come and get your stuff or it was on its way to the dump.

What Ranger Dave really wanted of course was to get all of us out of the park. Not just our stuff, us. But getting us out of the park was a police department matter, not for Parks and Recreation. As long as the park was open, the homeless had as much right to be there as anyone else, provided we weren't breaking any laws, and we usually broke only those that could be broken quietly and out of sight. As long as you kept your nose clean, or were at least discreet, it was only after ten p.m. that the cops would chase you out of the park, and by that time Ranger Dave had long since finished his day and gone home.

He was always on the lookout for alcoholic beverages. If he caught you with an open beer he'd throw you out of the park for the day, and that was if he was in a good mood. If he was in a bad mood he'd write you a citation.

But like I said, he was a fairly agreeable sort; it's just that he would prefer to have our things, our beer and us gone. We always hid the beer when we saw him coming. On Tuesdays when he only came to tag things for hauling away, we usually waited until he was gone to go get some.

The police, on the other hand, would unhesitatingly cite you for "open container" if they so much as caught you with a can of Coors, and were seldom lenient about it.

I'd gotten one of those tickets myself, late one night when I was camped alone on the far side of the library and I had not finished the last of the plastic Ten High flask on the sidewalk beside my sleeping bag, and a bored cop cruised up with his floodlights on at 1 a.m. and woke me up. Maybe a swallow of whiskey was still in the plastic bottle and it cost me $180.

On most Wednesdays the police department's Homeless Outreach Team would show up just about the time Ranger Dave was leaving, usually between ten a.m. and noon. As its name indicated, the HOT team was a city-mandated initiative to get homeless people off the streets by means other than arrest and detention. The parkies expected their visits. During the two hours on Wednesday mornings when they were expected, the controlled substances and alcohol were hidden under blankets or stashed in the bushes.

The cops knew the stuff was around of course, but they had a schedule to keep, other parks to visit, and so left the shakedowns to the regular day shift. The team consisted of Sgts. Rudy Payne and Fernando Solis, plus their entourage: Nancy Verdugo from the city's Chemical Addiction Response Team (CART) and volunteers from Health and Human Services who could help with applications for housing, drug and alcohol programs, disability and EBT.

"What time is it?" Cyrus asked.

I looked at my watch. "A quarter past nine. Want to go see if we can find Chantal?"

"What for?"

"I don't know. It would give us something to do."

"She's probably at Lion's Gate grabbing some free coffee. No, there she is."

Chantal, wearing extremely short shorts and a yellow halter top, was walking barefoot, very fast, toward the tree where Yvonne had already spread out their stuff.

"Look at her, she's *marching*," Cyrus sneered. He didn't approve of Chantal's meth use any more than he did Marianne's. Since he himself had kicked, he was contemptuous of those who didn't want to bother.

8

Jessie and her husband flew out from Oklahoma City for the "celebration of life," what funerals are called now. It was held at a local Methodist church, not because the family was Methodist but because the organist at the Methodist church was an old friend of his mother's who had also known his father and had even met Edith once or twice.

A small group of Edith's friends, most of whom had not seen her in a long time, showed up for the funeral, people she had known when she was a waitress around town. She never held any of these jobs for more than a year or so, probably because of her drinking, but he was in no position to say for certain, having been around rarely in recent years, before their mother's death and the prospect of having to live alone with her father had driven her to retreat into the granny flat and the brandy bottle.

She died in September, and for two months after that the family had no clear idea what exactly had killed her.

She was a walking billboard for unhealthy living, with her boozing, cigarette smoking, painkiller abuse, fondness for fatty foods and couch-potato ways. But once the medical examiner's van had carted her body away, he and his father had received nothing from the county other than a death certificate. He assumed that she had died of heart failure, having lived the sort of life that invited it. Maybe cirrhosis was also involved; surely she had invited that too.

She was cremated, her remains returned to the family in a sealed metal box. He and Jessie then had to decide where to disperse her ashes. Edith had always loved the mountains and never cared much for the beach.

They rented a Ford Fiesta and drove with her ashes up to Tehachapi in the mountains between the Mojave Desert and Bakersfield, and furtively scattered them in a field just outside of town.

In November the toxicology report came in the mail. Reading it carefully, he was surprised to learn that although they had found small fatty deposits in her liver, it was not as diseased as might have been thought.

But the autopsy also found fifteen milligrams of Methadone in her bloodstream. So, when the old man's doctor had changed his painkiller prescription from Vicodin to Methadone, she had indeed started popping this new stuff that was now in her top dresser drawer.

He checked on the Internet and learned that fifteen milligrams is not necessarily a lethal dose of Methadone – his father's prescribed dose was five milligrams; people had been known to take more than she had taken and survive. But he also learned that Methadone was one of those prescription drugs that are dangerous when mixed with alcohol, and he knew her well enough: there was little doubt that she had chased down those three blue pills with a big gulp, or maybe two or three big gulps, of brandy, before lying down for what turned out to be her final summer nap. She was 47.

He and Jessie went into the granny flat the day after Edith died to clear out her room. They found (he counted) 75 empty E&J brandy bottles stashed in drawers, in the closet and under a blanket on the floor next to her bed. Edith was one of those drunks who rather than run the risk of letting themselves be seen disposing of their empties, hoard them instead.

Among the dust bunnies under her bed they also found fifteen empty Vicodin bottles.

The old man pretended to be unmoved by his daughter's death. From the way he shrugged it off, it appeared as if he regarded her sudden demise as an inconvenience, and a predictable one at that. Even the old man, whose hearing and eyesight had been getting steadily worse for a long time, was aware of Edith's drinking (although the family made sure he remained unaware that she was also helping herself to his prescription painkillers) and he had predicted aloud more than once that he would probably end up outliving her despite being 43 years her senior. He showed no outward sign of any grief.

"I can see that this has hit you harder than it's hit me," he said to son, who made no secret of his own grieving for his sister, and who knew very well, by the way, that his father was lying. All his life Patrick had watched the rancorous game of what he called "guilt tennis" that his parents played with such practiced skill, and when his mother died, he knew from Jessie that, in the absence of their mother, the old man, deprived of his tennis partner, had redirected his rage at his younger daughter.

Unlike their mother, who preferred innuendo and *sotto voce* mutterings to outright confrontation, Edith fired the old man's acrimony right back at him, harder when her own rage was fueled with brandy. It was clear to everyone that Edith had stepped (or been placed) into her mother's position in the house.

Jessie told her brother a story that left no doubt of that. On one of the occasions when the old man had to be hospitalized for two or three days, he had committed a sedative-induced freudian slip and introduced Edith to the nurse as "my wife" before being corrected.

Now, without neither his wife or his daughter around to abuse anymore, the old man began to lose interest in his surroundings. It seemed so to his son, anyway, who continued to bring home large-print paperback westerns from the public library, just as Edith had, but noticed that now they remained mostly untouched on the coffee table. When the baseball season ended and the Dodgers were no longer on TV every night, Patrick searched and found a cable channel that ran westerns 24/7, including nightly reruns of *Gunsmoke*. But when he switched on the program each night just as he was about to bring the old man his dinner on a tray, he noticed that his father, although looking at the screen, seemed to be off somewhere else.

With Edith gone, he found that being a primary caregiver was a proving to be a much more taxing job than being a secondary one. Still, he thought as he screwed the cap back on the Scotch jug and replaced it on the shelf above the water heater after a big slug, there was no way he was going to remand his father over to convalescent care. He and Jessie had talked about it in the dining room on the day after Edith's memorial.

"I know he's been a pain in the ass to the whole family for years," he told her, "but he did the best he could, and he deserves a chance to die in his own bed." For once Jessie decided not to argue with him.

He hired a caregiver three afternoons a week. He had to overcome the old man's loud objections of course. His father absolutely did not want a stranger in the house, not for three afternoons, not even for one. But he went ahead and called a local company called Age Advantage and hired a young man named Ralph to come in on Monday, Wednesday and Friday afternoons so that someone would be there between the time Patrick returned to the newspaper office after lunch and the time he came home four hours later.

Mornings were not such a problem—the old man usually slept in his chair between breakfast and noon anyway, and Patrick arranged with his editor to leave the office early on Tuesdays and Thursdays. Ralph was a big and somewhat ungainly twenty year-old whom Patrick could tell from talking with him was not the brightest bulb on the marquee, but he could watch television with the old man, open a can of soup, brew up a pot of coffee and make a phone call, and those were really the only things the job involved other than helping the old man get out of his chair to go to the toilet now and then.

His father's death was neither unexpected nor sudden. Over the months that followed Edith's Methadone overdose (which, he decided, could not have been suicide—Edith was depressed all right, but no more so than the rest of the family; she had never mentioned anything about wanting to take her own life; she had simply used the Methadone as she had used the Vicodin, expecting no more harmful effect) he was already showing signs of dementia, and now they became worse. He had often claimed, even when still lucid, that he never knew what day of the week it was. Once retired, he had no reason to think about it—one day was like another to him.

Now he began to get confused about what time of day it was. He got up from his chair one afternoon and, making slowly for his bedroom, asked his son to "lock up" as if he were turning in for the night. It was midafternoon and the and the sun was still out. The old man didn't seem to notice that it was still daytime.

Then one afternoon, the demadex doing its work in forcing him to pee, he began his slow walk toward the bathroom aided by the walker he now used, but when he reached the far end of the dining room where two doors stood, one leading into the kitchen and the other down the hallway to the bathroom, he couldn't remember which door to take.

That evening after Ralph had left and Patrick sat with his father watching the local TV news to which the old man no longer paid any attention, his father looked at him suddenly and asked, "Are we somewhere north of Los Angeles?" "No, Dad, we're at home in our own house, where we've lived for years," he answered.

"But what about that….that tree? And...those grapes?"

He knew what his father was talking about. The old man had always taken great pride in tending his garden, which included a grapevine and an apricot tree, planted years before along the driveway.

"They're right here, Dad. Right down the driveway where you planted them when I was a kid. Don't worry. We're home. We're in our own house." Then, rising from the sofa in the middle of the TV weather report and leaving his father where he was, he went into the kitchen, got the Scotch jug down from over the water heater, poured himself a big shot, drank it in one gulp, went to the kitchen sink and, leaned over in front of the sink facing the kitchen window through which he could clearly see his father's apricot tree over by the fence, and wept.

Then one night the old man began raving about "cows knocking over the fence" and said he had a sudden, urgent need to "call the chief of police of Springfield."

Alarmed, he went into the next room, took his cellphone out of his pocket and called his sister in Oklahoma City.

"He's really raving now," he told her. "I'm not sure what to do. Something about a cow knocking over the fence?"

"I think when he was young they had a cow. He's back in his childhood."

"And he said something about needing to call the Springfield chief of police."

"Yeah. I think he was also a motorcycle cop back there in Illinois, right after World War II. Long before he met Mom."

"What do you think I should do?"

"Call an ambulance. Get him to the ER."

"All right, but what about after that?"

"There might not be any 'after that.' I hate to say this, Pat, but there is the possibility that he might die in the hospital. He sounds awfully far gone." A pause. "I should come back out there I guess."

"You don't sound too upset."

"Well, we've both known this was coming for a long time."

Another pause. "You going to come?"

"You know I will."

"When?"

She sighed. "Oh, tomorrow. Thursday at the latest."

"What should we do if, you know, he doesn't...that is, if he comes back home? He has before."

Another pause. "We find a place with an available bed."

"He has a bed here."

"Oh, you are SO fucking stubborn! Okay, tell you what. I'll get on a plane as soon as I can. Meanwhile, you get on the Internet and see if you can find a place that provides hospice service on call. He has Blue Cross, right?"

"You know he does."

"Okay. I'll be there in a day or two. Keep me posted."

"You know I will."

His father stayed in the hospital three days for observation. Jessie flew in from Oklahoma and installed herself in the spare bedroom down the short hallway from the old man's. By the time she got there and accompanied her brother to the hospital, the old man was lucid enough for brief conversation, although his son did have to explain to him where he was and make up a reason why. He couldn't just say "We brought you here because you were talking crazy, Dad." He told his father that his blood pressure had dropped suddenly and gotten them all concerned. His primary care physician Dr. Victor Fuentes came, looked him over and talked with him, (the old man liked Dr. Fuentes, a big Dodgers fan – they always talked baseball during office visits) and told his children that they could take him home, needlessly adding "His days are short." Jessie nodded silently and glanced at her brother, who had remained firm that, short time or not, their father was going to spend however many days he had left at home.

Ralph had been dismissed about a month earlier when Pat quit his own job on the community paper. As little as it paid, the job was hardly worth it, and now his father needed someone at home to look after him around the clock, not just during the afternoons. Jessie's being there helped; they took turns on what they began calling "The Dad watch" so that one or the other of them could get out of the house, do some shopping or tend to whatever else needed doing. Mostly of course the "Dad watch" was an excuse to take turns getting away for a while and they both knew it. He was glad his sister was there. Neither knew, nor did either ask where, aside from Albertson's, the other one went when not "on duty." He assumed that his sister spent much of her off-duty time talking with her husband on her cellphone. When it was his turn he would usually take the family Buick and drive to the public library to look through that day's New York Times and Wall Street Journal, then walk around to the park behind the building to sit on a park bench under a eucalyptus tree with a book. Sometimes it got too noisy to read, between children playing and the occasional homeless people who would walk past, talking and sometimes arguing, one of them invariably playing loud rap or hip-hop on a Bluetooth speaker. They all seemed to have Smartphones or the equivalent. When it got too noisy to read he would put his book in his pocket and sometimes drive to the beach to walk along the pier, watching the seagulls troll for garbage and the always-present handful of people, silent, heads mostly down, watching the fishing lines that dangled down into the surf from the thin poles they held in their hands as they leaned against the pier railing with its rotting wood and graffiti scratched in with knives.

The old man died. It happened on Jessie's watch, one day in August shortly after noon. He was pulling into the parking lot at WalMart, where he was thinking about buying some polo shirts and maybe a pair of jeans, when his cellphone began playing "Take The 'A' Train," his ringtone.

"It's happened," Jessie said. "He's gone."

"When?"

"Just now. I went into his bedroom to turn him over and he was lying there on his side. Not breathing, his eyes half-open. I'm calling the time of death twelve-thirty."

He exhaled a long breath, shook his head. "All right. I'm on my way."

"Where are you?"

"WalMart. I'll be there in ten minutes. You call the coroner. I'll be right along."

So here it was all happening again. Less than a year since the last time. What now? Too early to think. He drove home.

9

One November day everything seemed to happen at once. It was a Saturday, normally a quiet day in the park because the medical, dental and insurance offices in the neighborhood were all closed on Saturdays, so there was less traffic than on weekdays and it was easier to park – I still kept my scooter at the curb along Canon St. I didn't ride it much, so it usually stayed in one place. I realize now that it was a good thing I didn't ride it much. I was so full of beer most of the time in those days that getting on the scooter would have been a very bad idea. Cage's mom, Jennifer, had warned me about it in no uncertain terms: "If I catch you climbing on that scooter drunk again, I'm gonna kick your ass," she said.

"Why, Jennifer! I didn't know you cared," I said.

In reply she threw a sneaker at me. I was fond of Jennifer and I think she was of me. Otherwise she wouldn't have threatened to kick my ass and thrown a sneaker at me.

Not much danger of her kicking my ass, though. She was seldom around. But she was right. I did wreck the scooter once, returning from a beer-run to the CVS pharmacy when Crown Liquor store already closed.

And did I get lucky that night! I wasn't going very fast, maybe 15-20 mph, but I lost control going around a downhill corner. I landed in someone's driveway. Somebody, maybe whoever owned the driveway, called an ambulance. I had my helmet on, but I think I was out cold for a few minutes even with the helmet because I don't remember the ambulance arriving. I only remember the EMTs putting in the ambulance and taking me to Scripps. I wasn't seriously hurt, just some scrapes and bruises along the left side of my body, which was what I landed on. They had to take stitches in my left hip. They kept me at Scripps overnight. The doctor who did the stitching told me that my blood alcohol level was .14 It only takes .08 to get you a DUI in California. That's where I was lucky. The police were also alerted of course, and they came, but by the time they got there the ambulance and I had already left. All they had was my scooter, which they impounded of course. But $258 to retrieve my scooter from the towing yard was a lot cheaper than the $5,000 plus jail time that a DUI would have cost me.

I was in my usual spot under my usual tree facing McKinley Ave. that Saturday morning. I'd bought myself a folding chair at WalMart, a director's chair. It cost me $15. It was red. I was tired of those hard park benches, and also of trying to get comfortable sitting on the ground. Eucalyptus trees have large, knotty roots that protrude above the ground and make it hard to get comfortable sitting under one of them, even if all you're doing is sozzling yourself into blessed oblivion. The director's chair was an improvement; it even had a little hole in the right armrest with webbed netting inside where you could put a cold drink. I was reading and sipping on a Hurricane, which of course I had in a brown paper bag just in case the police should cruise by. I was reading *The Shadow Line* by Conrad. I loved Conrad's stories of the sea, although he's no barrel of laughs, as anyone who's read *Heart of Darkness* knows. I was deeply into it when a racket arose just off to my left. Feminine voices, shouting, even screeching. I looked up. I rolled my eyeballs silently. The Fighting Dykes, as Cyrus called them, were at it again. Chantal and Yvonne. So much for peace and quiet. I closed my book and took a deep gulp of my beer.

They were less than fifty yards from where I sat, and as usual I had no idea what they were fighting about. Their shouted exchanges provided no clue. All I heard was a lot of "You fucking bitch!" "You lying whore!" "You're nothing but a fucking pillow princess!" The usual stuff.

I looked around for Cyrus. As a close friend of both women, but especially of his "cousin" Chantal, Cyrus was usually able to restore the peace by getting between them. Cyrus often stepped in to mediate drug-or-alcohol induced arguments before they got out of hand. His first and foremost priority was always to make sure things got quieted down before any police showed up—the last thing any of the parkies wanted around, ever, was cops.

But there was no sign of Cyrus, or of Marianne either. Where would they disappear on a Saturday morning? A local church group regularly came and set up a table in the library parking lot on Saturdays, handing out coffee, bottled water, fruit, hard-boiled eggs, cookies, that kind of thing. Cyrus always wandered over to get his share and Marianne's. But the church people came around at 7:30 a.m. It was 9:45 now and they were long gone. Cyrus and Marianne's stuff was stacked and covered under their usual tree across the park from where I sat, but a quick scan of the park showed no trace of them.

The Fighting Dykes were such a pain in the ass. Obviously I had to find a quieter place. I drained the last of my beer, stuck the Conrad paperback in my hip pocket and folded up my chair.

As I was about to hoist the chair over my shoulder and head over toward Avenue D, away from the noise, suddenly Yvonne lunged at Chantal. She got her hands around Chantal's neck. But Chantal was no beginner when it came to street-brawling; she broke Yvonne's grip and shoved her backwards on to the lawn. Yvonne stumbled and fell and Chantal was immediately on top of her, pummeling away with open hands.

I'd seen those two going at it plenty of times, but never had I seen one of them actually put hands on the other. Fearing that one of them might actually hurt the other one, I pulled out my phone and dialed 911.

Although the police department was right across the street from the park, it took a patrol car almost fifteen minutes to get there. In the meantime the two combatants broke and went to neutral corners. Yvonne went across the park to a bench next to the sidewalk that led to the library. Chantal remained under the tree where the fight had broken out. She began brushing her hair.

I felt like a damn fool: now I had the cops on the way and the squall had blown over. I decided to make myself scarce and walked toward the library. I could duck in there, look at the newspaper and pretend I didn't know any of these people. The police were accustomed to Yvonne and Chantal's domestic squabbles. They had broken them up before. More than likely the officers would give them a scolding about disturbing the peace and a threat about the next time, and it would all be over. Still, I thought it prudent to get myself out of the picture. I leaned my folding chair against a tree, tossed the empty beer can into the trash and went on my way. It was still early, so it was very unlikely that anyone would steal my chair, although in the park you never knew. Anything that could be sold for drugs was fair game. I remembered Sandy's remark on the first day I met her, "They'll steal anything that ain't bolted down, and sometimes if it is."

It was not quite ten; the library had not opened yet. A half-dozen people milled around in front of the door, playing with their cellphones, looking at their watches, talking quietly among themselves. That was the library for you: sometimes they opened a couple of minutes late, but never a second early. I decided to go back to my tree. The girls didn't know that it was I who had called for help—it might have been one of the perennially-nosy park neighbors. And I already had a book to read.

But as I re-entered the park and headed back to my chair, it appeared as if the bell were about to ring for Round Two. Chantal and Yvonne faced each other across the grass, too far apart for grappling but within easy shouting distance, and continued their mouth fight. "I'm sick of you lying to me!" Yvonne shrieked. "I know what went on that alley! Bitch! You think I'm fucking STUPID? You think I'm fucking blind and DEAF?" "I wasn't lying! I was telling the truth! Fuck you and your fucking jealousy! Cunt!"

And they rushed at each other again. Bang, and they were back on the ground wrestling. This time Yvonne somehow got the advantage; she was on top. Chantal was on her back receiving the blows.

I looked around. Dammit, no sign of the cops *or* Cyrus. Myself, I've never been any good at fighting. I had two fights in junior high school and lost both of them. There wasn't any point in my trying to intervene. It wouldn't solve anything and I might just come away with a black eye myself, not to mention both of them hating me for sticking my nose into their lovers' quarrel.

But a patrol car finally pulled over to the curb on Davidson Street. Two cops got out and walked quickly over to where Yvonne and Chantal, not having noticed that they had company, were still grappling on the lawn. When they saw the cops, they stopped and stood up. Yvonne dropped her hands to her sides. She had been arrested before and knew better than to put them in her pockets. Chantal straightened her hair with one hand.

The shouting had stopped. I was too far away to overhear conversation. I retrieved my chair, set it back up, opened my book and pretended to read, although of course I was keeping an eye on the situation.

Yvonne had obviously been told to sit down. She sat on the grass, her legs folded Indian-style. Chantal was still standing. One police officer led Chantal a few yards away while the other stayed behind, talking with Yvonne. Then he went around, squatted down and put handcuffs on her. After all, Yvonne had been on top having her turn at the pummeling when the police rolled up. So it was Yvonne who was going to spend the long weekend in the pokey.

I talked with Chantal later. She wasn't mad at me once I'd explained to her that yes, I had made the call, but only because I didn't want either of them to get hurt. She was less concerned about that than she was about what was going to happen next, insisting over and over that she would not press charges against her "wife." I nodded, happy to be off the hook and not knowing the law involved. Cyrus explained later that it didn't make any difference whether Chantal wanted Yvonne locked up or not. The police had witnessed an assault. The city would file charges.

Cyrus and Marianne returned early that afternoon. He didn't say where they had been but I figured probably the ER. I was surprised that Marianne was still walking around—she was very nearly due.

I gave Cyrus the short version of what had happened earlier. "Judge'll probably issue a stay-away order this time," he said.

"Chantal wandered off somewhere," I said. "I haven't seen her since about eleven O'clock."

"She probably went to visit Yvonne in jail."

Later that afternoon Cheryl and Rob showed up. They were recent arrivals on our scene. Cheryl was from Galveston, or had been in Galveston, or somewhere near there, before. It was never very clear where she was from because she was always drunk; the exact location shifted around. We figured Houston was close enough; she became "Cheryl from Houston." Her father was in Houston, anyway, or so I gathered from her shouting matches with him on somebody's borrowed cellphone – she didn't have one of her own, so she went around borrowing everyone else's. My guess was that Rob was probably a Texan too, since they had arrived together. Rob had been in the Army ("He was a Ranger. First in, last out!" Cheryl proudly told everyone again and again) and was still in the reserves. Cheryl was about ten years older than Rob. You could see it. Her face showed some lines that his didn't. ("His will soon enough, he stays with her," Cyrus observed.) The booze and the cigarettes had helped age her, but she was clearly older than Rob, who stood straight and didn't have any visible signs of wear on him. He had blue eyes and wore a light-brown beard with no gray in it. Yet, anyway. Cheryl wore her hair short and it was not just blonde, but platinum-blonde, draw your own conclusions about that. She was quite slender and liked to show off her bare midriff although it was a little flabby – again, probably the booze. Mostly Cheryl was voluble. Her own boyfriend Rob called her "The Mouth of the South." To most of us she was "Oh-no-here-comes-Cheryl."

She was particularly fond of me for some reason. She would flirt, punch me, jokingly put her arms around me ("Come here, homeboy!") and once even jumped into my lap as I sat in my folding chair smoking a pipe. She was drunk that morning of course. "Dammit, Cheryl, you're gonna break the chair! Get off me!" I said as I dumped her on the lawn. I think she was trying to make Rob jealous. It didn't work, though. He barely seemed to notice her foolishness. No doubt she had pulled this sort of thing before and he was used to it. We all wondered why he stayed with her. She was soused on vodka all the time (Rob drank his share, but less than Cheryl did) so they fought almost as much as Chantal and Yvonne. But with them it was Cheryl who did most of the yelling while Rob did most of the ignoring. Rob and I got along fine, although Cheryl repeatedly told me on the side that Rob didn't like me. I think that was wishful thinking on her part. It got to be a joke between Rob and me; we would be talking and he would suddenly stop and say with a grin, "I keep forgetting. I hate you."

So why did Rob stay with Cheryl? Alone with Cyrus, I asked the question out loud. He shrugged as if the answer were something that went without saying. "She probably fucks his brains out every night," he said. Probably he was right. We left it at that.

They came strolling up late in the afternoon, hand-in-hand. Rob, as usual, had his backpack on. He seldom took it off if he weren't sitting down. An Army thing? Cheryl was feeling no pain, as our elders used to say.

"This place needs some waking up, Texas-style!" she laughed as she walked over to Marianne and asked her for a cigarette. Marianne had not stopped smoking despite her pregnancy, but she was stingy with her cigarettes and anyway she couldn't stand Cheryl. She didn't offer her a smoke and walked off without a word.

Cheryl pretended not to notice. "Hey, Pat! Can I use your phone to call my dad?"

"Nope."

"Oh, come on, homeboy!"

"No. I thought the CART people had you in rehab."

"They did, but she didn't stay," Rob said.

"Pleeease, Pat! I'm out of money. I have to ask my father to send me fifty bucks."

"No way. I know you. You make one call, then you hang up and immediately start dialing again. Then you talk, then you hang up and start dialing again. I let you make one phone call, you make five."

"Come on. I'm sorry. But what do you care? It doesn't cost you any extra."

"It's called abusing hospitality. No."

"Spoilsport. Hey, you want to buy some Librium?"

"They gave her some Librium in rehab," Rob said. "She had it in her pocket when she walked out. She's been trying to sell it all day."

"No, I'm not buying any Librium from you," I said. "Knock it off, Cheryl. Rob?"

He sighed. "You know how she gets."

She then asked Cyrus if he wanted any.

"No thanks. And don't offer it to my girl. She'll be going into labor any time now. I don't want any drugs in her system when I take her to the hospital."

"Good luck with that," I muttered under my breath. Cyrus caught my eye and shot me a helpless glance, as if to say "Win or lose, I have to try."

Rob persuaded Cheryl to set up camp under a tree about a hundred yards away. He wanted to get her off alone, and she responded with a wink and a grin to the rest of us, but we knew that he was only trying to steer her away so that she might lie down and sleep off the booze. We had watched this *pas-de-deux* before. Rob selected a spot, took his backpack off, put it on the ground and drew a blanket out of it. He spread the blanket on the ground and lay down. Cheryl curled up beside him. She took off her Levi's jacket and rolled it up for a pillow. He gave her a cigarette. We saw him quietly talking to her . Within ten or fifteen minutes she was asleep.

Andrew and Frankie had joined us. They sat on a bench playing mumblety-peg with their pocketknives. Cyrus asked me to go and get us both a beer. Once I'd collected a buck-forty from him to pay for his, I started across the park toward the liquor store, passing Rob and Cheryl's spot on the way. She was still asleep. He sat smoking and looking out at the traffic on McKinley Ave.

I paused next to him and looked at her collapsed form on the blanket. "Snockered again," I said.

"What's new?"

"Why do you stay with her?"

He flicked ash off his cigarette. "Tell you the truth, I've been giving some thought to going solo," he said.

"We all kind of wondered."

"I know. Everybody does."

I went off to get a Hurricane for myself and a King Cobra for Cyrus.

That night our little group (myself, Cyrus, Marianne and – for tonight, anyway, Frankie) camped in our usual spot on the concrete next to the west side of the library. There was a roof awning there which provided some shelter, although no rain was in the forecast that night. The awning in front of the library was wider, provided better shelter, and was more popular when it rained, but a lot of noisy tweakers tended to gather there at night and we preferred our side of the building where it was quieter. Also, in the event of a flare-up between any of the druggies, which could, and occasionally did, bring police cars swinging into the parking lot with lights flashing, it was better to be a little bit away from the action so that the police, if they did come, were unlikely to ask us more than "Did you see anything?" If you were around on the other side of the building you could more honestly say no.

You need something under you if you're going to camp on concrete. I had a six-foot roll of foam rubber. I'd unroll it and lay my two sleeping bags on top of it, one as mattress and one as blanket. My backpack was my pillow—not the most comfortable pillow in the world, but it kept your things safe during the night. Cyrus and Marianne had so many blankets loaded up on their two shopping carts that all they had to do was make a layer of them and snuggle up on it. They even had real pillows. They would bed down and then, as Marianne fell asleep, Cyrus would get out his iPhone and watch *Gunsmoke* reruns, which brought back some unpleasant memories for me.

Frankie was never prepared for anything. Drugs were his first priority and his backpack was all he carried around with him. At the last minute he always lacked something he needed. Cyrus would lend him a blanket, then Frankie would go out poking through the neighborhood dumpsters for a flattened cardboard box, standard bivouac equipment for many homeless. Cardboard did not provide much cushion against concrete, but it was insulating. On a chilly winter night having a piece of cardboard under you helped you to keep warm. Or warmer, anyway.

The homeless tend to keep country hours for the obvious reason that if you're living outside there isn't much to do after dark except bed down for the night. Cyrus made sure that our little camp was always in place by ten p..m. when the park closed. He wanted to keep a low profile at all times. Technically the cops could chase us away for camping on city property, and sometimes the younger, more gung-ho ones did when it got to be late at night and they didn't have anything else to do. But most of the rank-and-file tolerated our presence as long as we didn't make trouble and were out of the park by ten. They had more important things to do than hassle us, and anyway most of them regarded homelessness as the city council's problem, not the police department's.

We settled down for a long November night. It was a little chilly, but we all slept in our clothes, most of us only removing our shoes. Even those we kept close – yes, shoes were sometimes stolen. I always leaned mine against the library wall next to my backpack. Cyrus hunkered down to watch TV. (The library had wi-fi and they almost always forgot to shut it off at night.) I had my volume of Joseph Conrad and a half-pint of Hiram Walker to help me get to sleep. I didn't like the taste of bourbon, but it was cheaper than Scotch. Vodka would have been cheaper still, but even as low as I had sunk by then, I wasn't about to join the Eds and Cheryls of this world and become a vodka drinker.

It got to be about 11:30 by my watch. Frankie had found a large piece of cardboard and was asleep. Cyrus was still watching westerns. I was about to take off my sneakers, switch off my flashlight and try to get some sleep myself.

Then Cheryl came back. She knew where our little camp was and she knew which spot was traditionally mine: at the end of the row near the corner of the building.

She headed straight for me and practically fell on top of me. She was drunk of course, and sobbing hysterically, the way she always did after a fight with Rob.

"He LEFT me! Oh, Pat, he left me!" She threw her arms around me and buried her head in my backpack next to my shoulder. She stank of Popov or Smirnoff or whatever it was.

"He'll come back," I said. "You've had these tiffs before."

"No, he WON'T! He LEFT ME! This time he really left me!"

"Did he say where he was going?"

"No."

"Then he'll be back. Where's he going to go at this hour of the night?"

Cyrus looked up from *The Rifleman*. "Can we hold down the noise over there?"

"I'm trying," I said. "Look, Cheryl--"

"Can I stay with you?" She sobbed and looked at me in the half-light. Even in the half-light I could see that her eyes were bloodshot.

"No. Come on, Cheryl! There isn't room for both of us under here. There's barely room for me."

"But I don't want to be alone! Oh, where did he go?"

She began burrowing, uninvited, underneath my nice, warm sleeping bag, and I got pushed out of it, on to the concrete.

I stood up. "Cheryl, goddamn it, you can't stay here! Go back to wherever you and Rob were camped. He'll come back. Come on, get out of my sleeping bag!"

"No!"

Some might say that what I did next was kick her. It really wasn't a kick. Because I wasn't angry, just very annoyed. Who wouldn't be at that hour of the night? Cheryl was hard enough to deal with in the daytime. Right now I only knew one thing: I wanted her out of my bed. I gave her a poke (okay, a strong poke) with the toe of my sneaker.

"Cheryl, get out of my sleeping bag!"

Marianne, who had been dozing, slowly got herself out from under her blankets. She did not like being awakened, especially at night and, I would assume, especially when she was eight months and some days pregnant.

"Goddamn it, you fucking whore, shut the fuck up!" Marianne shouted. She did not like Cheryl, not one bit.

Cheryl knew trouble was coming. She wasn't that drunk. She got up from my sleeping bag. I stood back, over near the trash can next to the library planter.

"I got a right to be here," Cheryl said. "I got as much right to be here as anyone else!"

"Shut up, you fucking drunken slut! GET OUT OF HERE!"

Now it was Cyrus' turn to get annoyed. "Knock off the noise! You're gonna attract the cops!" He put down his phone and stood up.

"Oh, fuck you, Cyrus!" Marianne yelled at him. "I want this bitch out of here! Now! If you don't get rid of her..."

"I got as much right to be here--"

That was as far as Cheryl got. Marianne stepped over and clocked Cheryl right in the face. Even that pregnant, Marianne could throw a punch. Cheryl fell against the side of the building, but managed to straighten up and tried to hit back. She was too drunk to defend herself, though. Marianne threw a right cross that knocked Cheryl down again.

"Cheryl, I think you better get out of here," I managed to say.

Cheryl wiped her mouth with the back of her hand. She wasn't bleeding, but she was shook, and for the moment, defeated.

She got up. "Oh, fuck all of you!" she said, and hurried off into the night, still sobbing.

"She needs to go sober up," I said. I was one to talk, with my slight Hiram Walker buzz which had been spoiled by Cheryl's intrusion, which come to think of it was one of the reasons I was so annoyed.

"She needs to go to hell!" Marianne yelled, still shaking with anger.

Cyrus put his hands on Marianne's shoulders. "All right baby girl. All right. It's over now. She's gone. Man, that was a couple of good punches you threw there, pregnant lady." Joviality to ease the tension.

"I hate that bitch."

"We know. Pat, would you go check and make sure she's gone?"

"Are you kidding? It was me she was looking for. She sees my face, I'll never get rid of her."

"Please. Just a quick look around. I don't want her drawing in the cops."

"All right."

I strode off slowly in the general direction of the street, hoping not to find anything. I looked east up the street. I looked west down the street. She was gone. Relief. Back to my bedrolls, my last swallow of Hiram Walker and then some sleep.

Another commotion, less noisy but enough to wake me up, started about an hour later.

Marianne was going into labor. Cyrus was on the phone calling for the paramedics.

"You think that dust-up with Cheryl brought on her labor?" I asked him.

"That bitch," Marianne gasped. "Oooh."

"Easy, sweet girl," Cyrus said, patting her back. "We're gonna get you to the hospital right now." He looked at me. "Could be. I need to get her over into the light where the ambulance can see us."

Marianne had a blanket over her shoulders. She stood, stooped slightly over, arms crossed over her swollen abdomen. Cyrus put his arm around her. "Come on baby, let's go around front," he said.

"Anything I can do?" I asked.

"Nah, I don't think so." Cyrus had been through this with Marianne before. "Just stay here and babysit him." He jerked his thumb at Frankie, who had not bothered to wake up.

"Sounds like an easy assignment," I said, glancing down at Frankie's sleeping form.

"I'll call you."

It was daylight when Cyrus called my cellphone. I was half-awake, just thinking about getting up, moving my stuff and heading to 7-Eleven for my morning beer when the phone went off and reminded me suddenly of what had happened a few hours earlier. I flipped it open. "Hello?"

"We had the baby."

"When?"

"About three-thirty."

I shook my head, briskly. "You don't sound too thrilled," I said.

"The county already took her."

"Which means--"

"Yeah. Marianne tested positive when we came in. I knew she wasn't going to stay off it."

"Did you even get a chance to give her a name?"

"Cyrania."

"Pardon me?"

"SI-RANYA. Spelled C-y-r-a..." he paused for a second, "n-i-a."

"Named another kid after yourself, I see." Cyrus' daughters all had names that were variants of his own.

"What else? Whenever I plant a seed on this earth, it bears my name." This was Cyrus strutting the boards, as when he declared "I'm a Cowboys fan, and I'll die a Cowboys fan." It was unlikely that he had ever heard the name of Thespis, but Cyrus was his pupil.

Cyrus returned to the park later that morning, alone of course. Marianne would be in the hospital for another day or so.

I was back in the same spot where I was when the fight broke out between Chantal and Yvonne twenty-four hours earlier: next to my favorite eucalyptus tree, facing the library, book in hand. The only difference was that now I was sipping 7-Eleven coffee instead of Hurricane – I'd decided to wait for Cyrus.

"So it's a *fait accompli*," I said as he came up to me.

"A what?"

"A done deal. Did you at least get to see the baby before they took her?"

"Sure. She's beautiful. Looks just like me."

"Oh, shut the fuck up."

"Well, she's beautiful anyway."

"You must have gotten a picture."

He took his cellphone out of his pocket, fiddled with it, and showed me. Yes, she was a beautiful little girl and I said so. "Half-white, half-black, they're always the prettiest babies," I said. Somehow the tiny pink ribbon that someone had put in the baby's hair made me feel sad.

Cyrus must have felt the same. He stuck the cellphone back in his hip pocket and put one hand over his eyes. He sat there on the grass like that for a long time. I sipped my coffee and waited. There was no question that he was setting the stage to tell me something.

"Man, I'm gonna get outta here," he said at last.

"You've said that before."

"I know. But I've been thinking about it since last night. I didn't take the bus back from the hospital this morning. I walked. Thought about it the whole way. I don't care what I have to do, I'll give up the beer, anything. But I'm gonna get the county to play ball with me, give me my daughters back. I want us to be a family. I want my family, my daughters under a roof. I want to be under a roof with my girls." Cyrus began to cry, something I had not seen him do before. "I want to have a home with my daughters."

"Why don't you just get a job? Work to make it happen." I could easily have said the same thing about myself. But I didn't have three daughters. I couldn't see things the way Cyrus did.

"Takes too long," he said. "The kind of work I could find, with my background, no education, been in jail. I'm fifty-six years old. Nobody gonna give me the kind of steady work I'd need to provide my girls with everything I want them to have. I'm gonna need the county's help. I'm going to go before the court, lay out my case, convince them I can be a good father. I want to be a good father! I want my girls back!" He stopped crying, sniffed, looked up at me from where he sat on the grass.

"I'm gonna have to write some letters," he said. "But I can't write worth a shit. Pat, you used to be a reporter. Could you write some letters for me?"

"Sure. Just tell me what you want to say. We'll get it written down."

"I want to do this," he said firmly.

"Well, do it. Tell you what. What do you say we make this … a sporting proposition?" I was trying to think of a small way I could encourage Cyrus. This was the first thing I thought of.

"What are you talking about?"

"You weren't planning to live in the park forever. None of us is. I want to get out of here myself eventually."

"Why don't *you* just get a job? You never been in jail. You don't have the strikes against you I do. You went to college."

"I'm older than you are. What kind of a job is anybody going to give me? Night watchman? Driving a cab? I already tried that. To hell with that. I'll be sixty-two next year. Once I get Social Security I can rent a room somewhere. I don't have any family. I could manage. I've managed until now. Eating up my savings."

"Yeah, you told me you been draining off your 401(k.) But what's this sporting proposition you're talking about?"

"Just this. Let's say, let's say"...(nothing *too* big, I thought) "whichever one of us gets out of the park first, the other one has to buy us both a steak dinner. Best place in town. Black Angus."

Cyrus stood up, wiped his eyes and grinned. "Just to play safe, let's make it Denny's. I don't know if if I could ever afford Black Angus. But make it Denny's, homie, and you're on."

"Done. To seal the bet, what do you say you buy us both a beer?"

"No. I said I was going to give up the beer. I meant it."

"Carne vale. One last one."

"I don't have any cash on me."

"What's new? All right, goddamn it, *I'll* buy us both a beer."

On our way to the liquor store we ran into Terry, Frankie's dad. When he learned where we were going, he tried to work me for a Hurricane. Terry was one of the biggest moochers in the park, even bigger than Ed. On an ordinary day I might have treated him. Terry and I had a reciprocal agreement: you buy this time, I'll buy next time. But this time I told him no. This was strictly between Cyrus and me. We were on our way to seal an agreement. No third parties allowed.

10

For most of his life the only thing the old man ever did with money was stash it in savings accounts. Raised in poverty in the midwest, Joe Donahy had taken his own father's tales of the stock market crash very much to heart. Having seen poverty first-hand as a child, then gone straight to work after high school, the old man's greatest fear all his life was that poverty might somehow leap out from nowhere and "get" him again. His education did not include anything about handling money other than how important it was make sure you always had some saved. The very word "investment" had a sinister, fear-invoking sound to him; it carried the evil echo of *risk;* it was something dangerous and not to be fooled around with. The stock market, to him, was that mysterious and dreadful house of cards that had collapsed in 1929, causing the bank failures, foreclosures, hobo jungles, people selling apples and pencils on street corners and all the other ghastly things he had seen growing up. No "investments" for him. Banks and savings and loans, protected by the FDIC, were the only places he would ever put his money.

After more than forty years of this, his savings account balance was well into five figures. One of his brothers-in-law, an uncle of Patrick's who had done well for himself and his family and for that reason had the old man's trust, convinced him that letting all that money just lie there collecting the five or six percent interest was foolish. He talked the old man into putting some of his money into mutual funds and annuities. Hence the loose-leaf binders that would come out, one, two, three times a week and be spread on the dining room table.

But it became obvious, not too long after Edith's death, that he understood less and less of what he was looking at in these binders. The brother-in-law who had steered him into this was dead now. His son glanced through the binders one day and saw that the pages were out of order, superfluous cover letters and receipts mixed in with the actual statements, and everywhere were the old man's and margin notes in ballpoint pen which made no sense at all. Perhaps they made sense to the old man; to his son they were gibberish. At one time his father had written an elegant cursive hand. Now the scribblings were so shaky and crabbed that they were hard to read even if they had made any sense.

Well, he decided, so what? Now it was Jessie's problem, Jessie's and the lawyer's. She had been designated trustee in the event of the old man's incapacity or death. She was going to have to sort all of this out, and there were some other big decisions to be made as well, such as what they were going to do with the family house.

Which left him wondering where he himself was going to live. When Edith was alive they had discussed (when she was sober enough) the possible next moves for both of them when the old man finally died. They had talked about staying on at home, the two of them. The house had been in the family for more than fifty years, and no one was in a big hurry to see it leave the family.

Now Edith was gone and that problem had, sadly, taken care of itself. But his problem remained. Although he and Edith had talked about staying on the property together, he wasn't about to consider staying there by himself. The place was too big for one person. Even if they fixed up the granny flat and he rented it out, he would still have the three-bedroom front house to deal with, and he didn't like the idea of living alone there. He had never been a homeowner and did not want to become one at this stage of life. Property taxes, home repairs, upkeep...how would he pay for all of it? It was a moot question; he simply didn't want the expenses or the headaches involved in being a property owner. After a conversation that ran from afternoon well into the evening, during which they consumed two-and-a-half pots of coffee, he and Jessie decided to put the place up for sale.

It took six months to find a buyer. He stayed in the house until it was sold.

With his father gone he needed something to fill his days, and also, when the old man's life ended, so did the retirement pension that had been providing for both of them. He would have to find some kind of work.

He checked. His old job at the newspaper had been filled, and even if it hadn't, the ten dollars an hour that it paid would not cover the living expenses of a man alone in a three-bedroom house. He called around to some other papers in the area, but the answer was always the same: either they had all the people they needed or what editorial openings they might have were entry-level jobs for kids just starting out in the business. He was fifty-nine and not about to start covering city council meetings, at night, for a few hundred bucks a month, something he had willingly done when he was twenty-four and full of ambition, but not now.

He started driving a cab. When he called to ask about driving, the dispatcher who took his call told him he could make "pretty good" money at it if he were willing to work long hours. Now that he was alone with nothing else to do, long hours were not a problem. In fact they appealed to him more when he considered the alternative: sitting around the old house watching *The Young and the Restless* and *Wheel of Fortune.* He leased the cab. As long as the company got its weekly cab-rent it didn't care what hours he worked.

In the beginning he started out driving early in the mornings, but between six a.m. and early afternoon there was practically no business. Things usually began to pick up around three. then got busier at night. He quickly learned that between five p.m. and two a.m. things really got busy if they were going to get busy at all. He would leave the house around two p.m., drive until at least midnight and, if there were enough business, somewhat later. He would not drive after two in the morning. Experienced drivers told him that if some drug-crazed loony were going to hit you over the head for your cash, it was going to happen between two and five a.m. He took their advice and always made sure to go off-duty no later than one.

He got into a rhythm, going to bed toward dawn, sleeping until 11:30 or noon and then going back out to put in another ten or twelve hours. On the Fourth of July, Halloween and New Years' Eve it was closer to fourteen hours – lots of parties and lots of late revelers too drunk or too cautious to drive themselves home. There were plenty of groups wanting rides on holidays and weekends, which meant good tips, especially if they had been drinking. Drunks get very free with their cash.

His own drinking had picked up. He noticed it. Often after coming in from driving after midnight and finding himself both tired and wound up, wanting to sleep but too wound up for sleep, his father's jug of Scoresby Rare was still atop water heater in the kitchen. He'd fix himself a Scotch-and-water, sometimes a sandwich to go with it, take a seat in the living room at one or two O'clock in the morning and switch on Turner Classic Movies and swozzle himself to sleep with the Duke, Humphrey Bogart, the two Hepburns, Glenn Ford or another of his favorites. Often daylight would be seeping into southern California by the time he turned it off and went to bed.

It was a lonely existence, but he was used to that. He had once been married, but it had been a dozen years now since his divorce. His marriage was part of his earlier life, those days back in Maryland when a marketing job with a technology firm had enabled him to keep a continent between himself and his too-often bickering family. He remembered his wife mainly as a figure at the other end of the house. Valerie was a real estate broker and worked mostly from home, on her computer. (The computer was where they had found each other: both had gotten bored or fed up with their respective dating lives and resorted to Match.com.) She went all the time out to show properties, but usually by the time he came in from work late in the afternoons she would be in her office, once one of two bedrooms the house had, doing business on the computer and on the phone. Papers and loose-leaf binders were stacked and scattered all over her office among empty or partly-empty Diet Coke cans and ashtrays littered with the remains of Marlboro Lights. He seldom went into his wife's office. He found the clutter somehow depressing.

Real estate was Valerie's passion. She liked to "flip" properties – buy a place, move in and spend thousands remodeling it, then put it up for sale, buy another property and do it all again. This seemed to him a bit peculiar, but since real estate was clearly what she was passionate about, (she pored over the real estate section of the Sunday paper with the zeal of a Talmudic scholar while showing little or no interest in the rest of the paper) he regarded this as simply part of what she was, and hence, part of being married to her. But after they had moved twice within the first two years of their marriage, he began to suspect that something peculiar might be going on. Valerie took a cocktail of pills every morning and he never asked what they were for, but one day she jocularly referred to her regular-care physician, Dr. John Howard, as "my happy-pill doctor." Not alarmed but curious enough to want to know more, he examined the pill bottles while she was out on a real-estate call. At least three of them were antidepressants or mood-regulators. Could this be the reason why they were moving every year or so? If his wife were indeed bipolar, it might not be such a paranoid idea that their marriage might be just another of her enthusiasms-of-the-moment, and that he might find himself being flipped like a condo.

By the third year of their marriage, any disinterested observer would have drawn the conclusion that that was exactly what was happening. Valerie spent more and more time away from the house, and even when she was home, her "office time" would increasingly eat into the evenings which had once been held aside for dinner, music, conversation, laughter, argument, movies, sex or some combination of them. He started coming home, and, seeing that she was either gone or encloistered with her computer, would pop open an MGD, then another, mess with his own computer, read or watch TV as he waited for her to come out of the spare bedroom and join him.

He confronted her about it at last one night and to his surprise, instead of arguing or dissembling or even getting annoyed, she came right out and ruefully admitted that she was bored with the marriage and wanted it over with. Just for good measure she called him a drunk, but she needn't have bothered. (Valerie drank nothing but Diet Coke—eight or ten cans per day.) He knew perfectly well that he had been drinking too much beer lately, but as little as she had been around, what difference could it make to her? It wasn't as if his beer-swilling had spoiled any otherwise-lovely evenings. They hadn't had any such evenings lately.

Thinking things over later, when the beer had worn off, he derided himself for having overlooked (or willfully ignored) the most glaring fact of all: he was Valerie's third husband. If she had been unable (or insufficiently willing) to make two previous marriages work, what chance could theirs have had?

11

When Cyrus told me he was going to get out of the park and find housing, I didn't take him too seriously because he was always saying things like that. Every time he got mad about something, we'd hear his "I'm gettin' the fuck outta here" speech. Like that time at the library when a big scene with Marianne got him booted out for a few months. But somehow he never followed up on the gettin'-the-fuck-outta-here speech. That very Sunday that I took him to the liquor store for his "last beer," three guys from the another park a few blocks away showed up. Cyrus had hung around that other park for a while before we met. He told me about it. He'd finally gotten fed up with the constant trouble there and moved to our park. But he knew these guys all by name. And these were at the bottom, losers, you could tell by listening to them talk. No ambition anywhere that you could see – they lived for the next fix, the next beer, the next disability check, the next fight. Cyrus mostly avoided them anymore, and probably would have this time, but they had brought along a 12-pack of Bud Light and Cyrus made himself right at home among them, seated on a milk crate under a tree, cold brew in one hand, (the remainder of the beers hidden in the bushes nearby) and, after a few cans, shooting off his mouth like he always did. So much for his teary resolution of that morning, I thought.

But when the HOT team came around on Tuesday, Cyrus buttonholed Sgt. Rudy Payne and began an earnest conversation with him. Although Cyrus usually had a hearty greeting for the HOT team officers when they made their weekly visit, (part of his general policy of maintaining good relations with the police in order to avoid trouble) he didn't often engage them in actual conversation. Usually he confined himself to a good-morning-nice-to-see-you, a friendly wave of the hand, and then he'd withdraw to the far end of the park so as not to have to communicate with them any more than necessary. Cyrus had been in his share of trouble and was wary of getting too chummy with cops.

But today was different. That's why I noticed. Cyrus went right up to Rudy Payne and started talking with him. I was too far away to hear what they were saying, but if Cyrus was going to have a serious conversation with the HOT team, I had a pretty good idea what it was about.

Sgt. Payne was a black guy, stout like Cyrus, and very dedicated. He took his job seriously—he wanted to help the homeless get off the street. Rudy would do small things for you if he thought you needed help, such as the time my wallet was stolen and with it my driver's license, my only ID. I reported the theft to the police, but expected nothing and of course never saw that wallet again. But when Rudy heard about it he took me in his patrol car to the DMV so I could apply for a replacement license. He stood next to me while I filled out the form and then walked me right through. Had I gone there alone I would have had to wait more than an hour. But if you walk into the DMV accompanied by a police officer you're going straight to the front of the line. Rudy knew that, and knew he was doing me a favor. He was that kind of guy, serious about maintaining good relations with the people who were, theoretically anyway, in his charge.

After the HOT team left that morning, I asked Cyrus if housing had indeed been the subject of his téte-a-téte with the police. "Yeah," he said.

"And?"

"Oh, the usual bullshit, you know. They want me to get into a program, get on a list."

"What program? You told me you haven't used tweak in more than a year."

"I wasn't in a program, though. They don't know that I been clean for a year. It was something I decided to do for myself. They ain't gonna take my word for it, even though I'm clean now."

"Well, why don't you just humor them? Get in a program if that makes them happy and gets you what you want."

"Fuck that. For one thing, I don't need it. For another thing, we're back to *waiting lists."* he crinkled up his nose and pulled down the corners of his mouth like a child telling a friend that he can't play after school because he's on restriction. "Fuck that bullshit. Takes too long. You know how long Sandy's been on the waiting list for section eight? At least two years. I don't want to wait that long. I want my daughters back."

"What are you going to do?"

He walked a few steps toward the sidewalk, stopped, whirled around suddenly and faced me. "I'll tell you what I'm gonna do!" he said. "I'm gonna do what I said I was gonna do two days ago. Only I ain't gonna just write just one or two fuckin' letters, I'm gonna *bombard* them motherfuckers with letters! The mayor, city council, CPS, municipal court, county supervisors, HHSA, TV, radio, the newspapers. Everybody! I'm gonna make myself *such* a pain in the ass that they'll give me what I want just to get rid of me! Hee hee hee!" He pumped his fist like he'd just hit a home run at Yankee Stadium.

"Hold on," I said. "We both know you can't write a letter. You couldn't write a grocery list. I know I said I'd help you, but I thought we were just talking about a couple of letters. You're talking about a whole PR campaign."

"I'll make it worth your while."

"How? You don't have two nickels to rub together."

He was looking off beyond the trees now. "I'll get you a date," he said absently.

"I don't want a date. Besides, I can just see the kind of 'date' you'd come up with. Some gal who's in the roller derby. Some babe who drives a salvage truck and sells crack out of the cab. No thanks."

"You'll help me, won't you?"

Had his voice risen at the words "won't you" it would have been a plea. But his voice went down at those words, an affirmation of something already known, like someone saying "You went to Vegas last week after all, didn't you?"

I sat down in my director's chair, took my paperback book out of my pocket, and sighed. "Yeah. You know I will."

"You're a good person, Pat."

"I'm a goddamn pushover, and you figured that out real early."

I was, too. Despite having kicked Cheryl out of my sleeping bag two nights ago just before Marianne punched her and then went to the hospital to have a baby, I did have that reputation around the park. Everybody seemed to just know somehow that old Pat was a soft touch. Word probably got around the first time I bought a beer for Terry or a taco at the corner roach-coach for Ed. "Ask the newbie, he'll help you." Only I wasn't a newbie anymore and should have developed at least something of a carapace by now.

That same day Yvonne got out of jail. And just as Cyrus had predicted, a judge had already issued a stay-away order; Yvonne was not allowed within fifty yards of Chantal. Of course they ignored the order and went right back to being as lovey-dovey as they always were when they weren't trying to kill each other. It was only when the HOT team came around, or when a police car on some errand that had nothing to do with them was spotted in the library parking lot that Yvonne would quickly make herself scarce for a couple of hours.

Of course Yvonne was gone from the park a lot anyway in her role as chief bread-and-dopewinner for herself and Chantal. Yvonne reportedly did a lot of canning to raise a couple of dollars here and there. ("Canning:" Verb. Collecting aluminum cans to redeem at a recycling center.) But of course canning was chickenfeed—the recycling center paid only about 50¢ a pound. You had to collect cans all day to make as much as ten bucks.

She also did a lot of petty stealing. Everyone knew it. A rumor had gone around that Yvonne was seen one afternoon grabbing Amazon boxes from peoples' porches. I tended not to believe that, though. She was too smart and too cagey to go around ripping off FedEx deliveries in broad daylight. Yvonne was well-connected in the neighborhood network; she participated in its subterranean economy in which goods were bought and sold and nobody asked where they came from. One evening she overheard me tell Terry that I would like to own a sportjacket. I even described the one I'd get if I had the money: dark blue with gold buttons. Yvonne came around two nights later with a sportjacket draped over her arm. Dark blue with gold buttons. Stolen of course.

"Where did you get that?" I asked her, smiling. We all knew where she had gotten it.

"I have my suppliers," she smiled. "So. What do you say? Five bucks?"

I right away regretted opening my big mouth to Terry. Although I saw this sort of thing go on every day, and wasn't above paying a couple of dollars myself for a pocketknife or a Bluetooth speaker to use with the Obama phone which, by the way, I had acquired on the front porch of the library from some guy I didn't know by swapping him a pack of Marlboros for it, this was different. Receiving stolen goods was bad enough; some part of me did not want to be seen *wearing* stolen goods. Not wanting to disappoint Yvonne, I went ahead and tried on the jacket she had "found."

My sigh of relief at finding that it was way too small was almost audible.

"Honey, I can't wear this," I said to her.

"Too small, huh?"

"I look like Don Johnson on *Miami Vice.*"

"So, no sale?"

"Sorry, but come on. It's too small! You can see that."

She shrugged and smiled. "No worries. Somebody'll want it." With that, she draped it over a nearby bench. Obviously it hadn't cost her anything, because a few minutes later when I went my way, Terry went his way and Yvonne and Chantal went their way, she left that jacket on the bench. It was getting dark by then. Forty-five minutes later I walked past that same bench on my way to the drinking fountain and sure enough the jacket was gone. Either someone with a slighter build than I had come along, or what was more likely, someone needing weed money had come along.

Early Thursday morning, after Cyrus and I had had our sunup beer together, he said to me, "Let's get started on that letter."

"Where are we going to work? It's not even eight O'clock yet. The library doesn't open until ten."

"We can work right here. You got something in your backpack to write with, don't you?"

He knew perfectly well that I did. Even if I didn't have pencil and paper, I did have my laptop. My Lenovo laptop was my most valuable possession and the main reason I always used my backpack for a pillow at night. Usually I didn't take it out unless I were inside the library. No reason to flash around that highly salable, highly stealable item out in the open. Cyrus knew about it but by now I trusted him. In fact I wouldn't be surprised if he had prevented it from being stolen once or twice already when I was passed out on the grass in the afternoon sun after a little too much beer.

It was still early and practically no one was around. I took out the laptop and powered it up, but almost immediately the "battery low" light came on. "Needs recharging," I said unnecessarily. Cyrus could see the screen as clearly as I. "That takes care of that until the library opens."

"You got paper and a pen?"

I rummaged in my backpack as I put the laptop away. I found a gray Bic pen beneath my laptop, socks and underwear, plastic toiletries box, hand soap, an uneaten bologna-and-cheese on whole wheat in a Ziplock bag, (women from a local church had been through the park the previous afternoon handing out fruit, water and sandwiches) and a copy of *The Good Soldier* by Ford Madox Ford. (Ford was a friend of Conrad's.) "I got a pen," I said, "but..." (more rummaging) "no paper. Wait a minute. Wait a minute. Here we go." I found a handout sheet that I had wedged into *The Good Soldier* to use as a bookmark. I opened it. There was only printing on one side, the other side was blank.

Using my backpack as a desk, I prepared to take dictation.

What we wrote:

> "To Whom It May Concern,
>
> My name is Cyrus Williams. I'm 56 years old. I have no address at the moment, but I am seeking help in acquiring one. I am homeless, but hope to change that soon. I have four daughters. They are currently all in foster homes. I want to have my daughters back with me so that we can be a family again. For us to be a family, I need a home. I have had some problems in the past, but have been drug-free for more than a year now. I am willing to do whatever it takes to have my family back. I need your help in finding a home where my daughters and I can live. I sincerely want to get off the street and am willing to do anything the county or the state require. I am a religious man and believe that the Lord Jesus will help me in this, what I am praying for with all my heart. I know I can be a good father if given a chance. God bless you.
>
> Sincerely,
> Cyrus K. Williams"

Now all we had to do was wait for the library to open, get on one of its public-access computer terminals, type out the letter in Word, print eight, ten or a dozen copies (15¢ a page, which I was going to make Cyrus pay.) We would also have to look up the addresses of the various offices to which his letter would have to be mailed. I agreed to run down to CVS and buy some mailing envelopes for this project, but I drew the line at paying for postage. Cyrus would have to handle that and the printing costs himself.

"There's Bob," I said. Cyrus merely grunted in reply.

Yes, there was Bob, under a tree halfway across the park from where Cyrus and I sat scribbling, crossing out and correcting. He was doing a crossword puzzle and had a can of Steel Reserve beside him. I wondered who had bought it for him . Bob did crossword puzzles all day long when he wasn't cadging smokes or beers or sleeping under a tree. Cyrus called him "Bob the Bum."

I met Bob at the police station the morning I went to report my wallet stolen. He had just gotten out of jail and didn't seem one hundred certain of where he was. When I walked back across the street to the park that day Bob trailed after me. He didn't have any other place to go. I understood how he felt; it hadn't been such a long time since I hadn't had any other place to go myself. For a few months after that Bob and I were like Butch and Sundance – he simply went where I went, camped where I camped. He had no other place to go. He explained to me that his mother lived nearby but had a restraining order keeping him off her property, like Jennifer had with Cage. I couldn't imagine what Bob's mother would look like – he was easily past sixty himself.

But Cyrus didn't want Bob around. He wished Bob would just take his crossword puzzles and disappear. To Cyrus Bob smelled like trouble (in addition to all the other things he smelled like.) Besides, Bob was so obviously a *bum* in Cyrus' eyes, a ragged, shiftless moocher unable or unwilling to do anything for himself, that the way Cyrus saw things, he deserved neither respect nor sympathy. Bob sensed Cyrus' disapproval and stayed away from him. I, in turn, picked up quickly on Bob's desire to stay away from Cyrus, and started camping with Cyrus and Marianne's little band because I knew that Bob would go sleep somewhere else.

When I met him at the police station that morning, Bob said he was looking for his pickup truck. He couldn't remember where he'd parked it. He never did find it, and I suspected that the truck was imaginary. It was just as well if it was—Bob behind the wheel of anything would not have been a good idea.

I walked over and spoke to him. "Hey, Bob."

"Hey, Pat." He put down his pencil and crossword. Bob couldn't do two things at once. "What're….you up to?"

"Cyrus and I just finished drafting a letter. We're waiting for the library to open so we can print it."

"A letter … about what?"

"Cyrus wants to get a place. He's going to ask for help."

"Help...from who?"

"The county I guess."

He took a pull on his beer. "Good luck...with that," he said. "County ain't gonna help nobody with anything."

"The city, then. I don't know. He's asked Rudy Payne for help."

"Who?"

"You know, Sgt. Payne. The cop from the HOT team."

"Cops?" Bob looked around in alarm. "Are there any cops around?" Hurriedly he slipped the Steel Reserve 211 he was sipping on back into its paper bag and stashed it behind his back against the tree, which would have fooled nobody if they had been looking for it. Like half the parkies, Bob was on probation, and he was terrified of the police. Going to the police station to report his truck missing on the day he got out of jail must have taken just about all the courage he had.

"Relax. They were here yesterday. They probably won't be back until next week."

"I...don't like cops." he grimaced and looked around again.

"I know. But they're not here."

"I once...punched out a cop."

I had heard such bullshit stories before. “You couldn’t punch yourself out,” I said.

He had gone back to his crossword puzzle and now chose to ignore me. “Well, Cyrus and I have things to do. I’ll see you later, Bob.”

“See….you later.”

About an hour later, the sun well up, a police car pulled into the library parking lot. Whatever their business was, the officers went inside the library. They didn’t even enter the park. We saw them pull in, but it was obvious that whatever the reason for their visit, it had nothing to do with any of us. Nevertheless, Cyrus poked me with his elbow and said, “Look over there.” He pointed to where Bob had been sitting under his tree working on his crossword just a few minutes earlier. Suddenly there was no sign of Bob anywhere. “Bob left in a hurry,” Cyrus said.

“I didn’t see him go.”

“You were looking the other way. Look, there’s his beer can. As soon as he saw that police car pull in, he emptied his can on the grass and ran off. Probably ran up a tree somewhere,” Cyrus laughed. “Scared as a rabbit.”

“He told me this morning he once punched out a cop,” I said.

“And I’m Dennis Rodman. He’s scared of his own fuckin’ shadow.”

“Come on. The library’s open. Let’s see if we can get on one of those terminals before the videogame hogs grab all of them.”

As we entered the library, two police officers came out, a man and a woman. We didn’t recognize either of them and they didn’t give us as much as a glance. “Bob’s probably two blocks away by now, hiding behind a dumpster,” Cyrus laughed again. “Oh, well. He still has his crossword puzzle with him. He didn’t leave that behind. He can work on that until the coast is clear.”

The idea of Bob hunkered down behind a dumpster working on a crossword puzzle and keeping an eye out for the cops really tickled Cyrus. He laughed again. I laughed too.

12

The house was sold the following spring. Jessie was responsible for its sale, but she was in Oklahoma. She flew out at Christmas and again in early March, but for the most part the direct dealing with real estate agents fell to him. The final decision as to which offer they would accept was of course his sister's. But when a prospective buyer suggested that his intention was to tear the old place down and put four – or maybe it was six – condominium units in its place, Patrick was horrified. It had taken him a long time even to get used to the idea of strangers living there. The idea that someone might want to demolish the house and put something else in its place had not occurred to him. The offer was a good one, but one that he would have rejected outright had the decision been his. Moreover he knew that his sister's chief concern in the business of the house was to get the sale over and done with.

He agonized over calling her. After letting it go for two days, he fortified himself with a few Scotch-and-waters, called her up and told her about this latest development. Fearing that his thoughts in the matter would be peremptorily vetoed, he nevertheless made it clear to his sister that he was against the idea of allowing the house in which they had both grown up fall to developers' bulldozers.

To his surprise she agreed immediately. "Oh, yeah, fuck that," she said. "That house was built in what, 1925? 1927? It's a Craftsman house, by rights it should have historical designation. No, no, we're not going to let somebody tear it down and put up apartments. Are you all right?"

"I'm fine."

"You sound funny."

"I...I was up late last night. Driving my cab. I haven't slept too well. Especially what with worrying about this."

"Well, don't worry about it. A decent buyer can't be hard to find, not with that place. It's southern California real estate, and it's not like it's out in the boondocks."

"What did you say it was worth? I forgot."

"The appraiser said four hundred thousand, give or take. That's what we'll be splitting up when it's sold. The government will take its share of course. There are the cousins back in Illinois who are in for a share, and there's Aunt Bernice in Colorado. But you and I should each get, I don't know, maybe seventy-five to a hundred grand. I told you that already."

"You did. When was that?"

"Months ago. Are you sure you're okay?"

"I'm fine." He took a sip from the half-Scotch, half-water, one ice cube-filled glass on the counter next to him. He was glad that he had only put in one ice cube. She wouldn't hear two cubes clinking together and ask if he were drinking.

"So, I'll tell the realtor to tell the guy with the bulldozer that it's no sale."

"Have you started looking around for a place of your own?"

"I've made some calls, looked at a couple of apartments. Goddamn, they've gotten expensive. On what a cabdriver makes I'm not going to be able to afford very much."

Although he did not tell his sister this, he had all but abandoned the idea of renting an apartment. Even a one-bedroom place would cost a lot, and he didn't really need much space, being alone, driving the cab; he worked long and irregular hours. His personal possessions didn't amount to much. A rented room would suit him fine. Jessie had already supervised the sale of almost everything in the house. Furniture, kitchenware, china, linens, drapes, paintings, rugs … all he had left were a few tables and chairs and his bed, all of which could be put into storage. Beyond that, his clothes, the TV, a computer, a small desk that he had brought back from Baltimore and a few boxes of books were all he had.

He had thought about joining his sister in Oklahoma City of course. She was just about all the family he had left, and in Oklahoma City an apartment would cost considerably less than in greater Los Angeles. But he had ruled that out. Jessie had a bumptious side to her which made him feel that they probably would not coexist well under the same roof. Besides, he didn't want to move again, and certainly not to the plains states. He liked being on the coast. The fact that the house was about to pass out of the family would have made many people feel that the time had come to sever ties with what had up until now been "home" and move along. He knew that, but somehow the idea of leaving every vestige of his childhood and youth behind and drifting off like an astronaut cut loose in space gave him a feeling akin to vertigo. It was different when he lived back east; the family and home were still right where they had always been, right where he had left them, giving his life an anchor. A line of Yeats that he had read when he was in college came back to him: "I am thinking of a child's vow sworn in vain/Never to leave that valley his fathers called their home." His own father had once called Illinois home, but his only contact with his father's state of birth had been driving across its southern half once on I-70 between Indianapolis and Kansas City on his way back to the west coast from Maryland. He hadn't even gotten out of the car that day. His father left Illinois in his twenties and never went back. No, for the foreseeable future he would remain in California.

He searched the Internet, made some phone calls. Everything seemed to be either too far away or—he couldn't believe it—too expensive. Some were asking almost the same monthly rate for a room that a one-bedroom apartment would cost. And it didn't seem to matter if the available room were in South Gate, Inglewood, Torrance, Santa Monica or one of a half-dozen other places he looked at, everything seemed outrageously overpriced. Baltimore County was nothing like this. He'd had a two-bedroom apartment in Towson for less than some of these people were asking for a room over their garage or a 250 square-foot granny flat in their backyard. For now he postponed a decision about where to go.

He was driving along Sepulveda Boulevard on a Wednesday afternoon when the dispatcher radioed in and gave him an address to pick up a fare.

He went to the address and parked across the street. It was a duplex apartment, one of several on that block that looked alike. He double-checked the address – he had it correct – and was about to get out, walk across the street and ring the doorbell when a woman came out and walked toward his cab. She had obviously been watching for him.

She was attractive, a blonde, maybe in her mid-to-late thirties, wearing patched jeans and a gray zip-up sweatshirt. She had a tattoo on her neck. Nothing unusual about that, the kids all had them nowadays.

She was also obviously drunk. She made it across the street okay, but her hand slipped as she grasped the passenger-side door handle. She swore softly. She slid into the cab, not in the back seat as most customers would, but in the front seat next to him. No question about her state now; her eyes were glassy and she seemed confused. She leaned back, stretched and put her hands in her lap.

"Where would you like to go?" he asked.

"I want to find my car. Don't remember where I parked it."

Great, he thought. A drunk who forgot where she parked. This could be a major time-waster. The car had to be right around here somewhere, which meant a cheap fare, although drunks did often tip well. Then again if they were drunk enough, sometimes they forgot to tip at all.

"Is it on this street?"

"I think it's around the corner somewhere. I don't exactly remember."

"What color was it? What make?"

"I think it's blue. Maybe green. Make? Oh, shit, I don't know. It's rented." She coughed, a smoker's cough.

So. A rented car, and she didn't know what make it was, nor was she even sure about the color. This might take a while.

"I'm going to cruise around the block," he said. See if you can remember."

It was obvious that she was too drunk to drive anywhere. If they found her car and if she got behind the wheel, the result would almost certainly be a DUI or worse, with the cab company liable for letting a drunk drive.

"Do you have a friend around here who could come pick you up?" he asked. "I think you might have had too much to drink to be driving yourself. Now don't get mad when I ask this, but how much have you had?"

She was not offended by the question, in fact she looked like she was about to doze off and his question had merely interrupted her dozing. "Me and my friend, we were drinking vodka-tonics."

"For long?"

"All afternoon," she mumbled.

"Then your friend obviously couldn't drive you anywhere. Do you know anybody else around here?"

"Where's 'here?'"

"You don't even know where you are? This is Hawthorne."

"She drove from here. I just parked. … We went to lunch."

"Look, you're in no shape to drive. Maybe I'd better just take you home and you can come back and look for the car tomorrow."

"S'rented."

"An extra day's rent would be a lot cheaper than a DUI. Let me take you home. Where do you live?"

She nodded as if to indicate that all of this was merely keeping her awake, and gave an address in Torrance. After helping her fasten her seat belt, he began to drive.

"We might as well know each other's names," he said. "I'm Patrick."

"I'm Brandi."

"Not 'Vodka-tonic.'"

"No," she laughed sleepily. "Brandi. They call me Brandi."

"That's your real name?"

"My real name's Melissa. Brandi's my stage name. I'm a singer."

"Where do you sing?"

"Around. Bars, clubs, you know."

Any further attempt at conversation was probably useless. He knew he should have instructed her to get in the back seat, but damn, she was pretty. He hadn't been this close to a pretty woman in a long time, drunk or sober. He had programmed her address into the portable GPS unit on the dashboard—he still did not possess a phone with that function. She slumped down a little deeper into the front seat, the afternoon sun on her face, her eyes closed. He followed the instructions on his GPS and drove in the direction of Torrance.

He glanced down. Her left hand lay open across the two drink holders that separated the front seats. She seemed to be asleep now.

Impulsively, and against any better judgment that he had ever had, (but damn, she was pretty) he reached down and took her hand in his, steering with the other. It wouldn't wake her, not as drunk as she was. And it had been such a long time since he had held a pretty woman's hand.

They drove on like that for a few minutes. Then she stirred in her seat, but didn't open her eyes. Obviously she was awake. But she didn't pull her hand away, so he asked her, "Do you mind this? Me holding your hand, I mean."

"No," she said. "I kind of like it."

They rode along like that for a few blocks. Neither spoke. Brandi continued to half-nap, or seem to. He kept his eyes on the street. He squeezed her hand just a bit.

She squeezed his hand back, and even moved a little closer to the driver's seat. He looked over at her. Her eyes were still closed, but after a few moments she began slowly raising his hand in hers.

She guided his hand to her right breast and pressed it against her sweatshirt. He felt her soft breast under his hand. She *wanted* him to touch her breast! Extremely surprised, but also very pleased, he was happy to oblige.

They rode along like that for a few more blocks, she pretending to doze, he steering with one hand and squeezing her tit through her sweatshirt with the other, trying to keep his eyes on the street.

Then she reached up to her sweatshirt again. Slowly, shifting in her seat, she unzipped it. She took his hand and guided it inside.

She wore no bra. She placed his hand on her naked breast and wordlessly encouraged him to go on squeezing it. This attractive blonde, drunk or not, wanted him to play with her tits, or at least with one of them. He looked around to see if anyone in the traffic had noticed what was going on in his cab.

Everything rushed inside of him at once, blood and adrenaline. He felt a stirring in his pants that he had not felt in a long time, and, still in disbelief, continued squeezing her breast as she clearly wished him to do, but he also began looking around for a place where they might pull over.

He turned on to a side street, looking and looking. Brandi, clearly enjoying what he was doing with her breast, made no objection to his right turn off the main drag. The side street was lined with palms, but also with parked cars. Where could they find some privacy? It would have been easier if it were nighttime, but it was afternoon. Broad daylight.

Brandi moaned very softly, eyes still closed. No question, she wanted more. But where? Ah, there was a shopping center, and an Albertson's supermarket! Out back, behind Albertson's where the dumpsters were, maybe nobody would be around. There might be a truck making a delivery. That would spoil everything. But maybe there would be no truck. It was worth a try. Steering with one hand was difficult now that he was trying to make turns, but he got into the Albertson's parking lot and cruised past the rows of parked cars to the back of the store. Fortunately there were no shoppers making their way back to their cars, no one around to notice a taxicab pulling in with its driver and his passenger engaging in foreplay.

They were in luck; the loading dock was vacant. Not a truck in sight. He pulled over behind two dumpsters lined up next to each other. It wasn't much shelter, but it blocked the view from the other end of the alley.

Within seconds they were all over each other: kissing, groping, tongues intertwining. He unzipped her sweatshirt the rest of the way. Now she was bare-breasted. More tattoos: as he plunged his mouth on to the nipple of her left breast, he saw what looked like a white dove tattooed there. She put her hand behind his head and pulled him to her. He had heard long ago that booze made some women horny, but had dismissed such tales as the sort of male locker-room bullshit guys hear all the time. He had never on his own found such a thing to be true. Valerie was a firecracker in bed, (at least in the beginning) but she'd never been much of a drinker. Now here was Brandi, full of vodka-tonics and not only enjoying with gusto this fooling around with a total stranger, but clearly wanting it to continue. In fact, clearly wanting more.

She got her hand inside his pants, worked it past the elastic waistband of his underwear, grasped his now-swelling cock and began squeezing it. Without thinking he reciprocated, unbuttoning her jeans (tight of course) and getting his hand inside her panties. She was wet. Her head on his shoulder; she breathed into his ear. She squirmed, helping him work his fingers around inside her panties. She wanted to fuck someone, now. Him, since he was there.

But it was the middle of the afternoon. As the only sober person in the car, he knew that it wasn't going to happen. Not there, not then, not at 4:30 in the afternoon in a parking lot behind Albertson's. Other guys might have taken the risk; he would not. Summoning every ounce of willpower, perhaps more than might be expected in a man who hadn't had sex in as long as he hadn't, he kissed her one more time, very hard, then pulled his lips away from hers long enough to say, "We can't do this."

"Just a little?" She still smelled strongly of booze.

"Brandi...Melissa...it's four-thirty in the afternoon. We'll get arrested."

Without answering, she put her head back on his shoulder. She had taken her hand out of his pants and put her arms around his neck. She clung to him and remained silent, waiting for him to do or say something. As drunks often will, she had decided to leave the problem-solving to someone else.

He thought for a full five seconds. "Can we go to your place?"

"My sister will be there. She lives with me."

"Does she care? You have your own room, don't you?"

"I won't do anything with her around. She has a big mouth."

More thinking. What was left? His own house was miles away in the other direction. Too far and it would take too long. Besides, by the time they got there she might have sobered up enough to change her mind. Be out of the mood. There were plenty of motels around. Why not take her to the Super 8 or the Del Amo Inn? They weren't far away.

No. No. Now that he was thinking, he was thinking like his father, whose watchword was always "caution," who had told him more than once, "Act like you trust people, but don't." In a flash he envisioned taking Brandi to a motel, enjoying himself with her, taking her home and dropping her off, and then...and then...tomorrow morning when she was fully awake and fully sober, regretting the whole incident and feeling embarrassed by it, her calling the cab company and complaining that he had taken advantage of her when she was drunk. She would claim that she had been raped. And then...

He dropped her off at her apartment in Torrance. But when she had paid the fare, just before she got out of the cab, she leaned over and kissed him. She was still pretty drunk, but she understood. She appreciated his discretion. Most of the men she knew wouldn't have bothered to exercise that much self-control. Perhaps she felt a little foolish already.

"Wait a minute," he said, fumbling in his wallet. Why hadn't he thought of this before? He had some business cards that he'd had printed up; he always kept a dozen of them in his wallet. "Here," he handed her a card. "If you still feel like doing this when you're sober, give me a call." Then he remembered that she would have to return tomorrow to the neighborhood where he'd picked first her up in order to look for her car. "You want me to come get you tomorrow, take you back up and look for your car?" he asked.

"Yeah," she nodded as she read the card in her hand. "I think so. I'll call you."

"You don't have to call the cab company. My cellphone number's on the card. Just call me."

He drove until one a.m., feeling very good. He still felt good when he went back home that night, poured his usual half-Scotch-half-water-three ice cubes drink, switched on TCM and sat down to watch Elizabeth Taylor and Montgomery Clift in *A Place In The Sun*.

But she did not call, not the next day, or day after that or the day after that either. He had neglected to get her number when he dropped her off at home, so he couldn't call her. He considered that problem. If she'd called the cab company from her own cellphone, it might be possible to track down her number by going through the dispatchers' database.

He decided not to. What for? Obviously his presentiment in the front seat of the cab that afternoon had been accurate. Sobered up in the privacy of her own apartment, she decided that she had made a complete fool of herself and didn't want anything or anyone to remind her of it. He imagined what she'd done with his business card: left it on the kitchen counter or a coffee table overnight while she slept off the booze, then tossed it in the trash the next morning. That was that. Let it go.

Business was always brisk on Halloween, one of the biggest party nights of the year. Everyone knew the cops had DUI checkpoints all over the place; during the afternoon and early evening of Halloween, Facebook,

Twitter buzzed with tip-offs about where the cops were or where they had been last year.

He had been on the road since three p.m. It was now twenty minutes past eleven and he had easily made enough money to clear $200 on the night. He knew it. Should he decide to stay out for another couple of hours, the tally might climb closer to $300 – between midnight and two a.m. on party nights like this, the drivers really raked it in.

It began to drizzle, then to rain a little harder. He switched on his windshield wipers. Rain was almost as good for business as parties.

The muffled strains of *Take the A Train* sounded from deep in his hip pocket. He dug for his cellphone. Was it a call for a ride? He didn't get many "personals" as the drivers called them—nearly all of his business came from radio dispatch. The business cards he'd ordered from Vistaprint were attractive—he had designed them himself. On the front of each card was a photo of a taxicab like his, a yellow Ford Crown Victoria, above which were the words "Patrick Donahy, Taxi Service" and beneath, his cellphone number and email address. On the back of the card, bullet-points:

- Prompt, Courteous Service
- Clean Cab
- Driver Speaks Perfect English

Was this going to be a business call, or his sister wanting to talk about the sale of the family house? (unlikely—it was now 1:25 a.m. in Oklahoma City and Jessie had never been a night owl.)

"Hello?"

"Hello, Pat?"

"Yes, this is Patrick Donahy." Businesslike; at this hour who would be calling except a customer?

"This is Brandi."

He pretended not to remember. "Brandi. Brandi. Oh, yeah, the customer who misplaced her car! What was it, two weeks ago? Did you find it?"

"Yeah, we found it the next morning."

"Glad to hear it. So. I take it you need a ride somewhere."

"Yeah. Home.....you know where that is."

"Sort of," he replied.

He knew: 22515 Reynolds Drive, Unit 17, Torrance. "Do I assume you're at ... a Halloween party?"

"Sort of," she echoed him. "It's at my work. Shanghai Jake's, do you know the place? Where are you? How long will it take you to get here?"

"I'm in Santa Monica, around the corner from the DMV. You?"

"You're not far. We're over here just the other side of the 405. On Westwood."

"I don't know Shanghai Jake's, but I know Westwood Boulevard. Give me a street number and I'll find you."

He found the place. The rain had stopped already and she was waiting out in front on the sidewalk. She was dressed much like she was the last time he saw her: jeans and running shoes, only now she wore a bulky, cream-colored turtleneck instead of a sweatshirt. Nothing there to unzip and slip his hand inside of. She carried what looked like a gym bag under her arm.

He pulled up to the curb and she climbed into the cab. She got in the back seat this time, not the front. She had been working, obviously. Probably what she'd told him about being a singer was a lie; more likely she tended bar in this place. Maybe they had a band and they let her sing now and then. The important thing was, she was now sober. There wasn't going to be any groping, squeezing or French-kissing on this trip. Maybe just as well. But why had she called his cell number instead of just calling the cab company, or Lyft, if she needed a ride? He decided to make no mention of their previous business encounter.

"You going to the gym?" he asked casually as he pulled away from the curb. He glanced at her in the rearview mirror. She appeared puzzled by the question. "The bag," he said, "the gym bag. That's what it looks like, anyway."

"Oh. This is my costume. It was a Halloween party, you know. We had to wear costumes. Look," she pulled what was obviously a slinky black outfit from the bag and a big, very big, black wig. "I was supposed to be Elvira, remember her? The sexy vampire from those beer ads back in the eighties?" She held up and shook the wig. "That's why the hair. Remember? In the eighties everybody had BIG hair!" she laughed as she stuffed the costume and wig back into the bag. He tried to imagine what she would have looked like in that getup. She was right; the Elvira character in those old beer ads had been very sexy. Brandi would have been, too.

"Some sort of nostalgia party?"

"No, not really. Well, sort of. Most of our customers are guys over fifty. They all remember Elvira pitching Coors Light back when they were all guys in their thirties."

"I remember her well, although Coors Light wasn't my brand. I'll bet you looked great in that getup."

"I looked like an idiot. But the manager insisted."

Maybe she didn't remember telling him she was a singer. A singer would not have been expected to wear an idiotic (and skimpy) Halloween costume. A blonde bartender with large breasts, that was another story, even nowadays, when sexism was practically outlawed everywhere you looked. But neighborhood bars operated under the political-correctness radar.

"You remember my address? 22515 Reynolds?" she asked.

He remembered all right. "22515. Yeah, I think I remember. I remember the street anyway."

He drove her back to her apartment, continuing to wonder why she had called him. She had been so bombed the last time that, after waiting hopefully for a few days and getting no call from her, he decided that either his instinct had been correct and she was too embarrassed to be reminded of the encounter, or she didn't remember him at all, had come to after sleeping it off and remembered *possibly* having had sex with a cab driver (but most likely not; a woman knows when she has been penetrated recently, and that day she had not been) and preferred to just forget about it.

But she had, in fact, called him. Him, and not some other hack. She had not thrown out his business card, but kept it and called him.

He glanced back at her again in the rearview mirror. She wasn't asleep, she was looking out the window at the passing lights of businesses. He would never in this lifetime, he thought, even begin to understand women. He turned his eyes back to the street.

She turned her gaze from a Dunkin' Donuts sign to the back of her driver's balding head. He had to be well past fifty, like most of the guys at the bar. Did she feel safe with him because he was a little older? Or did she feel safe with him because he had had an opportunity to fuck her and had not? There was no question but that he could have; older or not, she remembered his cock when she put her hand in his pants. He was as capable as any man. But he had not done it.

By leaning forward in her seat just a little, she got a glimpse of his profile and decided he didn't have such a bad one. No weak chin. Slightly high cheekbones. Not such a bad-looking older guy. He seemed to be... what, a gentleman? Gay? No, he couldn't be gay. Things wouldn't have gotten as far as they did if he had been. There weren't many gentlemen around anymore, not judging from her experience. Most of the guys she knew would have taken her to a motel and reamed her good. And she would have enjoyed it, at least while it was happening. It was almost always afterward that she decided she didn't like it, or them. But he had taken her home. Okay, he was no Hollywood star, no GQ cover boy, but how many men in the real world were? There had been one real hunky guy who'd come into Shanghai Jake's one night and flirted with her. "Dino," he called himself. (His real name was Frank; why he was known as "Dino" was something she hadn't bothered to ask.) Yes, he had the good looks and the ripped body, and he was good in bed, but had turned out of course to be as selfish and inconsiderate an asshole as most of the rest she had known. She decided after two weeks that she was going to dump him, then discovered that she didn't have to because he had already left town without a word.

They reached the apartment complex where she lived. Neither had said much since their bit of banter after they pulled away from Shanghai Jake's.

He reached for the clipboard that he kept between the front seats on which he kept his driver's log and put on the CVS drugstore reading glasses that he kept around his neck on a piece of string. "So. Looks like….uh--"

"Would you like to come upstairs for a few minutes?"

He paused and broke off scribbling in his log. I'll-swap-you-ass-for-a-ride was not unheard-of among the cabbies. Such an offer had never been made to him, but he had heard from other drivers, including a couple whom he actually trusted not to be throwing around sea stories, that such monkey business did go on. Who knew? Maybe that was what she really had in mind the other time. Still, she had told him of her misplaced rental car; no reason to make up a story like that if she'd planned to offer a trade.

"Didn't you say your sister lived with you?"

"Yes. But she and her boyfriend are on a cruise. They went off to Cabo San Lucas. I don't expect her back until next weekend."

"One or both of them must have money."

"He does. He's a real estate broker. He's with Coldwell Banker downtown."

"My ex-wife was a real estate broker," he said. "Well, um...I'm still working," He didn't want to appear eager, it wouldn't look good. But he was more than ready to quit for the night, the after-midnight business be damned, if she would only say the right thing.

"How long have you been driving today?"

That was the right thing. "Since three. So..." he looked at his watch. "Almost nine hours."

"Well, I won't tell you your business. But if it's almost midnight, and you've been on the road for nine hours, don't you think you're entitled to take a break?"

She went ahead of him upstairs. He radioed in that he was going off duty.

By the time he went up and reached the apartment door that she had left open, she was already standing at the kitchen counter, mixing two of what looked like vodka-tonics. She had pulled off the bulky turtleneck and laid it over one of the breakfast nook chairs.

Beneath the turtleneck she wore a black camisole that left little to the imagination. She had lovely big breasts all right—he had already felt them. She was obviously well aware of her breasts and not at all self-conscious about them; how could she be, one who made her living pouring beer for a lot of leering middle-aged drunks?

She smiled as she handed him his drink, then went over to the TV and switched on the Tonight Show. She left the sound low so they could talk. Jimmy Fallon was interviewing some actress, or maybe she was a singer; he couldn't tell one of these kids from another anymore. It didn't matter, because he wasn't interested in the TV. As for Brandi, she had obviously only turned it on for a minor distraction. She knew there was no point in letting things get too hot too quickly.

13

I have to say that Frankie and Andrew were a couple of odd ducks. They were about the same age, late twenties, younger than most of us in the park, although there were a few people, their fellow meth-heads mostly, who were in the same age group as they, sometimes younger. The two of them didn't have much in common beyond being twentysomethings and sharing a fondness for controlled substances. But they were friends of a sort.

Andrew had a job at Lion's Gate, or said he did. He spent a lot of time there and was on a first-name basis with Steve, the heavyset guy who ran the place (and was incidentally the neighborhood computer guru—if you had a computer problem, Steve was the guy to go to.) I don't know if or how much Lion's Gate paid Andrew for his services. But he was a fixture there, usually around performing some chore, whether it was taking out the trash or painting the front porch or cooking hamburgers or whatever else they had for him to do. If you were trying to find one or another of the parkies, Lion's Gate was a good first place to look. If whoever you were looking for weren't there, chances are that Andrew would have some idea where to find them. You could get a free cup of coffee at Lion's Gate, and sometimes they gave away food. They also held Narcotics Anonymous meetings there every week. Many of the parkies were required to attend N.A. as part of their probation; others just went to Lion's Gate for the coffee, or for company, or to get some sleep on one of the two enormous leather couches they had in the foyer.

Andrew was always there, except when he wasn't. Sometimes he would disappear for days at a time. He claimed to be bisexual. I always suspected that it was just part of "the act" – Andrew loved to appear outrageous, changing his fashion style from goth to grunge and then to something else, growing a beard and then shaving it off, ditto his hair; once he even started using eyeliner for no reason any of us could see except to attract attention. Telling people he was bisexual might have been just another of his poses. But who knew?

What Andrew most clearly liked, though, was weed. There was very little he wouldn't do for weed money. One night when I got wet sleeping out in front of the library in the rain, I paid Andrew a couple of bucks the next morning to take my sleeping bag down to the Wash N' Dry and throw it into the dryer.

And he would sell things. In the park people were always selling things, and as already mentioned, it was park protocol not to ask where they came from. I bought a small AM/FM radio from Andrew when baseball season started. No Red Sox games of course unless they were playing the Angels, but I could get the Angels on AM 830 or the Dodgers on KLAC.

Sometimes I would buy things from Andrew that I neither needed nor wanted, just to get rid of him. He could be a very persistent salesman when he needed weed money. His most reliable technique was whining. He knew that if he whined long enough, I'd usually buy what he was selling just to shut him up, unless it were something I *really* couldn't use, like an automobile tire, a kid's-size desk, a bicycle pump or something else that he'd found in the alley.

He approached me one late spring evening when I was seated under my usual tree in my director's chair, a Hurricane nestled in the cup holder, listening to an Angels-Seattle Mariners game on the radio that he had sold me.

This time he wanted to sell me a rather wicked-looking knife. A knife was a handy thing to have in the park, and I don't necessarily mean for self-defense. If you needed to clean mud off your shoes or dirt from under your fingernails, open a can of tuna or ream out your pipe it was good to have one around. I had a folding knife which hadn't cost me anything. Marianne found it on the grass one day. She had no use for it and I had been standing there talking to her when she found it; she handed it to me. So I already had a knife. But that didn't deter Andrew.

"What do you say, Pat? Ten bucks for this knife. Comes with the sheath, see?"

"No."

"Come on, man. It's a nice knife." He held it up between his two index fingers for me to behold. The blade was six inches long, serrated near the fake-leather handle. It would have been perfect for cleaning fish. But I hadn't cleaned a fish since the last time I'd angled for spotted bass with my late father. Years ago.

"I don't need that pig-sticker. I have a knife."

"Eight bucks."

"I don't NEED it."

"But I need the money. Randy said he'd drive me up to the dispensary if I can scrape together ten bucks. Come on, buy the knife."

"No."

"PLEEASSSE?"

"Andrew, I'm trying to listen to the ball game!"

"Please?"

"No."

"Pretty please with sugar on it? Seven bucks." He smiled at me with his crooked teeth, his best, big-phony-salesman smile. I knew he wasn't going to leave me alone.

The problem was that the parkies knew I had a little money stashed away. Not much, but I had paid into a 401(k) while I was working in Baltimore and there was the hundred grand that was my share of the sale of the family house, although I had already spent a large chunk of that. Now I was eating up my IRA while I waited to qualify for Social Security.

I was doling it out to myself, trying to make it last. As my late father would have. Unlike, for instance, Frankie's dad Terry, who after waiting for more than a year, had gotten a $26,000 insurance payout from the apartment fire in which his wife had perished, leaving him and his son Frankie on the street. This happened before I came along—Cyrus told me about it.

Terry had gone through that money like a maniac. He bought a car, wrecked it and bought another. He splurged on hotel rooms for himself and (only sometimes, I'd heard) his son. He ate in restaurants, drank expensive liquor...and spent a lot on drugs. Within six months the wad was gone and Terry was back to sleeping in alleys, eating lunch at the Salvation Army and cadging beer and cigarette money from everyone he knew. Terry was mental. Half the parkies were. I probably was too. In those days? Yes, I must have been.

I took a deep gulp of my beer. It was the bottom of the seventh inning, Mike Trout was up to bat with two out and runners on first and second. The score was 6-5 Seattle. I wasn't a fan of either team, but I did want to hear what happened next and Andrew's imitation of a squeaky door-hinge was making it difficult. I got out my wallet, which never had more than ten or twenty dollars in it at any given time in those days. I found a five and two ones and handed them to him. He gave me the knife.

"Will you leave me alone now?" I said.

"Thanks, Pat!" he said, and he was off, presumably to raise the other three bucks somewhere else. I slipped the knife into my backpack and promptly forgot I had it. As I was doing that, Trout swung at a hanging slider, whiffed and the inning was over.

Frankie drifted in and out of the park depending on who had what mood-altering substances available, and he was much less discriminating about what he ingested than Andrew was. Frankie was willing to swallow or inhale just about anything as long as it yielded some form of fucked-up. If Cheryl were on hand with a bottle of vodka she was willing to share, Frankie would be found sitting on the grass with Cheryl and Rob. If the crowd around the tweaker tree were taking turns throwing blankets over their heads, Frankie would be found in the midst of them. He took almost any kind of prescription pill he could get his hands on, didn't much care what it was, and if there were also alcohol around, he would mix them without thinking twice about it. With Frankie, staying as bombed as he could as often as he could was always top priority.

I was pleased to learn that he liked to read. He saw me reading in Gogol's *Diary of a Madman* one day and, attracted by the title, asked if he could borrow it. I lent it to him.

When he was in the park, Frankie usually sought out the little group that included Cyrus, Marianne and me. He knew all of us, felt comfortable enough in our company, and also knew that I was usually good for a Pepsi or maybe even a beer if he caught me in the right mood. He had been in jail several times, for possession of drugs, assault, occupancy of property without the owner's permission, and once for chucking his skateboard through the plate-glass window of the liquor store down the street. (Frankie and his dad were both banned from the liquor store, Frankie for his skateboard stunt and Terry for shoplifting and passing bad checks.) He claimed the broken window was an accident. He probably threw the skateboard because he was pissed off about an unsatisfactory drug deal.

One person with whom Frankie was seldom seen was his father. We had all noticed the way they tended to avoid each other. Once in a while they'd be spotted walking down the street together, but most of the time if one were around, the other was elsewhere. Frankie complained to me about his father's unwillingness to stand him to a beer or share his weed, and of course I heard repeatedly from Frankie how his father had blown his way through that entire insurance wad without treating his own son to much more than a few nights here and there in a motel room instead of on the street. We were all acquainted with Terry's tightfistedness. But it struck me as odd, and Cyrus also noticed, the way he seemed to be as stingy with his own son as he was with everyone else.

Sometimes when Andrew was hanging out with our little band, Frankie would show up and they might start playing mumblety-peg with their pocketknives or giggling druggily together at some belabored joke, or one of them, having heard that Marianne had some drugs, would try to get her off by herself for a moment to see if she might share. Cyrus pretended not to notice this busines

Sometimes the two of them would get into a scuffle over something, probably drugs. They'd go at it, swinging fists and spewing filthy-mouth rage Neither resorted to his pocketknife, and seldom did either land a punch, and then they would go their separate ways, each vowing never to have anything to do with "that motherfucker" again. Eventually one would apologize to the other and everything would be normal again. Cyrus laughed at these hijinks of theirs.

"Did you see that?" he said to me after one of their scuffles.

"Why wouldn't I see it? I was standing right here. "Another fight between Frankie and Andrew. So what?"

"Fight?" Cyrus spat. "You call what that *fighting*? Shit, I call that line-dancing." He leaned back on his bench and crossed his arms over his paunch. "*Line*-dancing." he laughed at his own humor. I laughed too.

And now suddenly Sandy was gone from the park. The state and county had come through after a wait of more than two years. She had her own little cell at Bayview Towers, a fifteen-story subsidized concrete beehive for seniors.

After that we almost never saw Sandy except sometimes at the liquor store early in the morning. She would show up when the day guy came to open the place and help clean up. For that he would give her a break on her daily flask of cheap vodka. She never invited us up to her place and nobody ever wondered about that either. When someone left the park, they left the park.

"She got a place," Cyrus shrugged. "Why would she want to have anything to do with us anymore?"

I could think of no response.

"Any answers yet to that first bunch of letters we sent out?" I asked.

"Just one. HHSA says they don't deal with that, but they referred me over to FCS. Family Court Services. Which means I need to write another letter. Which means I need your help again."

"Why don't you just send them a copy of the first letter we wrote?"

"No, I want one that has more...details, you know. Proof of my honesty and intentions. Proof of my...sobriety."

"You're not sober. Not completely. You're not using anymore, but you still drink beer. And those shots. Yes, I know you told me you were going to swear off completely, but I saw--"

"Yeah, I know. You saw me partyin' with those guys from the other park. That was just a slip. That won't happen again."

"You're sure."

"I'm sure. From now on if I want a drink, I'm stickin' to Monster." Monster was an energy drink. El Mercado and Crown Liquor both carried it.

"Well, okay."

"I'm serious."

"Well, show me." I shrugged.

"And what about you? Why don't you get sober too, while we're at it?"

"What for? I don't have any children I'm trying to get back."

"For your health."

"Oh, screw my health."

It wasn't bravado. I meant it. At the time, anyway. At that I really wasn't all that much interested in what happened to me. The way I was feeling in those days, I was past sixty, and after the business with Melissa I thought that my life was pretty much over and done with anyway. I'd actually been thinking about it, insofar as I was able to think at all back then. I even staged a show for the parkies one afternoon.

One day, quite full of Hurricane, fuller than I knew, I told Ed and

Chantal, who were standing there, that I had decided to go off and kill myself.

Of course they thought I was full of shit and they told me so.

"You think I'm joking? Watch me," I said. "I'm gonna get on the 960 over there, go downtown and get on a Greyhound. I'm going to … New Mexico. That's it. Taos, New Mexico. I'm gonna kill myself when I get there."

Naturally, they didn't believe me. "Why Taos?" Chantal asked. She wore a half-grin and she was looking off at the trees, not at me.

"I've always wanted to see New Mexico. Never been there. I'll finally see New Mexico. Then I'll kill myself. It'll be the first and last time. Taos, yeah. That's where D.H. Lawrence died. It's good enough for him, it's good enough for me. I'll take the bus to Santa Fe, then another one to Taos. I think it's about fifty miles from Santa Fe."

They went right on talking to each other, telling me in side-comments what a complete bullshitter I was. But then I suddenly took my wallet out of my backpack, stuck it in my pocket and handed the pack, laptop and all, to Ed. "Here, I won't be needing this anymore." I said.

The guffaws stopped. A joke was a joke, but a guy giving away his backpack—and his laptop—was a pretty expensive joke.

"Okay, Pat, you've had your fun," Ed said. "I don't want your backpack. Come on, buy me a beer. Let's walk over to the liquor store, you and me."

"I'm serious, you guys. You don't seem to get it. Keep the backpack, Ed." I turned with a flourish and began walking toward the bus stop.

"Cyrus!' Chantal shouted across the park. "You better get over here!"

The 960 bus, which went downtown, had just left. I wound up sitting on that bus bench for close to forty-five minutes while my friends, now genuinely alarmed, tried to talk me out of getting on it, including Cyrus. Chantal went so far as to whip out her cellphone and call 911. Officers Payne and Solis actually did show up in a patrol car, but by the time they arrived, so had the 960 and I got on, using the bus pass I had in my wallet. As I took my seat I watched out the window. I heard Chantal say to Fernando Solis, "Stop him! He says he's going to kill himself!" And I heard Solis answer, "I can't arrest him! He hasn't done anything!" Then the bus pulled away, with me on it.

The Hurricane had done its work well—I was not thinking clearly at all. I rode the bus all the way downtown, got off and, after asking directions, found the bus depot on East Seventh. I walked in and bought a one-way ticket to Santa Fe. $199.50. Of course I didn't carry that much cash; I charged it on my bank card. What the hell, I wouldn't be using it much longer, right? Somewhere in the depths of that high-gravity fogbank I was walking around in, a voice kept whispering to me that this would sure show Melissa. What it was going to show her I wasn't in any shape to know.

My ticket paid for, I actually did get on the bus. But L.A. to Santa Fe is about 850 miles, out I-15 to I-40 and then through Needles and on into Arizona. It's desert. It's flat and dull. It gives you plenty of time to sober up and think. I got as far as Needles and then had to buy a ticket back. It was two-fifteen in the morning when we got back to Los Angeles and I had to hang around the bus depot until the city buses started running and I could catch the 960 back to the park. It was the most expensive joke of my life, although of course I hadn't realized I was joking until the money was spent. The fare back from Needles was no joke. Well, at least Ed was nice enough to return my backpack—and my laptop—to me. Probably he would have sold it for booze as soon as he was sober enough to do so, but I got back early enough the next morning to prevent him from doing that.

"I know what I'm going to do," Cyrus said. "Before we write another letter, let's go over to St. Lucy's and see Sister Paula."

"What can Sister Paula do for you?" I said.

"Make a couple of phone calls, maybe. Besides, she's Sister Paula. As in *Sister.* If you're trying to convince people that you're gonna turn your life around, it can't hurt to have a church behind you, right?"

This was Monday, one of the two days each week that Sister Paula handed out food at St. Lucy's in the morning. We waited until after ten O'clock before walking over there. Sister Paula and her volunteers opened the doors at nine, and for the first hour or so they had a line of people waiting for handouts. But by ten or ten-thirty the crowd was thinning.

Of course we saw people we knew there. Terry was always there, and sometimes Ed if he were sober enough make the walk.

Chantal was there this morning. She and Yvonne had adopted a scruffy little brown-and-white puppy that they had named Simba. The puppy, on a leash they had found somewhere, crouched between Chantal's sandaled feet. Somewhere they had found a leash for him. Counting Chantal, there were four or five people still waiting.

"Hi, Chantal," I greeted her. "Hi, Simba!"

The puppy knew me; he strained at his leash, wanting to come over and take a sniff to make sure I was who he thought I was. Cyrus and I were not there to get food, so we didn't take places in line. We lingered by the doorway, indicating to all that we were only waiting to see Sister Paula, and they should go right past us when their turns came.

"Yvonne must be out hustling somewhere. The pillow princess came over by herself," Cyrus muttered under his breath.

Sister Paula, seated at her desk inside, noticed Cyrus and me poking our heads around the door. Still dealing with "customers" and at the moment on the phone, she waved to us and then held up her index finger, signaling that we should wait and not run off. Sister Paula always made you feel that she was glad to see you, even if she were in the middle of something. I never saw her turn anybody away unless they were acting so crazy that the cops had to be called in, which didn't happen often, but sometimes did.

"Come in! Come in!" Sister Paula hung up the phone and waved us to chairs in front of her desk. "Haven't seen either you two in a long time!"

Sister Paula was an imposing woman; not fat or tall, just imposing.

She was a few years older than I, in her mid-sixties anyway, with short, reddish, graying hair, a ruddy complexion and blue eyes. She had been an elementary school principal for many years. I had never seen her in a nun's habit. Usually she dressed as she was dressed now, in a flannel shirt with the sleeves partly rolled up, and always with a small crucifix around her neck. She was a good listener; many of the locals who came by for the free food packages she gave away (donated by the local Ralph's supermarket) also came in to sit and tell her their troubles for a few minutes. She never made you feel rushed, either, although you had to be expect to be interrupted as you were talking with her; people were always coming in and going out, and the phone on her desk rang all the time.

"How've you been, Cyrus? I heard Marianne had another baby."

"Yeah, over a week ago."

"She still with you?"

"Pretty much, but she's been over at her mother's a lot lately. The baby's in a foster home."

"I heard that." Sister Paula waited. She had known Cyrus for a long time. She knew about his three daughters in foster homes.

"That's why we come over. Sister, I'm tired of the way I've been living. I want to get out of the park, find a place. 'Course you already know that. But now I'm more determined than ever. Pat here knows, he was there when I made the decision."

Sister Paula had heard this before. She smiled at me. "How've you been, Pat?"

"Hanging out. Reading a lot. Keeping a journal again." There wasn't much I could tell her, although that part about keeping a journal again was true. I had bought a couple of scribblers and a package of Bic pens at the CVS and was jotting down occasional thoughts and observations. It was something I had started doing in my teen years. Lately I had lost the habit. Sister Paula knew about my drinking. She knew about everybody's. The drugs too. She never brought things like that up, though, she waited for you to do it. I didn't. I wasn't ready to talk about it. In any case we were there on Cyrus' account, not mine.

He explained what he wanted: a letter from her, on parish stationery, that he could include with the next batch of letters he was planning to send out. "If they know I have you behind me, it'll help convince them how serious I am," he said. "The thing is, I want to get my daughters back. I want us to be a family again, you know? Not that we ever were much of one. Maybe you can also make a couple of phone calls to…somebody? I don't know who. But somebody." He shrugged and looked down at his lap.

She nodded. "Well, I'll do what I can. But you know I'd have to get the pastor's approval. It's like the bus passes, you know." Sister Paula was sometimes able to get thirty-day bus passes for people who requested them. But unlike the food handouts, they had to be approved by the church office.

"I know. But I thought it would be worth a try. You'll talk to Father Jay, won't you?"

"Of course, of course. Take some food before you go."

Cyrus didn't have to be asked. He had already risen from his chair and was dipping into the cardboard boxes filled with plastic bags, each containing a loaf of bread, some two-day-old pastries or half a cake, a can of chicken or some tuna, a Cup O' Noodles, one or two granola bars and a bottle of water.

Sister Paula motioned for me to take some food also. "Pat?"

"No, thanks, I don't need anything."

"You sure? Take some food. Come on."

Sister Paula and I had had this exchange before. I almost always turned down her offer of food. Not because I'm a saint or anything, but because I really didn't think I needed it. And I wasn't hungry, you see. I was living on beer. Besides, I had EBT if I got hungry. Besides, I didn't like taking charity. My father never would have.

"Give it to somebody who needs it more than I do."

"Take one, man," Cyrus whispered. "You can give it to me." Cyrus had long since embraced the code of the street; pride had no real place out here. So I accepted a bag, and as soon as we had left Sister Paula's office, gave it to him. He took it without a word, probably thinking that I was a sap. But since we were friends, maybe he was also thinking that sooner or later I would learn.

While we waited to see if Sister Paula could deliver on Cyrus' request for a church endorsement, we wrote more letters. That is to say, I wrote them and Cyrus affixed his crabbed signature to them.

Then Bob the Bum turned sixty-five and got his first Social Security check, which was not as simple as it sounds. With Bob the Bum nothing was ever simple. More about that shortly.

14

Later, as Brandi was falling asleep in his arms, he noticed by the electric clock next to the bed that it was almost four a.m. But he could not fall asleep. He was unaccustomed to having a woman's body nestled up against him. For a long time now, ever since the divorce from Valerie, he had slept alone and was used to it. Not that he preferred sleeping alone, but it had gotten to be a habit and he was, as he often reminded himself, a creature of habit.

Brandi's soft, steady breathing told him that she was now asleep, but he couldn't shut his mind off. He thought of what a wonderful surprise it was to discover that Brandi seemed genuinely attracted to him, enough to go to bed with him anyway, how equally wonderful and long-missed had been experiences like this, and of how his life, up until then running along on the accustomed and comfortable steel rails of daily habit, might just possibly have now shunted over to a new set of rails.

He looked down at Brandi, more beautiful in sleep even than she was awake. He thought of that old song by the Doors, *The Crystal Ship*: "Before you slip into unconsciousness/I'd like to have another kiss..." He would truly have liked to have another of Brandy's delicious kisses, but she was asleep, and for the moment there was no question of his going to sleep.

He slipped out of bed and, without bothering to put on his underpants, walked back to the kitchen and made himself a double vodka-tonic. As was so often the case at home after a late-night session of cable movies, dawn was getting underway when he finally slipped back into bed and fell asleep next to Brandi, who had not moved since he'd gotten up to make another drink, and then a couple more after that.

Brandi. He was going to have to start calling her Melissa. If they were going to be lovers it would be pretty silly for him to keep using her stage name.

Despite having stayed up in the kitchen and living room after she had gone to sleep, he awoke before she did. Ten minutes past nine. No doubt with the hours she worked, she was used to sleeping until late in the morning. He was too, but had always been a light sleeper, even more so when sleeping in unfamiliar surroundings. To leave before she was awake was out of the question. He didn't want her to get the idea that the night they had just spent had meant nothing to him, and that he was in a big hurry to get off and on his way.

He was in no such hurry; it had been a long time since he had had sex with anyone but himself. Gazing at her as she lay there in the morning light, warm beside him under the sheet and still deliciously nude, he got horny very quickly. But it would be churlish to wake her up for that, he thought. Surely when she did finally awaken there would be time for another fuck before breakfast.

There was. And since he had already been up and around for more than an hour by then, when they had finished their vigorous bout of morning lovemaking he already had the coffee ready in the kitchen.

Sitting on the sofa the night before, drinking and talking before the groping and kissing, they had told each other about themselves. She had told him that she hoped to have her sister, whose name was Sharon, out of the apartment soon. They did not get along well at all, and Melissa hoped that Sharon would either marry the boyfriend with whom she had gone off to Acapulco, or at least move in with him, but get out of Melissa's hair one way or the other.

"Why don't you two get along?" he asked.

"It's not that we don't get along. But she's a year and a half older than me, and she acts like, I don't know, she acts like those nineteen months give her a higher rank. She tries to tell me what to do. Tells me what men I should or shouldn't see, what I should do with my career. I just get sick of her bossing me around. I mean, she's my sister and I love her, but sometimes I wish she'd quit trying to be my mother."

"Now there is something I can relate to," he said. "I have an older sister myself, and she also sometimes needs to be reminded that she's not my mother. But, your mother's still alive? Mine died a few years ago."

"Yeah, Mom is alive and well. Dad too. They live in Colorado Springs. What about you? You have any other sisters? A brother, maybe?"

"We had a younger sister but she died."

"I'm sorry."

"Yes, it was tough for a while. Then our father died a few months ago, and now we're trying to sell the house. My one sister—Jessie's her name—lives in Oklahoma City with her husband. His name's Ray. He's retired."

"So you're alone now. I sometimes wish I was. I *often* wish I was. Like you say, when we were kids Shari kind of appointed herself Lieutenant Mom. She thinks she still is. So. You ever been married?"

"Once. I've been divorced for about five years. You?"

"Yeah, I was married. Just divorced last winter. My ex-husband lives in Louisville. And I have a son, Tommy. He's four. Tommy Jr. Named after his father."

Something familiar there. Ominous for him, as he thought later, gloomily remembering his Joyce.

"Where is he? Your son, I mean."

"In Kentucky with his dad. Tom and I agreed when we split up that Tommy would stay with his dad until I got settled out here on the west coast. Now that I have a place and a job, I'm trying to get him back. But my ex-husband and his lawyer are making trouble. Tom is such an asshole." She paused and smiled ruefully. "Here I am, telling my life story to a guy who probably listens to a lot of people tell their life stories. In your cab I'm sure you hear a lot of women call their ex-husbands assholes."

"Yeah, and I hear a lot of men call their ex-wives worse things than that. But it's okay, I don't mind your telling me. Like you said, I'm used to it."

"Do you have children?"

"No. My ex-wife didn't want any. She was an only child. She got used to being the center of attention very early in life. She wanted to keep it that way. I'll give her this much: she was honest about it. I was her third husband, and she told me before we were married that she had never been pregnant and never wanted to be. She didn't even like dating divorced men who had children, having to play second fiddle to someone else's kids."

"Sounds like your ex was a real piece of work," she said as she took his glass and got up to refresh their drinks. "I hate so much being away from Tommy," she said. "I want to have him back with me so bad. His father is fighting not to let me have him, says the idea of him living in an apartment in L.A. with his mother and his aunt, and his mother working as a bartender at night...let's face it. I'm a bartender. They let me sing with the band now and then, when they have a band, but mostly I tend bar at that place."

"I kind of guessed that," he said. "I mean, you can tell from the street that Shanghai Jake's isn't exactly the cocktail lounge at the Airport Hilton."

She sighed as she poured more vodka. "I know. But it's where I have a job for now."

"How do you get to work? What was that business with the rented car? I mean the day we first met. If you can remember that day. You were a little drunk."

"I was *shitfaced*. I'm sorry about that."

"I'm not," he laughed.

"It was my day off and I was at a friend's place and we were drinking, and I got to talking about, well, you know, the whole situation with my life, my ex, my son...I drank way too much, I know. The rented car was because my own car was in the shop that day. It's at work. I called you for a ride tonight because I stayed on for about an hour after my shift ended, had a few drinks, you know, it was a party. It was safer to call you."

"But," she added as she handed him back his glass and sat again beside him. "I wanted to call you. Something told me you were a very sweet guy, someone I could trust. Maybe--"

"Maybe because I didn't drill you in the back seat of the cab when I had the chance? Maybe that?"

She laughed and nodded. "Yeah. That. But other things, too. I could sense that you were a nice person, that's all. I haven't met many nice people lately."

He didn't want to delve into that. "So. You're looking to do what? Move up to a better work environment, obviously," he said.

"Oh, yeah." She sipped her drink. "And I've worked a few clubs around, you know, singing with bands. If I can just earn enough money...get to where I don't need my sister to help with the rent, maybe get a bigger place, and get my little boy back. That's really all I want. I want my son back."

Those last four words of hers dominated his thoughts the next day as he drove home. It might turn out to be Diane all over again. And he didn't want that.

After driving back to his own house, he worried over it all afternoon and for most of the night as well. As he drove his cab that night he continued to think about it. He got home at 12:30 a.m. and while he made the first of his usual string of Scotch-and-waters to go with the late-early movies, he was still thinking about Melissa...and about Diane. It was too late now to call his sister and discuss it with her. He would call her tomorrow before going out to drive.

He made the call and as soon as he had Jessie on the phone, got right down to what was on his mind. He told her about Brandi/Melissa and their night together, leaving out the part about how they had first met.

That would have required too much equivocation and he didn't have a lot of time for explaining.

"Do you remember when I was going with that girl back in Maryland? Diane Kosley?" He asked.

"Mm. Sort of. I do remember that it didn't last very long. Was she the one with the big boobs?"

"Yeah. I must've mentioned that detail."

"More than once."

"Okay, she had boobs like cantaloupes. She was the blonde with tits like cantaloupes. Can we move along now?"

"What do you want to tell me?"

"I met her when I worked for the Cyserve company. You remember when I worked there. She worked for the old guy who owned the building where corporate headquarters was. That's where I worked, corporate. Their office was right across the hallway from ours. We met, started talking, and you know."

"You got yourself some big-boobs nookie."

"Would you be serious? Something's bothering me and I want to find out what you think."

Jessie's joking tone vanished. "Tell me. I have all afternoon."

"I don't." He looked at his watch, "but I don't have to go out and drive for a little while, anyway, so...here's what it is. Diane was a musician, a pianist. A pretty good one, and she was serious. She went to Peabody. That's a prestigious music school. Anyway, that's what she wanted to do, play music, and the job she had in the Bavar office—Old Man Bavar owned the building—was just something she was doing for now, you know, to pay the bills. We started seeing each other, Diane and I, and pretty soon, you know, you were going pretty hot and heavy. She had a second job two evenings a week, playing Broadway tunes and standards in a cocktail lounge in Timonium-Lutherville, out there in the suburbs. I used to go hear her play, take her home, stay the night, you know the drill. Now

Brandi—Melissa, she's also a sort of musician, wants to be a singer. So there's a similarity there."

"Yes, but I don't see why that has to be a problem."

"I haven't gotten to the problem yet. Diane lived by herself. She was divorced. Her ex-husband, Dave, I think his name was, lived in Philadelphia. But they had a four-year-old daughter. Diane and Dave were in the middle of a custody fight over their little girl when she and I were dating. A lot of flamethrowing going back and forth. Lawyers. I heard about it, you can bet. I tried to be sympathetic, but of course there wasn't much I could do except be there and let Diane bend my ear about what a jerk her ex-husband was and of course how badly she wanted her daughter back.

"Well...guess what, sister dear? Br-Melissa is also divorced, and also embroiled in a dispute over child custody It's a little boy this time, but exactly the same age as Diane's daughter Lucy was, four. I'm having deja vu here."

"That's not unusual these days," Jessie said. "I'll admit, the coincidence is a little eerie, one being a piano player and the other a singer, and their children being the same age, but still, why does it have to be a problem? If you like this woman and you think there might be something there, stand by her. Be supportive in her difficult time. She'll appreciate it, and you."

"Apparently you don't remember how the thing with Diane ended. Or maybe I never told you, maybe I only told Edith."

"You and Edith were always very close."

A slight edge in Jessie's tone. It was true; Patrick and Edith had been very close, and sometimes, when the three of them were growing up, Jessie had felt shut out by her two younger siblings, who shared confidences and a repertoire of inside jokes that neither shared with her.

"Okay, so maybe I only did tell Edith. You were already married by then and Edith was still at home. We talked on the phone just about every Sunday. I even let her talk briefly with Diane once, when I called home from Diane's house. I was happy, I wanted to share my discovery of Diane with Edith. But Edith wasn't impressed. After talking with her for just two minutes, Edith decided that Diane was fundamentally an idiot, musical talent or no, and started giving me the business about it on the phone every week. "You were only attracted by her big boobs," she'd say. "Come on, admit it. Sister knows!" But anyway, that's past. Here's what happened. Diane and her ex-husband finally arrived at a joint-custody agreement. Diane got Lucy back. I don't remember the details of the agreement, how much time each parent got to spend with the little girl, but Lucy came back to live with her mom. Well, of course that put a crimp in our seeing each other. Diane didn't want her boyfriend around all the time while her daughter was there, although I did meet Lucy of course, and she was a very sweet child. I would talk and play with her when I came to pick up her mom for a date, and Diane would leave her with a babysitter. That wasn't a big problem. Sex, yeah, that was a problem. Her place was out now, but we could be together at my place sometimes There was no question of her spending the night anymore, she had to get back home to her kid. But I was developing some real feelings for Diane by then, and I was willing to work around all that."

"So what happened?"

"What happened was, Diane popped up one fine morning not long after she got Lucy back, and in the nicest language she could manage in such a situation, basically told me to hit the road."

"She give you a reason?"

"Yeah, in a way. Naturally, I thought right away it had to be another guy. But it wasn't that. Diane had dated a few guys before I came along of course—with her blue eyes, blonde hair and those twin volleyballs of hers, it goes without saying that a lot of guys were...well, let's not mince words, a lot of guys wanted to get into her pants. But it wasn't that. She had just decided she was going to give up the whole dating scene. She was going to make Lucy the focal point of her life. No more men, no more dating. At least not for now. Diane was closing up shop."

"So, you never saw her again?"

"THAT was a huge problem. There wasn't any "not seeing her again." Not just then, anyway. Remember Bavar Properties and Cyserve were right across the hall from each other. After such a dramatic break-off of relations, obviously the best thing for me would have been to get as far away from Diane as possible. But it wasn't possible. She was right there under my nose, day after day, week after week. I had to walk past the glass front door of Bavar to get to the men's room. I tried not to look at her. I think she waved at me once or twice, but I was too hurt to wave back. In fact it hurt so much, just having to walk past her to get to the john, that I started using the back stairs, going down to the use the restroom on the floor below ours. I would sit at the window in the company conference room in the mornings, watch her pull into the parking lot, park and walk into the building. I knew she was right across the hall. How do you get over someone when they're sitting seventy-five feet from where you're sitting all day long? Even if you can't see them? I probably should have listened to Edith. Maybe it was just her big tits. Maybe she was an idiot, like Edith said. Maybe I was an idiot. But isn't 'idiot' just a euphemism for someone in love?"

"So how did it finally work out? I mean, what finally happened?"

"Cyserve had been planning for months to move to a bigger office. Old Man Bavar had another building going up in that same business park, identical to ours but, (and it's a big but), because the new building wasn't finished yet, the penthouse was up for grabs. Our president/CEO, Dan Hawkridge, was an egomaniac who wanted to have his very own crystal palace on the top floor. Play King of the hill, you know. They got the new building finished and we all moved into new offices. The same place really, but now another building. If I still had to watch Diane pull in, park and get out of her car every morning, at least now she wasn't across the hall all the time. Still, it was a bad time for me."

"And you're afraid the same thing is going to happen again with – what did you say her name was?"

"Melissa. Melissa Spears. When she's tending bar and/or singing in clubs, she goes by 'Brandi Spears.,"

"Catchy."

"Yes. And yes, of course I'm afraid the same thing is going to happen again. Wouldn't you be?"

"Have you talked about this with her?"

"No. I only found out about it last night. I mean about the divorce and the kid."

"Well, you don't need to be discussing this with me. You need to talk about it with her."

"But don't you think it's kind of a dark coincidence?"

"It is, but still, you need to talk with her."

"You're right. But...last night was only the second time I've seen her."

"And you're already worried about the long term? How do you know she isn't going to dump you next week?"

"Thanks for the vote of confidence."

"Oh, you know I'm just teasing you. Seriously, though, if you're that concerned about all of this, you need to discuss it with her. Explain what happened. If she's worth bothering with at all, at least she'll hear you out."

There was no point in waiting. He called Melissa's cellphone as soon as he got off the phone with Jessie. Like himself, she was getting ready to go to work. He repeated the whole narrative that he had just shared with his sister. Melissa did not interrupt him once, which could have been either a good or a bad sign, he knew.

When he had finished, she exhaled a long breath. "Well, you've certainly had some experiences," she said. She paused. "I have too, you know."

"I know. For heaven's sake, Melissa, I didn't get to be the age I am without learning a little bit about people. Believe me, you don't have to share," he laughed, though his laughter sounded somewhat forced, even to him. "I'm not sixteen. I know you've been around. But have you ever heard a story like that before?"

"Believe it or not, yes. I've had a couple of divorced friends who dropped out of the dating scene to devote all of their time to their children. What Diane did isn't that unusual. That she did it suddenly, after letting you get that deeply involved, that does kind of surprise me. She probably had some emotional problems you didn't know about."

"Probably. My younger sister, the one who died, thought Diane was an idiot. From just talking to her once. She thought I was wasting my time with Diane. Looks like she was right, don't you think?"

"Maybe. And now you're afraid I'm going to do the same thing to you that she did."

"Melissa, I –"

"No, you're right to be cautious. I respect you for telling me all of this, Pat. Most men would keep things like that to themselves. The ones I've known wouldn't want to rock the boat, give things away, take a chance on blowing a surefire piece of ass."

Her choice of words shocked him for a moment. She knew it had; she had intended to shock him.

She gave it a second to sink in, then said, "You know I really like you. I honestly was surprised when I woke up sober after you dropped me that other time and realized that you hadn't touched me. I was so drunk. You easily could have."

"Well, before you start making me out to be Saint Anthony, I was seriously tempted, you know." He laughed again, and again it sounded forced. "It's true I didn't want to take advantage of you being plastered, but my motives weren't entirely...well, saintly. I could see at least a couple of ways that we, or I anyway, could have gotten into serious trouble."

"I know that, but, well, like I said, I do know men who wouldn't have hesitated, who would have taken me to a motel or a deserted road or something like that without thinking twice. You didn't even do that. You gave me your business card and drove away. By the way, were you expecting me to call you? Because I was sort of expecting you to call me. Even in this day and age it's usually the man who does the calling."

""Expecting' is kind of a strong word. Let's say that for a couple of days I was hoping you would call. But you didn't. If I didn't call you, it's because I decided you weren't interested. It was just a drunky thing. I mean, come on. I'm past the age when I could even fantasize about looking like a TV star, which by the way I never did."

"The thing is, I was. Interested, that is. I am. I am very interested in you. You're a gentleman, Pat. The only other gentleman I know is Tony, the manager at the bar. He's never tried to touch me or come on to me or anything. He's always very nice. You are too. I can feel it somehow. And by the way, you're not a bad-looking man. I think you're quite handsome."

"Thank you. But what about...my story?"

"I didn't know Diane," Melissa said. "I don't know what was going through her head. I have some idea, but I really don't know. The only thing I'm one hundred percent sure of in my life right now is that I love my son and I want him back. If what happened between you and Diane makes you worry about that, well, maybe you should worry. But at the same time I am very much attracted to you and I do want to see you again. Is that good enough for now?" She stressed the word "am."

He thought it over for a second or two. Maybe Jessie was right. Maybe it was far too early to be obsessing about things. Maybe, in worrying about problems that might or might not come up in the future, he was once again thinking the way his father had, his father who used to sit on the front porch smoking cigarettes and concocting disasters that might happen two, three or ten years from now. The unpleasant consequences that might follow if he switched the house from gas to electric heat. Or if he allowed his nine year-old daughter Edith to have a dog, which he did one Christmas, only to take it away from her a few months later and give it to the pound because he was worried that its barking might be bothering the neighbors, although no one had complained.

"Yes," he said. "It's good enough for now. More than good enough."

15

Bob had put in for his Social Security retirement benefits while he was still in jail. He didn't understand the process of course; the county caseworker who helped him fill out the application had to explain everything to him (more than once, would be my guess.) But his 65th birthday was coming up, he did understand that much, and they also made him understand that, having been a postal employee for nearly twenty years, (his drinking cut his career in the Post Office short) he had become entitled to $750 a month in benefits when he turned 62, but he hadn't applied at that time. That became $950 a month after he turned sixty-five, which he did a few weeks after arriving in the park.

But when he put in for his benefits from jail, Bob needed an address to give the SSA. He didn't have one. So he gave them the address of his eighty-eight year-old mother, without telling them that she had already gotten an injunction to keep him off her property. When Bob's birthday had come and gone and he, curious to see if his first check had arrived yet, slinked up to her doorway to ask, she shouted at him to get off her porch and would not listen when he told her that he had only come to see if his benefits were coming in yet. "I thought that…would make her….happy," he told Cyrus and me. "If I was...you know...gettin' a little money every month … she'd figure I didn't need to ask for her help anymore."

Bob's mother had threatened to have him thrown back in jail, so, without finding out one way or the other about his Social Security check, he retreated to the park and went back to doing crossword puzzles. When we asked him what he planned to do about getting his benefits at last, he scratched his head with his pencil and looked out at the street, Bob's way of saying "I don't know.". When Cyrus raised the possibility that Bob's mother might be receiving the checks and tearing them up or throwing them in the trash, Bob became so upset that he started to cry, but still could not think of what to do. I suggested calling the police and asking them to go and check on the matter, but that would not have been within their jurisdiction and anyway, at the first mention of cops, Bob nearly ran up a tree. No, if we were going to help Bob we would have to do something ourselves.

Why were we even interested in helping Bob? Because we figured that if he had $950 a month coming in and the county could find a place for him to have a roof over his head, which the HOT team kept telling us they we were working on, then he would be somewhere else. Bob was like that friendly mouse that lives behind the refrigerator in your kitchen: you want him gone, but killing him seems too cruel. You just want him … moved.

We went over to St. Lucy's and spoke with Sister Paula. She suggested that Bob get a post office box. We explained to her the problems with that idea, not the least of which was that Bob would have to pay a monthly rent on a P.O. box and he was sure to forget to do it. He might also forget where the post office was. There was no question of his opening a bank account, either—for one thing you need an address to do that too, and for another it was a virtual certainty that once he had opened a bank account, Bob would promptly forget which bank was his.

"I think what we need to do first is find out if his mother's getting them checks, and if she is, what she's doing with them," Cyrus said.

Sister Paula agreed. One of her volunteers in the food program, she said, was an old retired lawyer named James. She saw him twice a week when he pitched in to load the donated food at the grocery store and then helped to sort and package it at the parish center for the Wednesday giveaways. "He might have some idea what to do," she said, picking up her phone to call him while Cyrus and I stood and watched her make the call. This was Tuesday, and she told us to come back in the morning when James would surely be there.

We were back the next morning. We brought Bob with us. He wasn't much help, and we didn't expect him to be. But Bob did have his mother's phone number in his wallet, so we got him to call her. She hung up on him. Then Lawyer James tried calling her. She didn't hang up on him, but their conversation was short. He explained about the checks and she said that two had already arrived. But when he asked if Bob might come by and get them, she was adamant. No. She didn't want Bob anywhere near her.

"Man, what did you DO?" Cyrus whispered to Bob. "Your own MOTHER won't even let you pick up your check? What did you do to her?"

Bob couldn't remember. Well, maybe his mother was as crazy as he was.

James asked Bob's mother if she would give the checks to someone from County Social Services. She agreed to that, but James told us when he got off the phone that she had also said that from now on she wanted Bob's Social Security checks sent somewhere else, not to her house.

Some more phone calls. Social Services agreed to send somebody along with Bob to his mother's place. Then we had to wait for Lawyer James to type and print out an authorization on Sister Paula's computer for the county to pick up Bob's check for him. Bob had to sign it. It took him a long time to write down his name; two practice tries were required. It was agreed that when they went to get his money, the social worker would ring his mother's doorbell and Bob would wait in the car. Then Lawyer James called the police department and left a message for Officer Solis asking if Bob might, for now, receive mail at the police station. "They've done it for other people," he assured us. "I don't think Fernando or his boss will have a problem with it."

"Bob won't go to the cops to get his mail, he's scared of the police," Cyrus said.

"I'll talk to them. Maybe the HOT team can bring him his mail at the library. It's only across the street."

Cyrus nodded. "Yeah, they did that for Marianne for a while."

We took Bob back to the park, and he went back to his crosswords. A day or two later Sister Paula called Cyrus on his cellphone and told him to tell Bob that if he would get himself over to the Social Services building, someone would take him to his mother's house to get his checks. I was delegated to accompany Bob to Social Services. They took him off my hands and I went back to the park. Two hours later Bob wandered back (the county must have dropped him off nearby) with the two government checks, still in their envelopes, folded in half and stuffed into the hip pocket of his dirty, baggy pants.

But Bob couldn't cash either of those checks. Not without some form of I.D. He had lost his driver's license a long time ago, and by now it would have expired anyway.

The HOT team came to the rescue again: Officer Payne drove Bob to the DMV and shepherded him through applying for a state I.D. card, which looks exactly like a driver's license but doesn't entitle you to drive. He then took Bob to the nearest check-cashing place. Probably they would not have let Bob cash a refund check for five bucks if he had come in alone. But there's something about having a uniformed police officer standing next to you that convinces people you're genuine, or at least that they should do whatever they need to do to get rid of you, and the officer, as quickly as possible.

And that was how Bob the Bum came to have $1,900.

Well, I did say that it wasn't going to be simple.

Obviously Bob could not be allowed to walk around the streets with $1,900 cash on him—whatever he didn't immediately spend on beer would last seven or eight minutes. Back to Sister Paula, who talked with Father Jay, who agreed, after much cajoling, to let Bob temporarily leave some of his cash in a safe in the parish office, and gave him a receipt for it. "You'd better make two copies, Father," I said. "Give one to me, because he'll lose his." The Monsignor knew me and decided I could be trusted with this. "But we're not running a bank here, you know," Father Jay said. "This is only until he finds another place to put his money. When he comes back, he takes all of it." Agreed. So Bob took his receipt, I took my copy, and off we went, Bob with $300 in his pocket and the other $1,600, for now, safely in the hands of God.

Cyrus urged Bob to recompense all the parkies from whom he had been bumming cigarettes and beers up until now. I wasn't a cigarette smoker, but he owed me four or five beers easily. He owed several other people, but of course he couldn't remember who or how much of what. Then Cyrus had an idea. "Why don't we have a cookout?" he said. "I know somewhere in that pile of junk Marianne won't let me get rid of there's an old hibachi somewhere. We can get some charcoal, Bob can pay for some carne asada and stuff, and we'll just invite everybody to a little picnic, say it's Bob's way of paying everyone back."

That's what we did. The meat department at El Mercado down the street from the liquor store was well-known in the neighborhood for its carne asada, said to be the best in town. Bob sprang for five pounds of it, plus beans, rice, chips, guacamole dip and two 12-packs of Bud Ice. Cyrus and I split the cost of a bag of charcoal, and we got some styrofoam plates, plastic forks and a roll of paper towels.

We hauled all of this stuff back to the park. Cyrus dug up the rusty hibachi that Marianne had found in the alley off Canon Street and insisted they keep because it might come in handy, which it did tonight. Ed, who had joined us by now, found an old iron skillet in the back of his car that we could use to heat up the beans and rice. He had brought Chantal and Yvonne with him, and Cage, who was with Chantal that night, (which couldn't have pleased Ed very much) and of course Terry was around. Cyrus had put out the word around the park that we were going to have a picnic, but even if hadn't, Terry would gotten wind of it. Terry could sense free food the way some birds are said to be able to sense the approach of a tsunami. I didn't see Frankie anywhere, but Andrew showed up after about an hour, lit his weed pipe behind a tree and joined in the fun. Someone had a Bluetooth speaker connected to their Smartphone and started playing that rap garbage, which annoyed me at least as much as having Cage around must have annoyed Ed. In fact I took a couple of beers and my director's chair and placed myself far enough on the perimeter of the gathering so that the "fuck-my-bitch, fuck-yo-ho'" bullshit was at least a decibel or two less below earsplitting. But I thought to myself, as I popped open a beer, that if that goddamned racket stayed that loud just one minute after it got dark, somebody across the street was going to call the cops and complain about the noise.

They didn't have to bother. A police car came cruising along Canon and everyone scrambled to put out their cigarettes and hide their half-full beers under blankets and in the shadows behind trees. One or two deftly and quietly got rid of the cardboard cases filled with empty cans – the parkies always made sure that they did their partying close to a trash can in case they had to get rid of the empties in a hurry. The rap was suddenly turned down; the shouting became a pulsing buzz.

The police car pulled over to the curb. Two cops got out and walked over to speak to us, but it was nothing too serious; they informed us charcoal fires weren't allowed in the park and would have to put it out and get rid of the hibachi. "Butane is okay, but no charcoal fires," one of them said. The coals in the hibachi still glowed, but most of the food had been eaten by then. Cyrus stepped up, apologized to the two policemen, said we didn't know about the charcoal rule and told them that certainly, we'd put the coals out and clean up right away. "Next time we'll go down to Eucalyptus," he told them. Eucalyptus Park, about a half-mile north of us, had barbeque grills and picnic tables. It even had restrooms. Probably we should have gone there in the first place. No citation was issued, but the two cops walked around for a few minutes, talking with people, checking for outstanding warrants, the usual stuff. Cyrus, Ed and I cleaned up the picnic mess and then the two cops finally drove away.

The party was over. Well, almost. There was still beer left. The smokers lit back up, the beers came out of hiding and the rap came back on, but not as loud as before.

I looked around and there was no sign of Bob. "Where's Bob? Anybody see where Bob went?"

"He headed for the power station when he saw the cops coming," Cage said. He and Chantal were passing a weed pipe back and forth. Where was Yvonne? She probably wouldn't like that. Ed wouldn't like it either, but Ed was already passed out drunk on the grass.

The power station was what we called the locked building down behind the library where there was a generator used for I-don't-know-what. It had a chain-link fence around it with signs that read "Danger: High Voltage." We used the area around it as an emergency outhouse. If you suddenly had to take a crap at night, and the library was closed, the power station stood at the bottom of a steep embankment that concealed it from the rest of the park and the street, so you could do your business and count on at least a little privacy if you were careful.

I found him. He hadn't bothered climbing down to the power station. He sat alone on a bench at the top of the embankment, a can of Bud Ice in his hand.

"Are you okay, Bob?" I asked.

"Yeeaah." A long pause. "I just didn't … want to be around … any place where there was cops." He squinted like he did when he was thinking, or trying to.

"I kind of figured that," I said.

I sat beside him. "How come you're so afraid of cops?" I asked. "You got a warrant or something?"

"N-n-no. I just don't like cops. I don't … trust 'em."

"Rudy Payne was pretty nice to you today."

"Yes....he was," he admitted.

"And you were walking up to the police station the morning we first met."

"That was....different. I'd just....gotten out of jail and I was....tryin' to find my truck. And it was a Sunday. There was no place else...I coulda gone." It surprised me that he could remember that much.

"Bob, do you have any family? I mean besides your mother."

He thought about that for a couple of seconds. "Yeah? Yeah?" he nodded. "I have...a daughter?"

He squinted at me as if checking to see if his answer were right.

"You have a daughter?" Great, I thought. Now we sounded like a vaudeville team.

After thinking for a moment to make sure he'd given me the right answer, he said again, "Yeah? Yeah. I do...I have a daughter. Her name is....uh, uh..."

"Do you know where she lives? Is it anywhere near here? In California, anyway?"

"Elena. Her name is Elena."

"Where does she live?"

"I can't...remember. I think...maybe..." he trailed off.

"Think."

He took a deep gulp of his beer. "Why is it ....important? God, I haven't seen my daughter... in...five years?"

"Do you have your wallet?"

"Yeah." He pulled it out.

"Is your money still in there?"

He checked. "Yeah, yeah. Still there, what's left after....this hootenanny we just threw."

"Listen, Bob. You can't handle your own money. We all know it. So do you. You got sixteen hundred bucks in safekeeping with Father Jay now, but that's not going to solve the problem. You're going to be getting a check every month now. You're going to need some kind of a conservatorship."

"A what?"

"That's where you appoint somebody to handle your affairs for you. Like your money. It's best if it's a family member. Your mother won't have anything to do with you. If you have a daughter, I think we should try to find her. She might be willing to at least manage your money for you, if not take you in. You'd have an address where they could mail your check, anyway."

"But I…don't know where she lives!"

"I'm sure your mother knows. After all, it's her granddaughter."

"My mother...won't talk to me. You...saw for yourself."

"Maybe Sister Paula can talk to her. I'll ask, anyway. And maybe we can talk to that lawyer friend of hers, James, about how to set up a conservatorship. Listen, we can talk about this some more in the morning, okay? Now come on back, the cops have left."

"Okay." He stood up slowly, clutching his beer. "You're sure … they're gone."

"They left fifteen minutes ago. There wasn't any trouble. They just told us we couldn't cook in the park. By the way, have you eaten?"

"Yeah. Yeah, I had something to eat."

"Good. Tonight before you go to sleep, try to remember where your daughter is. What city, at least what state. You'll try?"

"Yeah, I'll try. Don't know if….there's any point. But I'll….think on it."

I went back to rejoin Cyrus and the group, which was already beginning to scatter now that most of the food and beer were gone. I reported to Cyrus the conversation I'd just had with Bob.

Cyrus scratched his ample stomach. "You think they can find his daughter?"

"I don't know, but now that there's money involved, somebody's got to handle things for him. There's only so much *we* can do. By the way, I hate to think of him going to sleep tonight in some parking lot or alley with over two hundred dollars in his pocket."

Cyrus nodded. "Well, yeah," he said, "but he's still Bob the Bum. Nobody would think, lookin' at him, that he had more than twenty-eight cents."

"He wouldn't have to be robbed. He could just lose it somewhere." I looked around the park. "All right, where the hell has he wandered off to now? I brought him back from the power station with me. Yvonne!" I shouted. "Have you seen Bob? He was here a minute ago."

Yvonne sat on the ground with a blanket around her shoulders. She might have been cold, but it was more likely that she was planning to duck under that blanket pretty soon and smoke some crystal.

"He went that-a-way!" She pointed toward the intersection of Davidson and McKinley. The liquor store was around the corner at the end of McKinley. Bob had probably gone to get more beer, now that he had the money to pay for it, and probably cigarettes too. A whole pack this time, more smokes than he'd had in his pocket at any one time since jail, and probably before that.

Cyrus, Marianne and I made camp that night in our usual spot along the west side of the library. Frankie appeared out of nowhere just before midnight. He had come prepared this time, with a blanket and a flattened cardboard box to sleep on. Like me, he used his backpack for a pillow. His sudden arrival brought me out of my doze.

"Frankie, where have you been? You missed food. We had a picnic."

"I know, My father told me. No worries. I was over at Lion's Gate. They served pizza tonight."

"And you were out in the alley smoking weed with Andrew."

"Yeah."

"Well, go to sleep."

But Frankie didn't go to sleep. He often became animated when he had been smoking weed, and he wanted to talk. Stoned or sober, Frankie had a tendency to babble, and none of us really wanted to listen to him just then. He sat on his blanket and talked his usual gibberish for a long time, giggling at his own jokes. Then Cyrus, watching westerns on his Smartphone as usual, told him to shut up. He went right on talking. Then I asked him to shut up. He ignored me, too. Then Marianne told him to shut up and that was when he finally shut up.

In the morning after we had broken camp as usual, piled everything up around Cyrus and Marianne's tree and tied down a tarp over it, I went off alone to get my breakfast beer. (Cyrus no longer joined me in the morning-beer ritual; he was sticking to his resolve to stay on the wagon now.) But by now I knew there was going to be a midmorning beer later anyway. Maybe Cyrus would care to join me on that next jaunt to the liquor store and get himself a Monster.

It got to be ten O'clock. The library was now open. According to the morning routine I had established by then, as soon as the library was open I would go in and try to get on one of the computer terminals that were open to the public. Many people wanted to use the Internet, so I had to move quickly as soon as the doors opened.

There was a one-hour-limit on the use of the workstations, but that was more than enough for me. I would check the news headlines, the weather forecast and, during the baseball season, last night's scores. Then I might spend a few minutes chatting with my Facebook friends, check to see if I had any emails to answer, and then log off. Unlike some of the parkies, who used the library as a lounge/toilet/siesta spot/phone-charging facility, I didn't like to hang around inside the building for very long. Believe it or not, I found it too noisy. The old days of "Shhh, this is the library" were long gone. Nowadays so many used the library for purposes that had nothing to do with books, there was a steady murmur of voices, the jarring sound of ringtones and cellphone conversations, and the occasional screaming child which no one tried to silence unless its mother were embarrassed enough to do so, and most weren't anymore.

As I left the library that morning and sauntered back out into the sunshine, thinking I would find Cyrus and ask if he wanted to walk around the corner to Crown with me, I saw that there were two police units there. They had not parked at the curb, but pulled right up into the park itself. A small group of people and police had gathered around a spot right at the edge of the bushes at the top of the embankment that led down to the power station. I was too far away to see what was going on, but I noticed that Cyrus was among the small crowd.

I drew closer and saw Bob sitting on the sidewalk next to the bushes. He was soaking wet. The cops were trying to talk to him and everyone else, including Cyrus, stood around gawking. I walked up and stood next to Cyrus. "What the hell happened?" I asked.

"The cops are trying to find out. Bob's kinda...incoherent."

"You mean more than usual."

Cyrus grunted. "Looks like he fell asleep in the bushes and they turned on the sprinklers." he said. "He was too passed-out drunk to even notice he was getting wet."

"So what are they going to do?"

"They'll probably take him to the hospital. We'll see."

One of the officers was trying to ask Bob questions but wasn't getting much of anywhere. "Do you know where you are?" "Uh, I think so," Bob said, looking around. "Do you know what year this is?" "Umm.... Damn. Uh...no. No, I don't." Bob shook his head. "Do you know who the president of the United States is?" Bob couldn't answer that one, either.

I went up the policeman who was asking him questions. "Did you check to see if he still has his wallet?"

"Now, who are you?"

"I'm a friend of his. His name is Bob. Did you check to see if he has his wallet? Because last night he had more than two hundred dollars in it."

"We checked. Yeah, the money's still there. How do you know about his money?"

Cops.

"I helped him get it. Do you know officer Payne? Rudy Payne?"

"Yeah, of course we know Rudy."

"He helped Bob. We were here. He took Bob to cash his Social Security checks. He has another sixteen hundred stashed over in the rectory at St. Lucy's. Here, look." I pulled the receipt out of my backpack. The cop took it and looked it over. "Father Jay, the pastor over there, he's holding the rest of Bob's money. We wanted to make sure it was safe."

"Okay, we'll look into that," he handed me back the paper. "You guys take pretty good care of your friends, don't you?" There was some suspicion in his tone, even though I had dropped Rudy Payne's name. Cops.

"Cyrus and I, that's Cyrus over there," I jerked my thumb in my friend's direction, "we kind of figure if we don't look out for each other, ain't nobody else goin' to." Listen to me, will you? I was talking like Cyrus.

"Good philosophy," the cop said. Then he turned back to Bob. "Mr., uh, Mr…what's the name on that state I.D.?" he asked his partner, who held Bob's wallet.

"Wallenski," the other cop said.

"Mr. Wallenski, we're going to take you to the hospital. The ambulance is on its way. Do you have any family around here?"

"He has a daughter," I said.

"Do we know where she is?"

"No. He doesn't either, unless he remembered last night. I asked him. But from the looks of him, he probably doesn't remember much about last night."

"My guess would be you're right," the officer nodded.

The ambulance came and they took Bob away. I saw him one more time, much later, after I got out of the hospital myself.

The same week that Bob fell asleep in the sprinklers, Yvonne left the park suddenly and for good. She and Chantal had one more big screaming match, but with no fisticuffs or smackdown this time. We heard the yelling. It seemed to have something to do with a battery charger, but with those two, things like battery chargers were excuses. The real *casus belli* was elsewhere.

After Yvonne disappeared I asked Chantal what had happened. She explained that she and Yvonne had agreed that Yvonne should move back up to San Jose where her brother lived and stay with him for a while. "We knew she was going to get in trouble again if she kept breakin' that stay-away order," Chantal said in her usual machine-gun-speak that I had trouble following. "So we decided that she should just get out of here for a while. She has to come back in three months for court anyway."

But Cyrus being Cyrus, he dug deeper into the story than I did. He knew the principals better for one thing, Chantal being his "cousin." Also, he did pride himself on knowing more about what was going on around the park than the rest of us. So, when I mentioned to him that Chantal had told me that Yvonne's sudden departure was about the stay-away order and her fear of more trouble with the cops, he made a snuffing noise through his nose and said, "She told you that? That ain't the reason." Then he sat silently, waiting for me to ask. (Cyrus loved the dramatic pause.)

"So," I said. "Are we gonna sit here all afternoon while you wait for me to say, 'Well'?"

Cyrus stretched and yawned for stage effect. "Chantal's pregnant," he said at last.

"How do you know?"

"She told me."

"She didn't tell me."

"I've known her longer than you have, remember?"

"Another pregnancy in our little park," I said. "Do we know –sorry, Maestro-- do *you* know who the father is?"

He acted surprised that I should ask. "Cage," he said.

"That skinny little meth-head?"

"I told you that, too. I told you Chantal would do just about anything for twenty bucks worth of crystal. Just what to do you think them two have been yellin' and screamin' about for the past year? Phone chargers? No, this is all about Cage. Chantal was fuckin' Cage for a while and Yvonne caught them at it in the alley. I'm sure I told you that."

"You mentioned Cage. But you didn't mention Yvonne catching them in the alley. I would have remembered that. And you said it was just hearsay."

Cyrus shrugged. "Well, Mr. Hearsay is gonna be a daddy."

"At least this time the daddy's gonna be somebody besides you."

"Somebody say Amen."

16

It was getting to be a familiar pattern: he always woke up first. Melissa faced him on her right side, still asleep, hugging her pillow, her head pressed against his shoulder. He gently propped himself up on his elbow to look at his watch, trying not to wake her. But she stirred at even that slight movement, opened her eyes, smiled, kissed his shoulder and went back to sleep. The glance at his watch told him it was eight forty-five. He went into the kitchen to make coffee, as he had on the other two mornings that week when they had been able to spend the night together. . He didn't mind. But now he was thinking about her sister. They had had Melissa's place to themselves all week, but this was Saturday, and Sharon was expected back from her Mexican riviera cruise tomorrow afternoon.

A half-empty bottle of Jose Cuervo and a plastic bottle of margarita mix stood on the kitchen counter from the night before. They had made margaritas while he cooked dinner.

He unscrewed the top of the Cuervo bottle, sniffed at it, took a sip and grimaced, (tequila was not his drink) put it back in the cupboard and put the margarita mix back in the refrigerator. He went to the sink and filled the Norelco carafe with water for coffee, leaving the water on to fill the sink for washing dishes, got out a scrub sponge and some lemon Ajax and went at the dishes from last night's meal while the coffee brewed.

Melissa came up behind him. She was barefoot; he didn't hear her approach. She put her arms around him from behind and kissed his neck. "Thank you for cleaning up," she said.

"Habit. There wasn't much to clean. When I'm alone, I almost never leave dishes in the sink at night. I don't like getting up in the morning and facing a sinkful of dishes. But this wasn't much," he said again.

"You're some woman's dream man."

"I wasn't Valerie's."

Her robe hung open and she was nude under it. "Come back to bed," she said, then added in a kind of cross between a purr and a command, "I want morning cock."

He kissed her, ran his hand through her hair. "You *do* like sex first thing in the morning, don't you? By the way, do you always talk like that? 'Morning cock?' "

"Does it bother you?"

"No, but it does make me think of a line from the movie *Patton*. You know, George C. Scott?"

She laughed. "'Cock' makes you think of the movie *Patton*?"

"A reporter asks him about his language when he's talking to the troops, and he says. 'Well, when I want 'em to remember it, I give it to 'em loud and dirty, so it'll stick.'"

She smirked, reached into his briefs and gave his already-stiffening prick a squeeze. "That loud and dirty enough for the troops?"

"Dirty enough, loud and clear. I think I'm done with these dishes," he said, smiling as he wiped his hands on a towel. Then, a little embarrassed at feeling himself respond so quickly to her touch, he looked over at the bubbling Norelco on the counter. "Coffee's ready," he said.

His attempt at nonchalance did not fool her. "It'll wait a few minutes," she said, and led him by the hand back down the hall. For the first time in recent memory he felt very happy.

She dropped her robe in the floor, lay on her back nude and pulled him down on top of her,

"You know what?" he said, "this makes me think of another great quotation."

"Not now."

"No, this is good."

"Oh, all right. Patton again?"

"No, Foghorn Leghorn, you know, the rooster from Bugs Bunny?"

She gave him s slap on top of head. "You're kidding! We're about to *fuck* and you're thinking about *cartoons*?"

"Sorry. I'm a Looney Tunes fan. You might as well know that about me."

"I think that's cute. Okay, what'd he say?"

He cleared his throat and tried to imitate Foghorn Leghorn's voice. "'You're about, I say, you're about as subtle as a hand grenade in a barrel of oatmeal!"

"You asshole." she smiled up at him, locked her hands behind his neck and kissed him very hard.

As they finished breakfast, his laptop, which he'd brought over with him, was on the table, extolling music by Thelonious Monk. Melissa had turned out to be a fan of classic jazz. She directed him to a website that streamed 1950s jazz, the likes of Monk, Coltrane, Dizzy Gillespie, Stan Getz and company. That was her favorite period.

"What's this song?" he asked, sipping coffee.

"*Round Midnight.* It was recorded at a club in New York City called The Five Spot. Very famous jazz hangout back in the day."

"I like it. Kind of sexy."

"I find Monk's music very sexy," she said.

"I find you very sexy."

"Well, you needn't," she smiled..

"What do you mean, well, I needn't?"

She smiled and put down her coffee cup. "He also has a song called *Well, You Needn't.*"

"I don't know a hell of a lot about jazz. But now that I know you like it, I want to. Mozart's always been more my speed."

"He's sexy too."

"You think so?"

"Sometimes, yes."

"Give me an example of Mozart you find sexy."

"I can't name anything. Just...I don't know. He has this one thing where....it was in that movie, you know? The orchestra comes in, low and slow, and then there's this oboe, playing a single note that kind of just hovers in the air..."

"The Serenade for Winds in B-flat. That's what you heard if you're talking about the movie *Amadeus.* How do you come to know so much about jazz?"

"My daddy was a jazz musician. He played in a combo and had hundreds of jazz records. So tell me how you came to be an expert on Mozart."

"I'm not an expert. I don't play an instrument. Always wanted to, but never had the patience to learn. Tried the piano, the guitar. Gave up. But I had a buddy in high school who was a very good pianist. He knew a lot about the classics. We used to hang out after school. He'd play records, sometimes play the piano a little bit. I picked up a lot from him. I liked the music, so I started listening on my own. That's about it."

"I loved the movie. I felt so sorry for...what was his name? The bad guy?"

"Salieri. Only he wasn't really a bad guy in real life. The movie took a lot of liberties."

A thin, tinkling tone, some song he didn't recognize, came from the counter top next to the refrigerator. "Is that your phone?" he asked.

She got up from the table. "Shit, I hope that's not Tony wanting me to come in early."

She picked it up, spoke into it, and whispered, "It's Tom. My ex."

He withdrew to the the couch, giving her as much space as he could in such a small apartment without withdrawing all the way to the bedroom. He turned on the TV but left the sound off. NCAA basketball.

Then there was a sudden change both in her tone and her volume. "Hi, BUDDY!" she squealed, her voice shooting up into the baby-talk register as her face blossomed into a wide smile. "It's my son," she said to him. Then back to the phone: "How are *you*, sweetheart? Mommy misses you! What?""

Now that she was obviously talking with her son Tommy Jr., and nothing of a sensitive nature was going to be discussed with a four-year-old, he went back into the kitchen and quietly began clearing the breakfast dishes off the table as Melissa went on with the high-pitched gushing of a mother who has not been with her child in months. He was happy for her of course, but at the same time a tiny wisp of cloud flitted across his sky. He suddenly wanted a drink, but it was too early in the day for it, and given the moment and the fact that he and Melissa had already discussed his anxiety about divorced women with small children, it would not have looked right. He went to the sink and silently cursed himself for his pettiness. "Quit acting like a kid," he thought. "That business with Diane was a long time ago, and you were already far past being a kid then."

And Jessie was right. If Melissa meant anything at all to him, and he had already decided that she very much did, he should give her his emotional support now rather than feel threatened by her love for her little boy, which was of course more powerful than any love she could, or ever would feel, for him or anyone else. Things had been this way for maybe a hundred thousand years now. It was among the most deeply-established and hard-wired of all the traditions on the earth, wasn't going to change, and shouldn't. There was no question in his mind what Melissa represented, either. Not now. The role of Eros in nearly anyone's life makes a bell-curve: he knew that this was, at his age, the merest fluke, and probably the last chance he was going to get for anything resembling happiness before he was too old, too washed-out, just too far gone to attract anyone, or offer them much. What did he have left now? It remained to be seen even what he had left that Melissa might want. He was more than twenty years her senior and certainly not rich. What could she possibly see in the likes of him? Money was the only thing that could beat Nature's odds once you were past a certain age. Years of simply watching what went on around him had taught him that. You could be old and rich and you would never lack for companionship. But to be old and poor, or even of modest means? He didn't want to think about it. An aging cab driver, even one like himself, about to come into his share of the sale of a house, was still an aging cab driver and probably not going to get another shot at establishing a bulwark against loneliness this late in life. Since his marriage to Valerie had broken up several years ago, the great gate-crasher had hovered nearby, always closer, its shadow getting slowly but steadily larger with the changing of the seasons, the turning of each year. And if there was one thing he knew as surely as he knew that those seasons were changing and that that shadow was indeed getting longer every time he cared to think about it, it was that having witnessed the deaths of both his younger sister and his father, he did not want to die alone.

When Melissa got off the phone she threw herself into his arms. He was sure that she was going to start crying over being separated from Tommy. He was prepared for that, prepared to follow Jessie's advice, hold Melissa, stroke her hair while she cried, offer reassurances and his firm, unquestioning support.

But she appeared to be very happy.

"I'm going to see Tommy! He's coming for Thanksgiving, and he'll be staying right through Christmas!"

"His father agreed to that?"

"He wants to go to England for Christmas. I told you he was British, didn't I?"

"I don't think you did."

He has family in Manchester. He wants to spend the holidays with his family. He's going to let me have Tommy right through New Year's. Isn't that wonderful?"

"Absolutely. So...I guess I'll get to meet the little guy. Of course that means I'm also going to have to meet your sister, doesn't it?"

"Oh, don't worry about that. Shari won't be a problem. I think she'll like you just fine. I know I complained about her, but she isn't that bad. In fact, why don't you come over and meet her next week? Maybe around Wednesday? She'll be back tomorrow afternoon. Come and have dinner. I won't even make you cook." She kissed him.

"You sure?"

"She'd better get used to you being around, because I want you around." She kissed him again. "Besides, if she can go waltzing off on a cruise with her boyfriend, why shouldn't I have my boyfriend over?"

"Am I your boyfriend? I'm old enough to be your uncle," he said.

"Yes you are, my boyfriend that is, if you want to be, and I don't care about the other thing. I think you're wonderful. I've never met anyone like you."

"You mean, no one as old as me?"

"Don't be silly. I've dated older men than you. No, I think I can size people up pretty fast, and there's something very special about you, Pat. You're kind, you're a good listener and you're a good…cook."

"That's it?"

She smiled. "You were expecting me to say 'a good fuck' of course. You men. I don't have to say it. I think we both know it. *You are a good fuck*, Pat Donahy. I don't care what your ex-wife might have said. Did you and she have problems in bed? I can hardly believe you did."

He was happy. "That's a little personal, don't you think?" he said.

"I guess yes. I'm sorry. Sometimes I let my mouth run without thinking. It's gotten me in trouble before."

"I have the same problem, and it's gotten me in trouble before, too. But there were other problems. It wasn't all just her. It was as much my fault. Really, Valerie and I shouldn't have gotten married in the first place. We were too much alike. Each of us had his or her...well, it doesn't matter now."

"I'll make some more coffee."

"Mind if I have a smoke?"

"Not if you open the window. I didn't know you smoked cigarettes."

"I don't. But sometimes I enjoy a pipe." He went to get his pipe and tobacco out of his jacket.

She looked at him as she set up the coffeemaker. "So you smoke a pipe. Well, they would say that we're in the 'discovery' phase of our relationship, wouldn't they? Listen to me. 'Discovery phase.' I sound like a fucking paralegal," she laughed. "You know I once started a paralegal course, but didn't finish it. There's a discovery for your side."

"I used to smoke cigars, but I had to give them up. I can't stand cheap ones and I can't afford good ones." He puffed at his pipe to keep it lit.

Back to the sound of Thelonious Monk's piano, no longer solo now but backed by a large band.

"Oh, this is from *Monk's Blues*," she said.

"Is that the song?"

"No, that's the album. It's the only album he ever made with a big band that I know of. The song is *Just A Glance At Love."* She hummed along with the music. "It's one of my favorites."

"Do you think this one is sexy? Because speaking just for myself, I think it's kind of sad. Wistful."

"It is. But sad and wistful can be sexy, don't you think?" she said.

"Maybe he was thinking of a lost love when he wrote it. It sounds like something someone might write after a failed romance."

"He didn't write it. Teo Macero wrote it. He was a saxophone player, composer. He worked at Columbia Records. I think he produced for Miles Davis and Dave Brubeck, big names."

"Oh, my. You really do know your shit, don't you?"

"Do you always talk like that?"

"Touché," he grinned at her.

"Like I said, my daddy was a jazzman. He played the clarinet."

"That's probably where your love for music comes from. How are things going on that score, by the way? You have any gigs lined up soon?"

"One of the regulars at the bar says he knows the manager of the Café Ciel."

"Where's that?"

"On Sunset. It's a fancy place, and they have live music." She poured coffee into his cup. "It's probably bullshit," she said. "If he hangs out at Shanghai Jake's, how would he know the manager at a fancy place like that? Likely just some horny old bastard who thinks he can talk his way into my pants."

This time her language really stung. "Well, there's a lot of us out there," he said.

"Oh, Pat! No! No! I didn't mean you!" She put down the coffee carafe and placed both hands on his shoulders. She looked him squarely in the face. "I didn't mean you," she repeated. "Of course you're not like that. If I thought you were, do you think you'd be here?"

She took his face in her hands. "I want you to stop this. This being so obsessed with your age. You're a kind, thoughtful man, and anyone can see you're intelligent."

"And a good listener."

"And a good cook." She smiled. "And other things too. That's all that matters to me."

"Have a seat. If I'm so damned thoughtful, let me pour your coffee."

"Thank you, baby." She sat. She had called him "baby." Joy.

He had forgotten his cellphone when he went out to drive his cab the afternoon before. When he got back to the house, he picked up the phone from the coffee table to check for calls or messages.

There was a text message from Jessie. It said to call her right away. The house had been sold.

Although it was perhaps not a good idea since he planned to go out and drive later, he fixed a double Scotch-and-water and sat in the kitchen, thinking and staring out the window at the Cup-o'-Golds which had been his father's particular pride.

Of course the sale of the house came as no surprise. He and Jessie had been working on it for months now. But he hadn't done much to prepare for the impact it was going to have on his life since that afternoon about two weeks ago when he had taken a call from dispatch and gone to pick up a very drunken fare who turned out to be named Brandi-Melissa Spears. Since then the train of his thought had circled primarily around her. Now it had to shift back to the problem of what he was going to do when the family house was pulled out from under him, which was now about to happen.

He called his sister right away. Yes, a couple who were moving to California from Ohio, and had looked at the house on Wednesday, had made an offer and Jessie had accepted it.

"You remember that couple, the Bierschwels. You met them three days ago when the real-estate agent brought them around."

"Of course. They were nice. So they want the house?"

"They made a good offer and I took it. I'm sorry I didn't consult with you, but I tried to reach you and all I could get was your fucking voicemail. I had to act fast."

"I know. My fault. I left my cellphone here yesterday when I went to work, and then--"

"And then you went and spent the night with what's-her-name."

"Brandi. Melissa. Yeah, yeah, I did. So what's next?"

"We'll have a closing. You'll have to sign all the papers since I'm back here. Then you'll have to get your ass of out that house. I hope you have a new place lined up."

"As a matter of fact I don't. I kind of got sidetracked with Melissa. I looked around at some places, but I haven't actually done anything yet."

"They're going to want to move in right away. You'd better do something quick or you're going to be sleeping in your cab. Or in the park."

The idea of renting a room instead of an apartment had gone out the window. Now that Melissa was in the picture they were going to need a place where they could be alone. That ruled out his becoming someone's boarder. Even a granny flat might not be good enough. Coming and going from a third party's property, even if he had a separate roof, might be uncomfortable for her and certainly would be for him. There seemed no alternative but to rent an apartment and bear the cost. And he had no time to shop around, now. Since he had to move anyway, he wanted to move as close to Melissa as possible. But he had to do it now.

"Thank God for the Internet," he thought to himself early on Monday morning as he drove south on Interstate 110. It had taken some searching, but he'd found a studio in San Pedro, with kitchen and bath, for slightly less than $1,100 a month. It was about the best he was going to be able to do, at least on such short notice. San Pedro. Well, it wasn't exactly Bel Air, he thought. But he would only be about fifteen minutes down the freeway from Melissa's place, which might not be of any importance in six months or maybe even in three, but for now it was important enough.

He met at Coldwell-Banker with Allen and Rhoda Bierschwel, the couple moving in from Dayton, Ohio, two mornings later. The real estate company had already arranged everything with Jessie. All he had to do was sign the papers. He did that, then rented a U-Haul truck and cleared the last of his things out of the home that the Donahy family had occupied for more than fifty years. He noticed that he didn't feel especially sentimental about it as he drove the loaded truck away. It had all happened too quickly. There would be time for that later, much later, like around two O'clock the next morning when he turned his cab toward home and realized that he was going the wrong way.

17

We had an very rainy winter in the park that year. El Nino? I don't remember, and wouldn't have cared if I had known. All I knew was that it was wet, wetter than SoCal usually is.

Our little band of gypsies, myself, Cyrus, Marianne, Chantal (Cage, after Yvonne had left) sometimes Frankie and once in a while even Ed huddled on especially wet nights beneath the awning in front of the central library instead of in our usual spot over on the west side of the building. The main awning was wider and provided more shelter from the rain. But it leaked in some places; you had to learn where they were. I learned that the hard way on one of my first rainy nights in the park when I spread my sleeping bag in the wrong spot and woke up at 5:30 a.m. miserably wet. Cyrus lent me a dry sweatshirt and a pair of old jeans (which didn't fit; Cyrus was both shorter and wider than I.) I had to hold them up with one hand as I dragged my wet clothes and nearly-soaked sleeping bag down to the Wash N' Dry to throw everything in the dryer. Later Andrew would offer to do such chores in exchange for a little drug money, but at that time I hadn't met him yet.

Cyrus got the letter he wanted from the pastor of St. Lucy's, and a few other written recommendations, including one from Officer Payne, in support of his efforts to get at least some of his daughters back with him. He managed to get a hearing before a family law judge, who naturally asked Cyrus why he was asking for custody of his children when he didn't even have a job. Cyrus protested that he was more than willing to work but that there hadn't been much work for him lately. He told the judge, truthfully, that he had recently worked part-time baking at Dunkin' Donuts, and done some general contracting work. But his hours at the bakery, few to begin with, had been cut, and the one or two contractor acquaintances that he had in the flooring and drywall businesses hadn't been giving him many jobs lately. Rudy Payne's letter confirmed that Cyrus was on a waiting list for subsidized housing. Cyrus swore that he had stopped drinking, (to which I could have testified if asked) and stressed that he had not used drugs in well over a year. The judge told him to come back in a month and show documented proof that he had been seeking regular employment during that thirty-day period.

"Well, it's a start," I told him the morning after the hearing as we sat on our usual bench, me nursing a beer in a paper bag and him sipping on a Monster. "So. Are you going to look for work? And by the way, where's Marianne?"

"Asleep, as usual. Yeah, I'll look for work. I'll go down and apply at Human Resources, check the county job board. I gotta find something steady, though. No more of this a few hours here, a few hours there shit."

"You have any special skills? I know you can bake doughnuts and lay down carpeting."

"I've done a little house painting, worked as a plumber's assistant for a while but I'm not a plumber."

"Something'll turn up," I said. "For now the judge just wants you to show him you've been looking. Nothing's really going to happen until you get a place anyway. Speaking of places, I have to do something for myself, and pretty soon. I'm getting sick of sleeping out in the rain. I really am."

"Get yourself an SRO somewhere. You still got some money left from the sale of your dad's house, you told me."

"I don't really want to go for the single-room occupancy thing," I told him. "I've checked, and that's going to cost five, six hundred a month. Even when my own Social Security kicks in like Bob's, which won't be for a while yet, that would take half of it right there. Rent's just money down a rathole anyway. And what would I get for it? Sure, I'd be out of the rain, but probably in some wino hotel downtown. If I want to be miserable, I can be miserable right here. It's just the fucking rain. I'm tired of the rain."

"We all are," Cyrus said. "But the rainy season's just about over. We probably won't see any more until next fall. I plan to be gone by then." He squeezed and crushed his aluminum can for emphasis. "You gonna owe me a steak dinner, homie."

"I probably will," I agreed. "But in the meantime I have to do something. Sleeping under the stars is fine in the summertime, but even when it doesn't rain, you know it can get pretty damn chilly on a January night, even around here."

"Why don't you get a van like Bill's?"

Our friend Bill had a van that he slept in, an old gray Chevy badly in need of paint. Reverse didn't work on it—it would only go forward. He almost always kept it parked in the same spot on Canon Drive, but the city had an ordinance that you couldn't leave a vehicle parked in one place for more than 72 hours, so every other day or so Bill would pull the van around to McKinley Ave., stay there for one day and then move it back to his regular spot on Canon. The van had a slightly cracked rear-view mirror on the passenger side which so far the police had not bothered him about. Inside it, Bill had an actual bed with a mattress, not just a cot—the van was long enough for that, but not by much. To cook his meals on his butane stove he had to squeeze in between the end of the bed and the back of the two front seats. Bill was a Vietnam vet, and he had done prison time, not just county jail time. The word was that he had been a feared figure in the yard when he was in Atascadero, but we didn't see any behavior on his part that would support such a rumor. He was soft-spoken, liked to joke, read his Bible a lot, never drank and sometimes shared his food with whoever was around. We all liked Bill. He told everyone over and over that he was sick and tired of living in that van, which was easy to believe since he claimed to have been living in it for two and a half years. But complaining or not, he didn't sleep in the rain.

It was the best advice Cyrus had given me yet.

So I bought a van. It took a sizeable bite – about three grand – out of what I had left in my 401(k), but it turned out to be one of the best purchases I ever made.

I didn't have to look far, or for long. The hunt for my van turned out to be almost incredibly quick and easy.

A guy named Miguel Herrera, known as "Mexican Mike," attended N.A. meetings at Lion's Gate. Of course Andrew knew him, and as soon as he heard that I was thinking of buying a van, introduced us . Mexican Mike had a 2002 Ford Econoline he was looking to sell.

Naturally I wanted to know why he was selling it. He said it was because he wanted to get a newer one. Andrew took me over to look at it. Cyrus came along. The van was ugly, with a faded coat of what had once been burgundy paint, a few dents in the fenders and a small crack in the passenger-side mirror. The seat covers were ripped and the heater/defroster didn't work. The a/c never had worked, at least as long as Mexican Mike had owned the van. It was a high-top, once used as a medical transport vehicle. The commercial lettering on the van had been removed, but you could still see the ghost of "KopMed Mgmt" and a phone number. The electric lift for getting wheelchairs in and out of the van was still in place, up against the back doors. The seat covers in the front were torn.

On the plus side, the tires looked almost new and when Mike and I climbed in so I could take it for a test drive, the engine started right up and ran smoothly. It climbed hills just fine. The brakes were good. I looked under the hood. The engine was clean, no worn-hoses. The battery appeared new. Mexican Mike claimed that the van hardly burned any oil at all. It had 158,000 miles on it, but he insisted that a van like this one wasn't considered "high-mileage" until it hit 200,000. And I wasn't planning to drive to Oklahoma anyway. Mostly I just wanted a place to get out of the rain and have a little storage as a bonus. I wouldn't be lugging my earthly goods estate on my back or strapped to that orange scooter anymore.

Rob, Cheryl's boyfriend, (remember Cheryl?) bought the scooter for $100. We hoped he would use it to run away from Cheryl. But I saw them cruising along Sepulveda about two months later and there she was, sitting on the back, her arms around his waist. At least they both wore helmets.

The purchase of that old van changed my life. At WalMart I bought a camping cot and one of those thin foam-rubber pads you put between a mattress and a box spring.

Now, for the first time in ages, I had a bed. Not much of a bed, but a bed. I had been keeping a couple of milk crates filled with books in storage. I fetched them and put them in back of the van. Now I had a bed and my small library with me. I put the radio in there, and of course my director's chair, and at WalMart I also bought a folding TV tray, which gave me a sort of a desk to write on, and a battery-operated Coleman camping lantern so I'd have some light in there in the evenings.

Cyrus and I talked about the wheelchair lift. I wanted to get rid of it. Cyrus said I could probably sell it for $300. I considered that carefully. $300 was nothing to be sneezed at it in the world of the park. But I finally decided not to bother. I just wanted to get rid of that thing ASAP. Not only was it heavy, but without it I'd have a few more square feet in the van. Andrew borrowed some tools from Lion's Gate and we took it apart, hauled the pieces down the alley and left them there. We knew someone would haul it away for scrap. Someone did.

Now, for the first time in what seemed like ages, I had a home of my own. Not much of a home, no running water or electricity, but a home. I could go inside the van, close the hatch and sleep without having to put up with tweakers playing rap music around the corner or fighting among themselves, nor with Cyrus' endless late-night marathons of *Gunsmoke* and *The Rifleman* on his Smartphone, nor with Frankie showing up late at night stoned and wanting to deliver one of his monologues, nor with bored cops prowling around, waking everybody up to make us move or to nail someone for open container.

But best of all, now, whenever it began to rain, the sound of rain on the roof of the van was a lullaby, no longer an alarm. I was snug and dry inside my little shell in a blissful late-night beer-haze. Often, when it rained or even sometimes when it didn't, the Beach Boys' classic *In My Room* ran through my head as I drifted off to sleep.

Before lights-out I liked to sit in the van, read, listen to the radio, and smoke my pipe while tossing down a nightcap in the form of a couple of MGDs or maybe a Hurricane. I parked on Davidson in front of Bill's van, but Bill was a crank when it came to smoking-- if he so much as picked up a whiff of tobacco smoke he would complain about it, citing his "asthma." He wouldn't allow anyone to light a cigarette within ten feet of him; he even objected to the smell of my vanilla-scented Virginia Gold. So I kept a few extra yards between his van and mine.

If I wanted to turn in early and there was still partying going on among the nearby trees, all I had to do was pull around the corner and find a spot over on the east side of the park, on McKinley Ave., away from the noise.

Moving into the van also improved my social standing in Parkland.

Before I bought the van I was just another guy hanging around, either reading in his director's chair or sleeping off his beer under a tree. But the van quickly became a place to gather, and I became a cross between Lucy in the *Peanuts* column, dispensing psychiatric advice from her lemonade stand, and Sam Drucker, the old man who ran the general store on *Petticoat Junction* and *Green Acres* back in the 1960s. Pat's van suddenly became something like Drucker's Store. Cyrus dubbed it "The Café Patrick" after I bought a butane stove like the one Bill had and started brewing my morning coffee on the sidewalk. Parkies began to show up for free coffee.

At first it was just Cyrus and Marianne, then gradually others drifted over or dropped by, sometimes on foot and sometimes on bicycles, when they saw me fire up the butane stove and put on the percolator. Café

Patrick was open for business. People brought their own cups. One or two more folding chairs appeared out of nowhere. Cyrus went into the van and got out my radio. Coffee was poured. Cigarettes were lit. Jazz Groove played Dizzy Gillespie and McCoy Tyner. Park news was discussed. The café closed when I put the butane stove back in the van and took the empty coffeepot over to dump the grounds in the garbage and rinse out the pot in the drinking fountain.

Of course it was only a matter of time before Ranger Dave noticed all this and made a point of pulling up in his truck to tell us to quit blocking the sidewalk (not that there was much foot-traffic at that hour.) And of course he also reminded everyone that smoking wasn't allowed in the park, and tut-tutted at me for having my butane stove on the sidewalk. But as long as we were only drinking coffee and not beer or wine, (by then I'd had my sunrise brew) he confined himself to cajoling and finger-wagging and didn't issue any citations. I moved my stove to the grass, we got the folding chairs off the sidewalk, the smokers went out into the street where smoking was allowed, and Ranger Dave drove off. He had another seven years until retirement. He'd done his duty.

It was about this time that Yvonne began making a long-distance pest of herself. She had moved in with her brother in San Jose, but now, quite apart from putting Chantal, the park and all of us behind her, she began checking back regularly. It didn't seem to matter to her that Chantal was pregnant with what I had been told was Cage's child. Yvonne was already a Facebook friend of Cyrus'; now she added me. Often in the morning when I went into the library to read the newspaper and check my messages on the public workstation, I found Yvonne waiting for me, on FB, 340 miles to the north.

And we would have these chats, Yvonne probing for information about Chantal, me not being much help. I preferred it that way. I didn't want to get too mixed up in Yvonne and Chantal's version of *As The World Turns.*

Of course Yvonne was also pumping Cyrus for information. He

and I compared notes. Cyrus was sanguine about it all: "Yvonne'll find another girlfriend up there. She's still young. This time next year she won't remember any of this."

"I hope so, because this time next year Chantal will be nursing," I said. "And by the way, even with what little I know about Cage, this time next year he might be in jail."

"Or worse, and probably sooner than that," Cyrus said.

My new van also made me the park's unofficial ride service. I already had a reputation as an easy touch; now that I had four wheels instead of two, people started coming at me wanting rides to the doctor, the courthouse, their bail bondsman, HHSA...yes, they usually offered me some gas money for these lifts, but with gas hovering between $3.50 and $4.19 a gallon, how much good were their four-and-five-dollar offerings going to do me? I pocketed the dollar bills they gave me and used them later for beer. In the meantime I was still eating my savings, and now that I had bought the van, which used a lot more gas than the scooter did, I was even more acutely aware of that fact. I was looking forward to my sixty-second birthday when I could put in for Social Security.

Andrew had been hitting me up for rides to the dispensary even when I was still getting around on the scooter. I've already pointed out that he was an odd duck; here's another example. When I told him one day that I didn't want to take him to the dispensary on my scooter because among other things I'd had a few beers, and suggested that he take the 704 bus instead, which went right by there, he gave me a pained look and said, "I can't ride the bus."

"And why *can't* you ride the bus?"

"It's...I can't stand being that close to people. On the bus you have people jammed up against you, squeezing into seats. I'm not comfortable with anybody touching me. I won't take the bus. I'd rather walk."

"When you ride on the back of my scooter you have to hang on to me."

"I know, and I don't even really like that either. But it's over a mile, and I'm not going to take the bus. Never mind, I'll walk."

He knew I would give in. I always did. I'd bought a knife from him that I didn't need just to get him to leave me alone, hadn't I?

I took him to the dispensary about once a week. A beat-up old van was lower-profile in traffic than a bright orange scooter, so as long as I stuck to the speed limit and went along with traffic, I didn't worry so much about attracting the cops' attention, although given my past experience I certainly should have.

When it was just the gallon-a-week scooter, he paid me off in beer. It was a *quid pro quo*. He paid me for rides, I paid him to run the occasional errand such as doing my laundry or, now, sometimes waxing the van. I didn't want mine getting to look as crummy as Bill's. And like I said before, Andrew would do almost anything for weed money.

Sometimes Andrew showed up just to hang out with me for a while, usually because he wanted to get away from Lion's Gate, where so-and-so or so-and-so (I never remembered the names) had been "talkin' shit" about him. What this "talkin' shit" was all about I never knew, never asked and he never gave particulars. You didn't have to be a psychiatrist to recognize Andrew's borderline-schizo personality; it was surprising that he hadn't been bounced from that place long ago.

One evening when it wasn't quite dark yet, Andrew showed up while I was sitting on the park lawn in my director's chair, reading, smoking and drinking a beer. The side-door of the van was open. Andrew climbed wordlessly inside with a wave at me first. I got up and, leaving my chair on the lawn, climbed into the van because I knew that once he had settled himself in there, next he would light his weed pipe. If my friends wanted to smoke weed they had to do it outside. It was my rule; I didn't like the smell of it in the van. He had a black vinyl notebook tucked under his arm which I recognized as the journal he kept sporadically. He filled it with random jottings, mostly written when he was stoned, and drawings, mostly grotesque cartoons. Andrew had a pretty good eye for drawing, actually. His cartoons were not to my taste, but he did draw well.

"Just thought I'd hang out with you for a while," he said. "Is that okay?"

"Yeah, I suppose. Just don't smoke weed in the van."

"Where's that Bluetooth speaker?"

"It's in the box between the driver's seat and the passenger seat."

He dug the little speaker out, connected it to his phone and in moment we had Tracy Chapman (Andrew's current favorite) singing *Give Me One Reason.*

"You played that the last time you were here," I said.

"Don't you like it?"

"Turn it down."

Andrew had obviously been smoking weed before he got there. Like Frankie, it made him hanker to talk.

"Hey, I was writing in my journal today," he said. "Would you mind taking a look at it?"

I didn't want to. I was familiar with Andrew's cannabis-fueled Goth ravings. I think he fancied himself a sort of latter-day Rimbaud, or would have if he had known who Rimbaud was. Andrew wrote a lot of stuff about violence and death, but I think it was all part of the act, like his claim of being bisexual.

He was obviously going to make a nuisance of himself as usual, so I decided I might as well get it over with. "Okay, give me your notebook," I said. He handed it to me and I sat on the cot to read.

While I was poring over his morbid, nihilistic palaver one more time, Andrew started rummaging in a Rubbermaid container that I had behind the driver's seat, squeezed in at the foot of the cot. "I'm looking for a lighter," he explained.

I glanced up to make sure it wasn't his weed pipe he was getting ready to light. No, he had a Marlboro 100 between his fingers.

He found the lighter. He also found the knife he had sold me that other time. He took it out of its sheath and started playing with it. It was easy to see that he would now like to have it back.

I read his mind. Or he read mine.

"Would you sell me back this knife?" he asked. "You're not using it, are you?"

"No, I'm not using it, and I'll sell it back to you for exactly what I paid you for it. I think it was seven bucks."

"Can I give it to you next week?"

"Sure, if you want to take the knife next week."

"Oh, come on, man."

"I know you. You're hoping I'll let you have the knife and then I'll forget that you owe me for it."

"I won't forget. I'll remind you. I'll pay you. You know I always do."

I had to admit that yes, Andrew usually did pay people sooner or later.

"All right. Yeah, I'm not using it. Just remember you owe me seven bucks."

"I'll remember." Andrew opened his belt and hung the knife and sheath on his hip.

It got to be dark. I wanted another MGD. Andrew walked to the liquor store with me and tried to get me to buy him one too. He shrugged off my refusal with a giggle; he knew that, since he already owed me for the knife, asking me to buy him a beer was pushing things a little.

By the time we got back to the van it was getting cool outside, so I decided to move indoors for my next beer. I left the director's chair on the grass for the moment and stepped back into the van, popping open my beer and reaching over to turn on the radio. As I reclined on the cot with my beer, Andrew walked off into the darkness of the park by himself. Going to smoke some weed away from me, no doubt. I left the hatch of the van open. Jazz Groove was playing Miles Davis. *Jeru.*

Then I heard shouting outside. I recognized Frankie's voice. He and Andrew were at their "line dancing" again, as Cyrus called their fights.

I was inclined to just let them settle it like they always did. But I heard a metallic clatter. I got up, looked out the open door and saw that Frankie had just thrown my director's chair out into the middle of Davidson St.

I jumped out and shouted at him, "Dammit, Frankie, you don't throw my chair in the street!"

He ignored me. Frankie had his skateboard in his hands and he was swinging it at Andrew. Andrew backed up against the side of my van, trying to protect himself. I noticed the knife lying on the sidewalk.

Frankie struck Andrew on the left arm with his skateboard. I leaped in behind him and threw my arms around his shoulders. "Frankie! Stop this! Right now!" I shouted.

His reply was to violently shake me off, whirl around and start swinging the skateboard at me. Now it was my turn to receive a whack on the arm as I, like Andrew, tried to fend off a blow.

"That's it, Frankie!" I yelled at him as he turned back to attacking Andrew. "You hear me? You don't hit *me* with a fucking skateboard! It's bad enough you hitting Andrew, you don't hit ME! I'm calling the cops, you little bastard."

"Fuck you!" he shouted, still swinging his skateboard at Andrew.

I climbed into the cab, where my cellphone lay beside the driver's seat. One leg still hung out the passenger-side door as I leaned over to grab the phone and flip it open. Frankie saw me with the phone and slammed the van door on my ankle. I had two injuries now, but I was too mad to feel the pain, just yet anyway. I dialed 911 and told the dispatcher to get a unit across the street right away.

"What is your name, sir?" she asked.

I told her.

"And your address?"

"Goddammit, I don't have time to sit here and tell you my life story! Get a unit over here! There's an assault with a deadly weapon going on!"

"I'm not asking you your life story, sir. I need an address."

"The address is the park across the street! You know? *Across the street from the police station?* Davidson and McKinley! Get a unit over here!"

The moment I began punching numbers into my cellphone, Frankie took off at a dead run across the park, screaming "I'm gonna kill both of you fucking faggots!" as he disappeared into the darkness.

"What was that all about?" I asked as I came back from the middle of the street with my director's chair in my hand.

"He asked if he could stay overnight at Lion's Gate," Andrew said. "I told him 'No' and he went berserk."

"Why'd you tell him no?"

"Are you kidding, man? Did you see the way he was acting just now? They don't want that shit over there. They'd blame me for bringing him. We've let him stay there before and he's been a problem."

The police finally showed up and took our report. They caught up with Frankie later, in the parking lot in front of El Mercado. Cyrus was there and saw the whole thing.

"When they put the cuffs on him he was still screaming that he was going to kill you two faggots," Cyrus said with a grin.

"He was tweaking in orbit. When he comes down he'll just be Frankie again, and I'm about as scared of Frankie as I am of Bob the Bum."

"He's going to do ninety days for this, maybe six months," Cyrus said.

"You think so?"

"Oh, yeah. Assault with a deadly weapon, and him with priors? Maybe a year. He told the cops Andrew pulled a knife on him."

"If that happened, I didn't see it. I was in the van when the ruckus started. All I saw was the knife lying on the sidewalk. I didn't see anybody use it."

Frankie got six months in county jail. Andrew and I were both subpoenaed to testify against him, but Frankie copped a plea so we didn't have to go to court.

About a week later the police department played host to "Coffee With The Cops," a community-outreach thing they did a couple of times a year. They staked out a street corner, roped off the sidewalk for a couple of hours, hung up banners and signs, and invited one and all to drop by, have coffee and schmooze with the cops, including Police Chief Candace Rawlings (whom I thought rather cute. She was married of course, and the cops thought it was funny: "Pat has the hots for the chief.")

Cyrus and I stopped by for a free cup of coffee. Rudy Payne and Fernando Solis were both on hand.

"Hey Rudy," I said, "want to see my red badge of courage?" I showed him my cut-and-still-slightly-bruised left arm. "Frankie hit me with his skateboard."

"I know. I read the report," he said. He fixed me with a serious eye. "You know what this means, don't you, Patrick?"

"Yeah, yeah. I gotta get outta that park."

As I said "I gotta get outta that park," Rudy said, "YOU gotta get outta that park." We said it in unison, like we were doing stand-up. Of course this was a regular refrain with the HOT team. They wanted us all out of the park, sooner rather than later.

18

Tommy, perched on Patrick's lap, turned away from the screen and looked at him. "That's not cool," he said.

Wile E. Coyote had just tried to drop a piano on the Roadrunner and wound up plummeting into the canyon, clinging to the piano lid. Crash.

Next, the Coyote tried a boulder on a giant catapault, yanking the cord as the Roadrunner sped past. The catapault didn't work of course, and the boulder fell on the Coyote. Thump.

"That's not cool," Tommy said again. He must have picked up "That's not cool" from television. At age four he would be breaking in new expressions, expanding his vocabulary at that alarming rate kids have. The little boy was clearly enjoying himself.

The laptop was on the dining table. It was still daylight, but the Christmas tree lights were on in the corner of the living room. It was a time of year he had always liked, and he found that having Tommy there made it more pleasant still.

The cartoon ended. "Can we watch another one?" Tommy asked.

Patrick looked at Melissa, who was passing into the kitchen. "I had to introduce him to the Coyote and the Roadrunner."

"He sure likes them! Of course you realize that now every time he sees you, he's going to want to watch the Coyote and the Roadrunner again." she laughed, happy to see that he and the boy were getting along so well.

He clicked around on You Tube and came up with another cartoon with the same two characters. "I'm getting him off on the right foot," he said firmly. "Heck with that stuff on Nick Jr. Looney Tunes are the real deal."

"The Coyote never gets the Roadrunner," Tommy said.

"That's right. He never gets the Roadrunner."

Melissa's cellphone jingled as Sharon came down the hall. Unlike her sister, Sharon was dark-haired, and a little shorter. She shared Melissa's high cheekbones, green-gray eyes and slightly stubborn mouth.

As her sister took the call, Sharon took a seat at the table where he and the boy were watching cartoons. "You like the old classics, I see."

"I grew up on Bugs Bunny and Daffy Duck," he said, glad to have an adult across the table so he would have something else to look at besides the Coyote's spectacular fails, which he had seen hundreds of times since his own childhood.

"You like children," Sharon smiled.

"I do."

"How come you never had any of your own?"

"I married late and my wife didn't want children."

"That's unusual," she said. "For a woman not to want children."

"Valerie didn't want any. She told me once she had never been pregnant. I remember thinking it was odd, the way she said it. She made it sound like some sort of distinction. I was her third husband and she never had any kids."

"Some people aren't meant to have kids. Some people aren't meant to be married."

Was this aimed at him? He shrugged. "How about you?"

"I was married once. No kids. It didn't work out. Seems like most of them don't anymore. Marriages I mean, not kids." she smiled.

"Melissa says you're seeing someone now, though."

"Yeah, Stanley. He's very nice. Makes good money."

"I heard he's in real estate. That's what my ex-wife did."

"We'll have to see what happens," she said with a kind of half-smile that suggested she was, anyway, hoping for the best.

But he was getting tired of small talk and wished Melissa would get off the phone. Sharon seemed all right; certainly he had not seen the kind of tension between the two sisters that Melissa had complained about before. But there was no telling with siblings. Maybe she was putting on a "company" face for him.

Thanksgiving had gone well enough. It was his second meeting with Sharon. He hosted dinner at his new apartment, which was cramped but the three adults and child managed in the one room. He lived not far from the harbor now and Tommy had been thrilled when he took him out to look at the boats and the docked ships. Visiting San Pedro harbor made him remember his own childhood. He had an uncle who had had a boat harbored here, the kind that used to be called a cabin cruiser. His uncle was a pilot for United Airlines who flew back and forth between L.A. and Honolulu. His boat was called the *Hali Kai*, Hawaiian for "House on the Water." He had been taken out fishing on it when he was six and had gotten seasick. The only other thing he remembered about the harbor was a huge sign advertising Canada Dry soft drinks. When you're six the whole world looks huge.

Sharon had lit a cigarette when she sat down. Now she crushed it out as her sister finished her phone conversation.

"Was that Tom?" she asked.

"Yeah. He's flying out tomorrow and wanted to make sure we had everything straight as far as when he's coming back, when he can expect Tommy, you know." Naturally she sounded sad.

The next cartoon had ended. Tommy climbed down from Patrick's lap, went to his mother and complained that he was hungry.

"I'm going to feed him and then go out to do some Christmas shopping if you can stay with him for a while," she said to her sister, who nodded. "Patrick, do you want to come with me?"

"Sure. And while you're making Tommy's lunch, come here, Tommy."

Patrick lifted the child back into his lap. "Since your mommy and I are going shopping, what would you like for Christmas?"

"Santa brings presents," the little boy replied.

"Well, that's right, he does. But if you haven't told him what you want yet, Santa and I are on very good terms. He rear-ended my cab last week. Rudolf put a dent in the fender. I agreed not to call the insurance company. Santa owes me a favor."

"Really?"

"Pat," Melissa said from the kitchen, where she was preparing to make a grilled-cheese sandwich for Tommy. She grinned at him.

"So. What can I tell Santa you want?"

"Actually, he saw Santa on Thursday," Melissa said. "Didn't you, Tommy? Did you tell Santa what you wanted?"

"A Hot Wheels garage," the boy said.

"Well, then. If Santa already knows, Pat doesn't have to tell him."

"I want to come with you."

"This trip is just for grownups. You stay here with Aunt Shari."

He suggested that they take his cab to the shopping mall. Like many cab drivers, he used it as a personal vehicle when off duty, and he had just filled it with gas, so it made sense that he should drive.

They got in the car. Melissa, putting on her sunglasses, slid in on the passenger side of the front seat.

"You remember what happened the last time you rode up front," he said with a grin.

She kissed him. "I'm sober now. Drive."

It was Christmastime; the mall was crowded. A decorated, fully-lit tree that must have been twenty-five feet high stood inside the main entrance. Down the corridor to their right as they came in, carols were being played on a piano, obviously live, not a recording. Sure enough, as they moved in the general direction of Macy's, they saw a young man in a tux seated at a Yamaha grand, tinkling out *Sleigh Ride.*

Melissa wore tight Levis, knee-high boots and a bulky pale blue sweater. She had put on a bit of peach lipstick. She looked beautiful. Absently scanning the window displays in the stores as they walked by, she seemed to read his mind, reached over and took his hand. It was such a pleasure having her beside him and feeling her hand in his that he wished they could remain there all afternoon.

"I have an idea," he looked at his watch. "It's uh – twenty minutes to one. I haven't had lunch and I'm hungry. If you're hungry, what do you say we have a bite somewhere and then do our shopping?"

They went into B.J.'s Brewhouse. Their server, a young Asian woman who gave her name as Lili, handed them menus and asked if they would like anything to drink. Melissa ordered iced tea and he ordered a Bass Ale. "You know, these places make most of their money off the bar, not the food," he told Melissa when Lili had gone to get their drinks. "That's why they always ask if you want a drink before they take your food order."

"Well, maybe I should have ordered a Mai Tai," she said, "but it is a little early in the day for me."

When they had ordered and Lili had once again gone off to see to their food, he looked around the restaurant. It was crowded; that was to be expected on a Saturday afternoon, especially during the holidays. But it reminded him of something he had read not long ago. "I saw that these malls are in trouble. Some of them might start closing soon."

"This one looks like it's doing fine."

"Well, it's Christmas. I read that the long term doesn't look so good for them. Amazon's kicking everybody's butt. Most people are doing their holiday shopping online now. Which brings up the question of, what are we doing here?" he looked around. "Didn't you do most of *your* shopping online?"

She sipped her tea. “I did, but it’s too close to Christmas now to order anything for Tommy. It wouldn’t come until after Christmas.”

“You didn’t order anything for him already?”

“Oh, sure, a couple of things. But that Hot Wheels garage, I didn’t find out he wanted that until I heard him tell Santa on Thursday. We were here to pick up a couple of things I had ordered at Penney’s, and he wanted to get on Santa’s lap, you know.”

“Why don’t you let me buy him that toy?” he said.

“I couldn’t ask you to do that, Pat.”

“You don’t have to, because I’m going to do it. He’s a great kid and I want to give him something. I have a niece and a nephew—Jessie’s kids. I used to love buying them toys at Christmas. But they’re grown up now.”

“I do enjoy seeing the way you and Tommy get along. He really likes you.”

“I like him. He’s a great kid,” he said again. The idea that she might already be thinking of him as a possible stepfather gave him a pang of pleasure. After his divorce he had resolved never to marry again, but now the idea didn’t seem so unthinkable. But the memory of what had happened with Diane lingered at the back of his mind like a notice of an unpaid bill.

Lili came with their food. He ordered another Bass Ale.

“Maybe you shouldn’t have a second one,” Melissa said. “You’re driving. And speaking of driving, aren’t you driving your cab tonight?”

“Yeah, yeah. You’re right. I’ll just have one more. We’re going to eat and then we’re going to walk around the stores. I’ll be okay.”

As they ate, Melissa talked about her son. Of course she didn’t want to send him back after Christmas. “He’ll be back in June, but that seems so far away,” she said.

“Not for me it doesn’t. When you get to be my age, six months gets to seem like two weeks. It gets worse as you get older, you know. My father used to pop up on the Fourth of July and say, 'Well here it is, almost Christmas!'"

"Stop harping on your age, Pat. You know it's not important to me."

"I was just trying to lighten the mood a little," he said. "I hate to see you sad."

"Well, there is one good piece of news. I might be singing after the first of the year, and I don't mean at Shanghai Rick's, either. This would be a much better gig."

"You mean at that place on Sunset?"

"Oh, you remembered that! Yeah, Barney came through. He was the old guy at the bar –"

"The horny old guy."

"That's what I thought. But it turned out that he wasn't bullshitting after all. He really does know the manager at the Café Ciel . He got me an audition right after New Year's. If it works out I'll be fronting a jazz combo over there for a week in late January."

"A jazz combo. That sounds right up your alley. Can you get the time off from work?"

"Tony will let me take a week. I have a week's vacation coming anyway. And..."

"And?"

"Well, it's all just talk at this point. Hardly even worth bringing up." She shrugged and gave an embarrassed little smile. "Maybe I shouldn't even mention it, I might jinx it."

"What is it? Come on, don't be mysterious."

"Well, if the gig downtown comes through, and if it goes well, there's been some talk that I might be able to land a gig at one of the hotels up in Vegas."

"Vegas? That's the big time."

"Oh, come on. It won't be Harrah's. Probably not even a place on the strip. But, still...you know, Las Vegas. It could be a break for me. Oh, but, hell, it probably won't happen."

"I don't know," he said. "I've known life to pull some funny stunts. Usually they're bad, but sometimes they're not."

"I'm not even going to think that far ahead," she said. "For now let's just see if I can land that job downtown."

When they had finished shopping they drove back to her apartment. Tommy lay on his stomach beside the Christmas tree, scribbling with crayons in a coloring book. Sharon was watching a movie on cable, which he recognized immediately as *Die Hard* with Bruce Willis. The eighties. What a time for crash-and-boom thrillers they were.

"Did he take a nap while we were gone?" Melissa asked as she hustled a bag of presents down the hallway and into the closet.

"Not really. I put him down, but he didn't sleep more than ten minutes." Sharon said. "I'm sure he's excited about Christmas."

"He'll probably fall asleep during *Rudolf the Red-Nosed Reindeer* later. Darn it, I know he'll love that. He's never seen it."

"Are they still running *that*?" Pat asked.

"Yes, it's on every year now, like *A Charlie Brown Christmas.* That was on last week."

"I saw both of those when they first came out. I was maybe...nine? Ten at the most. Long time ago."

"They're classics, all right." Melissa went to make coffee.

"Like me," he thought.

He joined Sharon on the couch and stared absently at Bruce Willis, his mind wandering back to the Christmases of his childhood, of which television had always been such a large part. Not much had changed in more than fifty years as far as that went, anyway. Of course they still ran programs like *Charlie Brown* and *Rudolf* largely as a sop to his own generation, already beginning to die off now; more than a handful of people he had known in high school were dead, as he learned two years earlier at his 40-year class reunion. One by one, like the musicians leaving the stage in the last movement of that Haydn symphony, the filaments connecting him to his childhood and youth were vanishing. Once his memory had been crowded with accurate details of those days. He could remember the color of the polo shirt he wore on the first day of fifth grade; the exact printing on the inside of his baseball glove when he was in Little League playing shortstop for the Hornets; the moment in the school cafeteria that November afternoon when he first heard that President Kennedy had been shot; the moment three months after that when he first heard of the Beatles. Now all of that was beginning to seem like something that had happened to someone else, in another life. And the details were beginning to fade, even to blur. It was frightening. Once he had been able to recite the names of his Hornet teammates right down the roster. Now he couldn't even remember their faces.

Melissa kissed him on the forehead as she handed him a cup of coffee. "So what time do you think you think you'll go out to drive today?"

"I might not," he said as he took a sip.

"It's Saturday," she reminded him. "That's your busiest night of the week."

"I know. But I'm entitled to a night off now and then, don't you think? I'd like to stick around and watch *Rudolf the Red-Nosed Reindeer* with Tommy."

"Well...wonderful! We can order a pizza or something."

"In my family we always had pizza on Christmas Eve. It was kind of a family tradition."

"But you can't skip Christmas Eve. You said yourself that's one of your busiest nights."

"Yeah, it's a warm-up for New Year's Eve," he said. "New Year's I'll probably be driving until three a.m."

"You can have your Christmas Eve pizza tonight. I'll make a nice big salad to have with it."

"Sounds good." he put down his coffee, stretched and yawned. "Yeah, I'm going to take the night off."

Their eyes met and he knew right away what she was thinking. "I'll head for home after *Rudolf*," he said. "What time is it on?"

"Eight."

"Yeah, I'll take off after that. Nine O'clock's too late to start driving."

She kissed him again.

When Melissa got ready to order the pizza he told her not to bother having it delivered. He would pick it up. That would be faster. He drove to Domino's, picked up the pizza and then stopped at 7-Eleven on the way back for a pouch of Carter Hall and a six-pack of MGD. If he had one and Melissa and her sister each had one, that would leave three to stick in the fridge, or two if he decided to have a second.

They had pizza and watched the Christmas special together. As Melissa had predicted that he would, Tommy fell asleep with his head on her lap just about the time Burl Ives was telling about the big snowstorm that one year which forced Santa to ask Rudolf if he would help him save Christmas for all the children of the world.

19

I groped for my flashlight and looked at my watch. I counted back the hours in my head and knew right away what was going on.

Cold sweat. I hadn't had a beer in twelve hours and I was already going into withdrawal. I had been through it at least a dozen times before and knew the symptoms: cold sweats, the shakes. Sometimes a headache. Always a sort of panic.

And here was the problem for the moment: according to my watch it was 3:12 a.m. That meant two hours and forty-eight minutes until the 7-Eleven around the corner unlocked the beer cooler. There was nothing I could do except roll myself into as tight a wet ball as possible in the freezing August night and shiver until the State of California declared the bar open.

There was no question of any more sleep. I lay there and shivered, turning now and then in the hope of getting warmer or of dozing off. Neither happened.

When it got to be six O'clock I was reluctant to crawl out from under my damp cover. It was going to be cold, and my teeth were already close to chattering. But it had to be done. I forced myself to sit up, peeled off my wet polo shirt as fast as I could and groped around among the milk crates for a sweatshirt, cursing that I had to dig for it.

I found one and pulled it over my head in a hurry. At least it was dry. I got out of the truck and walked as quickly as I could, which wasn't very quickly, to the 7-Eleven.

After downing a 24-oz. MGD in four or five long pulls I felt better. The sweating and shaking stopped. But I knew the fix was temporary, and

I didn't really feel good, just less bad. In fact, as I stopped to think about it, overall I felt pretty lousy.

It was Wednesday, the day the HOT team always showed up. I'd had the presence of mind to buy two MGDs, and after downing the second one around eight-thirty I continued to feel okay, but my crack-of-dawn beer-walk had done me in; there was no way I could have walked farther than the sidewalk without having to sit down and rest. The liquor store and El Mercado were both less than two blocks away, but I knew I wouldn't make it to either one if I tried.

Besides, I didn't want any more beer. Not now. I wanted something else. Milk actually sounded good. I hadn't drunk milk in ages. But I wasn't going to make it to the store. I sat on the grass and looked around for someone who might help.

Luckily Chantal was about two trees over. She and her group had their usual blanket spread on the ground. They would be tweaking soon, but with the HOT team expected any minute, they didn't want to take the chance just now. They milled around among the trees. A bicycle lay on the grass. As usual someone had Bluetooth hip-hop going.

I called over to Chantal. "Chantal! You got a minute, honey?"

She walked over to me. She wore a flowing, light-blue ankle-length dress and flat-heeled sandals – one of the summer outfits she had picked up at a church clothes-giveaway somewhere.

"What's up?" she asked.

"I need you to do me a favor. Here," I got out my wallet and handed her my EBT card. (I knew I could trust her with it; we all took turns running to the store for each other.) "Would you go down to El Mercado and get me a pint of milk? Whole milk, not that two percent shit. Get yourself a Mountain Dew while you're at it. I just don't feel like I can walk down there."

"Milk?"

"Yeah."

"Can I get a Payday bar too?"

That was just like Chantal. She was pushy, always wanting a little more than you were offering. I answered with my hand, gesturing yeah, sure, fine, just go get the milk. I reminded her of the PIN code for my EBT card and watched her walk off across Davidson.

She didn't ask me why I wanted milk, nor did she ask why I felt incapacitated. Parkies were often under the weather from drugs or booze or both. It wasn't unusual. Besides, we generally didn't ask each other a lot of questions. It was the code of the park: when the police came poking around, the less everyone knew the better off everyone was.

Chantal brought me my milk and I drank it right down, but I still felt weak, not like moving much. I could have gone back into the van and stretched out on my bunk, but there was no sun in there. Mexican Mike had taped aluminum foil over each of the windows when he owned the van, and I had left them in place. Sometimes in the park, especially at night, you didn't want people to know you were home.

But it was a warm, sunny morning and, probably because I wasn't feeling well, I decided to stay out in the fresh air for a while.

Pretty soon officers Payne and Solis were making their weekly rounds along with Nancy Verdugo and the usual pixies from Social Services. They went from tree to tree, camp to camp, slowly, making chitchat with everyone, offering help and keeping an eye out for any unauthorized activity, contraband, weapons, open beers, drugs, the usual stuff.

I knew it would be a while before they got to my tree, and they were sure to check out Chantal and her little coffee-klatsch before they bothered with me.

I pulled an old paperback from my pocket, a tattered copy of St. Augustine's *Confessions* that I'd picked up from the library's discard shelf. I'm not especially religious anymore, but I have a weakness for the sound of people telling their own stories. If I were to give you a list of my ten favorite books, I'll bet half of them would be memoirs and autobiographies. (When

I was twenty-five I began reading Anais Nin's diaries and immediately fell in love with her. Then I continued reading, and after a couple more volumes I fell out of love with her. Just like real life.)

The HOT team worked its way across the park. I looked around and spotted Cyrus walking over to talk with Rudy Payne. He had gotten a lot chummier with the cops, or least with Rudy, since mounting his campaign to get Section 8 housing.

Then, still reading, I heard Chantal arguing with Fernando Solis. He wanted her to show him what she had in her bag and she was giving him some guff about it. That was also just like Chantal. Yvonne had spoiled her. She was used to being treated like royalty and sometimes got bratty over little things. Officer Solis even used that word: he told her she was "acting like a brat."

"You're going to have to grow up, Chantal, and soon," I heard him tell her. "Look at you. You're going to have a baby. You have to stop acting like a child yourself."

Sulkily, she opened her bag for him, and of course it contained nothing but makeup and candy wrappers. She wouldn't be stupid enough to carry around drugs in her tote bag with the police expected any moment. Chantal, being bitchy just for the hell of it. What had Yvonne called her? "Pillow princess." No more of that.

Then Payne and Nancy walked up to me. I put my book down, lay back on the grass with my hands locked behind my head and smiled, a little weakly I suppose, up at both of them.

"Morning, all," I said.

"Morning, Pat," Rudy said. "How are you feeling?"

"I feel okay. No worse than usual."

"You don't look so good."

"I don't?"

"No, you don't. Have you been drinking?"

"No more than usual."

"This morning, I mean."

I shrugged. No point in bullshitting him.

"Couple of beers."

"You know there's no alcohol allowed in the park."

"Do you see any?" This was protocol.

"You gotta get out of this park, you know," Rudy said. "I saw the report about Frankie taking his skateboard to you and Andrew."

"I know. You told me about it at Coffee-with-the-Cops, remember? And like I told you that same morning, he was drunk and stoned when that happened. I wasn't."

But I really did feel crappy. I was putting on an act and they knew it. And I probably did look awful. I hadn't seen my own face in a mirror since the last time I'd shaved in the library men's room. I'd been wearing the same clothes since…well, yeah, since that same day, which was also the last time I'd bathed, giving myself a sink bath right after shaving. In the absence of showers that's what we did: douched ourselves off with soap and hopefully warm water in front of a handy sink, then dried off with hand towels. In the past four days I hadn't even changed my socks. I must have smelled like a goat.

These two people had been coming around the park for a long time. They knew me as well as they knew anyone else here. I sensed that they considered me not entirely beyond redemption. Don't ask me why. Maybe it was because I was the only person in the park who had never been in jail, never been in any kind of trouble except of course the trouble that had brought me to the park in the first place. Of course that was their job. But they were right. I couldn't spend the rest of my life in the park. I never intended to. I hadn't thought much about what my next move should be, hadn't wanted to bother thinking about it. Cyrus' quest for housing had pricked my conscience, at least into making me feel as though I should be making some effort in the same direction. Some effort of some kind, anyway. I wasn't quite ready throw it all up and follow in the footsteps of Bob the Bum.

As if on cue, Nancy stepped in and asked me, waving the clipboard in her hand, "Pat, if we could get you into a detox program, would you go?"

After a long pause I replied, "Yes. I would."

Right away I had second thoughts. But I was indeed truly sick of feeling like shit. "That's all the facts when you come to brass tacks, something something something." T.S. Eliot I think. I felt more-or-less okay for the moment, but I knew that wasn't going to last. It never did.

"Yeah," I sat up. "You make the arrangements and I'll go."

The first place they took me was the hospital. A doctor looked me over and gave me the usual three-day supply of Librium. That's how long it generally takes to detox; the Librium is to help you avoid the shakes. I had dried out before; it was all familiar.

They found a detox facility in Van Nuys that said it would take me. They didn't want me to drive myself there, though. They wanted to chauffeur me. I didn't argue with them. Having given myself up to this, I was past caring much about the details. Maybe they were afraid I'd throw down a few beers and get another DUI on my way up there. Or maybe they just didn't want it to be too easy for me to give up before the ten-day program was finished, jump in the van and drive off.

That created one small logistical problem: there was a city ordinance against parking in one spot for more than seventy-two hours. That was why, every second day or so, I would pull my van around the corner from Davidson Street to McKinley Avenue, park there for one night, then pull back around to my regular spot first thing the next morning. To get around this while I was gone, I went and found Bill, who was charging his phone inside the library, and asked if he would move my van for me every forty-eight hours while I was away. He agreed and I gave him the keys. Then I put some clothes, underwear, toiletries, my copy of St. Augustine and my notebook into my backpack, and they drove me in a police vehicle to the Greater Los Angeles County Substance Abuse Center in Van Nuys.

You had to surrender your cellphone when you checked in. That part was no big deal, I wasn't planning to call anybody anyway. It was explained to me that they didn't want the hard drug users to be able to call their suppliers from inside. It had happened before. No skin off my nose, as they say; I there to kick booze, not smack. It wasn't very likely that I was going to call Cyrus and ask him to take the bus up there and slip me a six-pack of beer or a bottle of Mad Dog under the fence. I handed them the phone and got a receipt for it. You also had to turn in any medications you were carrying. All I had was the Librium; I gave it to them.

You weren't locked up, you just couldn't leave the grounds. It wasn't like jail, it was more like a rather grim summer camp for mostly-grumpy adults. The grumpiest were the ones who were there because of a judge's order.

We slept four or six to a room depending on who was coming and going. Each of these mini-dorms had its own bathroom.

They roused everyone at 6:30 a.m., after which came twenty minutes of milling around in a common room where a television set droned out the Channel 7 Morning News, and you could drink tepid coffee which was the only coffee you were going to get all day.

At seven everyone was lined up and herded down to the mess hall for breakfast. The food was atrocious, but peanut butter, jam and Wonder Bread were provided – I got through most of my ten days on peanut butter sandwiches, as did some of my fellow drunks and dopeheads.

You got fifteen minutes for breakfast, and then everyone was herded back upstairs for cleaning detail. Mops, brooms, rags, toilet brushes and cleanser were broken out and we policed the living area.

After clean-up came a 90-minute counseling session in which everyone sat in the common room in a big circle on folding chairs and shared boring stories about their addictions, their dolorous lives and their hopes for the future. Lots of jail stories. You couldn't just hang back on the perimeter and keep silent (which I tried to do.) Everyone had to contribute. I didn't want to talk about Melissa, so I told park stories and kept them as short as I could. I explained why I called my recent home "Hurricane Park" and that got a laugh, at least from some of the alcoholics, who knew exactly what that joke was all about.

At ten-thirty a.m. there was a smoke break outside, which you had to take whether you smoked or not. They meant it, too. I tried to skip the smoke break one morning and sit in the "dorm" reading instead, but they chased me outside. "You can't stay in here by yourself." I'd left my pipe in the van, and I like cigarettes, so while everyone else puffed away, I'd take a seat on the curb alongside my fellow unhappy campers and join in the talk, most of which was grumbling.

At eleven forty-five we were herded downstairs for lunch. After lunch came another cleaning session. (I always tried for a mop; mopping the hallway floor was quicker than dusting and less disagreeable than emptying trash or scrubbing toilets.)

We had a break until two O'clock, then there was another counseling session. Often they brought in guest speakers for these afternoon shows, who talked about breaking the cycle of addiction or dealing with the family problems that often led to addiction, or related topics. Prayers at the end, just like A.A.

Dinner, preceded by another smoke break, was at five p.m. More jail-quality cuisine. (It got to be a running joke between myself and the kitchen staff: they would load a plate and push it across the counter at me; I would take one look at it, push it back and go off to make a peanut-butter sandwich. They were not insulted by this, they found it funny.) For beverages you had your choice of water or iced tea from plastic pitchers. There was a soda machine in one corner if you wanted to pay for a drink.

In the evening there was a third group meeting, then another clean-up session, and then we were pretty much free to do what we wanted until lights-out at 10:30.

Evenings were a problem for me. Most of my fellow campers would gather in the common room for a movie before the nightly curfew. But I've never been big on the sort of movies they tended to like, action-adventure flicks with lots of bang-bang, kaboom, shouting and squealing tires, or with galactic warriors zooming around in spaceships blowing up planets, weird-looking aliens and each other. My idea of a great movie was such fare as *Sabrina* or *Mr. Roberts,* not *Green Lantern*. Pass.

There was a small shelf of books tucked away in one corner of the common room. Not surprisingly, most of the titles were self-help volumes about overcoming addiction. There was some paperback fiction: horror classics, romances and thrillers along the lines of Stephen King, John Grisham and Danielle Steele. Books with raised print on their covers. Nothing to interest me.

But way down at the bottom of those shelves where it would be easy to miss it if you weren't looking for it, someone, at some point, had stuck an old, blue, faded, clothbound, beat-up, incomplete set of Shakespeare.

I made this discovery just as I had taken the last of my Librium. "There is a God after all," I thought.

I spent each remaining evening of my self-imposed sentence unsystematically plowing through *Henry IV Part I, Richard III, The Tempest, Twelfth Night, Hamlet, A Midsummer Night's Dream* and *King Lear.* So thoroughly did I bond with these aging, threadbare blue volumes (as, down the hallway, my fellow substance-abusers enjoyed *300* and *Guardians of the Galaxy*) that when my ten days at the detox center ended, and Nancy Verdugo and Fernando Solis were due to pick me up in a police car, I seriously considered stealing those books. There were at least a dozen plays I hadn't gotten to yet, and what the hell, I asked myself? I didn't know who left them there or why, but it was a cinch that nobody else in this place was ever going to have any use for them.

But I left them there. Who was I to be such a damned snob, assuming that no other soul, suffering through the divorce from drugs or alcohol, would ever find themselves needing the consolation of the Bard? Besides, I lived behind the public library. Back home I had access to all the Shakespeare anyone could want.

On Day Nine I prepared to leave the detox center. I was dried-out, finished with the shakes and sweats, and I assured one and all, myself included, that it was going to be like this from now on. There was no way I wanted to go back to feeling as awful as I did that morning when I had to send Chantal to the store for milk, the morning I agreed to go to detox.

When Nancy and Fernando came to pick me up on the morning I was turned loose, we had an argument in the patrol car on the way back to the park.

For the time being there was no place they could take me except the park, if for no other reason than the fact that my van was still there, with Bill babysitting it. And I had no other home. But both were adamant: under no circumstances, they insisted, would it be a good idea for me to stay there.

"We can't force you to leave the park, of course, Pat, but I kind of wish we could," Solis said. "The park's not a good place for you."

"That's what I keep hearing. But what you all seem to forget is that I don't have any other place to go, except maybe another park. Or the beach. What am I supposed to do? I have no job and I have no income. I can't just waltz out and rent an apartment. Oh, I could, I suppose, but that would wipe out the last of my savings pretty fast. I don't want to do what Terry did with his insurance settlement. I'm sure you heard that story."

They had heard Terry's story. "Are you on Social Security?" Nancy asked.

"I won't be until this fall."

"What if we could get you into a rehab facility?" Solis asked. "You'd have a roof over your head, counseling services if you need. And meals."

"I don't know. I just got out of boot camp. Do I want to go back?"

"If you want to stay sober you'll probably have to go into some kind of facility.There's a faith-based place downtown, Genesis Recovery. We've done some work with them in the past, if you don't mind that it's faith-based."

"You mean it's –"

"Run by a church group, yes," Nancy explained.

"Oh, I see. In a word, NO. I'm not going off to cool my heels for six months or a year in some religious jail where they follow you around spouting Bible verses all day. That's out. Not even three squares and a sack are worth that."

"You're not religious," Nancy said.

"Not THAT religious, or maybe I should say not religious in that way."

"Are you Catholic?" Solis asked me.

"Who wants to know?"

"Just asking, that's all. I'm Catholic myself."

"Well, yeah, I'm Catholic. I wasn't raised in it. I got baptized in college."

"Something to do with a girl? You wanted to get married and she was Catholic?"

"No, nothing like that. I just decided to become Catholic, that's all. Like Dave Brubeck did."

"Dave Brubeck?"

"You know, the great jazz pianist. He joined the church as an adult. He told people that he didn't convert, 'convert' means you switched from another faith. He never belonged to any church before, he just walked in one day and announced that he wanted to become Catholic. It was like that with me. I had to no religious upbringing at all. Why did you ask about a girl?"

"Because that's what it usually is when a guy converts in college, or at that age anyway. It's because of a girl," he said.

"You sound like you speak from experience."

"I'm a deacon at St. Lucy's" he said. "You didn't know that. I'll bet even Sister Paula never told you."

No, I didn't know that. And Sister Paula had never mentioned it either. Officer Solis, a Catholic deacon? I had no idea. But then why would I? "Don't you need a theology degree to be a deacon?" I asked.

"I have one. Loyola Marymount."

"Still waters run deep," I said.

"Catholic Community Services runs a rehab program. Think you might like that better?"

"I don't know." I didn't want to pursue this any further. Not now. I was in the back seat of the patrol car, and I waved the back of my hand at him, an impatient gesture I suppose. "All I know right now is that I want to get back to my van."

They took me back to my van all right, but they kept after me the whole way. The subject of rehab centers was dropped for now. They shifted gears and talked about A.A. instead.

It was not a new idea and I told them so. "I've been to A.A.," I said. "My...former girlfriend talked me into attending a couple of meetings. And just now, I mean, here, while I was at this detox center, they took us on a couple of field trips to A.A. in Burbank."

"What did you think?" Nancy asked me.

"Same thing I thought the other times, that it's just like church," I said. "Some guy gets up and says 'I'm Joe Blow or Sam Schmuck or Harry Horsehide, and I'm an alcoholic.' Then Joe or Sam or Harry, or Jane or Jeanette or Thusnelda tells everyone some horror story about how demon rum ruined his or her life, and how the twelve steps are helping them to stay sober, and blah-blah-blah, and happy, happy, happy, and then everybody joins hands and says the Lord's Prayer and then goes home. The only thing I liked about A.A. was the free coffee."

"But you know you can't do it alone, Pat," Solis said. "You need a support group of some kind. If you try to do this yourself, without help, you're just going to start drinking again."

"Two is a group," I shrugged. "I have Cyrus."

"Cyrus? Oh, come on! I've seen you and Cyrus together. You bring out the worst in each other."

"You didn't know Cyrus is on the wagon? He hasn't had a beer in months. He only drinks sports drinks now. He's trying to get a place and get back with his daughters. He's serious about it. He's staying sober. Honest to God. You didn't know?"

"I heard that he was trying to get into a place, but I still don't believe it. Cyrus?"

"I'm not saying he's a changed man. He's still Cyrus. He's still old full-of-shit, you-can't-count-on-him-for-anything Cyrus. But he's got this. He's doing this. He got off the tweak last year, now he's staying off the brew and the shots. I'm telling you, Cyrus and I can support each other. In fact we have a bet going. First one out of the park the other one has to buy a steak dinner for both."

"Either one of you gets out of the park, I'll buy you both a steak dinner," Fernando said. "If you stay sober, that is. But I still think you need A.A., Pat, even if you don't like going."

"Waste of time. But I'll tell Cyrus about your steak dinner offer."

They dropped me at the park and I went looking for Bill. He wasn't hard to find. He spent most of his time in the library even if he didn't need to charge his phone. Bill had a bad knee; he walked with an aluminum cane and naturally didn't like to wander very far. He spent hours in the library every day, reading the papers, charging his phone, studying his Bible and making endless notes in ballpoint pen in a wirebound notebook he carried around with him, just like Andrew carried his. I never asked what he was writing about – I assumed it had something to do with his religion. Bill had found Jesus while in prison.

I found him in the main reading room at a long table empty except for him, making notes as usual. A thick book lay open on the table beside him, probably a Bible commentary.

"Hey, Bill," I said softly.

"Pat! Good to see you back! How did it go?"

"It went."

"You staying sober?"

"I only got out of detox an hour ago. But that's the plan. Do you have my keys?"

"Yeah, here they are." He pulled my keys from the black leather vest that he wore over a T-shirt that advertised Triumph motorcycles, although Bill didn't own a motorcycle that I had ever seen.

"Any trouble with the van?"

"No. Just moved it, like you asked."

"Thanks so much for that. You seen Cyrus today?"

"This morning."

"Anything happen while I was gone?"

"Not much. Cyrus had another court date."

"And?"

"I only knew he was going. Last Wednesday I think. Ask him about it."

I went looking for Cyrus, but he wasn't around the park anywhere. Neither was Marianne. Well, that was normal. She almost always went wherever he went. Wherever they had gone, I knew they'd be back eventually.

I walked to the liquor store for a Mountain Dew. That would be my drink of choice from now on. Alcohol-free of course, but rumored to have plenty of caffeine to make up for it.

The van was right there in its usual spot on Davidson in front of Bill's van. I spent part of that afternoon cleaning it out. It hadn't had a good sweeping and airing since long before I'd gone to the detox center and I decided it was overdue. Why not? It was a warm, sunny day. I took my sleeping bag and pillowcase to the Wash N' Dry – Andrew wasn't around to do it for me, unfortunately – and on the way back, stopped at El Mercado for a roll of paper towels and some Windex. I took the radio out, tuned in KKJZ and put it on the sidewalk to listen to jazz while I cleaned the windows and mirrors.

Cyrus returned after dark, alone. I was sitting inside the van reading. He saw the light of my lantern and came over.

"So you're out," he said. "Welcome back, homie."

"Thanks."

"Staying off the brew?"

I held up my Mountain Dew by way of reply. "You?"

"Same."

"Where's Marianne?"

Marianne had gone back to her "place," the small apartment in Long Beach that she shared (on paper anyway) with three other heads. She didn't like going back there, but she had to go now and then if only to pick up her mail. If she disappeared for too long the county would assume that she had left the area or died and they would put someone else there. Marianne would not have minded that so much, but she had some things stored in that little apartment and it gave her a mailing address for her disability check. Cyrus had accompanied her there that day because she didn't like to go anywhere alone.

"She'll be back tomorrow. She'll have to find her own way back. I'm not going to go get her."

"Bill tells me you had another court date while I was gone."

"Last week. Now the judge wants me to attend a parenting class."

"How long will that be?

"Twelve weeks. Once a week. I'll do it."

We were walking across the park now, back to the tree where Cyrus kept his and Marianne's stuff. I glanced up at the sky, between the trees. There, in the otherwise dark sky, was something very bright.

"What the fuck do you suppose THAT is?" I said. "Up there. Look." I pointed..

It was a bright white light, too bright to be an airplane, moving across the sky from north to south very slowly. Crawling across the sky. It looked like one of those flares you see in World War I movies, the ones they would shoot out over No Man's Land at night to see if there was any enemy activity going on out there. It seemed to have a sort of translucent tail behind it, like a comet's tail.

"It's a rocket," Cyrus said. "Gotta be a rocket."

"Vandenburg?"

"Yeah, probably the Air Force up to something."

We stood there and watched the bright light. It continued to move slowly. It got brighter. Then it turned toward the southwest and began a long, slow descent, still burning brightly. Whatever it was, it was obviously supposed to come down in the Pacific.

We watched the bright light continue to move lower and lower in the sky until it disappeared behind the trees and buildings across the street. "Well," said Cyrus, "It's either going into the ocean or somebody's dropping a bomb on Marineland."

"I can't think of anything the dolphins have done to deserve that."

It was in the L.A. Times the next morning, with photos. Hundreds of people had lined up all along the coast that night, on beaches, roadsides, cliffs and in parked cars to watch this thing fly over. The rocket had indeed been launched from Vandenburg AFB, but the Air Force wasn't behind it. It was one of the SpaceX experimental rockets that billionaire Elon Musk was still sending up, working on his own private space program.

I told Cyrus that I'd seen the story on the front page of the paper about that thing we saw. He greeted the news with a throat-clearing, a "hmm," a nod and a shrug. He had bigger things on his mind than SpaceX, Elon Musk's ego or future missions to colonize Mars.

20

You would never walk or drive along Sunset Boulevard in West L.A. and mistake that street, the very quintessence of postcard California, for the Boulevard Saint-Germain.

He had been in Paris once, on a one-week vacation back in the Baltimore days when a trip to Europe was still within his budget. Paris was resplendent with linden, horse chestnut, mimosa and even American honey locust trees, but no palm trees. There were definitely no palms on the streets of Paris, unless they had them in an arboretum somewhere that he hadn't seen. Sunset Boulevard is lined on both sides with tall palms, all the way from downtown L.A. to Hollywood. You would have to go on into Hollywood and take a tour of a movie studio back lot before you would have even a chance of seeing anything that would make you think of Paris.

Unless you dropped in at the Café Ciel. Someone had gone to a great deal of trouble and expense to make the visitor to this restaurant/nightclub on the Sunset Strip feel that he or she was about to enter The Brasserie Lipp or some other famous Parisian eatery. He had made a point of stopping at Lipp's when he was in Paris, as do many thousands of American tourists every year. Its popularity probably had something to do with Hemingway. Hemingway had eaten there in the 1920s and written about it. Even now, he thought, with fewer and fewer people bothering to read Hemingway anymore, the romantic appeal of that "Lost Generation" era between the two World Wars, when Paris was full of artists of every stripe, many of them Americans, still drew in the tourists. Woody Allen had even made a movie about it a few years ago.

Hence, the Café Ciel sported a dark wooden facade facing the street, with a green-and-white awning over the entrance, beveled glass windows in front with *CAFÈ CIEL* emblazoned on them in white lettering, and even a few small tables out on the sidewalk on either side of the revolving door that led inside. A waist-high ironwork grille surrounded the sidewalk tables.

Once you got inside the Left Bank ambience continued, with tables along the walls, carpeting of a burnt-orange color, wooden columns reaching from the carpet to the wooden ceiling, and ceiling fans. A bar stretched along the wall on the right side of the dining room. An arched doorway led to a wide room in back, behind the dining room, where the nightly entertainment was held. A small stage with a proscenium faced a roomful of tables where patrons could sit and order drinks during the show as in any nightclub.

He entered the restaurant accompanied by his pal Sam, a fellow cab driver. Sam was Ethiopian. He had been driving for Yellow Cab for about five years. When Pat began driving for the company he and Sam had struck up a friendship right away. Sam enjoyed taking Pat, who had never driven a cab before, under his tutelage and showing him the fine points of the business, primarily the little things you could do to make the best tips, and to engage "regulars," customers who would call the company and ask for you by name, or bypass the company dispatcher and call your cellphone directly And of course the best places to go at the best times to find business. The two cabbies often met late in the afternoon, joining the line at the cab stand in front of the Marriott. Sometimes they would cruise down to LAX in tandem, conferring by phone as they drove down the 405. Sam always greeted Pat at the cab stand in the afternoons with, "Patrick, my Patrick, we're gonna make some money tonight, my friend!" smacking the palm of his left hand with the inside of his right fist as he did so. He liked Sam a lot, and had asked him to come along tonight. Going to hear Melissa – he had to remember to call her 'Brandi' when she was performing – at Shanghai Rick's was something he had done several times, but tonight was a special occasion, her opening night on the Sunset Strip, and he wanted to bring a friend along. Sam was the logical choice, being the closest to a friend he had at work.

He informed the host at the door that they had come for the evening show and did not intend to dine. They took seats at the bar. Through the wide entrance to the back room they could see that the club part of the cafe was still dark except for a single light over the empty stage.

He looked at his watch. "Eight-fifteen. We're a little early," he said. "The show starts at eight-thirty. Let's have a drink."

"That your girlfriend?" Sam pointed at a small cardboard marquee mounted on an easel alongside the entrance to the back room.

Why hadn't he noticed that right away when they came in? It had two black-and-white photographs on it: one of the jazz ensemble, five black men with their instruments, piano, saxophone, drums, double bass, and Fender guitar, and the other of Melissa sporting a white off-the-shoulder gown and glittering earrings. "The Café Ciel Presents The Marshall Osgood Quintet … with special guest Brandi Spears," the sign announced.

"Yeah, that's her," he said, suddenly even more impressed than he had been when they came in and he got his first look at the place, a venue more than one notch above Shanghai Rick's. Although he had seen Melissa perform before, he had never seen her features on a marquee, even a small one. It was very professional. And she did look beautiful in the photo. Where had she had that portrait made, he wondered? And when?

"I thought you said her name was 'Melissa.'"

"It is. 'Brandi' is her stage name. She thinks that sounds better on a singer."

"You say you met her in your cab?"

"I sure did. I told you that story. She was as drunk as a fiddler's bitch."

"And she wanted to fuck you right there in the cab."

"I did tell you that story. Understand, that was unusual."

"I'd say it was *very* unusual. I've never had a customer want to fuck me in my cab."

"You know what I mean, wise guy. I mean about how drunk she was that day. I've never seen her that drunk since."

Sam grinned, shook his head and looked down at where he was twisting a cocktail napkin in his fingers. "So what's that beautiful singing sensation doing with an old fuck like my Patrick?"

"I've wondered myself, believe me."

The bartender approached them. "What can I get for you gentlemen?"

He ordered a bourbon-and-soda and Sam ordered vodka-and-grapefruit juice.

As the bartender put their drinks in front of them, Patrick saw out of the corner of his eye, through the drawn-back curtains at the door of the back room, that additional lights were beginning to come on in there. "Must be almost showtime," he said unnecessarily. For some reason he felt slightly nervous.

They took their drinks and moved to a table in the back room. Most of the time, either at the movies, a concert or at any kind of show, he tended to seat himself in the back, but tonight he wanted to be close enough to the stage so that Melissa would see him and know for certain that he was there. He had told her that he intended to come, but he wanted to make sure she saw him. He and Sam seated themselves three tables back from the stage. He wanted to her see him but he also wanted to be able to talk to Sam between numbers. A few people he had seen in the dining room drifted in. He finished his drink and signaled a waiter for another. Sam was still sipping his.

On the small stage were a Yamaha grand piano, a set of drums, four microphones on stands and three large amplifiers. A man in black jeans and a T-shirt with "Acapulco" lettered across the front came out and adjusted the microphones as more people came in and took seats.

Then the lights went down, a spotlight from the back hit the front of the room and the members of the Marshall Osgood Quintet, all welcoming smiles, bounced onstage, took up their places and instruments and launched into the Dave Brubeck standard *Take Five.* In a pause after the first chorus, riffing rhythmically on the piano to introduce a long drum solo, piano player Marshall Osgood said good evening to the crowd and presented the members of the group, who each took a bow, and then the drummer, Osgood's brother Kelvin as he had been introduced, promptly launched into his solo. The saxophone took one more chorus, then the group faded out *Take Five* and segue'd smoothly into another classic tune, *Billie's Bounce,* of which he remembered hearing Stan Getz' version at Melissa's place. The saxophone player acquitted himself quite well, Patrick thought, with some satisfaction that the time he had spent with Melissa so far had enabled him to appreciate a well-played tenor sax.

"So where's your girlfriend?" Sam said softly over the music.

"I'm starting to wonder myself," he said. "Did we come on the right night?"

"They wouldn't put her picture on that sign outside if she wasn't going to be here," Sam said. "And there's a mike set up in front of the band. You finished that drink pretty quickly."

"And I want another one. Where's the waiter?"

He looked around the room for the waiter. "She'll probably come on after this number," Sam said.

Just as the waiter had put his third drink in front of him on the table, the spotlight came up again and Marshall Osgood at the piano began playing a lead-in to Cy Coleman's *The Best Is Yet To Come.*

"Ladies and gentlemen, welcome to the Café Ciel! We are more than pleased this evening to introduce to you a remarkable local talent whom we met the other day!" Osgood said. "I know a fine voice when I hear one, and this girl has a way with a song, let me tell you. Would you give a warm welcome to...Brandi Spears!"

Melissa strode out from the wings and into the spotlight. He had expected that she would be dressed and made up fancier for this stage than she had ever bothered with at Shanghai Rick's, but he was astonished at how beautiful she looked tonight. She wore a fitted red satin off-shoulder gown with a slit skirt. (Many years earlier he had seen Diahann Carroll wear an outfit much like this one on The Tonight Show with Johnny Carson, and was so knocked out by how stunning Diahann Carroll looked that night that he never forgot it.) She wore diamond earrings (surely fake, but fabulous anyway) with a matching choker. Red nail polish and black, spike-heeled sandals completed her ensemble.

"Baby, you look like a million bucks," he whispered. He was feeling his whiskey. Fortunately no one heard him, including Sam.

With a smile and a thank-you, first to the audience and then to Marshall Osgood and his musicians, she began the song: "*Out of this tree of life I picked a plum...You came along and everything started to hum...*"

She spotted him in the audience, made eye contact, smiled at him slightly and turned her attention back to the small crowd. Good; so she knew he and his friend were there. He'd have to introduce her to Sam after the show, he thought. Or maybe when they took a break, if they took one. He didn't know how long her first set was going to be.

When the song ended, Sam leaned across the table and said over the applause, "Your girlfriend sings very well, but I think Frank Sinatra did that song better."

"Maybe, but Sinatra never looked that good in his life."

Sam laughed. "From me you will get no argument about that. Yes, she is lovely. And-you-met- her-in-your-cab! You did tell me you tell me you were Irish, didn't you?"

"'Patrick Donahy.' Names don't get more Irish than that."

"Then I would say that you surely have the luck of the Irish, my friend."

"Slainté." He drained off the last of his drink and signaled for yet another.

"You should take it easy on that stuff," Sam said. "I can drive, but you want to be reasonably sober when we go to congratulate your friend after the show, don't you?"

"I'll be fine," he said. "But you're right. I'll hold it after this one."

Melissa continued her set with covers of Cleo Laine, Ella Fitzgerald, Natalie Cole; she did a Diana Krall number, *Narrow Daylight,* which he found particularly moving.

He wanted another drink, but Sam was right; it was more important to be fully in control when he introduced her to Sam later. He really wanted to talk to Sam first, though. He had some things he wanted to tell him when they first came in; now the booze had made him naturally more inclined to talk than earlier. But not while Melissa was singing.

When Melissa and the band finally took a ten-minute break, she came over to Patrick and Sam's table. All eyes in the room followed her. Because people were watching, she kissed Patrick lightly on the cheek. "Oh, darling, I'm so glad you managed to be here tonight!" she said.

"Mondays are slow in our business, you know that," he smiled and squeezed her hand. "Mel—*Brandi,* I'd like you to meet my friend Sam Fasil. Sam and I are kind of partners-in-crime in the cab racket. He's been driving for years, and he's been a really good friend to me, taught me a lot."

"Sam, nice to meet you," she shook his hand. "Fellas, I have to go backstage and talk with Marshall. We just have a few minutes. But we'll see each other after the show, okay?"

"Yeah, we're not going anywhere," he said.

"Your voice is lovely, Ms. Spears. I very much enjoy your singing," Sam said.'

"But he says you're not as good as Sinatra," Patrick said.

"Patrick, my Patrick!" Sam said. "You know I was only joking."

Melissa smiled. "Oh, he's right! I'm no Sinatra,"

"You're much, much prettier," Sam said.

Patrick laughed. "Good save, partner."

"Thanks, you're sweet," she said. "I'll see you guys after the show, okay?" She gave Patrick another peck on the cheek and went backstage.

"She is really something extraordinary," Sam observed.

"Yes. No question. Sam, I've pretty much told you my whole story, haven't I? While we've stood around our cabs waiting for business in the evenings, I've more or less told you everything, right?"

"Everything? Well, I don't know. Let's see, you've told me about your failed marriage, some things about your life back east, working for that company in Baltimore. You've told me about the death of your younger sister and of your father, and you've told me about how this beautiful, classy and talented young lady we have come to hear sing this evening came close to tearing her clothes off in your taxicab one afternoon--"

"Can we drop that? I'm sorry I told you about it. Geez, someone might get the idea she does that sort of thing all the time."

"You haven't known her that long. Maybe she does."

"Knock that shit off! I'm serious, now. If I thought that way about her, I wouldn't be telling you what I'm about to tell you. In fact I wouldn't be having anything to do with her at all. I'm not a teenager anymore, Sam. I think I've learned a few things about people. She's definitely not a whore."

"I'm sure she isn't."

"And she was really, *really* plowed that afternoon. She had a good reason. She was upset about her kid."

"So you've told me. Now, what is this thing you're going to tell me?"

"I want another drink."

"That is not what you were going to tell me. And no, you don't. Want another drink, that is."

He picked up his empty old-fashioned glass from the table and rattled the ice in it. "I told you about my marriage to Valerie," he said.

"Yes."

"I told you what a total train wreck it was."

"Yes, you told me that too."

"And I told you that I would never, ever consider getting married again. Once was enough. Hell, with me, once was too many."

"But now you're thinking about trying it again, right? And with this girl."

He sighed. "Yeah. I guess I'm about ... as subtle a hand grenade in a barrel of oatmeal."

"What?"

"Never mind. The truth is, I've been thinking about it ever since I heard that she'd landed this gig."

"Have you asked her to marry you?"

"That's a stupid question, man. If I had, either she would have said no and I wouldn't have anything to tell you about, or she would have said yes and I would have told you already, or she would have said something like 'it's-too-soon-to-discuss-marriage-let's-wait-and-talk-about-it-later,' and I wouldn't be on tenterhooks – as wound up – as you can see that I obviously am."

"May I take a guess that this might be why you're drinking so much tonight?"

"It might be," he conceded.

"Logical." Sam sipped his drink. He was still on his first one. "But you say you began to think about this when she landed this job. If you don't mind my asking, my friend, what does the one thing have to do with the other?"

"Now, that's a very *good* question. What does the one thing have to do with the other? Well, I'll tell you. She said something about Las Vegas--"

There was a sharp drum roll. Kelvin Osgood was back behind his drum set and the other musicians were taking up their instruments to continue the show. The combo went straight into *Take The A Train.* It was too loud for conversation, especially sitting as close to the stage as they were. Further discussion with Sam would have to wait at least until after the show, or maybe for the next time they were hanging around the stand in front of the Marriott together waiting for someone to come out of the hotel and need a ride to the airport.

Melissa came back out on to the little stage. There followed another thirty minutes or so of Rodgers and Hart, Cole Porter, Stephen Sondheim... and then Melissa-Brandi paused and looked over at him before turning to speak to the audience.

"Folks, I'm going to do a special song now," she said. "It's kind of a sad song, but it's a wonderful song, written by Mr. Teo Macero, who's not a household name, but he was very big in jazz circles in his day, saxophonist, composer, producer… worked with some of the greats, Miles Davis, Dave Brubeck, Thelonious Monk...Monk recorded this song in 1963, and I'd like to do it for my someone now. I love this song. Hope you do too."

With that, Marshall Osgood played the piano introduction and Melissa went into *Just A Glance At Love.*

Of course he remembered it. He had heard it for the first time in her kitchen. "*How would I/know that you/meant just what you said?/How could I be so wise/To your smile to understand?…We knew we took just a glance at love,/We knew we looked so askance at love...*"

This was the first time he had heard words with the tune. His observation about the song on that morning over coffee, when all he heard was the melody played on Monk's piano, had been right, just as the composer intended. *Triste.* It was indeed a song about a failed romance. But what difference did that make? It was a little incongruous, but so what? He knew perfectly well that she had not chosen it to sing for him – and she could only be singing it for him – because of its melancholy tone. No, clearly she had picked that song as a reminder of their morning in the kitchen together listening to jazz, which obviously had meant something special to her. She picked it because it was something they had shared. He couldn't have been happier if she had chosen the most ardent love song ever to come out of Tin Pan Alley.

She did not glance his and Sam's way again for the rest of the song. It didn't matter. Neither did it matter when she reached the line, *"We knew/ we threw/away a chance at love."* She might have had her ex-husband in mind as she sang those words, or some other former lover, or nobody in particular. But not him. Definitely not him.

21

Cyrus' parenting class met on Tuesdays and Thursdays. He had to sign in and sign out so he could show the judge that he had actually attended. The classes were held at a Presbyterian church in Gardena. Sometimes I gave him a ride to class in the van.

Not long after I got out of detox and Cyrus had begun his classes, I drove back to the park from dropping him off and found the HOT team there, which did not surprise me because it was Wednesday, but did surprise me because it was getting close to twelve O'clock and usually they had come and gone by then. Payne, Solis and Nancy Verdugo were making their rounds, with their usual HHSA helpers, going from tree to tree.

Nancy spotted me. She waved and I waved back. Then, as Payne stayed behind to talk with Ed, Chantal and Cage, who were hanging out together that morning, she and Solis came walking toward me. I knew what they probably wanted, and it wasn't anything I particularly wanted, but they had been pretty nice to me so far and they meant well; there was no point in being rude.

"Morning, Pat!" Solis said.

"Welcome to my backyard," I said. I was being deliberately jocular because I knew what was coming. I bowed to Nancy. "Good morning, Ms. Verdugo, you little barrel of laughs, you."

She laughed and replied with a curtsey, her clipboard in hand.

"Cyrus around?" Solis asked.

"He's at his parenting class. I just got back from taking him there."

"How's that going for him?

"He's determined to stick it out. I have to give him credit for it."

Nancy didn't have time for chitchat today. She had her agenda and got right to it. "Have you given any more thought to going into rehab?" she asked me.

"You really have that stuck in your craw, don't you?"

I was careful to frame this with a laugh. It was okay if they thought I was being a smartass – they were used to that – but I didn't want them to think I was being resentful, defiant or ungrateful. I really wasn't. But I'd gotten myself detoxed now and I wasn't drinking anything stronger than Mountain Dew. Wasn't that enough for them?

No, of course it wasn't. They wanted me out of the park. Like Ranger Dave, all they really wanted was for all of us to simply not be there anymore. To be off their beat, someone else's problem. Yes, I'm sure they wanted me to stay sober, (for my own good of course) but more than that they wanted a name off their checklist. Another little success, one less body taking up space under public trees and on park benches.

They weren't bad people. They were good people. But when they said "We want to help you," (and I have no doubt that they were sincere) what they really meant was, "We want you to go away. We want you to go away healthier, happier and better-adjusted than you were when you got here, but *stop being a problem by being here.*"

I had no intention of making it quite that easy for them. What was it to them if I stuck around or went away? If I went away it was one little problem solved, after which they could go home to their houses and families. All I had was my van. The way I had it figured, anywhere I went on the globe I was going to be taking up space. You only stop taking up space when you're dead. What skin was it off their noses if I chose to take up space in Aurora Park in L.A. County, California? I wasn't involved in any criminal activity (outside of purchasing probably-stolen property now and then); I didn't do drugs; I wasn't even drinking beer anymore (at least for "for today," as A.A. thinking goes.) No park neighbors had made any complaints about me or my van that I knew of. I wasn't bothering anybody. If anything, people bothered me: Cyrus wanting rides; half the neighborhood coming around for morning coffee; Andrew hustling for drug money; Frankie coming around stoned and refusing to shut up; Yvonne bugging me on Facebook for progress reports on Chantal and Cage. Until we got rid of her, Cheryl trying to squeeze me out of my own sleeping bag. Like Byron's Don Juan I was more acted upon than acting. Like D.W. Washburn in that old song from the radio, I wished they would "go save somebody else."

"We just want to help you, Pat," Solis said.

"Uh-huh. And I suppose you two have found a place for me, right?"

"You weren't interested in a faith-based facility," he went on, "So we talked to Southland Trailblazers and Bud Antley. that's the guy in charge over there, said they'd be willing to take you. Do you know that place? It's only about a mile from here."

"I know that place. That's A.A. I've been to a couple of their meetings. I've met Bud."

"He's a nice guy."

"He's okay."

"Then you know they have a six-month rehab program, right? They even have a few permanent sober-living apartments over there if you qualify for one."

"I know about those. I also know the county doesn't subsidize them. Guys who live there pay $500 a month."

"If you look around the market these days, that's really cheap."

"You don't have to tell me. I was paying close to eleven hundred for a studio in San Pedro."

"See? It would be a bargain. And you did say you're about to put in for your Social Security."

"Yeah, and that 'bargain' of yours would eat up half of it. And what'd be in it for me? Living among a bunch of guys whose proudest achievement in life is that they don't drink anymore? Doesn't sound like a lot of laughs."

"It's better than the park."

"You assume that. But how do you *know* it's better than the park? How do you *know* that I'm not just fine living in my van, a stone's throw from all the books I could ever want to read, able to pull the damn hatch shut any time I don't want to deal with any of you? You take it for granted that having a permanent roof of some kind over your head is the *summum bonum*. And I'll grant you that it's better than sleeping on the ground. But I have my van now. I have a cot in there. I have a place out of the rain. Nobody bothers me, except when this crowd wants me to make coffee for them, buy the junk they steal or give them rides."

I made a sweeping gesture toward the entire park, my domain, with a wave of my arm. "I don't have it so bad," I said. "Socrates lived in a rain barrel, you know."

"But Pat," Nancy said in her most earnest tone, "you know that you're not going to stay on the wagon without some help. I know, I know, you told us that Cyrus is staying clean and that you two can encourage each other, but you and Cyrus aren't exactly a support group. And he's trying to get himself out of this park. One day this week, or next week, or next month or the month after that, somebody or something is going get you so upset or so stressed out that you're going to head right back for that beer cooler. We've seen it a thousand times."

"And those do-gooders at Southland Trailblazers might be just the ones to drive me to it."

She laughed in spite of herself. "Oh, you're impossible!"

I only said that I wasn't going to make it easy for them; I didn't say I wasn't going to let them have their way. I just wanted to make them work a little for their money. While I had no intention of trying to get into one of the Trailblazers' permanent sober-living apartments and turning into one of those sobriety-is-joy zombies I had seen in the parking lot over there, cigarette in one hand and styrofoam cup of coffee in the other, talking in low tones about football and gas mileage, I already knew that there had to be a next thing, some form of a next thing. I hadn't figured out what it was going to be yet. Cyrus had a concrete goal; I had none. All I knew was what was obvious. I could verbally fence with the HOT team until the middle of next week, but I agreed with them that I could not hang around the park forever. There had to be something down the road. There always has to be something down the road unless you're ready to go jump in the cemetery right now, and I wasn't quite there yet.

So it was back to the Army for this particular Mr. Jones. Cyrus would have to find someone else to give him rides to parenting class. Solis met me at Southland Trailblazers the next afternoon and I checked into their rehab program. At least I didn't have to ask Bill to look after my van this time – Trailblazers was only a few blocks away and they had plenty of parking.

Again, as with the detox program I had just finished, some of the guys were there because they had been ordered there by a judge. I was there of my own free will and could leave whenever I wanted, but despite all of the regimentation and the checking-up on you they did, (not much different from the detox program) I found it pleasant enough being indoors, having clean sheets to sleep on instead of a sleeping bag, plus hot showers and three meals a day.

I decided to stick around at least until my sixty-day grace period ended and they began charging me rent. Then I would probably pack up and scoot, because I wasn't about to go out and get a job pushing a broom somewhere. I had worked hard for years at plenty of jobs. I'd been a reporter on newspapers and on radio, an office clerk, a marketing writer, a business news editor, a store clerk, a security guard, a cab driver and a teacher. I had had quite enough of working and now would wait for my Social Security benefits, thank you. I didn't have that much longer to wait, anyway. I was almost sixty-two.

I met a few guys who really liked it at Trailblazers and wanted to stay on, guys who apparently felt that they really needed the facility's summer-camp routine to stay clean and sober. These were the ones who talked of eventually getting into the sober-living apartments at the east end of the compound, where some guys had actually been living for years. If you stayed and kept your nose clean long enough, you might be moved from the dormitory which I was now sharing with half-a-dozen others into a single-occupancy room.

But I didn't last sixty days. My sojourn among the dedicated sober didn't even last two weeks.

It was a Tuesday morning and I was on the crew that cleaned and mopped upstairs. There was a guy on my team named Robert whom I had already decided that I did not like. At all.

Robert had no sense of humor. I couldn't get a laugh out of him for anything. He was about my age, a skinny guy with a graying crew cut, and I don't know what kind of personal problems he had – we all had personal problems or we wouldn't be in rehab, but he constantly went around with a look like he had been weaned on a slice of lemon, and any time I spoke to him I got only monosyllables in reply. I can deal with just about any type of person, but no-sense-of-humor is something that really rubs me the wrong way. I guess I just can't see anyone taking themselves that seriously.

I finally just started avoiding Robert. If he was mopping, I'd clean the shower stalls. If he was cleaning the shower stalls, I would mop. Anything to keep him a few feet away from me and avoid having to speak with him.

That morning our crew was preparing to go upstairs and start cleaning. I was getting ready to mop. There was a fence along the back of the patio area where we hung the mops to dry every night. I had taken one and was sloshing it around in a bucket with water from the hose and some Mr. Clean. I squeezed the mop and looked at my watch. 7:26. Four minutes until we hit those floors. Everything in this place was timed like *Mission Impossible.* You didn't start mopping until the crew chief told you to, which would be exactly at 7:30.

Robert was at one of the patio tables talking with a couple of the other guys. All three had styrofoam cups of coffee in front of the them on the table. Robert had a half-smoked Marlboro between his fingers. He looked at his watch.

"Well, almost show time," I heard him mutter. This was as close to levity as he ever came.

Thinking I was being nice, I spoke to him. "We still have four minutes. Go ahead and finish your coffee."

Without looking at me, he grunted, "Don't tell me what to do, friend."

'Don't tell me what to do, friend?' All I had told him to do was relax and finish his coffee.

I already didn't like him. And it was early in the morning, and I really didn't feel like mopping the floors, and my coffee, as usual, had not been hot enough or strong enough, and he just shouldn't have said that, that's all. Wrong thing to say. Wrong time to say it.

Something snapped. I'd had enough of Robert. Maybe I'd had enough of Southland Trailblazers already and up until that very second didn't know it.

"Don't tell me what to do, friend?" I repeated what he'd said.

"You heard me."

"In the first place," I said, lifting the dripping mop out of the bucket, I'm not" – WHAP! – "your friend!"

Yes, I did it: I hauled off and smacked him right in the side of the head with that wet mop. I didn't swing hard, but he was unprepared. The styrofoam cup flew out of his hand and coffee went all over the table, mixed with a big splash of water and Mr. Clean. The half-smoked cigarette went to the pavement in a mini-shower of sparks. The other two guys at the table with him jumped up and got out of the way.

He got up from his plastic chair, water and Mr. Clean dripping from his face. The front of his shirt was soaking wet.

"I'll make you pay for that, asshole!" He growled, squaring off as if to fight.

"Yeah? Here's a down payment, you skinny little prick."

I hit him again with the mop, this time a bayonet-thrust, a soggy uppercut that caught him square on the chin. I put all my weight behind it. The pavement was wet; he slipped, fell over backwards and crashed into the table. He came up with his fists ready for battle, but I had the mop.

"Put down that mop and fight fair if you're a man!" he sputtered, still dripping. His thin, gaunt face was red.

But I wasn't interested in any Marquess of Queensberry crap. All I wanted to do was knock him on his can again.

"I'll 'tell you what to do, 'friend,'" I said. "I'll tell you 'what to do,' you skinny-ass dickhead motherfucker." I thrust the mop at him again. He took a step or two back, but he had his fists up in front of his face like John L. Sullivan. We must have looked like two of the Three Stooges. I don't know why all of the guys standing around weren't laughing. Well, it had happened pretty quickly.

Then the crew chief, a burly Mexican and fellow alcoholic named Miguel, rushed over, grabbed the mop out of my hands and got between us.

"Pat, are you fucking crazy? What are you doing?" he shouted. "Somebody go get Bud!"

But the moment had passed. Either Robert's courage had failed or he had realized the supreme idiocy of the situation. After all, he had brought this on himself with his don't-tell-me-what-to-do remark. His pale blue eyes flamed with ruffled pride and whatever dislike he already had for me, for which I could think of no explanation, by the way. Even now, I had thought I was being nice to him, letting him finish his coffee. But like they say, you can't be nice to some people.

Robert had to avenge his ruffled pride, though. Instead of continuing the brawl, he pulled his cellphone out of his pocket, dialed 911 and told dispatch that he had just been assaulted and wanted the police to come and arrest his assailant.

Did a couple of smacks with a wet mop constitute assault with a deadly weapon? I'd find out when the cops got there. But I knew that my time at Southland Trailblazers was up. Whatever that next thing might turn out to be, I was going to have to go look for it somewhere else. Might as well go get my things and prepare to leave, whether behind the wheel of my van or in handcuffs.

Bud Antley came hurrying out of his office as soon as he'd heard what happened. When he came out on to the patio, what he saw was a bunch of guys standing around who should have been at their morning cleanup chores, one of them already leaning on a mop and one of them visibly wet. The rest were standing around muttering in little groups. Looking at us. Probably waiting for the next flare-up. Glad to have morning cleanup delayed.

"All right, all right, break it up!" he said. "Come on you guys, get to your cleaning! Except you two, I guess." He pointed at Robert and me. I handed my mop to one of the other fellows who was on his way upstairs. He shoved it into my bucket and wheeled it off.

"What happened?" Bud demanded.

"This sumbitch hit me with a goddamn mop!" He was wiping his face with a paper napkin now. "You're goin' to JAIL, asshole!" he roared.

"*This* son-of-a-bitch said something I didn't like," I said. "And if he says it again, I'm going to smack him with a mop again. Or some object less soft and wet."

"What did you say to each other?" Bud asked.

"I told him we still had a couple of minutes and he should go ahead and finish his coffee," I said. "And he says, "Don't tay-yell me what to do, Freyend." I mimicked his hick accent, and he didn't like that either. He glared at me and groped his wet shirt front for his pack of Marlboros. Bud suddenly hung his head and for a second I thought he was going to cry.

"Well, DON'T you tell me what to do," Robert growled.

"I'm not your friend and you're a fucking moron."

"Say that again."

"Moron. You. Are. A. Fucking. Moron."

He took a step toward me and this time I raised my fists.

"Knock it off! Both of you! Simmer down!" Bud got between us. "Pat, can I see you for a minute?"

I nodded. Bud took me gently by the arm and led me back toward his office. Miguel stayed with Robert, who found a smoke, lit it and stood by the fence, looking out at the hill behind our building.

"Listen, Pat," he looked around to make sure no one could hear us. "Robert has been...well, let's just say he's been a problem before."

"You mean stuff like this?"

"Well, yeah. He's started trouble with a couple of other people. As you can see, he's not easy to get along with--"

"He's a redneck moron. I can't stand the son-of-a-bitch," I said.

"I know, I know." Bud spoke as if he had already heard this. "There have been complaints about Bob. But he's trying to stay sober, and it's been really hard for him. His wife left him because of his drinking. He lost his house. It's been harder for him than it is for some others."

"I've heard those my-wife-left-me-and-I-lost-my-house stories before," I said. "It doesn't excuse him being an asshole."

"You know it is harder for some people."

"Yes."

"I can see that you're recovering nicely. Or you seem to be. How long have you been sober?"

"About four weeks now, I think. Yeah, there was the ten days in detox, then a few days in the park I didn't have any beer, and then here. Be a month next week, I think."

"Robert's coming up on four months. But he has been a trial. This is maybe the tenth time he's called 911 since he's been here. Once he called

911 because he thought someone had taken his watch. Listen, we don't want any trouble around here."

"I know. Sorry. Well, the cops are on their way by now. I'll be arrested and your problem will be solved. Because I can assure you that when I get out of jail I won't be coming back here."

"Would you hang on a minute while I go talk to Robert?"

"I'm not going anywhere," I said. "I'm already facing assault charges. I don't want to add leaving the scene to that."

Bud walked back out to the patio. I sat at one of the long tables used for the daily A.A. meetings. There was no one else in the hall; they were all either upstairs cleaning or off at their day jobs.

I looked out the window at the parking lot. No sign of any police yet, which did not surprise me. They seldom responded to a 911 call in less than fifteen minutes. That had been a sore spot among the cabbies when I was driving. We weren't allowed to carry any form of protection, not even pepper spray. If a cab driver got robbed or assaulted, all he or she was allowed to do was call the police, and it sometimes took them 45 minutes to an hour to show up. "You're supposed to let them kill you, then call the cops," the saying went. Some defied the rules and carried baseball bats in their trunks, for all the good that would do in an emergency. I never had.

Bud came back. "I talked to Robert and he says he's not going to press charges," Bud said. "He's already called dispatch to cancel the emergency call, but it's probably too late for that. They'll be here in a minute or two. We'll just explain to them what happened, maybe they'll let it go. They must have more important things to do."

"Maybe."

"But there's one thing. Robert only agreed not to press charges if you leave. Permanently."

I nodded. "I just said I wouldn't come back here even if it meant jail. Fact is, nothing personal, but I think I've already had about enough of this place," I said. "It was nice having a clean, warm bed and a roof over my head for a couple of weeks, but I don't want to live like this, and I'm certainly not going to pay $500 a month to live like this. I'll just be on my way."

Two patrol cars pulled into the parking lot. The police always sent a backup. Three of the officers, two younger male cops and a young woman, I didn't recognize, but the fourth was Fernando Solis. My bet would be that he'd heard Southland Trailblazers mentioned on the radio and thought it might have something to do with me.

Solis came over to where Bud and I were standing. The other three, the younger cops, wandered around as cops do, looking for anything unusual, looking busy, waiting for instructions.

"Okay, what happened?" Fernando asked.

"Pat here clocked Bob Korzep with a wet mop," Bud told him.

Solis looked at me. "You didn't."

I nodded. "Afraid so."

"Pat," he said in the sad tone of a high-school football coach who's just found out that his star quarterback got caught shoplifting. Then he looked at Bud. "Where's the other guy?"

"That's him out there on the patio, smoking," Bud pointed through the window.

"Is he okay?"

"How hurt could he be? It was the business end of a wet mop, not a fireplace poker," I said.

"He's agreed not to press charges," Bud put in.

"Oh, yeah? Miles, Bishop, go talk to him," Solis said. The two young male cops went out to the patio to speak with Robert. The young woman cop continued poking about silently in the background, looking official, looking busy, thumbs hooked in her gunbelt. Waiting.

Solis didn't run me in, but decided it would be a good idea if he and the other officers hung around until I'd gone upstairs, gotten my things together and walked out the door.

There wasn't much to gather. I'd come in with my backpack and I left with my backpack. What few other belongings I had were locked up in my van.

Solis and his comrades waited. They didn't mind. Cops do everything slowly. I'd once watched them take twenty minutes to put the cuffs on Yvonne.

Fernando walked me back out to the parking lot. He sighed. "We're disappointed in you, Pat."

"Why? I hit a guy with a mop. I didn't fall off the wagon."

"You were one of our success stories."

"I'm still sober," I repeated.

"But you won't stay that way. I suppose you're going back to the park now."

"You suggest maybe the waterfront instead? I'd get into more trouble there and you know it. Faster."

"Let us try to find you another place. Someplace where they only let you have a dry mop."

"Why is this so important to you?"

"It's my job. And believe it or not, Pat, I like you. I think you're worth salvaging."

"Not everybody would agree with you. Maybe I don't."

He put his hand on my shoulder as I prepared to climb into the van. "I also think you're full of shit," he said.

"I never denied that."

"What are you gonna do when you get back to the park?"

"Find Cyrus and see if he got someone else to take him to class."

"You care about Cyrus, don't you?"

I shut the van door and put the key in the ignition. "Be safe, Officer Solis, sir. And give my love to that hotsie-totsie Chief Candace."

"Tu viejo sucio," said Solis.

"Huh?"

"You're a dirty old man." He grinned, turned, waved a hand at me as if brushing away a fly and walked back to his patrol car.

22

Melissa's gig at the Café Ciel went better than she or her friends had hoped it would. After the one-week engagement ended and she had returned to her regular job at Shanghai Rick's, she told Patrick over a dinner of braised salmon and white asparagus at his tiny place, a meal he had prepared special, by way of celebration, that the manager of the Ciel definitely wanted her back again.

"He told me it might be before Easter," she said as she poured out more Taittinger brut champagne, for one bottle of which he had paid $59.95, but what was a celebration without champagne (even if he himself didn't especially like the stuff?) On his laptop The Modern Jazz Quartet, with Milt Jackson's signature vibraphone, doled out *A Night In Tunisia.*

"Would you be fronting the same group?"

"He didn't say."

"Because I thought they were great, and you all had an excellent blend. The tenor sax guy is really good. He blows a mean chorus."

She laughed so suddenly and so hard she spat out champagne. "Well, you dig the most, Daddy-O! I'm turning you into a real hepcat!"

"Stop that right now!" He too was laughing. "I don't believe this. You are *way* too young to remember beatnik talk. That was almost before *my* time."

"You forget, my father was part of that scene."

"Yeah, your daddy was one of the daddy-Os. Classic Danny Thomas spit-take, by the way," He said.

"What?"

"Danny Thomas used to do that. The spit-take. It was one of his routines."

They went back to working the beatnik-talk joke, him throwing in a few lines from what he remembered of the Maynard G. Krebs character on the *Dobie Gillis* TV show in the 1960s.

"Well," he said, getting up to open the door before lighting his pipe, "and have you heard anything more about Las Vegas?"

He had been afraid to ask this question.

"Barney – you remember, the guy who knows the manager at the Ciel – came in two nights ago and we talked about that, about the future anyway. I don't really think Barney has any connections in Vegas," she said. "That was just bullshit, he was trying to impress me. Then again, I did think that his claim to know the manager at the Café Ciel was bullshit too, didn't I?"

"You did."

"I think there's a better possibility that Dave might have connections, whether in Vegas or somewhere else. Dave Aaron, that's the manager at the Ciel, the one who says he wants me back. Of course I wouldn't bring that subject up with him, not now. For now I just want another shot at working his place. I think for now any talk about Vegas is going to stay just that, talk. Anyway it doesn't have to be Vegas, right? My next job could be anywhere. It might be better if I did just work around southern California for a while. You know I do want to get full custody of Tommy. It would be better if I had something like a home to offer him. It would look better to a judge too."

He hoped the deep pleasure these words gave him did not show on his face.

Melissa couldn't stay overnight. "Sharon went off with Stanley this evening and forgot her key. I'll have to be back before she is so I can let her in."

She left at ten-thirty, and as soon as he was alone he poured a

Scotch-and-water to get the taste of champagne out of his mouth, then cleaned up the mess from supper. With Melissa gone back to her own place for the night, he went back to his usual routine: once the dishes had been washed and put away, he made another Scotch-and-water, a double this time, then went to TCM and found Gregory Peck in *The Bravados.*

But he was only half-following the movie. He thought about the evening just concluded. Should he have popped the question over dinner? No. It was best that he had stayed away from the subject. The evening had been to celebrate her triumph; the mood was just as it should have been, light, cheerful, laughter-filled. They made love before he cooked the dinner, in the same spirit of celebration, the simple delight they took in each other's bodies, with the underscoring it gave to Melissa's recent success. To bring up the subject of marriage on such an evening would not have been right and might have ruined everything.

Another double Scotch and he tried to concentrate on Gregory Peck doing his revenge thing, chasing down and killing the bad guys one by one, on his inexorable way to the horrifying discovery that they were innocent after all. He had seen this film and knew how it ended. Joan Collins was one hot number in 1958, all right. But his thoughts were still too much on Melissa and what possible shape their future might take, or if they even had one. The western wasn't holding his attention as it normally would. He got up and made one more drink.

The couch was an IKEA fold-up futon. His new place had no separate bedroom. The sofa-bed was unfolded and open now, as he and Melissa had made love on it before dinner. He liked the futon. It was firm, firmer than most mattresses and better for sleeping than some beds he'd been in. He was lying on his back as he watched the movie, head propped up on two pillows. The hour and the liquor finally combined to overpower his train of thought. He put his empty glass on the floor, turned over and went to sleep. When he awoke it was daylight and the TV was still on. TCM had moved along to Irene Dunne and Cary Grant in *My Favorite Wife.*

He was a fan of Cary Grant, but turned it off.

Late that afternoon he and Sam were in their usual places, standing beside their cabs in front of the Marriott Hotel.

"We're gonna make some money tonight, Patrick!" Sam said, looking out at the traffic on South Beverly.

"You always say that."

"I feel it in my bones."

"You always say that, too."

"So. How is your girlfriend doing with her nightclub engagement?"

"It ended last Friday. She's back at her regular job now. But the place wants her to come back. They said maybe in the spring, which isn't far away now."

"You said you were thinking of proposing to her. Have you done it?"

"No."

"Have you seen her?"

"I saw her last night. What is this, Twenty Questions? I cooked dinner for her last night at my place. Kind of a celebration of her wrapping up this gig on Sunset. We had champagne, the whole celebration bit."

"Just the two of you."

"Of course. My place isn't big enough to host a banquet. It's hardly big enough for a sit-down dinner for two."

"Oh, look." Sam pointed toward the valet parking entrance to the hotel, where an Audi and a Lexus sedan were being driven in. "My cousin is doing very well, it would seem."

"Your cousin parks cars?"

"My cousin Abraham parks cars in a very big way, Patrick my friend. He owns Gold Star Valet Parking Service. Those men parking cars over there, they all work for him."

"No kidding! He's an entrepreneur? YOU have a wealthy cousin?"

"Quite wealthy. He has the valet parking contracts for all the big hotels in town. See, he can underbid all the other services because he flies workers over here from Ethiopia by the planeload. They're happy just to be here. And he puts them to work parking cars."

"Nice guy. Why don't you work for him?"

"Because I don't want to park cars for the next to nothing that he pays. He didn't bring me over here, I got to the States by myself. I don't owe him anything. I like him, decent enough fellow I suppose. But I don't owe him anything."

"But since you're family, and if he's as rich as you say, I wouldn't think he'd have you parking cars. He'd put you in some sort of executive position, wouldn't he?"

"Hmm, yes, I suppose. But I don't want to sit behind a desk shuffling paper, either. I like being outdoors and I like being my own boss. So." Sam wanted to change the subject. "You have not asked this, uh, what was her name again? Brandi?"

"I told you that's her stage name. Her real name is Melissa."

"Right. You have not proposed to Melissa, but you are still thinking of it."

"That's right. I thought about it for a long time last night after she left. I'm just not sure it's a good idea. She's just a little more than half my age, and she's...well, she's in that business."

"You mean you look down on her because she wants to be in show business? I'm surprised at you, Patrick. I would have thought you more democratic than that."

"Don't be ridiculous. It's just that it's such an unsettled business. Singing in lounges isn't selling real estate, you know. She says she doesn't want to go on the road. She has a son – I've met him and he's a great kid – and she says that she wants to make a proper home for him. Right now he spends half his time with his father and half with his mother. She hopes to persuade her ex-husband to let her have full custody. I think a big part of her just wants to live a normal life."

"Then what is the problem?" Sam asked.

"The problem is, whether she admits it to herself or not, the music biz *isn't* going to be a normal life. I should say the odds are against it. I hate to resort to clichés, but I'm afraid Melissa might be looking to have her cake and eat it too. The music business, from what I've read and heard about it anyway, is a much crazier, dicier and even more dangerous roller coaster in terms of drugs and all that shit, even than acting is. I don't know if there's any place for me on that roller coaster or even if there should be. And what about Tommy?"

"Tommy?"

"That's her son. What about him? If the idea of being married to her – which does mean being married to her *life*, by the way, that's what the word means – if that looks like it could be a minefield for an old guy like me, imagine what it could be for a little boy who needs his mother around. I know she has the best of intentions, and I know she loves her son. I have a strong feeling that if it came down to that, and she had to make the choice, no doubt she would give up the singing career for her son. Most women would. And that would be a good thing. But where do I fit in? Should I try to?"

"It sounds like you're truly worried about little Tommy."

"Well, I am. He's just a kid. He doesn't understand any of this. Right now he's dealing with what it's like to be with one parent for a while, then the other for a while. That's bad enough. What's it going to be like if he finds himself getting yanked out of bed every now and then and told 'Come on, Mommy has a gig in South Lake Tahoe and she's gonna stick herself and you in a motel for a couple of nights.' Of course I know she wants to avoid anything like that. She told me so. But given the nature of that business, it could happen."

"Patrick, Patrick," Sam said, tamping down the air in front of himself with both hands. "You know that you should be having this conversation with Melissa, not with me. I will only ask one further question. Do you love her?"

"I...I think so."

"No, no, no, my friend. This is not the kind of question that can be answered with 'I think so.' This question requires a yes or a no. Take a deep breath, don't look at me, look across the street. Look at that truck parked down at the end of the street. Okay? Now. I will ask one more time. Do you love her?"

He stared at the truck for a full fifteen seconds. It was unloading office supplies at the CVS Pharmacy.

Then, "The old fool says 'Yes.' The old punchline is ready to become the old punchline."

Sam raised his hands like a priest consecrating the host. "Go in peace with my blessing, my children, live long and prosper and all that shit."

"Well, you're a romantic son-of-a-bitch, aren't you?"

He drove until just after midnight, then radioed in that he was going off duty. It was starting to rain, but he didn't feel like driving anymore and he didn't feel like going directly back to his studio. He drove instead to Shanghai Jake's, where he knew Melissa would still be working at this hour.

The rain was coming down fairly hard by the time he turned on to Westwood Blvd. and pulled up a few yards down the sidewalk from the bar. He got slightly wet dashing for the door, and once inside he stamped and batted water off himself as his eyes adjusted to the darkness.

Melissa spotted him from behind the bar and waved. She appeared to be in conversation with an older man at the bar.

He went over and took a seat two stools down from the man with whom Melissa was talking, a very thin, older guy wearing a Dodgers cap, corduroy pants and a checked flannel shirt. He had a beer in front of him, half-finished, and a cigarette in one hand.

"Pat, this is Barney Devereaux," Melissa said. "Barney got me the job at the Café Ciel."

"I didn't get it for you," the thin man said. "I introduced you to Dave.

You got the job yourself. Glad to know you," he shook Donahy's hand. "Brandi's told me about you. You drive a cab, right?"

"Yes, I just came off duty. I wasn't ready to head for the barn yet, so I decided to come by and say hello, have a drink," he said to Melissa, who leaned across the bar to give him a kiss. Barney Devereaux turned his attention to Jimmy Fallon on the television screen.

Melissa didn't need to ask him what he wanted to drink. She went off to make him a Scotch-and-water. Barney Devereaux flicked cigarette ash into the ashtray on the bar and took a sip of his beer.

"I'm surprised guys like you are still in business," he said. "I've been reading that Lyft and Uber have just about driven the cab companies into the ground."

"They have made it a lot harder," he admitted. "But they're starting to have their own problems. Uber took off like a skyrocket a couple of years ago, but their business has leveled off. They don't train their drivers in anything, not customer service, nothing. They just sign them up, give 'em the app and off they go. There's no quality control. They've had a lot of complaints. And there are still people who prefer an old-fashioned taxi. They see the familiar car, they see the brand. They know who they're getting in the car with."

Melissa put his drink in front of him.

"Did you sing tonight?" he asked.

"Tonight was karaoke night," she smiled. "Barney here got up and sang *Stairway to Heaven.*"

"You must be close to my age," Donahy said. "I remember that song."

"Saw Led Zeppelin in concert twice," Barney said. "Lessee, '76 at the Forum and '81 in San Diego. I used to go to a lot of concerts in them days. I saw the Doobie Brothers, Chicago, Fleetwood Mac –"

"Nostalgia acts, now," he said. "You see them playing the Indian casinos, where people older than you and me go by the busload to gamble."

"Yeah," Barney said ruefully, "When we was kids we used to make fun of our parents watching Lawrence Welk and playing their Glenn Miller and Artie Shaw records. Now we're the ones poppin' Geritol and going off to see Van Morrison and Steely Dan. God, Van Morrison. He looks older than us now."

"That's because he is. When he was with the group Them, I was in the Cub Scouts."

"Remember Them? 'G-L-O-R-I-A, Gloria.'" Barney started playing an air guitar. "G-L-O-R-I-A, Gloria!"

He nodded, remembering the song. But he wasn't sure how he felt about having this conversation with Melissa standing right there, especially considering the talk he'd had with Sam just a few hours earlier.

Then, perhaps sensing his unease, the age thing being a subject they had discussed before, Melissa interrupted Barney's reminiscing.

"Pat, you came in wet," she said. "Excuse me, Barney. But you know I don't like to drive in the rain, honey. Do you think you could drive me home after we close?"

"Sure, but the rain may have stopped by then. What about your car?"

"It's parked out back. I've left it here overnight before. It'll be all right. I can have Shari bring me to work tomorrow afternoon."

"Or I can pick you up."

"You're a love."

He went on to have another drink, and a third, while Barney, soggy with nostalgia after who-knew how many beers already, drew him into a trivia contest to see who could name the most one-hit wonders from the 1960s and '70s. Barney beat him easily at this game. He knew them all, from The Surfaris (*Wipe Out)* to Norman Greenbaum (*Spirit in the Sky*) to Frank Mills (*Music Box Dancer.*) Amazing. Barney had them catalogued in his head: artist, year, label, even the highest each went on the Billboard charts. What other libraries of information, he wondered, might this skinny little fellow who may have casually launched Melissa's career in the music business through a just-as-casual attempt to get to first base with her, have in his head?

It was just after 2 a.m. when they left the bar. Melissa, dressed in denim jeans and jacket as she had been on the afternoon when they first met, linked her arm in his as they came out the door into the street. It was still raining, but less hard than it had been earlier. Without unlinking her arms from his, Melissa pulled her Levi's jacket up over her head.

"Come on, it's not raining that hard now," he said.

"I don't want to mess up my hair."

"Oh, fuck!"

"What?"

"Look."

He pointed. The taxicab's right rear tire, next to the curb, was flat. "Wouldn't you know? It would have to happen in the rain."

"What are you going to do?"

"What can I do? Change the tire. Get in, no need for both of us to get wet." He opened the door for her.

"No, I'm going to help," she said.

He tried to tell her not to be silly, to get in the car and stay dry, but she insisted.

"Okay, then, let's do it," he said. "Wait a sec while I make sure the parking brake is on."

He set the parking brake, they went around to the trunk and he got out the spare tire. He bounced it on the shiny asphalt a couple of times to make sure it, too, wasn't flat, then got out the small hydraulic jack and the lug wrench from the trunk. She helped him position the jack under the rear Ford's rear axle, then squatted beside him on the sidewalk as he pulled off the hubcap and removed the lug nuts one by one. She dropped them into the hubcap one by one, then steadied the tire as he went around and raised the jack a little higher, clearing the tire from the ground so he could make the change.

It took about five minutes. Both were quite damp by then. As he put the flat tire, jack and lug wrench back into the trunk, he pulled out a dirty old towel that had been left there by whoever had to change the tire the last time. They wiped their hands on it, and she smiled up at him and gave him a kiss.

"We're not exactly the pit crew at Ontario Speedway, but we got that done pretty fast," he said, returning her kiss.

He suggested that they go and get some coffee before proceeding home. Since both were accustomed to late hours, going for coffee at 2:30 in the morning didn't seem out of the ordinary to either.

"Good idea," she said. "You've had a few drinks. You could use some coffee before driving home."

"I only had three, and they were spaced over an hour and a half."

"But I was making them, so they were more whiskey than water."

"Yes, you do spoil me, don't you?" He kissed her again.

"And you know how the cops are around here. Let's go get some coffee."

They drove to a nearby Denny's and went inside. Despite the hour and perhaps because of the rain, Denny's was busy. Most of the booths were occupied, but they found a vacant one and slid into it. Melissa began patting her hair with napkins.

The drinks he had had at Shanghai Jack's emboldened him to clear his throat.

"Well," he said, "I had a talk with Sam this evening. You remember Sam, my cabbie buddy? You met him at your opening night."

"Of course I remember Sam. And what did you two talk about? Competition from Lyft and Uber?"

"No. As a matter of fact I talked about those things with your friend Barney while you were fixing me a drink." He smiled, but was looking away from her, toward the window.

Then he looked at her across the table. She was looking directly into his eyes. The booze-courage ebbed slightly. But she reached across and put her hands in his.

"Sam and I were discussing," he began again. "That is, we were talking about, you know, your recent engagement. And we talked about...well, the music business, in general. And I talked about Tommy, and, uh--"

"My Tommy?"

"Yeah. Well, you know. You have this son, and he's a great kid, and I was thinking about, you know, the career you're trying to get started, and domestic life, and all that sort of thing, and I was kind of thinking out loud, you know."

"No, I don't know. Honey, what are you babbling about?"

"I was wondering if, you know, you might...think about marrying me."

He winced as he said this, then braced himself for the expected 'are-you-out-of-your-mind?'

He half-thought he *was* out of his mind. Should he just get up and leave now, before the waitress came with menus and made the moment even more embarrassing?

But she said, "You want to marry me?"

He finally worked up the nerve to lock eyes with her. "Yeah," he said.

"Oh, honey, I--"

"Yeah, I know. I know. Forget I mentioned it. The hour. The booze you fed me. Never mind. It was a dumb idea. I told Sam--"

"You're an idiot. You know that, don't you?"

"Yes, I know that. Guy my age ought to know better. Just...chalk it up to temporary brain-death. Forget I mentioned it. I knew you'd think I was crazy. I am crazy. No fool like an old fool and all that."

"Will you SHUT UP?" she squeezed his hands more tightly. "Of course I'll marry you."

"What?"

"You heard me."

"Why?"

She laughed and shook her head. "Honey, you are really something. You propose to me, I say yes, and you want to know why. You're a piece of work."

"I suppose I thought--"

"You overthink. You do that all the time. Like the way you obsess about your age. As if that were important. I love you. And I'm pretty sure you love me, or you wouldn't be proposing in the middle of the night after changing a tire in front of a bar in the rain."

He drew a sideways figure eight with his index finger on the tabletop.

"It's true. I do love you. I must admit that I like the sound of that. I haven't said it to anybody in a long time."

"Say it again."

"Well, I love you."

"Don't put 'well' in front of it."

"I love you."

"I want to hear it with my name."

"I love you, Brandi."

She slapped his hand. "Say it right, smartass!" she said with a grin.

"Okay. I love you, *Melissa*. Patrick loves Melissa. Find me a tree and I'll carve it in a heart. One of those palms on Sunset, out in front of the Café Ciel. Couldn't get more romantic than that. Or cornier, for that matter."

"Or more perfect." She squeezed his hand again. "I love you, Patrick."

The waitress interrupted them, bringing menus which they waved away, thank you, just coffee please. The waitress, in her fifties from the look of her, was obviously sleepy and glad not to be bothered taking orders. But she was pleasant. "Two coffees," she smiled. "Cream and sugar?"

"None for me," he said. Melissa also shook her head. The waitress went to get their coffee.

He stared at his hands, not quite convinced yet, despite the endearments they had exchanged, that his idea was such a good one.

"Think about it," he said. "You're going to marry a cab driver, pushing sixty, who drinks too much?"

"Well, we will have to talk about that. I'm glad you brought it up and I didn't have to. You *do* drink too much, Pat. I think you know it. If we're going to be married you're going to have to quit drinking or least severely cut down. For Tommy's sake if not for ours."

She was right. But he had to say something in his own defense, so he said, "You drink. You were two sheets the afternoon we met."

"But that was unusual for me. You remember that day. I was upset about Tommy. You've never seen me that drunk again, admit it."

"I told Sam that. But you've never seen me out of control either."

"No. That's true. You don't binge. But you drink all the time."

"I don't drink in the morning, and I never drink when I'm working."

"I'm not saying it's been a problem, honey. But it could become one. You mentioned Tommy. I don't want a boozer around Tommy."

"I don't drink around Tommy."

"I know. And I want to keep it that way. So let's talk about my son. You said you had told Sam about Tommy. I think Tommy means a lot to you, and I love you for it. I've seen you playing with him. You know what I think? You told me all about your marriage to Valerie. You said that she boasted that she had never been pregnant. She didn't want children. Maybe you thought at the time that you didn't want children either. Or you convinced yourself that you didn't. But I think there have been times when you have really regretted never becoming a father. It shows in the way you are with Tommy. The way you played with him when he was here at Christmas. I think you would have been a great father."

"Are you trying to convince me or yourself? Because Tommy is a big factor in this."

"The biggest factor. He's all of it," she said. "He's all of it to me."

He shrugged in assent. "That's as it should be."

"Patrick," she said, "I don't need any more convincing about you. I know you would be a good stepdad for Tommy."

"He has a father."

"He has a *father.* He needs a *daddy.* Someone who will be around for him, not someone two thousand miles away whom he sees every now and then. And like I said a minute ago, I really do think you would have made a wonderful father. Maybe if you had become a father you wouldn't drink so much. Did you ever think about that? You would have had something else to occupy your thoughts, something important. I know you've been around and I know you've read a lot of books and I know you've seen a lot of life. More than me probably. But I think there's been something missing from your life, and even though you were married, I think maybe you've been leaning on booze to try and forget about that missing thing."

The waitress put their coffee in front of them.

"Let me ask you something, babe," he said, running his finger around the rim of his coffee mug. "A second ago you said that Tommy had a father, but needs a daddy. Now I've told you all about my marriage to Valerie because I'm a natural-born blabbermouth. You've never told me much about your marriage to Tom. Why wasn't he a 'good daddy?'"

"Oh, Tom tried. But he was British. They're not the warmest people in the world, and I don't think Tom was really ever very comfortable being around children, even his own child. He came from a pretty cold-fish household over there, I think even by their standards. His parents never showed him much warmth or affection when he was growing up. He told me about it, trying to explain I think the reason why he was the way he was. Also, Tom had growing up to do. He was cheating on me left and right, you know. That's what really broke up our marriage."

"What? I can't believe it. Married to a beautiful woman like you and he went chasing after other women? I never would have thought about cheating on you. If I had you at home, I'd stay at home."

"Well, thanks. But that's where the immaturity came in. When Tom hit thirty he panicked. He felt himself getting old, and he didn't like it. He wanted to stay young. Maybe he thought he'd missed out on something. All I know is, he started chasing everything in skirts, and it finished us pretty quick."

"The seven-year itch."

"Yeah. He got it about five years early."

He stretched, yawned and sipped his coffee. He actually felt very happy. Now there was nothing to do but make plans. It was a good feeling.

She continued squeezing his hand.

"I'll say one thing for me," he said. "You might say that I obsess about my age too much, but I can tell you with confidence that I'm not going to have a mid-life crisis now. I'm past the age for that. No danger there."

"No danger there," she repeated, still smiling. She took a sip of her coffee and looked at her watch. "Three O'clock," she said.

"'The dark night of the soul is always three in the morning,'" he said. "Scott Fitzgerald."

"Not tonight it isn't."

23

Yvonne was back. She had already been back once, for her court date over the business with Chantal and the stay-away order months ago. But that had been settled, although somehow I never heard the details, (most likely I just wasn't paying attention) and Yvonne went back to her brother in Santa Clara County.

She knew about Chantal's pregnancy of course; there was no way that was going to stay a secret, even with her up in San Jose. Everyone was wired with devices, and you never saw such a gaggle of gossips as a park full of homeless people with nothing better to do all day but talk about each other when they aren't buying a selling, getting drunk or high or telling lies about their jail experiences.

But now the word was around that she was back in L.A. to stay. What had she come back for? She was avoiding our park, probably for the obvious and sensible reason that another scene with Chantal could only get her back in trouble with the law, and what would have been the point now? Chantal was very pregnant by this time and she and Cage hadn't been around much lately anyway. Cyrus told me that Jennifer was now in a Section 8 apartment of her own, and a temporary cease-fire between Jennifer and her son was in effect, at least until Chantal had the baby. Chantal was said to be staying at Jennifer's place. It made sense. After all this was Jennifer's grandchild Chantal was getting ready to have.

Once the initial dust-devil of tongue-wagging had dissipated, we all went back about our business. Once or twice Cyrus did bring it up that Yvonne was in the neighborhood – he had apparently seen her coming out of the am/pm mini-mart and they had exchanged a few words – but as good as Cyrus was at digging up tidbits of gossip and then spreading them around, he must have come away from this brief encounter with nothing to report, because he reported nothing. We only had it confirmed that Yvonne was indeed back in town.

The Café Patrick was also back in business now that I had screwed up my attempt at going to rehab and was back among my people. (And yes, I was drinking beer again. Solis and company knew about my relapse, but all they could do was cluck their tongues and go back to regarding me as the lost soul that we all knew I was anyway.) I was back to flinging open the van hatch most mornings after my sunrise MGD and brewing up a pot of coffee on the Coleman stove for anyone who wanted to come around and have some.

One morning Cyrus and Marianne were sipping away side-by-side in the open van hatch. I was in my folding chair on the lawn with my coffee, smoking my pipe and keeping an eye out for police cars because I shouldn't have been smoking my pipe right there on the lawn, but it was a nice morning and I liked the feel of the grass under my feet so to hell with the police. Nobody was going to complain anyway because aside from our little group there was nobody else in the park. It was too early.

Also present was my new friend Larry, an American Indian (so he claimed) whom I had just met because he had just gotten out of jail and wandered into our park as lost souls often did. My van proved a magnet, as it so often did, especially in the mornings when the hatch was open and there was fresh coffee to be had. So Larry joined us, with his long gray hair tied back with a rubber band and his girlfriend Bridget, who was a little bit crazy but in our neighborhood we weren't very choosy about crazy people as long as they remained peaceful.

Larry had been a drummer. He would play along to the music on the radio, using a pizza box for a bongo drum or his knees if he had no pizza box. My radio jazz was okay with Larry, but he preferred the golden oldies from Top 40 days, like Barney Devereaux in the days back at Shanghai Jake's. He was a year or two older than I, and loved to sing along with the Beatles and the Turtles and other 1960s stuff. That was fine with me because I remembered the same songs, and sometimes I sang along with him. Larry and I were quite a duo. Think Simon and Garfunkel if they were unable to sing in the same key.

So we were having coffee, Marianne was complaining to Cyrus (again) about his not being attentive enough to her. Larry was pacing up and down the sidewalk, barefoot, coffee in hand, looking for cigarette butts that might have a few puffs left in them. Bridget was sitting under the trees, shooting at the pigeons with an invisible pistol.

Then, along the sidewalk, strolling up Davidson Street, came Yvonne.

She was a bit heavier than I remembered. Beside her was a young woman, also on the heavy side, Mexican.

"Yvonne!" I got up and went over, pipe still in hand, and put my arms around her. "We heard you were back among us! How are you?"

"Hi, Pat." She hugged me tightly. "I missed you."

"I've missed you too, sweetie."

The surprise arrival broke off Marianne's attack on Cyrus. They came over from the van and there were hugs all around.

"Guys, this is Consuelo," Yvonne introduced her friend. "She's the reason I'm here."

Consuelo, whoever she was, shyly waved at all of us and smiled. So Yvonne had found herself a new girlfriend, as Cyrus had predicted she would.

"Consuelo, I'd like you to meet my friends Pat, Cyrus, and Marianne," Yvonne handled the introductions.

By now Larry had broken off his butt-search and joined us. Bridget had put away her invisible gun and left the pigeons in peace.

"These other folks I don't know," Yvonne smiled awkwardly. I took over and introduced Larry and Bridget.

"*Un gran placer conocerte,"* Larry said as he shook hands with Consuelo.

"Muchas gracias, señor amable," she replied with a curtsy and a giggle.

"I thought you said you were an Indian," I said.

"Indians sometimes speak Spanish."

"You got me there."

I offered them coffee. They accepted and I went into the van to rummage around for a second folding chair that I knew I had in there someplace. One of them could sit in my chair. Wherever Yvonne sat, I wanted to be close to her. I didn't want to miss any possible story.

They met on Facebook. Yvonne was still up in Santa Clara County at her brother's place and Consuelo lived in West L.A. Consuelo sent Yvonne a friend request and they began talking every day on FB and then on the phone. They met for the first time in May, when they had the Gay Pride parade on Santa Monica Blvd. and the two women decided that would be a good excuse for Yvonne to come down for a long weekend. They went together to the Dyke Day party out near Dodger stadium, had a wonderful time there and spent the weekend at the beach and at Consuelo's place where they cooked and played music and smoked weed and talked a lot and decided what the hell, why shouldn't Yvonne come on down and move in with Consuelo, since the job she had working security at a bank in Milpitas wasn't any great shakes and she could easily find that kind of work if she wanted to back here in L.A. which was her regular turf anyway? So Yvonne rented a Ryder truck and Consuelo went up to San Jose to help her pack her stuff and they trucked it all back down the coast together and now Yvonne was staying at Consuelo's place. Consuelo worked at WalMart on the evening shift, stocking shelves.

Consuelo sat in my director's chair. Yvonne sat cross-legged on the grass at Consuelo's feet. Larry tried to to talk to Consuelo some more in his halting Spanish, gave up and switched back to English. I scrounged up another coffee mug and a used 7-Eleven cup from the van, rinsing it out from my water jug.

I said to Consuelo and Yvonne, "I hope you take it black. I don't have any milk or sugar."

"No sugar?" Yvonne stage-whined.

"I had some, but it doesn't last long around here. Marianne puts about fourteen sugars in her coffee."

"Oh, man."

Marianne just looked at me, open-mouthed, and gave me a "Well?" like, "is it MY fault I like my coffee sweet?"

"I'll tell you what," I said. "Since this is an occasion, I'll go down to El Mercado and get some sugar and milk. Yvonne, will you come along with me? Give us a chance to catch up a little." I really did want to talk to her alone.

Yvonne looked up at Consuelo, who gave her OK by kissing the air.

With that, Yvonne and I walked across Davidson Street together and headed for the market.

"So how've you been, Pat? I heard you went through rehab."

"I went *to* rehab. I didn't stay long."

"What happened?"

"I got into a fight."

"You're kidding! I can't see you in a fight. You're the most un-violent person I've ever met."

"It wasn't much of a fight." I looked her up and down as she walked along beside me, then blurted out what I had noticed when I first saw her.

"Forgive me, honey, but you've put on a pound or two, haven't you?"

"Yeah," she said. "More than a pound or two. This is what I used to look like before you met me. Did I ever show you my driver's license?"

She pulled out her wallet and showed me. Yes, she had been heavier when that license photo was taken.

"That was me before you and I met," she said. "I'm clean now, Pat. When I was with Babe I was tweaking all the time." ("Babe" was what she called Chantal when they weren't trying to kill each other.) "That kept me thin. This is what I look like when I'm clean. Sorry," she smiled.

I put my arm around her. "So you are managing to stay clean, then. I'm proud of you."

"You can give Consuelo credit for that," she said. "She's been clean for two years now. She used to do heroin. Not anymore. We're good for each other. How about you? Staying sober?"

I shrugged off the subject. "Cyrus is."

"Really?"

"He hasn't had a beer or a shot in months that I know of. He's sticking to sports drinks these days. I have to hand it to him. He really wants to get back under a roof with his girls. He's doing everything the judge tells him to do."

"You think he'll make it?"

"*No se. Vamos ver.*" I shrugged again.

"You speak Spanish too?"

"No. But I took it in high school."

There was a pause. "Have you seen Chantal?" she asked. ("Babe" must have been a slip.)

"Not for a couple weeks. I think she and Cage are staying with his mother. You know the baby's due any time now."

"I'm glad for her. The baby will help settle her down. I just wish if this had to happen the father could have been somebody else."

"You really don't like old Cage, do you?" I tried to make light of it. But she wasn't having it.

"He's lower than dogshit. He was the guy who got her tweaking in the first place. I thought I could get her off it, but then I started using, stupid me. Then I went out and worked and scrounged to support both our habits. Then I caught them screwing one day."

"In broad daylight?"

"No, it was after dark. I just said 'one day.' I meant one night. He was right there, fuckin' my wife in front of God and everybody! I swear if I'd had something to hit him with I would have laid his skull open."

"And hers too, probably."

She sighed. "Yeah, hers too, probably."

"Well, that explains it. Why the two of you were fighting all the time. I knew it couldn't have been just because of whose charger it was or who owed who for drugs."

"I still love Babe. I'll always love her. But that was fucked up. It was because of the drugs, you know? I'm really glad to have all of that behind me."

"You're *sure* you do," I said. We had arrived at the store.

"Would I be here if I wasn't? Consuelo is so good for me. I'm so lucky. We're both clean and sober. And she has a job! I'll find a job and we'll do fine. One thing I'm sure of, she won't be out screwing her dealer behind my back. She's serious about staying clean. It's good."

We went into the store and bought a box of cube sugar and a pint of milk. I added a 22-oz. can of Icehouse for later, slipping it into my jacket pocket as we walked out to the sidewalk. Yvonne didn't say anything about it. We went back to the park and I gave her another hug before returning her to Consuelo.

And so it came to pass that the park had its second baby. That is, we in the park saw the second baby come along since I had been around. Which made everyone in our little gypsy band...interested parties of one kind or another. These things get complicated when you're on the street.

Of course we all wanted to see Chantal's baby as soon as we could.

It was summer now, and I was taking a nap under a tree, which I often did after lunch because lunch was usually followed my third or sometimes fourth beer of the day back then, which meant that a civilized siesta was in order. By that time of day it was too hot in the van for sleeping, especially at the beginning of August, which it was now. I would take thin rubber thin mat from the top of my cot and flake out under a tree.

Ed came weaving up and started talking to me. I drank beer all morning, but Ed drank vodka all morning, so he was drunker than I was and didn't care that I was napping.

I heard a sharp noise that sounded like my name, which jolted me up out of my pleasant doze, and don't we all just hate that?

"Pat," he said a second time.

I opened my eyes but didn't sit up. "Ed. Ed. What the hell?"

"What's that?" he pointed.

"What's what?"

"That."

I looked where he was pointing. A large plastic ziplock bag lay next to me on the grass. It had not been there when I drifted off to sleep.

The baggie contained a ham-and-cheese on white bread, an apple, a Juicy Juice with straw, two granola bars and a bottle of water. There were also a tube of toothpaste, toothbrush, razor, a mini-can of shaving lather, a bar of soap, some sanitizing hand wipes, and a comb. There was also a napkin for the food.

"Someone left me some stuff while I was asleep," I said.

People sometimes did this. People with good hearts, or on a mission of salvation, or both, would see us bums lying under the trees and assume that we were drunk, stoned or whatever, but visibly in need and presumably in despair.

Often, in addition to handing out food, they wanted to pray with you, or over you, or they would invite one and all to join them under a tree for prayer and Bible-reading.

I never joined in these grub-for-God sessions myself but Cyrus always did. He wasn't being a hypocrite, either. Cyrus was a loudly self-professed Christian and was perfectly happy to join in the prayer circle. He often prayed the loudest of the group. If he got a sandwich or a slice of pizza out of it too, so much the better.

But sometimes, like now, someone would just quietly leave things for us and slip away.

The sheet of lined paper was a folded-up note, block-printed in blue pencil.

"Hi. My name is Cheyanne, and I want to help you. I bought you some gifts that hopefully you will like and get some use from. There is no need to be scared or feel alone. From Cheyanne."

After her name she had drawn a little heart.

Cheyanne. What a pretty name. Probably a kid, judging from the writing.

"Her name is Cheyanne," I said. "She saw me lying here and left this stuff for me."

"Sweet of her. There are still some good folks around," Ed said.

"I wish I had been awake so I could have thanked her. I'm not as badly off as she thinks. I'm sorry she thinks I'm that badly off. I'm glad to have this stuff, but I feel stupid. She couldn't have known that that van over there belongs to me, that there are people here worse off than I am." I picked up the goodie bag with one hand and rubbed my head with the other.

"Goddamn it, bless her heart!" I cried.

"Bless her heart," Ed repeated with his familiar vodka-befuddled nod.

I still have that note. I carry it with me and I don't plan ever to lose it. And although I'm much too old to have a daughter now, when I think about it, I always think that if I did, by some fluke of nature, have a daughter, I would definitely want to name her Cheyanne. It's such a beautiful name. More girls should have such a name.

But back to Ed. He was here on bigger business than my little gift from an angel donor. .

"Chantal had the baby," he said.

"Huh?"

"Chantal had the baby."

Since we all knew what a crush Ed had on Chantal, it didn't surprise me that he had this news before anyone else. We all had our sources.

"When?" I sat up now and rubbed my head.

"About three this morning."

"How do you know?"

"I called Kaiser."

"Did everything go okay?"

"They didn't say it didn't."

"Was it a boy or a girl?"

His hands fell to his sides. "I forgot to ask."

"Good job, Bob Woodward. I'll never hire you to work on my newspaper."

"Sorry. I was excited. I hung up the phone too fast. But I'm going out there to see her and the baby. I'll let you know when I come back. You want come along?"

There was no way I was going to get into Ed's car with him begging for a DUI like he was now.

"No thanks. Not now. I'm going to go find Cyrus and Marianne. They'll want to see the baby too. We'll come out later."

You're wondering why I didn't discourage Ed from driving. I knew there was no point, that's why. There was no talking to Ed when he'd had a few. If he was going to drive, he was going to drive. Unless you were prepared to wrestle him for his keys all you could do was hope and pray that he didn't hurt himself or someone else. Or that the cops would get him. Luckily he never went far. And now, after giving me the big news, off he went, slowly, in the general direction of his bunged-up '95 Oldsmobile Cutlass, parked over on McKinley.

Maybe he would get behind the wheel and fall asleep. He'd done that before.

That got me rid of Ed. But then I looked around the park and there was no sign of Cyrus. His and Marianne's stuff was right there under their usual tree, covered with their usual tarp, but they were nowhere to be seen. Where did they keep wandering off to?

There was nothing to do but wait until they came back, which they had to sooner or later. I set up my director's chair under the same tree where I had been sleeping, lit my pipe (after a quick visual sweep for police cars) and sat down to read.

While I waited for Cyrus to return, Larry came ambling up the grass from the Davidson side of the park. He had an old-fashioned boom box with him, one with AM/FM radio and a cassette tape player. Sanyo. Vintage 1990 or so.

"Hi, Larry," I said. "Where's Bridget?"

"She has a class this afternoon. She's taking computer science, I think I told you."

"Yeah, you did tell me. Where'd you get that?" .

"Belongs to my friend Luis. He let me borrow it. He's a real oldies fan, like you and me. Listen to this."

He switched it on. Marvin Gaye was in the middle of *I Heard It Through The Grapevine.*

"I haven't heard that in years," I said. "I was in junior high when that was on the radio."

"Me too. He's got a whole tape here he made of this stuff."

We listened to music for a while, there on the grass. Oldies. But when the tape came to *Count Me In* by Gary Lewis and the Playboys, I suddenly felt like someone had punched me in the stomach. I asked Larry to skip that one.

"You don't like that song?"

"I love that song. But please, just don't play it. It reminds me...never mind. I don't want to hear Gary Lewis and the Playboys. Don't ask me why."

Larry fast-forwarded to the next song. We started singing along.

In a break between songs, I took another look around.

"I wish Cyrus would get here. I'd like to go see Chantal's baby and it just occurred to me that I'm going to need Cyrus to do that."

"Who's Chantal?"

"I forgot you're still kind of a newbie around here, don't know everybody yet," I said.

I told him about Chantal and Yvonne.

"But it just hit me," I went on. "I don't know Chantal's last name. If I go to the hospital by myself I won't know who to ask for. Cyrus will know her last name. You want to come with us if we go?"

"Sure. Bridget's in school and I saw my parole officer this morning. I don't have anything else to do."

Cyrus and Marianne finally did show up. They had been at the Salvation Army grabbing a free lunch along with Terry I gave them the news, told them I'd heard it from Ed.

"But I've been waiting for you because I don't know Chantal's last name. Do you?"

"Sure. It's Rickman," Cyrus said. "And Chantal isn't her real first name, either. Her name is Charlene. She goes by Chantal 'cause she likes the sound of it."

"Charlene Rickman. Well. Are we going?"

"Let's go."

The four of us piled into the van and off we went.

"Was it a girl or a boy?" Marianne asked me as I drove.

"Ed forgot to ask."

"Figures," said Cyrus, looking out the window.

At the hospital Cyrus asked for Charlene Rickman and we were sent up to the third floor. She was in Room 308 and the door was half-open and thus the Three Godfathers, plus Marianne, swept into the hospital room.

Cage was there, standing beside Chantal's bed holding the baby. Odd that he would be holding the baby and not she, I thought, but our attention turned right away to Chantal, who lay in bed in her hospital gown, looking tired of course. She wore glasses. I didn't know Chantal wore glasses. She never wore them in the park.

"Hi, guys," she smiled wearily. If Ed had already been there, she was surely expecting the rest of us.

"Where's Ed?" I asked.

"He came and went a while ago."

"I told him to leave," Cage said. "He was drunk."

"He's always drunk," I said.

"I don't want any drunks around my baby boy." Cage, a drug-dealer, didn't want drunks around his baby boy. Complicated world.

"Oh, so it did turn out to be a boy," I said, looking over Cage's shoulder as if the baby's face would confirm its gender. "Ed told us you'd had the baby, but he forgot to ask if it was a girl or a boy."

"Oh, sorry everybody," Chantal said. "Meet Malachi James Rickman. Babe, give him to me."

So now Cage was "Babe."

"Why'd you pick 'Malachi?'" I asked.

"I wanted him to have a biblical name."

"I like that," Cyrus nodded. "People used to name babies from the Bible, praise the Lord. I wish more people still did."

I couldn't resist. "Then why do you keep naming your daughters after yourself?" I asked.

"Aah," he waved me away like a fly. I stifled a laugh. Sometimes teasing Cyrus was so easy it wasn't worth the trouble.

"He was born at 3:25 this morning," Chantal said, "and he weighs seven pounds eight ounces. I named him James after my father. Come on, Babe, gimme."

Cage reluctantly handed her the baby.

"He's beautiful, Chantal," Marianne said.

"Women always say that," Cyrus said. "Look at him. He looks like Yoda." But Cyrus was visibly pleased as he said this.

"Newborns always look like Yoda," I said. "Can I hold him?"

"Don't listen to them, Chantal," Marianne said. "He's gorgeous, just like my last one was."

"Can I hold him?" I asked again. "I want you to take a picture of me holding him." I leaned over and kissed Chantal on the forehead. She handed Malachi to me. I cradled him in my arms. "Hi, Mal, hi, buddy," I whispered.

"You drop that baby and I'll kill you," Cage said.

"Up yours. I was holding babies when you weren't even a gleam in your father's eye."

"I can smell beer on you. Don't drop him."

I cuddled little Malachi, my left hand supporting his head, and rocked him.

"I ain't gonna drop him," I said. "I wouldn't mind dropping *you*. From about six stories. But I ain't gonna drop him."

This kind of banter was common among us. Cage ignored me, too much the proud papa to be offended just now.

"Got your cellphone, Chantal? Will you take a picture?" I asked again.

"Yeah, sure," she got her purse from the nightstand and fumbled for her Smartphone.

Just as Chantal was about to take a picture of Malachi and me, the little guy decided he wanted no part of these proceedings and broke out into a screaming fit. What Chantal posted on Facebook half an hour later was a photo of me grinning like an idiot with a red-faced infant in my arms yelling like a motorist who's been cut off in traffic.

"Is there something wrong with him?" Larry asked.

"No. All newborns scream like that," I said as I handed the baby back to Chantal. "I read an article by a pediatrician. Newborns come into the world pissed off. Think about it. They've just been kicked out of a nice, warm, comfortable place where all their needs were taken care of and now suddenly they're shoved out into our big, cold, dirty, noisy world. They don't like it. They get used to it after about the first three months. Doctors call it the fourth trimester."

"Thank you, Mister Spock," Cage sneered. He had to get back at me for my crack about dropping him from six stories. "What makes you so smart?"

"That's 'Doctor Spock,' genius. I read a lot. You ought to try it sometime. Of course you'd have to learn how first," I said.

Cage was in a good enough mood to just give me the finger and left it at that.

He wasn't to stay in a good mood for long. Because as it turned out, neither Chantal nor Cage nor Cage's mother Jennifer ended up losing much sleep over little Malachi. Chantal tested positive for drugs when she checked in at Kaiser, just as Marianne had the previous fall, and just as they had done with Marianne, Child Protective Services took the baby and put him in a foster home.

The last time I saw either Cage or Chantal they were both working on getting clean, hoping to get the county to give Malachi back to them.

When we returned to the park that day, the first thing I did, after popping over to Crown for my late-afternoon MGD, was go into the library to use the bathroom and check my email on one of the public terminals.

I saw Bill in his usual spot at one of the long tables, poring over what was most likely one of his books on religion. He looked up and saw me as I was passing, caught my eye and waved me over to him.

"Hey, Bill," I said. "What's up?"

"While you were gone there was a guy in the park looking for you," Bill said.

"Looking for me? Who would be looking for me? Was it a cop?"

"No. Definitely not a cop. But he was looking for you. He asked for you by name."

"Bob the Bum?"

"No. I know what Bob the Bum looks like. This was another guy."

"Well, what did he look like?"

"He was a black man, kind of tall. But he didn't look like...well, you know, I don't want to sound racist, but he didn't look like most black people – you know, most black people have the kind of flatter nose and thicker lips than we have? He had the dark complexion, but his face didn't look like an ordinary black person's face. Kind of, you know, more European."

"Did he give his name?":

"Yeah, he said his name was Sam. He told me his last name, but I forget what it was."

"Fasil," I said. Couldn't be anyone else.

I told Bill about Chantal and the baby. But now I was thinking about Sam. How in the world had he managed to track me to Aurora Park? And more importantly, why would he bother to?

24

It was a hot, dry day, at the beach. Usually at the beach there was at least a breeze. Not today.

They had a beach umbrella, and to get into more of its shade he moved closer to her. She was half-dozing and his moving around awakened her. She lifted the straw hat from her face. Under it she wore sunglasses.

"Sorry to disturb you," he said. "I wanted to get in some shade. It's not even cool at the beach today."

She smiled, shading her eyes with her hand. "I was thinking about going in for a swim anyway. You're right, it's very hot."

His glance caressed the length of her body. She wore a teal two-piece swimsuit. He had the urge to put his hands on her right then and there, but it was indeed very hot, and even if it weren't so warm, there were easily five thousand people milling around.

"Probably no cooler in the water," he said.

"Where are Shari and Tommy?"

"They walked up to the pier. She promised him ice cream."

"Rub some sunscreen on me, will you?"

"With pleasure. I've been sitting here wanting to manhandle you."

He got a tube of Neutrogena out of her straw beach bag and began rubbing the goo into her back and shoulders. "You should put some on, too," she said.

"I will as soon as I'm done smearing it on you. I'm giving myself a hard-on here."

"Down boy," she giggled over her shoulder. "We're not alone."

"So when did you say the wedding's going to be again?"

"Shari and Stan's? She said June. I don't know if they've picked a date yet."

He had only heard about any of this that morning.

"And where did you say they're getting married? At the zoo? Even if I had a thing for giraffes, I'd think that was crazy. I never heard of anybody getting married at the damn zoo."

"I thought the same thing when she told me. But I looked it up on the Internet. The Santa Barbara Zoo is a popular place for weddings. It's in a beautiful setting, has nice mountain views, it's spacious, they take care of everything. And Shari and Stan are both animal lovers, they go to charity events for animals. In fact they met at the Humane Society. Shari worked in the office there for a while and one day Stanley came in wanting to adopt a dog. So what the hell? Let 'em get married and pet the baby elephants if that's what they want."

"I'll go if I'm invited, but I'm not wearing a pith helmet."

"Oh, you're invited all right. I'm going to be my sister's maid of honor and I want you there for moral support. Also, I admit I want to show you off to Stan's friends."

"Why? I may be the same age as Bruce Willis, and I may be as bald as Bruce Willis, but I sure as hell don't look like him."

"I think you look better. And you're certainly better-looking than Stan."

"Everything has its compensations. Stan could buy and sell me ten times."

"I wouldn't sell you for anything."

"You're prejudiced."

"Kiss me."

He kissed her. "It really *is* hot," she said. "I'm going to go jump in the water. Care to join me?"

"Tell you what, you go ahead and I'll join you in a few minutes. I'm going to wait for your sister and Tommy to come back. Tommy told his Aunt Shari that he wanted to bring me back an ice cream too."

"It'll probably be all melted."

"Probably."

She strode off toward the surf. He watched her as she walked away, her body undulating with that rhythm and natural grace that seems to come built-in with some women. Although happiness was something that he had known so rarely in his life that sometimes he found himself wondering if he even knew what the word meant, just then he considered himself a very lucky man.

Sharon, wearing a yellow one-piece swimsuit and sunglasses (why not a two-piece? She had every bit as fine a figure as her sister) and Tommy in his Sonic the Hedgehog swimming trunks came walking up the sand from the pier. Each clutched an ice cream cone, and, true to his word, the little boy clutched one in each hand. He had brought along a half-melted but proudly unlicked one for Patrick.

"The ice cream man is here," Sharon smiled.

"Thank you very much, sir," he accepted the cone from Tommy, quickly wiping away some melted ice cream with his index finger. "Butter pecan?"

"That's what you asked for," Sharon said.

"If you could find it."

"Yeah, Scoops had it. They're up there by the boardwalk."

"On a day like this I'll bet they're doing a land-office business. Well, come on. It's hotter than h – blazes out here. Let's see if the three of us can scrooch in under this umbrella and enjoy our ice cream in some shade."

What he really wanted was an ice-cold beer. But true to his talk with Melissa on the night he had proposed, he was trying not drink in front of Tommy. Beer wouldn't taste good with butter pecan ice cream anyway.

The three of them crowded under the umbrella. He was half in the sun, but there really wasn't room for all three of them. "Where's Melissa?" Sharon asked.

"She went in the water. It got a little hot for her."

"It *is* hot."

"So," he said, looking at Shari and rubbing Tommy's head, "Getting married at the zoo."

She laughed and licked her cone. "I know it sounds insane!"

"No, no. Well, yes, yes. But Melissa explained that it's really a nice place."

"It's beautiful. And we both love animals. It just seems like the perfect spot. Melissa told you how animals were involved in our first meeting, Stan and I."

"She reminded me again just now. Bet it's gonna be expensive."

"Stan doesn't mind. He's had a good year. Besides, it's going to be a small wedding. We don't expect more than twenty-five or thirty people, counting you and Melissa. You are going to be there?"

"Melissa's gonna be maid of honor, right?"

"Yes, but I want you there too."

"I'll be there. Maybe after a glass or two of champagne I'll start feeding hors d'oeuvres to the giraffes."

"That's the spirit. Although I doubt the zoo allows hors d'oeuvre-feeding to the animals."

She leaned over and kissed him on the cheek. "Thank you, Pat."

"Thank you," he said.

"Where's my mommy?" Tommy asked.

"She went in for a swim," he told the boy. "She was hot and she wanted to cool off. She should be right back. Finish your ice cream."

"And what about you?" Sharon said. "I heard a rumor that you and my sister are getting married too."

"We have discussed it. It looks like it. Seems to be a season of weddings, all right."

"Well, let me offer these congratulations --" she kissed him on the cheek again – "and then let me be a nosey sister here. Where and when are you two planning to tie the knot?"

"We haven't really gotten that far yet. I mean, we've discussed it of course, but then when we heard about you and Stan, we decided not to steal your thunder. We'll probably wait until later this summer. Or maybe even fall. There's no hurry beyond the fact that I'm a lot closer to the cemetery than the rest of you."

"Oh, stop that. Melissa told me you get silly about your age."

"It's not that silly. If I were Melissa's age I'd say we had all the time in the world. But I don't have all the time in the world for anything anymore." He punctuated this comment with a smile. No point in being morbid.

"Then why wait at all?" she said. "Why don't we make it a double wedding? We'll all four get married in June."

"That's really very sweet of you, Shari," he said. "But I don't want to get married at the zoo. I'm kind of old-fashioned that way. I was thinking maybe a Chinese restaurant."

She crinkled her nose and waved her ice cream cone at him like she was going to stick it in his face.

"Are you going to marry my mommy?" Tommy asked him.

"Oh, come on, big guy," he said to the boy. "You and I already talked about that, didn't we? We had a real man-to-man talk, just us guys. Remember?"

"Oh, yeah."

"And we agreed that we're going to be a family, right? And your real daddy will still be your daddy. But you and I will be real good pals."

"I won't live with my daddy anymore?"

"You will sometimes. Your mommy and daddy are working that out." He looked at Sharon. "I'm staying out of it."

"Smart man."

"Will I have a baby brother?"

He looked at Sharon again, who stifled a laugh and looked away.

"Uh…well, don't count on it. Tell you what. We'll see." Best change the subject. "Hey, hey. You want to go find your mommy?"

"Yeah."

"She'll probably be right back, but finish your ice cream. If Mommy isn't back by the time you finish your ice cream, we'll go look for her, okay?" He had finished his own ice cream while talking with Sharon.

"Okay." Tommy turned his attention to his rocky-road cone. He gave it three or four good licks.

"How about a sand castle? Would you like to build a sand castle?" Anything to keep the talk away from baby brothers.

"Yeah!"

"We'll find Mommy and then I'll help you build a sand castle."

Sharon smiled at him as she licked up the last of her ice cream and bit into the sugar cone. "Fancy footwork," she said. "Oh, look. Melissa."

Melissa strode up from the surf, body water-droplet glistening, hair wet and bedraggled, feet covered with sand like breaded veal cutlets. She smoothed her hair back with both hands. "Brr, that was bracing!" She said. "Honey, hand me a towel, will you?"

He handed her both a towel and her sunglasses.

"The air may be hot, but the water's cold!" she said.

"Well, it's only the end of April," he said. "The water hasn't had a chance to get warm yet."

"I doubt if it's more than sixty out there. Hi, sweetheart!" she said to Tommy. "Did Aunt Shari get you ice cream?"

The boy held up his cone by way of reply. He had nearly finished it. "Are we still gonna build a sandcastle?" he asked.

"Of course. I promised him a sandcastle." he said to Melissa, unnecessarily. "Here, sit in the shade next to your sister." He moved away from the umbrella.

"Thanks. I'm still pretty cold. Let me sit in the sun for a minute." Still rubbing her hair with the towel, she plopped down on the sand and slipped her sunglasses on.

"Shari and I were just sitting here talking about this...season of weddings we're having," he said. "She knows you and I have been talking about it."

"Yeah, I suggested you guys should join us in Santa Barbara and we make it a double-wedding," Sharon said. "But Pat says he doesn't want to get married at the zoo."

"That wouldn't work out anyway," Melissa said. She turned to him and said, "I meant to talk to you about that, honey. What would you think about getting married in September or October?"

"I already told Shari we were probably going to wait until after the dust has cleared from her and Stan's nuptials anyway," he said. "Yeah, sure. Waiting until summer's over is fine with me. I kind of like the idea of getting married in the fall. October always was my favorite month, even if it does include my birthday."

"Why wouldn't June work for you, just out of curiosity?" Sharon asked.

"Oh, I was going to surprise Patrick with this little bit of news, but I suppose I can tell both of you at the same time. The Easter engagement that I just wrapped up at the Ciel went great. Of course Pat already knows that because he was there on my last night. But guess what? I have an agent now. That was going to be the first part of my surprise, Pat. Yeah, I've been taken on by the McCurry agency in Burbank. Marshall Osgood hooked me up with them. They're the agents for Marshall and his combo. Well, now they're my agents too. How about that?"

"You're on your way!" he cried, leaning over to throw his arms around her. "This is great news! I guess now you can get out of that dive on Westwood."

"I already have. I gave my notice last Thursday. The guys were happy for me. Tony even bought everyone a round of drinks. Of course there were only about six people in the place that night."

"Congratulations, little sister! I'm so happy for you!" Sharon said as she came over and hugged Melissa.

"So what's the other half of the surprise?" he asked. "You said that was the first part."

"Are we gonna build a sandcastle?" Tommy asked.

"Yes, yes, of course, big guy," he said. "But just a second. What is the other half of the surprise, baby?"

"The other half of the surprise," she said, still rubbing her hair with the towel, "is that they already got me a booking. I open June 1 at the Barona casino."

"Where's that?" Sharon asked.

"It's down in San Diego County. Up in the mountains."

"It's run by one of the Indian tribes," he said. "There's a couple of them down there. We also have them closer. Pechanga. Those Indian casinos are all over the place."

"I'm going to be the opening act for Gary Lewis and the Playboys," Melissa said.

"Gary Lewis and the Playboys?" he said, surprised. "Are those guys still alive?"

"Alive and touring."

"God. Gary Lewis. They were on the radio when I was in elementary school. But it makes sense. Barona. Remember the night I came to Shanghai Jake's and you introduced me to your friend Barney?"

"How could I not remember that night? It was the night you proposed," she smiled and touched his leg.

"Barney and I were talking about this while you were tending bar. Those casinos book a lot of nostalgia shows. Because they cater heavily to my generation, the sixties geezers. Retired people like to gamble, and since the tribes went into the casino business, people don't have to go all the way to Vegas to do it."

"So it turns out I didn't have to go all the way to Vegas either."

"You going to take Tommy with you?"

She gathered her son into her lap and kissed the top of his head.

"Are we going to build a sandcastle?" the boy asked again.

"Yes, yes."

"I won't be able to," she said. "He'll be back with his father by then. Of course, Shari will be on her honeymoon, and –"

"Probably best for Tommy," he said. "For now," he added quickly. "But we'll have to work that out. We will."

"Do you think you could stay with him? You know, at my place? I could talk to Tom."

"Wouldn't be a problem, except I work mostly at night."

"After we're married things will be different. You will give up the cab, won't you? Find something you can do in the daytime?"

"Guess I'll have to," he smiled. "Oh, hell, I'm not married to that taxi."

"Why don't you go back into journalism?"

"I'm a little old for that, I think. Besides, it doesn't pay squat. I make more money driving the cab than I did on that last rag I worked for, back when my dad was alive."

"You're not too old. Stop that. And I expect to be making pretty good money myself, soon." She rocked the little boy on her lap and gazed out at the ocean.

"We'll talk about it, honey. Right now," he said, getting up and brushing the sand off himself, "this young man and I have a date with some wet sand." He reached down and took Tommy's hand. "Come on, big fella. Let's go build the Escorial."

The two women watched as the man and the little boy walked off, hand-in-hand, toward the surf.

"He's a keeper," Sharon said.

"They both are."

"What about Pat's drinking? You told me you've discussed that with him."

"You haven't seen him with a beer in his hand today, have you? Of course he promised me he wouldn't drink when Tommy was around."

"I can see that he's very fond of Tommy."

"And Tommy's very fond of him. I hope things work out."

"They have a way of doing that, you know."

Tommy was obviously a precocious little boy. He had already noticed that the child would hear something once and remember it, and it was obvious from the questions he asked that when he got older he was going to be quite a handful to his teachers. Now, for instance, he spoke up as they made their way down to the wet, packed sand, asking what a "core-e-all" was.

"What?"

"A core-e-all. You said we were gonna build a core-e-all."

"Oh, the Escorial. That's a castle. A famous castle. It's in Spain. That's far away from here."

"Is it big?"

"Real big. They built it for the King of Spain."

"Does he live in it now?"

"No. He died a long time ago. Other kings lived in it after him, though."

"Have you seen it?"

"No. I haven't been to Spain. But I read about it." He had somewhere, sometime, maybe in a dentist's office, read an article on Spain in the *National Geographic* that had photos of El Escorial, not far from Madrid. He tried to remember some of what he'd read, that it was commissioned by Phillip II in the 1560s and that Spanish kings, Bourbons and Habsburgs both, had been buried there for the past 500 years or so. Then he tried to remember something about the castle that might be of interest to the boy, who had never heard of Phillip II or the Bourbons or the Hapsburgs, and had probably never seen a castle outside of a picture book or on TV.

"It took a long time to build," he said.

"Real long?"

"Real long. About twenty years, I think."

There was a pause while the boy figured that one out. "How long will it take to build our castle?" he asked.

"Not that long. I really don't think your mommy and your Aunt Shari want to wait twenty years for us to finish. But we'll take our time, right, big guy? We have the rest of the afternoon." He squeezed Tommy's hand. "We have all the time in the world, you and me."

They dropped to their knees and started scooping together wet sand with which to make walls for their castle. Suddenly he remembered that he had forgotten to put sunscreen on himself as Melissa had suggested he do. She had put some on the boy when they arrived at the beach. Still, he decided that they had better not stay out in the sun too long.

25

Frankie got six months in county jail. Part of it was for whacking Andrew and me with his skateboard that night at the van. A skateboard is considered a deadly weapon. Part of it was for last January's breaking of the window at Crown Liquor, with that same skateboard, and then not paying for the damage. He also had a handful of outstanding warrants on other things, including failure to meet with his parole officer.

He was about to be released, and there was some curiosity, even some minor concern, about what that might mean to me.

Frankie had assaulted Andrew and me, not just me. But no one seemed especially worried about Andrew. The consensus among the parkies was that since Frankie and Andrew quarreled all the time anyway, as far as Andrew was concerned this would be written off as just one more incident. More line-dancing, as Cyrus might have said.

But with me it was different, or so rumor had it. Frankie and Andrew's past scuffles were one thing, but it had been I who called the police that night. I turned him in. Therefore if Frankie were going to be mad at anybody when he got out of jail, he was going to be mad at me. So the story went.

I told all of this to my new friend Larry as we sat on the grass one afternoon watching the girls go by (if you remember that old song.) We had one in particular that we watched for, a pretty little Asian girl who jogged around the park, pods in her ears, every afternoon about four O'clock. The first time she jogged past us in her pink shorts, white tank top and headband, we were singing along to *Bluebird* by Buffalo Springfield on

Larry's borrowed boom-box. We promptly dubbed her "Bluebird." We would watch for Bluebird every time we sat there, oldies playing and cold beers from Crown or El Mercado in brown paper sacks in our hands.

Larry had not been among the park crowd long enough to know everyone yet, although he automatically became one of us honorary godfathers to little Malachi Rickman by virtue of having been with us when we went to see Chantal's baby for the first time. Larry also met Chantal that afternoon. He found her cute, as most guys did – it was all that hair. Of course that day she had also had the glow of new motherhood on her, until CPS took the baby anyway.

But Larry had not met Frankie yet, obviously, since Frankie was still in jail when Larry got out of jail and showed up in the park. Larry listened me tell the story of the Night of the Skateboard, and the details of Frankie's arrest, with wrinkled brow. Larry liked to appear street-savvy, and not knowing Frankie, he strongly suggested that I should be on my guard.

"I've seen plenty of guys come out of jail pissed off at whoever got them tossed in there, wanting payback," he said.

I repeated what I had said months earlier, that I was about as scared of Frankie as I was of Bob the Bum, which then required that I explain to Larry who Bob the Bum was. (We hadn't seen Bob the Bum since the day they fished him out of the bushes, soaked to the skin, and took him away. I hoped he was all right, or at least still alive.)

"You should get something to defend yourself with," Larry said.

"I don't need anything to defend myself with."

"You know what they say, better safe than sorry."

"I got a frying pan," I offered.

"How heavy is it?"

"It's cast-iron. Marianne gave it to me. She found it and said I might be able to use it, since I have the Coleman stove now."

"That's good. You could crack his skull with that. But you should probably get a baseball bat, or maybe a golf putter. Something you could really swing."

"I'm not going to need a baseball bat or a golf putter," I said. "I'll be okay."

"Well, you're my bro and I got your back," Larry declared. "You remember that. Just say the word, day or night, I'll be right here with my homeboys."

Cyrus knew Frankie just as well as I did, and like me he wasn't especially worried about what Frankie might do to me when the county turned him loose. When I told Cyrus of Larry's promise to come running with his "homeboys" if I needed rescuing, Cyrus rolled his eyeballs.

"His homeboys'll show up on their walkers," he said.

I laughed at this. Cyrus was referring to the obvious: Larry was the oldest guy in the park now, a couple of years older than I. He liked to tell war stories about his street fights. But Larry was only five feet six inches tall, and Cyrus had already figured him as one of those little guys who prefer their imaginations to their memories.

High Noon, if that's what it was going to be, arrived about eight-fifteen a.m. a week later.

Business was petering out at the Café Patrick. Everyone was finishing their coffee, smoking and either enjoying or ignoring John Coltrane on the radio. I went to the drinking fountain, dumped the grounds in the bushes behind it and rinsed out the coffeepot.

I was back in the van with the hatch open, stashing the coffeepot in the little storage area over the cab, when I heard someone out on the sidewalk say, "Hi, Frankie."

I stepped out of the van into the sunlight. Everyone suddenly became not exactly dead-quiet, but subdued, like they didn't know what to expect next. Coltrane was blowing a chorus of *My Favorite Things.* Frankie squatted on the sidewalk next to my van. I took a seat in my director's chair and lit my pipe, trying to be as cool as I could. I wasn't really afraid of Frankie, but it was an awkward, embarrassing moment. When I'd had Yvonne arrested, it was understood that I had only called 911 because I was afraid she and Chantal were going to hurt each other. It had not been my intention to get either of them arrested. This was different. Frankie had assaulted me and I'd had him thrown in the jug for it, and he hadn't just stayed for a weekend. It had been half a year. All eyes were furtively on Frankie, who looked up and down Davidson Street before he spoke.

"So, I guess I'm too late for coffee," he said.

"Yeah, I just cleaned out the pot," I said.

"Here, Frankie, finish mine," Cyrus said. "It's still hot."

"Got sugar in it?"

"Yeah."

"Thanks." Frankie accepted the 7-Eleven cup from Cyrus.

He finished the coffee, put the cup on the sidewalk next to the van's right rear tire, stood up, brushed off his jeans, said he was going to go look for his father and see if he had any weed that he might share, (fat chance: Kenny never shared) and with a "See you guys later" and a general wave to all of us, he wandered off across the park.

"I knew he wasn't gonna do shit to you," Cyrus said as he picked up the cup from the sidewalk.

"I'm glad you were right. I'm glad we were right."

"He's been in jail so many times, what's one more stay to him? Besides, he's on probation again. He fucks up one more time, they're gonna throw away the key. In fact next time it could be prison, not county jail. I think you're good."

Just another quiet morning in the park.

I was reading the Wall Street Journal in the main room of the library. I liked the Journal, especially the Saturday-Sunday edition, for its feature stories. Down at the bottom of the front page a feature always began, often on an interesting and unusual topic. This morning I was absorbed in a lengthy piece about how the Amish in Pennsylvania maintained their

19th-century lifestyle in the age of Amazon and Google when I heard the sound of someone theatrically clearing his throat in front of me.

I lowered the newspaper. The throat-clearer was my friend Bill. Standing beside him was none other than my older friend, Sam Fasil.

"This is the man who was looking for you before, Pat."

"Sam!" I scrambled up out of my chair, the newspaper dropped and forgotten. "What in the – I mean, Bill told me you were here before, looking for me, but … What's it been? Two years?"

"Patrick, my Patrick!" Sam said as we shook hands. "Closer to three years, actually."

"I'm going to start charging you for being your social secretary, Pat," Bill said, grinning through his beard. "Now if you gentlemen will excuse me, I'd like to read the paper myself." He reached down and snatched my Wall Street Journal from the chair.

"Take it, take it. Thanks, Bill," I said.

Although I had been expecting that Sam would return if he bothered to come that first time. I still had no idea why he had been looking for me. Seeing him again brought back a lot of things I had been trying to forget despite being resigned to the fact that I never would forget them. Of course nothing of what had happened was in any way Sam's fault, but in my mind I associated him with those times, and the pain was still there. Still, he was a friend, and he had come looking for me. Why? I suggested we step out into the morning air where we wouldn't have to keep our voices down.

"Before we get caught up, old friend, you have to tell me how you found me," I said to him. "I haven't exactly been keeping a high profile lately."

"It was not easy. You vanished from the earth quickly. I knew your old address because I was there that one time, afterward, remember?"

"I remember."

"I checked there, but you were gone and your neighbors had no idea where. So I checked with the city. The police had no record of you anywhere, and forgive me, but I also checked with the county and you hadn't been in the morgue, either."

"Lucky me."

"I even went to one of those websites where they give a complete report on somebody for $29.95. Criminal record, mortgages, all that shit. But after I had sat in front of the computer for five minutes while it gathered all this information – and I might not even have had the right 'Patrick Donahy' to begin with; you know you're not the only guy with that name – I decided that what they were offering to sell me was much more than I wanted to know. All I wanted to know was where you might be. Also I didn't want to spend the $29.95. I logged off."

"So how *did* you find me?"

"I remembered that you had told me you grew up around this neighborhood. And also that when you were growing up, you spent a lot of time at the public library. I decided to come by and see if you were still here and if you were still such a bookworm as you used to be. You weren't here, but I asked around and your friend Bill there told me that you and he both actually live here now."

"More or less. I got a van over there that I sleep in. He has one too."

"So you are...homeless?"

"Unless you count the van. Bill and I are among the lucky ones. Some people around here sleep in parking lots and behind stores. I did my share of that before I bought the van."

He looked at me, kind of puzzled.

"I can't explain, man," I said. "I guess I just sorta...gave up. Giving up is a hard habit to get out of. Besides, I don't do too badly here. It was tough at first, I was eating up what was left of my 401(k). But I'm getting Social Security now."

"I think I can understand. You don't have to explain. What was her name? Melissa?"

I nodded. "Mm."

"Such a dreadful thing."

I didn't want to get into it. "Fortunately I did have enough money left to buy a broken-down Ford Econoline and throw a cot in it," I said. "But what about you? Are you still driving your cab?"

"No. I stopped about a year ago. Sold my van."

"You could have sold it to me. So you're doing something else now."

"Yes. That's what prompted me to come looking for you, actually. Do you remember one evening when you and I were standing around in front of the Marriott, bullshitting as usual, and I told you about my cousin Abraham?"

"Sure. The parking-lot biggie. I asked you why you didn't work for him instead of driving a taxi. You had some reason for not wanting to, as I remember."

"I changed my mind. He wanted me to come into the company and finally offered me a salary that I would have been a fool to turn down. I handle employee relations for him. He wanted that off his hands, he's so busy with other things, and since I speak both Oromo and Amharic –"

"Oromo and –"

"Amharic. Those are the two main languages back in Ethiopia. I can talk to the guys."

"You want me to park cars? No thanks. I turned 62 a few months ago and I'm getting Social Security now. It's only about $1200 a month, but I don't have to park cars."

He laughed and clapped me on the shoulder. "No, of course not. It wasn't parking cars I had in mind. Not for you. I would not have come looking for you if it were that. I have something in mind that I think you would find more interesting, if you like the idea. Let's go have some lunch. Let's talk about it. My treat."

"It's a little early for lunch," I said, "but then again no parkie worth his salt ever turns down a free meal."

"Parkie?"

"That's what I call the people who live around here, of which I am now one."

"I see. So. An early lunch, old friend?"

"Lead the way."

We walked to his car, which turned out to be a late-model Mazda RX. Whatever Abraham had Sam doing, from the look of things he wasn't doing too badly at it.

Sam didn't know the neighborhood of course (except how to find the public library) so at my suggestion we went to Palumbo's, an Italian place on South La Brea that made the best hot pastrami sandwiches in town. I had not been there in a long time, but Palumbo's was a local institution. When I was a kid my family used to go there on Sundays now and then.

Palumbo's was still right where I remembered, and it was open. We sat in a booth, I ordered a half-carafe of chianti, Sam ordered iced tea and as we looked at the menu, which I didn't really need to, Sam told me what was going on.

His cousin Abraham had decided that he wanted to start his own weekly newspaper.

"He's tired of paying the Times' advertising rates," Sam said. "He has decided that if he starts his own weekly paper, not only will he be able to save money on advertising, but will also raise his visibility in the community. I told him about you because I remembered you used to be in that business. He doesn't know anything about running a newspaper. He needs someone who has some experience.

"I don't know anything about running a newspaper either," I said. "I was only a reporter. There's more to running a newspaper than reporters. A lot more. I don't know anything about the business end of it except that it involves selling advertising. In fact the advertising comes first and the newspaper comes later."

"But you did say that you won an award once … from the Valley Press Club, was it?"

"Yes. For investigative reporting. Not for anything that makes money."

"Don't worry about the money part of it. Abraham's a smart dude. Look how much money he's made out of parking cars. He wouldn't be considering a venture like this if he hadn't figured it all out. Let me set up a meeting between you two."

"Sure. I'll meet with your cousin. What the hell? As Harvey Keitel said in that movie, 'It ain't like I'm runnin' off to go to the opera.'"

The waiter came with my hot pastrami sub and dinner salad, and Sam's steaming plate of ravioli. He sipped his iced tea and I ordered another half-carafe of house chianti. The occasion called for more wine. I planned on taking a good nap in the park later, after Sam was gone.

"Do you mind my asking what has happened to you?" Sam said. "You can tell me to mind my own business if you want, but I am curious, old friend, forgive me for it. You disappeared so suddenly and then we didn't hear from you anymore."

"Well, after the accident … After Melissa died … Well, there's progress. For a long time I couldn't even say it. That she died, I mean. I can say it now."

"Understandable."

"After she died … You're a family man, aren't you?"

"Yes, of course. Two children."

"I wanted to be a family man. I really felt like I wanted that. My first marriage was a mess, as you know. I was hoping for, well, you know, something more."

"And you loved Melissa."

"Yes."

"Such a dreadful thing. What happened again, if you don't mind talking about it?"

"She was on her way back from Barona. That's in San Diego County. Lakeside. She had been singing there. The gig was finished and she was on her way back to L.A. She had just started the drive back – she was on the

52 highway heading for the 805. It was late. CHP said a drunk driver got on the 52 going the wrong way. There was a head-on … I wasn't there of course. I got woke up at one in the morning by a phone call. Her sister and I had to go down there. It was just … too awful. Even after all this time I really don't want to go into it, Sam. She was thirty-seven."

"Such a shame. She had a son, as I remember."

"Yeah, Tom Jr. Tommy. We would have been a family, Sam."

"I understand. If anything were to happen to my wife or children, I don't what I would do."

The waiter brought my second carafe of wine but now I didn't want it. This kind of talk and wine did not sit well together.

"What became of the boy?" Sam asked.

"He's back with his father as far as I know. He'd be...seven or eight now."

"And then...what I'm really wondering about, what became of you?"

"You're seeing it. At least the latest chapter of it. I kind of went to shit. Off the rails. Nothing mattered anymore. I didn't give a fuck about anything. Everything unraveled. It had to, nobody was minding the store. I lost control of the booze. I quit the cab company. You remember that part. I couldn't pay my rent anymore, but I wanted to leave anyway. I wanted to get the hell away from here, from any place or anything that reminded me. So I bugged out. I just bagged everything and took off."

"Took off to where?"

"Istanbul."

"*Istanbul?*"

"Uh-huh. I went on the Internet and found a website that was a clearinghouse for jobs teaching English overseas. Dave's ESL Café. It was called I got hooked up with a school in Istanbul that was looking for a few Brits and Americans to come and teach English for them. I applied, got myself sobered up enough to get through a Skype interview, and they hired me. So I put my things in storage, got a passport, packed a bag and I was off to Turkey. I got lucky. They needed teachers and as long as you had a college degree, they didn't care if you were TEFL-certified or not. They preferred it if you were, but they didn't insist. Anyway, that's where I went, believe it or not. Istanbul."

"Did you like it?"

I shrugged. "I wasn't there to like or dislike it. It wasn't tourist travel, I just wanted to get out of here. Did I like it? It's a place. Huge city. Spread all over the place, like L.A. It's the only city in the world that's on two continents. Lotta history of course. Mosques every hundred yards. Worst traffic I've ever seen. But I wasn't driving, so I didn't mind. Pretty hot in the summer, though."

"Istanbul."

"Yep. For about a year and a half."

"Learn any Turkish?"

"I learned how to say two things: 'I love you,' and 'I didn't order this.'"

"'I love you?'"

"*Seni Seviyorum.* My students taught me to say that."

"And the other?"

"That one's tougher. Let me see if I can remember. *'Ben bunu ısmar... lamadım.'* Tourist survival. The waiters over there are all crooks. My students warned me. Whenever I went to lunch with them, they always examined the bill like Sherlock Holmes to make sure we weren't being charged for something we didn't order."

"Two phrases. And you were there for a year and a half?"

"Hey, I wasn't there to learn Turkish, I was there to teach English. I was in Turkey for about a year and a half, then I got fired."

"What did they fire you for, if you don't mind my asking? I can't imagine that you were a poor teacher."

"No, my students loved me. I think I was a pretty good teacher. I didn't get many complaints from students, anyway. It was the administration. I could never get along with the office crowd. There was one in particular who, well, never mind. Not worth talking about. I decided to come home."

I wasn't about to tell him I'd been fired for drinking too much. He was my friend, but we weren't that close.

After I'd given Sam my cellphone number and he'd dropped me off back at the park and gone on his way, I found Cyrus trimming his fingernails on a bench near his and Marianne's tree. It was after twelve O'clock by now and Marianne was asleep under a dirty yellow blanket next to their pile of stuff. She almost always slept at that time of day.

"Marianne's out like a light I see," I said, sitting down.

"She was tweaking yesterday. She'll probably sleep all day. I got news, homie."

"Me too. You go first."

"I been approved for Section eight. All I gotta do now is wait for them to find a place. 'Course, that could take months. Might not, but it could."

"So you and Marianne will be parting paths."

"I think we both knew we would sooner or later. What's your news?"

"Kind of similar, actually. I just had lunch with my old friend Sam from cabbing days. His cousin wants to start up a newspaper, he says. I have dabbled in that business, if only on the editorial end. But he might want me to come work for him. I didn't think I'd ever want to go back to work. I'm still not sure I want that. But I told Sam I'd talk to his cousin."

"So we both might get out of this park at about the same time."

"Stranger things have happened."

"Well," he put his nail clippers in his pocket. "That means we might also be coming down to the finish line on that steak dinner. I mine medium-rare."

"I like mine *carbonado,* as they say in Brazil. Burned. Black. With lots of steak sauce."

"That's a criminal thing to do to a steak."

"That's me. A real desperate character."

26

He woke up too early. He nearly always did, here in Pendik.

It was the call to prayers. *Salat al-fajr.* It awoke him almost every morning just before dawn, which in summer meant very early, but it was already fall now. There was a mosque right around the corner. It had loudspeakers mounted on its minaret. A hundred and fifty years ago, he often thought when the sound woke him up, that would have been one guy up there shouting. With the window closed he might have been able to sleep through that. But a loudspeaker? No, that always woke him up. When it was over he went back to sleep.

The sun was up when he awoke again. This second-floor apartment had two small bedrooms, but he preferred to sleep in the sitting room, whose large window faced east toward the street below. The sitting room got the morning light and he preferred it to the bedrooms down the hall in back, which were rather dark. There was a large couch in the sitting room which made a comfortable bed, a red-and-black-patterned rug, presumably Turkish, on the floor, and a dining table in the corner on which he had set up his laptop and speakers. The café downstairs had wi-fi; he could tap into its network and get on the Internet from his sitting room. Sometimes when the signal was weak he would go downstairs, sit in the café, order a coffee and surf the Internet from there. But he didn't have to do that often.

He slept in his clothes so he wouldn't have to waste time getting dressed.

He got up, rubbed his head, went to the toilet down the hall, then padded into the kitchen to get a can of Efes beer from the refrigerator. He liked Efes, with its blue-and-white label. After this one he had only two more left. He would have to walk down to the corner market soon.

The electric clock on the back of the kitchen stove read 7:48. The old Syrian who ran the corner market would be raising his metal shutters for the day any time now, although this was Saturday and sometimes he opened late on Saturdays.

Booting up the laptop, when the date and time appeared he saw that today was also his birthday, about which he had forgotten. He counted back to the last time his birthday had fallen on a Saturday and tried to remember what he had done that day. All he could remember was that he had been in California then. He was in Pendik, on the Asian side of the Bosphorus, now.

The café downstairs was open and, having opened the sitting room window to let in the morning air, he could smell the cigarette smoke and hear the voices from the tables out on the sidewalk. The regulars were there as they were every morning, sipping their coffee, smoking and looking over the *Hürriyet* or one of the other dailies.

Morning papers. Why not? He went to Spotify and pulled up Strauss' *Morning Papers* waltz. He thought about the café patrons downstairs with their coffee and their newspapers, sipping, smoking, checking out the headlines. Just another ordinary morning for them.

He looked out the window at the morning street. Many apartments had Turkish flags hanging from their balconies and windows, and portraits of Mustafa Kemal Ataturk could be seen in many windows. They were everywhere in the city. "Ataturk is to us what George Washington is to you," one of his students had remarked. The founder of modern Turkey after the fall of the Ottoman Empire at the end of World War I, Ataturk was a national hero, judging from the ubiquitous presence of his face all over the city. Patrick had to admit that he had never heard of Ataturk until, after an eleven-hour flight from Los Angeles the previous year, he had landed at an airport in Istanbul that bore the man's name.

The condensation from his can of Efes was about to make a circle on the wooden table and he put a folded-up sheet of paper under it, but of course the circle had already been made. How long had it been since he had started his own day with the routine of coffee and a look at the newspaper instead of morning beer and staring out the window? Of course the newspapers here wouldn't be of much use to him; he couldn't read Turkish, hadn't bothered even to learn any. There was nobody to talk to except his students, and they were trying to improve their English. That's why he was here. Maybe it was the realization that this was his birthday, but suddenly he felt even more depressed than usual. The thought of Melissa didn't help of course. Thoughts of her always began within moments of his waking in the morning, if not immediately upon waking, so mostly he preferred being asleep, and beer made it easier to sleep so he drank beer all the time, or the cheap red wine available at the Migros store about ten minutes' walk from his place, just the other side of the big mosque that woke him up just before dawn every day.

He had one student on Saturday mornings, Mustafa, (probably named after Ataturk; it seemed as if half the men in the city were named after him) a tall, heavy-set Turk with a very large nose, in his mid-thirties, who came to the school at 10 a.m. once a week for a three-hour private tutoring session. He enjoyed his tutoring sessions with Mustafa precisely because Mustafa's attitude toward learning English was cavalier at best. He was only taking English lessons because his employer had insisted on it. Mustafa worked for a building contractor who had decided that if they could both speak English it would be advantageous for sales. Playing hooky wasn't an option, since both teacher and student had to sign in at the beginning of each lesson and sign out when they had finished. Hence, Mustafa's goal at each lesson was to steer discussion away from the textbook and turn the tutorial session into a three-hour social visit. His favorite subject was women. He loved to tell stories of his various conquests, and managed to get his point across even if he had to do it in broken, halting English. As for Patrick, he didn't particularly mind Mustafa's shilly-shallying. Three hours is a long time to fill and as long as he and his pupil were conversing in English, something, anyway, was being accomplished. Sometimes they even took their Saturday-morning lesson out of the building. Although the administration of English Time frowned on such *al fresco* teaching methods, the office was lightly staffed on Saturday mornings and no one ever paid any attention as they slipped down the back stairs and out into crowded Nisan Caddesi, the street where the school was located. They would hook left and head down along the sidewalks toward the harbor, where Pendik Marina lay with the Sea of Marmara beyond it, and where there was a large waterfront park that Mustafa had dubbed the "Party Garden." Stopping at a grocery store on the way for bottles of Efes or cans of Tuborg, (and him keeping an eye out for anyone they knew) they would sit on a bench in the park, drink beer, watch the boats come in and go out, and talk English. It was not a bad way to spend a Saturday morning, he thought.

Mustafa was already in the otherwise-empty classroom when he came in. He sat at a desk, playing with his Smartphone like everyone did nowadays.

"Morning, Mustafa."

"Morning, Teacher." Mustafa shut off his cellphone and put it in the pocket of his windbreaker. He touched a finger to his forehead, winced slightly and smiled a slightly embarrassed smile. "I got...a little bit hangover."

"Big night last night?"

"Yeah. Friends over at party apartment. Lots of girls."

"Party *apartment*? I knew about our little party garden down the street, but 'party apartment?'"

"Yes. Two apartments. One for...everyday stuff, you know...One for parties."

"I see. No, I don't. How can you afford two places?"

"Party apartment belongs to...a friend. We share it."

"So you take turns having parties."

"Yes. Sometimes together."

"You're deep."

"What?"

"Never mind. So...you're a tad hungover this morning?"

"Yes. I think I need … *kokoreç* about now."

"Koko –"

"*Kokoreç*. Kind of…sandwich. Made of sheep guts. Good for hangovers."

"I think if I had a hangover, the last thing I would want is sheep guts. Come to think of it, the last thing I would want is sheep guts even if I were feeling fine."

"No, no!" Mustafa laughed. "Is good! You want to try it? Instead of party garden, we'll go eat."

"It's a little early for lunch. Why don't we go after class?"

"I got hangover now," Mustafa said with a stage wince. As usual, Mustafa was not inclined to spend three hours sitting in the classroom.

We sneaked downstairs and out the back way.

Mustafa led the way to a grill where they could sit either inside or out, but not wanting to be spotted by anyone from the school, he insisted that they take a table inside and as far toward the back wall as possible. They ordered beers.

"This is actually nice, doing something a little special," he said. "You know, today is my birthday."

"Your birthday today?"

"Uh-huh. I realized it when I got up this morning."

"Your birthday today," Mustafa repeated. "We should have...party."

"You and your parties. I'm sixty. The big Six-O. Nothing to celebrate there."

"*Sixty*? Yes, yes! We must celebrate, Teacher!" His students always addressed him as "Teacher." He had tried to get them to use his name, but they seemed more comfortable with "Teacher." "After class, let's go to party apartment!" Mustafa said. "Not far away. Maybe fifteen minutes."

"You mean forty-five minutes, don't you? You forget Istanbul's traffic." It was true. Istanbul had the worst traffic he had ever seen. Even being from L.A., he had never seen such traffic. The problem was that the Turks were forever putting up new buildings but not bothering with new roads.

Mustafa placed their order. Knowing what he was about to try eating, he quickly drained his beer and ordered another. Although he had never thought of himself as a picky eater, he wanted to be well-fortified if he were going to face *kokoreç*.

The waiter put their food in front of them. Whatever it was, it came with fries. He could eat those, anyway.

It didn't look bad – rather like taco filling served on the now-familiar *ramadan pide* – Turkish flat bread.. The meat was ground, whatever it was. It didn't smell like taco filling, though. There was a pungency to it that ground beef didn't have. He would learn later, reading up on *kokoreç*, that in addition to the intestines of a sheep or goat, it also often included traces of heart, kidney and lungs. Kidney would account for the pungent aroma – he thought of Mr. Bloom's frying mutton kidney in *Ulysses* with its "fine tang of faintly scented urine." There were also bits of tomato and the unmistakable aroma of olive oil, oregano, black pepper and parsely.

Mustafa was already eating his. So, with another gulp of beer, he picked up the *kokoreç* sandwich and bit into it. He had to admit that it wasn't bad, although it certainly didn't taste anything like a taco. He decided it must be an acquired taste, but a taste he wouldn't mind acquiring if he were to remain in Turkey long enough.

"You like it?" Mustafa asked.

"Mmm, yeah, I guess," he said. "It's different, but it's not bad."

"Have some more beer."

He did have one more, but also knew that he probably shouldn't. He had already had enough to ward off the shakes for a few hours. To walk back into the school with beer on his breath would be risky. He had been warned about it once already. After all, these were paying students. They were money. Complaints about drunken teachers were something the school did not need. After Mustafa had examined the bill for anything they hadn't ordered and then paid the check, and they were on their way back to English Time, he made sure to stop off at an *eczane* for some breath mints.

Mustafa was on his cellphone all the way back up Nisan Caddesi, making one phone call after another.

"What are you making, business calls already?" he asked.

"No." Mustafa laughed. "I'm inviting people to...your party. Your birthday."

"I didn't say I would come to any party."

"Oh, you have to come! Your birthday! We'll cook out, drink some beer, dance, we'll have...good time."

"Where is this...party apartment of yours?"

"Tuzla. Not far. Ten minutes."

"Thirty minutes with the traffic."

Mustafa shrugged and gave the familiar What Can We Do smile.

"If your 'party apartment' is in Tuzla, where's your regular apartment? You know, the one that has your wife and kids in it? Where do you actually live? Also in Tuzla?"

"No. Kadikoy."

"Kadikoy! I used to live there! They transferred me to Pendik from Kadikoy. That must be...fifteen miles!"

"About twelve."

"Does your wife say anything about this 'party apartment?'"

"I tell her it's a business place. But I have to be very careful about... cellphone, you know?" He grinned. With his big nose and yellowed teeth, it was not an attractive grin.

"Yes, I've heard of that. People getting caught in lies because of their cellphones. Never had that problem myself."

"You never … been married?"

"Yes, once. But I didn't have a party apartment."

The place was in the hills overlooking the Tuzla-Pendik shipyard, on a mostly-dirt side-street with many buildings similar to Mustafa's but still under construction. Some were already occupied although obviously unfinished. There were a few clotheslines with laundry blowing in the afternoon breeze off the sea, and one or two chickens poking around in the yard of at least one building. Some kids in the street were kicking around a half-deflated soccer ball.

The drive was very twisty, with the expected heavy traffic. Mustafa made a stop at a market to buy cans of beer, of which they both partook as Mustafa piloted his Jeep Cherokee through the tangle of streets.

He had had nothing to eat all day, and with the drive along Pendik and Tuzla's serpentine, narrow, traffic-choked avenues, combined with the beer in his empty stomach, he was getting carsick by the time they reached Mustafa's place. He did not feel like partying now, not that he especially had before. All he wanted was to lie down somewhere.

"Mustafa, I don't feel very well," he said. "Is there a place where I can lie down for a few minutes?"

He really felt like he was going to vomit, which would have been a huge embarrassment.

"Sure, Teacher. Come inside."

Mustafa's phone calls had apparently been effective: close to a dozen people already milled around the area behind the building, essentially a dirt slope leading down to another terraced lot with another unfinished apartment building. The men had a fire going in a trash can, preparing to grill *kebab.* They had bottles of beer in their hands. Mustafa greeted them in Turkish as he led Patrick up the stairs and into the apartment, where, thank God, there was a couch long enough for him to stretch out.

"I get cold towel for your head," Mustafa said he he helped him lie down on the couch.

Mustafa brought the towel soaked in cold water and placed it across his forehead. "You just lie there, rest," he said. "You'll be okay soon. You want a beer?"

"Not now, maybe later."

But he could see concern on his pupil's face. If the guest of honor were to get violently sick, he too would be embarrassed.

Mustafa went out to talk with the group outside. Someone had music playing. Turkish popular music, not loud but tinny, and in his present condition, maddening. Any music at all is torture to someone who's nauseated.

He lay there forcing himself to breathe rhythmically, trying to fight down the queasiness. He could hear them outside talking in Turkish, and although he couldn't understand any of it, he heard the name "Erdogan" several times. The new president. Said to have an islamist background and to take a dim view of secularism, which presumably would include things like party apartments.

"He doesn't want Islamic republic, like Iran," one of his students had assured him, "But he wants Turks to be good Muslims. He's more popular in the countryside than in the cities, where people are more secular."

He had indeed noticed that in the stores the price of beer, wine and liquor had all risen noticeably since the election. While pulling up short of prohibition, the new president obviously wanted to discourage drinking without going so far as to spark demonstrations on Taksim Square, which had happened in the past over other issues. The police carried machine guns around, but in Turkey that was normal.

Out of the corner of his eye he saw two women come out of the kitchen, drinks in their hands.

He turned his head slightly to look at them. One was blonde, the other brunette, both dressed for warm weather and neither wearing a *hijab*. So

Mustafa had invited women, or perhaps they had come along with the other guys. They followed Mustafa outside and left him alone in the living room.

After about thirty minutes the nausea began fade. He sat up slowly. A few more people had come in, including two or three more women. The smell of cooking meat wafted in from outside, and although he had no appetite, at least it didn't turn his stomach. That was a good sign, as was the fact that the tinny music coming out of somebody's Bluetooth speaker or a radio or whatever it was no longer made him want to crawl away to someplace quiet and die.

Mustafa came in from outside, can of Efes in hand, and noticed him sitting up.

"Ah, Teacher! Feeling better?"

"A little bit."

"You want beer now?"

"Uh, yeah. Okay."

Mustafa went into the kitchen to get him a beer. At that same moment a young woman came in from outside. She was Turkish, and looked very familiar, but he could not place her. She almost had to be in one of his classes. He seldom interacted with anyone anywhere in Istanbul except at school. He racked his brain trying to place her in a classroom. She was petite, with the usual dark eyes, black hair, in her case very thick, and slightly dusky complexion of this part of the world. Quite pretty, actually. She was dressed western style in jeans, a sequined blouse, low-heeled pumps.

When Mustafa returned from the kitchen and handed him a can of Efes, the girl returned along with him and sat on the sofa. In a moment the first part of the mystery was solved.

She noticed the distracted look he was giving her, and she smiled. "Don't you know me, Teacher? It's me. Aysun. From your Level Four class. Tuesdays?"

"Oh, yes, yes, Aysun! Why didn't I recognize you right away?"

"I've changed to western clothes."

That was it. Aysun always came to class in traditional *djeballa* dress and *hijab* head covering. Some of his other women students did that too. Not many, but a few. He had never seen her out of traditional dress. He had never seen her hair before.

"Why the change?"

"I decided I wanted to change. I'm still Muslim, but I wanted to wear different clothes. And I'm going to live in Amsterdam at the end of this semester."

"What's in Amsterdam? A job?"

"Yes, probably. I have cousins there."

"I'm sure that President Erdogan would like you better dressed the other way."

She laughed. "Yes! And he is one of the reasons I'm leaving. I have been to Amsterdam before. I like it there."

"Big Muslim community there."

"Yes."

Muslim or not, as they talked Aysun began sending him unmistakeable signals that she liked him. She seemed in no hurry to leave his side, anyway. Although she did not drink, when he had finished his beer she cheerfully volunteered to go and get him another.

"Where do you know Mustafa from?" He asked her.

"He's also a cousin."

Now it was his turn to laugh. "You Turks! Every one of you has four hundred cousins!"

"Yes. We have big families. Mustafa goes to English Time because of me. I take classes there, so I thought it would be good for him too. I suggested it."

"Your English is much better than his. Of course you're Level Four. He's Level One, and not even very interested in that."

"I have traveled more. Mustafa has never left Turkey."

"Do you mind if I ask how old you are?"

"Twenty-six."

"Good grief," he thought. She was clearly getting a little flirty with him, an old guy, and she was even younger than Melissa had been. It was probably nothing to worry about. She had just told him of her plans for Amsterdam, so it was unlikely that she was casting around for a green card.

He had been warned about that. Teachers, especially from the U.S. Canada and the U.K. were always getting hit up for help in getting visas or emigrating. But the school had a firm unwritten policy about relations between teachers and students. Turkey was not a good place to get into trouble of any kind. He had seen the movie *Midnight Express.* This wasn't drugs, but it could be trouble just as big.

The food was ready, and now he was sufficiently recovered to feel like eating something. He and Aysun joined the others outside, sat on a wooden bench and ate *kebab.* He drank more beer.

It was then that one of Mustafa's pals from over by the barbeque, who had been casting sullen glances in Pat and Aysun's direction for some time as he sipped beer and smoked, came over to them.

He was visibly not happy. For a moment he stood in front of them, beer in one hand and burning cigarette in the other, looking around and not saying anything. Aysun would not make eye contact with him. So that was it. Second mystery solved.

Pat looked up at the glowering Turk, who couldn't have been more than thirty.

"Hi," he said, his mouth full of *kebab.*

"Hi," the guy said back. He didn't seem to know much more English than that, but he was just as obviously in no mood for pleasantries. He said something in Turkish to Aysun. She snapped something in Turkish back at him. Then she put down her plate, stood up and a verbal machine-gun duel in Turkish began of which he couldn't understand a word, but didn't have to. The oldest scene in film or popular song was being played out in front of him. Aysun had had a fight with her boyfriend, decided to punish him by making him jealous with the first guy who came along. He of course, being an idiot like all boyfriends, fell for it, and now the machine-gun duel.

He stood up because he felt it would be cowardly to remain seated, but he stood up slowly because it would be stupid to stand up too quickly and get punched.

Mustafa, the embarrassed host, hurried over and tried to break up the squabble. Now the barrage in Turkish became triangulated fire, and he couldn't follow a word of it, but he heard Mustafa say his name, "Teacher," a couple of times. Probably he was reminding his cousin and her boyfriend that this was supposed to be Teacher's birthday party and they were ruining it.

With everyone watching now, Mustafa persuaded the two lovers to at least back away a little and stop shouting at each other. Without another glance at him or their host, Aysun and Evrim withdrew into the house, still arguing but now in lower voices.

Mustafa apologized with a shrug. "I'm sorry, Teacher. That's...her boyfriend, and –"

He held up his hand. "You don't have to tell me. I've watched that scene in every Rock Hudson and Doris Day movie ever made."

Mustafa squinted and scratched his head. These names meant nothing to him.

"Never mind. It's not important."

"It wasn't about you."

"I didn't think it was."

"They...argue about her...she's going to Amsterdam at end of year."

"I know. She told me."

"He don't want her to go."

"I could see that."

Aysun and her boyfriend left the party soon after. She didn't say goodbye to him. He hoped she'd at least said goodbye to Mustafa. He was her cousin, after all. While glad that the mini-episode between Aysun and Evrim had turned out to be nothing more than a stupid lovers' quarrel, he wasn't sure how he would feel now about facing her in class next Tuesday. He hoped that she might feel a similar discomfort. She might be too embarrassed to show up in class. He hoped she would be. She was a good enough student that missing one class wouldn't mean much.

Not wishing to be rude to his host, he finished eating, but now wanted nothing more than to go home, and began to wonder how he was going to get there. He couldn't ask Mustafa to leave his own party and drive him. A taxi wouldn't work; he didn't know his own address in Pendik. He could recognize the street but didn't know the name of it, nor the number of the building.

He was a bit drunk now; he had lost count of how many beers he'd had.

Aysun, so young and so pretty, had made him think of Melissa. Now he could not think of anything else and he felt miserable and wanted to go back to his own apartment and crawl into bed. Suddenly he felt a million miles from anything familiar except lovers and their melodrama, and he had had more than enough of that.

He went to Mustafa and made excuses: he was beginning to feel sick again and wanted to go home. Actually this wasn't far from the truth. Mustafa went and found one of his other guests, a young man named Fuat who lived in Pendik and knew the neighborhood where the school was. Mustafa explained to Fuat what was needed and Fuat cheerfully agreed to give Pat a ride back to his place. "He'll drop you off and then come back," Mustafa explained as he pushed one more Efes – a nightcap – into Patrick's hand before they went off to Fuat's car.

Fuat's English was shakier than Mustafa's, but he gathered right away that Fuat was a soccer player. He listened to Fuat talk about soccer all the way back to Pendik, which wasn't far in terms of distance, but in terms of the route, with its traffic and twisting streets, seemed like a very long trip.

And sure enough he began feeling nauseated again. When Fuat finally dropped him off on a street that he recognized near his building, he managed to thank the young man for the ride, then stumbled past the café, into his building and up the stairs to his apartment just in time to get to the toilet and vomit.

He heaved three times. He remained on his knees in front of the bowl until he was sure that another heave would not be coming, and then he crawled off to bed on the sitting room sofa.

Next thing he knew it was time for *Salat al-fajr.* The mosque loudspeaker down the street began its slow, steadily-building drone, and as usual he woke up. It was still dark. The days were getting shorter now, daylight coming later.

When the echo of the call to prayers had faded away, he turned over and tried to go back to sleep, but knew right away that there would be no more sleep. He was awake for the day. What time had he gone to bed last night? It must have been early. Mustafa's party had begun in the afternoon. It couldn't have been very late when he'd asked to be taken back to his own place, no later than eight or nine. He looked at his watch. 6:24 a.m. About forty-five minutes until sunrise. He felt okay, having drunk nothing at the party except beer, too much beer, but only beer. He'd had no hard liquor or wine, and he had eaten food. So there was no hangover. That was good, anyway.

But he wanted a beer now. It was Sunday. That was no problem; except for the small Christian population, in Istanbul Sunday was just another business day. But the old Syrian on the corner wouldn't be opening for business until at least eight O'clock. An hour and a half.

He got up, still dressed as usual except for having removed his shoes last night. He shuffled in his socks to the refrigerator, opening it hopefully.

There was one tall Efes left. He popped it open, switched on the hall light, went down the hall to the bathroom, urinated, returned to the sitting room and sat on the sofa, looking out the window. Gradually the eastern sky was beginning to gray.

Then, beer in hand, he went to the sitting room table and booted up his laptop. Spotify again: he selected Miles Davis' *Birth of the Cool.* He listened to the entire album and sipped on his breakfast beer. Finally, looking again at his watch, he felt reasonably sure that the old Syrian down the street would now be open for the day. Leaving the music playing, he went out and locked the door behind him.

On Tuesday Aysun did not appear in class. That was good. No awkwardness to deal with.

The next day he got called into the director's office.

The director, a skinny little guy in his thirties named Hakan, annoyed him no end with his habit of smiling all the time. Good news or bad news, Hakan was always smiling behind his black-rimmed glasses.

"Well, Pat, sit down," Hakan smiled as he came into the tiny cubicle of an office that Hakan occupied. He sat.

"So what's this all about?"

"Pat, I'm afraid we're going to have to let you go."

"I'm fired."

"Afraid so." Apologetic smile.

"Mind if I ask why?"

"You've been warned about your drinking. We've had complaints." Confident smile.

He so much wanted to punch the little bastard. Now would have been the perfect time, since he was being fired anyway. But that would probably have gotten the Turkish police involved, and you didn't want to get involved with the Turkish police.

"You and your 'complaints.' From whom? Do I look drunk? Have I ever come in here drunk?"

"I have smelled it on you."

"That's what you say. You don't smell it now, do you?"

Hakan made a big show of sniffing. "No. But I believe there is something called....the party garden?" That smile. He wanted to come across that desk and throttle Hakan.

"Party garden?"

"We got a complaint that you and your...Saturday student, Mustafa, leave the building, and you buy beer and go sit in the park drinking beer. You've been seen."

I was obvious what had happened. "'Seen,' my ass," he said. "Someone ratted us out, and I know who, because she's Mustafa's cousin and she wasn't in class yesterday."

Mustafa must have told Aysun about the party garden, and she had to have told Hakan. What did she have to gain from playing stoolpigeon?

She must have had her reasons, but he had given up trying to figure out women a long time ago. It might have had something to do with the boyfriend. Maybe she just didn't want him telling the story of the lovers' spat around the school. Maybe she was mad at her cousin. Who knew? It didn't matter now.

Hakan shrugged, smiling relentlessly.

"So you admit it. I don't understand you people. You're always hard up for teachers, but you're also ready to fire them for nothing, on a moment's notice. This is a fucked-up place." He meant Turkey, not the school, although the school was bad enough.

Hakan's smile vanished at his use of "fucked-up." Whether this American meant the school or Turkey, it was an insult either way.

"You will have to go to the main office to collect your salary," he said. "I don't have any cash here." Hakan probably had thousands of lira in his locked filing cabinet, but knew that if he paid out any of it, he would have to submit a voucher to the main office across the water, near Taksim Square, and reimbursement could take weeks. Why put himself out for this drunk, whom he had just fired anyway?

But Patrick had already decided he had had enough of this place. The school and Turkey both. He had reached the decision on the morning after his birthday party at Mustafa's little party-nest in Tuzla. A year and a half was long enough for grieving. Long enough for this.

He made the one-hour trek on public transportation to the main office the next afternoon, picked up his money and instructed them to get him on the first flight back to Los Angeles. He was entitled to return airfare, having completed his first contract the previous June.

They got him on Etihad Airways, which meant a long journey: three hours from Istanbul to Abu Dhabi on Turkish Airlines, then the twelve hours back to L.A. on Etihad, plus the entire night he spent in the terminal in Abu Dhabi, napping on the carpet at the boarding gate, using his backpack as a pillow, until airport security awakened him at six a.m. and told him he couldn't sleep there.

He dealt with the overseas flight with a bottle of Teachers from the duty-free, which he picked up at the boarding gate and stuffed into his backpack. The rules were that it was not to be opened until destination was reached, but once the Airbus 380 had leveled off at cruising altitude and the "Fasten Seat Belts" sign had been turned off, he slipped into the lavatory with his backpack, tore open the seal on the bottle and took a long, long pull of Scotch. With two or three more trips to the lavatory, he managed to sleep most of the way to Los Angeles.

He knew that when he got back to L.A. he would have no place to go. He had given up his apartment and as of this moment, had no income.

Upon arriving back at LAX, not knowing where to go, he took what was left of the Teachers he had bought in Abu Dhabi and spent one night in the cheapest motel he could find. The next morning, still not knowing where to go, his homing instinct steered him via public transportation back to the old neighborhood east of the freeway in Bell Gardens where he had grown up.

After another night in a motel, he knew he was going to need wheels and found a motorcycle dealer that sold scooters. He bought the cheapest one he could find, an orange 150cc Tao Tao Lancer which cost a large chunk—$850—of what he had left in his savings account at Coast Federal. Not legal for the freeway, but good enough for the surface streets. It would be his last big expenditure for a long while.

He made his way to the public library, an old haunt from his youth. It would be a good place to sit and think about what to do next, and the library had a park behind it. On the way there he stopped at Target and bought a sleeping bag, thinking he would probably need it, if only for a few nights.

The scooter came with a trunk. He bought a six-pack of Miller Genuine Draft and tucked it into the trunk. He knew it wasn't legal to drink beer in the park, but he was sure people did it anyway.

A few hours later, after wandering in and out of the library and around his old neighborhood, and sitting under a tree for a while, furtively sipping beer from a brown paper bag, he took a seat on a bench next to an old woman and, seeing that she was reading the paper, struck up a conversation.

27

"We're thinking of calling it *Zip,*" Abraham said.

"*Zip*?"

"Yeah. It's short, catchy. People will remember it," said Ron, who sat next to Abraham. We were at a Starbucks on Hawthorne, where I'd agreed to meet Abraham.

Ron might have been the bouncer in a bar when he was younger. Maybe in some place like Shanghai Jake's. He looked about my age now, sixtyish, beefy, with a red face and thin, sandy hair. Too old for a bouncer. He was dressed as if for golf, in polo shirt and Dockers, but he wore a Rolex wristwatch, so he had to have money. But he also had that quasi-threatening way about him. After five minutes I had already decided I did not like Ron.

"*Zip* is a brand of bicycle tire," I said.

"Well, we like it," Ron said with finality.

Who's "we?" I thought. And who was this creep? Because if I were going to be expected to take orders from him, I'd already decided, it was no thanks, I'm outta here.

As for Sam's cousin Abraham Negassi, although I knew he was Ethiopian, I thought he bore a striking resemblance to Pedro Martinez, the great Red Sox pitcher. Not as tall maybe. Facially he looked strikingly like Martinez, right down to the wispy mustache. As a Red Sox fan I had to like that about him. But what was he about? And who was this red-faced thug sitting next to him?

Right away Abraham threw me a curveball. I had explained to Sam that my only background in newspaper work had been as a reporter – I knew nothing about the business end and not much more about the editorial end than pitching, developing and writing stories. So imagine my surprise when Abraham suddenly said, taking a sip of his coffee, "I know Sam told you that I was looking for a reporter. But the guy I had in mind to be my managing editor, to run the show, has already backed out. He has other things he wants to do. Do you think you might be interested in the managing editor job? I would pay you $450 a week to be the paper's editor."

It should have been a pleasant surprise. Kicked upstairs before I'd even started? More responsibility? Probably more *money*? What's not to like?

But I was my father's son. I saw problems. I had some prior experience with editing a publication, but not a newspaper. It had been *Cyserve News*, the company newsletter of Cyserve, where I worked in the marketing department for a couple of years. So I knew a little something about layout, but at Cyserve I had been using Pagemaker, an old and now-obsolete desktop-publishing program. Now I would have to learn a new program, probably InDesign, which I knew about but had never seen.

And what would I have to lay out and proofread? He would have to find another reporter if he no longer intended to use me for that. I might end up working with some journalism student fresh out of college, and I wasn't sure how I felt about training a young reporter. I assumed that Abraham had a tabloid in mind, but even if I had eight or ten pages to fill, copy from one reporter wasn't going to be enough. Abraham would have to pay for a subscription to the Associated Press or some other news service for filler. Did he know this? Had he already done it? Lots of questions.

But above all of that there was the larger question: whoever Abraham had in mind as managing editor of *Zip* (or whatever they might wind up calling this gazette if I could get them to change their minds about that dumb name) had already walked away. What did that say about the whole project?

It might be nothing but some house of cards that this Ethiopian parking mogul had constructed in his mind, which could fall down at the slightest puff of wind.

On the other hand, what did I have to lose? I was a homeless drunk sleeping in a van. If it took eight weeks (optimistic estimate) to get the first issue put together and into print, well, I did the math: two months on salary at $450 a week. I would get $3,600 out of this anyway.

I explained that, with my limited background in desktop publishing, combined with my slightly deeper experience in community journalism, I thought I could handle the job. Abraham made an offer then and there, and I accepted it. Even Ron seemed happy with that. He shook my hand, anyway, rather gruffly.

As Sam drove me back to the park I remembered what they had told me at the Social Security office when I applied for benefits. I could work part-time, they said, but if I were to make more than $1,400 a month, my benefits would most likely be reduced. But that was something I could worry about later. *Zip* probably wouldn't last more than one issue anyway.

Hare-brained scheme or not, I decided that this called for a celebration. After all, this might get me out of the park and back to something like a normal life.

I went to Crown Liquor and bought a pint of Jack Daniel's. I seldom drank whiskey anymore, but this occasion called for something better than Hurricane or MGD.

Frankie, who could smell free booze before a bottle had been opened, somehow managed to bump into me on the street when I came out of the liquor store.

On the possibility that I may have bought some hooch, he had a line ready: he asked if I had a copy of *Crime and Punishment* and if I did, could be borrow it?

He knew perfectly well that I had a copy of that in the van. He had thumbed through it and we had discussed it one evening when he was hanging with me before he went to jail. Smoking weed hadn't affected his memory that much.

He came back to the van with me and we drank the Jack together. I told him about Abraham and my offer of a job as M.E. of *Zip*. Of course Frankie offered congratulations, but he was more interested in the Jack. I had to remind him to take the book when he left.

We got to work a week later at Abraham's office, which turned out to be not an office at all, but a private residence on a cul-de-sac in Glendale. His valet parking empire was run from the living room of an ordinary-looking pale blue stucco house with white trim, whose front yard sloped sharply down to the sidewalk where Abraham's black BMW was parked. Sam didn't pick me up this time; he was busy with his own duties and I had to get myself there in the van, but Abraham gave good directions and I had no trouble finding the place.

Ron, whom I had already dubbed "The Bouncer," was there, and there I also met Javon Coulter, an amiable young black man, American, not Ethiopian, whom Abraham had taken on as his graphic designer.

Javon and I were shown what was to be our work space, a large room in the back of the house, down a hallway and past a bathroom, which I guessed had been used for storage before. It had an overhead light, but only one electrical outlet. The room was empty except for three wooden tables, two of which had PC computers sitting on them (one had an extra-large monitor.) On the third table, in one corner, were a Mr. Coffee and some styrofoam cups, a box of cube sugar, some plastic stirrers and a jar of Coffee Mate. The Mr. Coffee was on, the carafe half full – Javon and I would be sharing a room with the office coffee mess.

"Pat, that computer over there in that corner will be yours," Abraham said. "Javon's using this one." Javon had already been at work; the big monitor glowed with creative art images of some kind.

"Makes sense, the graphic design guy needs the big monitor," I said.

"Right."

"You got the publishing software?"

"Yes, it's already loaded on there."

"I'll just have to tinker with it and learn how to use it."

"The box is under your desk. I'm sure there's an instruction book."

"What about the AP? The wire service?"

"I paid for a subscription. You should be able to get right in there on your computer. The receipt's right there."

No question, we were starting out from scratch all right. Two guys in a bare room with two PCs, a coffeemaker, a new software package (Javon had brought his own software) and one electrical outlet which we would have to share until someone got to Home Depot and bought us a power strip. Javon would plug in his computer and printer for a while; I would sip coffee and go over the instruction manual for InDesign while I waited for my turn.

As Javon and I tried to get to work, down the hall I heard Ron yelling. He yelled a lot. This time his yelling had something to do with the guy Abraham had apparently hired to handle ad sales, who had not been around for days. Not a good sign. Without ad revenue we wouldn't be around for long.

Whatever answers Abraham was giving him, we didn't hear them because Abraham didn't yell.

"Who is that guy? Do you know?" I asked Javon. "I mean the muscle. The one making all that noise. I think his name is Ron?"

"He's Abraham's business partner," Javon said. "That's what he says, anyway. But I was here yesterday and Abraham treats him more like an employee. He sent him out to get office supplies yesterday. If a guy's your business partner you don't send the motherfucker on errands. So I don't know."

"Maybe he's just an investor in this little enterprise."

"Maybe."

"That would explain some of the yelling, anyway. If I was backing a project like this, I guess I'd feel entitled to yell."

"But when Abraham tells him to do something, he does it," Javon said.

"Strange. What do you think of all this? You, me, two computers, one outlet, an empty room. I'm sure there have been newspapers started under worse conditions than this, but this guy is rich, or says he is. What are we doing in the back room with the coffee pot?"

Javon shrugged. "Could be he's planning to run this at a loss so he can write it off his taxes."

"You might be exactly right."

"For now I'm just going to ride with it. He's paying us, or he says he's going to."

Abraham and I had a little private jam session in his living room/office (the Bouncer was happily not present) so I could get a get a clearer picture of just what kind of publication he wanted me to create.

What I learned from him eased my mind a bit, at least on the question of my hiring another writer to work on our fledgling newspaper.

I should have figured it out already. Since the only reason Abraham wanted to put out his own newspaper in the first place was to avoid the L.A. Times' ad rates, this was going to be a community hand-out, light and fluffy, a tabloid distributed on the street for free. We weren't looking to win awards for hard-hitting journalism. *Zip* was going to lean heavily on concerts, local features, sports and entertainment, restaurant reviews, movies, that sort of thing.

It made sense. I would still need to find some local writers to help me fill the editorial hole, but there were always plenty of wannabe writers dying to do things like concert, restaurant and movie reviews. See themselves in print. With only myself and a few freelancers we could surely make the thing as "local" as it needed to be. I could put an ad on Craigslist for contributors and I'd be buried in responses. There might not be much talent out there, but there were bound to be plenty of egos.

Tentatively, learning how to use InDesign by playing with it, I started putting together a "dummy paper," a model issue mostly filled with wire copy and photos, just to get an idea of what our product was going to look like and at the same time give Javon and me some practice at what we were expected to do.

Since I slept in my van, my bedroom went where I went. I could have parked right there in Glendale and stayed close to the task at hand, especially since I didn't know how many days it was going to take, though Abraham was antsy to get going.

But at the end of each day I drove back to the park. That's where my more-or-less "family" was anymore, and I wanted to keep Cyrus, Marianne, Larry and the rest of the gang up-to-date on what was going on with me. I didn't want to just disappear.

I was gaining weight. My pants were getting tight and I was developing a beer belly. Well, you drink as much beer as I was drinking in those days, you get a beer belly. But I was eating very little, practically living on beer. I had thought the two things would balance out. But no, I was clearly swelling up. Cyrus noticed it that night as we were sitting in the van, him with his usual sports drink and me with my usual MGD. He looked at my sneakers, which I always wore with white socks. "Your ankles are swollen," he said.

I looked down. "Damn, they are."

"I've heard of beer giving people a big stomach, even a big ass, but I never saw it give 'em fat ankles."

I remembered my father and his swollen ankles. My father had the edema which came with his congestive heart failure, which in turn had resulted from his fifty-odd years as a heavy smoker. His right ankle in particular, and his calf too, swelled up until they were as big around as a football. His doctor put him on Demadex to get rid of the excess fluid. That took the swelling down, but it also made him piss like an elephant.

Sometimes he wouldn't make it to the bathroom and would wet his pants, bringing on a volley of swearing.

"Maybe you should go to the doctor and have that looked at," Cyrus said.

"I will if it doesn't go away. Maybe I just need to lie down for a while."

The next morning the swelling in my ankles did appear to have gone down. There was still some swelling, but visibly less. I chalked it up to too much beer and not enough physical activity. I wasn't having any pain, so I went about my business.

I drove back over to Glendale to continue putting together *Zip.* (God, I hated that name! A newspaper that sounded like a brand of stain remover! Who could have come up with that? It couldn't have been Ron the Bouncer. He didn't strike me as having the imagination it would take name a puppy, much less a publication.)

Javon and I were busy at work in our back room a couple of afternoons later when the display advertising department of *Zip,* which so far anyway consisted of one guy named Byron whom I only saw once (he was tall, black and wore a leather overcoat) apparently came into the office. I say "apparently" because this time I didn't see him, I only heard him. Actually what I heard mostly was Ron, down the hall yelling. I heard little of what Byron said in reply, and as usual, not a word from Abraham, who spoke too softly to be heard at that distance.

Byron was not having much success selling ads. If Ron's audible meltdown was anything to judge by, he wasn't trying hard enough. Or maybe he wasn't devoting enough time to it. But sure enough, later that day when Javon had sent from his computer to mine a file containing display ad material which I had been instructed to work into the bottom of page three, (Abraham had bought us a power strip so we no longer had to share an electrical outlet) there were only two ads, one for a seafood restaurant and one for a gentlemen's club (strippers) somewhere on LaBrea

Ave. (Later I learned that the "gentlemen's club" was owned by a friend of Byron's.)

Of course a big ad for Abraham's valet parking business already took up half of page three. That had been Javon's first assignment. Nobody expected an advertising bonanza in our first issue, but this didn't look very good, and certainly didn't bode well for the second issue, if there were one. I was starting to sweat a little. I told Javon that I was going to the toilet, then slipped out the front door and down to my van at the curb to take an analeptic gulp or two from a pint of White Horse that I had stashed under the cot. As I passed Abraham's office, Ron was pacing up and down in front of Abraham's desk. Abraham, pencil in hand and concentrating on something in front of him, ignored Ron.

Sam came for a short visit in the next morning. He had personnel business with Abraham, but dropped in to say hello to me. It was the first time he and I had been in the office together. He came into the back room, greeted me and Javon, fixed himself a cup of coffee and sat in a chair beside my tiny desk.

"How's it going?" he asked.

"I'm not sure," I said. "I think I have the hang of this publishing program now, and Javon's doing an excellent job with the design, but Abraham wants to put out the first issue next Thursday and we don't have much to work with so far. I've put up a Craigslist ad for freelance writers, but so far I've only received three or four resumes. I haven't even had a chance to look at them yet."

"I'm afraid this is all something I don't know much about," Sam said, "but Abraham is no fool. I'm sure he knows what he's doing."

"Hey, Sam, let me ask you something," I said, lowering my voice. "Do you know who this guy Ron is? All I know about him is he's unpleasant and he's loud. But he seems to take orders from Abraham. Who the hell is he?"

"He's Abraham's junior partner. In the parking business. But he sticks his nose in everything. I guess he thinks Abraham's luck is his luck."

"Where does he come from? What does he do other than run errands for Abraham and yell a lot?"

"He's a commercial real-estate developer. Small-time, but I hear he does well enough."

"How did Abraham get involved with him?"

"That was before I got involved. But what Abraham told me was, when he was new in town and trying to get his valet parking business going, some of the bigger, already-established guys didn't want him moving in on their trade. They tried to keep him out."

"There's a *parking mafia*?"

"Nothing so bad as that. But they didn't make him feel welcome. Abraham, he's not a big guy, and he's not real brave either. Ron, he's been in a few bar fights and he's had a couple of scuffles with the law. I think Abraham keeps him around for safety. Like I said, Abraham's not a real brave guy. Smart, but not brave."

"So I was right. Ron is the muscle."

"In case Abraham needs it. So far he hasn't that I know of."

"He looks like he might keep a couple of baseball bats in his trunk."

Sam shrugged and smiled. "Who knows?"

Abraham hired a printer down in Orange County somewhere, and I learned that he was planning a press run of a thousand copies for the first issue. I also learned that in addition to selling advertising, Byron had also been charged with the responsibility of going around to local bars and restaurants and asking if we could place stacks of copies next to their cashier stands. Hopefully he was having more success with this than he was having in selling ads.

Meanwhile, I read over the resumes and samples of past work I had received so far, made some phone calls and lined up a couple of local freelance writers, although it was unlikely that I would have any local copy until the second issue. Both of the freelancers I took on were kids in their twenties. Abraham had authorized me to offer $75 for a 1,000-word piece.

For that kind of money, kids and retired old ladies were all I was going to get. But I couldn't be choosy. Not for now, anyway. I continued filling the first issue of *Zip* with fluff and photos from the AP.

Zero Hour was approaching for our first issue. I was still quite busy doing layout, and at Abraham's request I had written, for his by-line, a sort of Declaration of Principles, if you remember *Citizen Kane.* Well, yes, I'm joking about that. But he did ask me to write a short statement for page 2 of our first issue laying out who we were and what we planned to do for the community. Perhaps he wasn't just looking for a tax write-off after all.

Wednesday morning came around. We were scheduled to send the first issue to the printer the next day, which looked like it was going to be ten pages of fluff, but I had done the best I could with wire stuff. It was no kind of "local paper" yet and wouldn't be until I got some feet on the ground working up local stories. But Abraham was in a hurry to something on the street.

An eleventh-hour conference was called in Abraham's office. Javon, Byron, Ron and Abraham were already in there. I was making some last-second changes on page ten.

"Pat!" I heard Ron bellow. "Get in here! We're havin' a meeting!"

I really did not like Ron shouting commands at me. "Give me a second! I'll be right there!" I bent over in my chair to tighten the lace on one of my shoes and noticed that my ankles were swollen again.

Ten seconds went by. I heard Ron's voice again. "Pat! Get in here!"

I wanted to slip out to the van for a quick one before facing this, but there wasn't time and anyway, that would have required that I walk past Abraham's open office door. I went into his office and pulled up a chair in front of Abraham's desk. We were all huddled in a little circle. Crowded together. Not a good thing, not in an atmosphere like that. Still, Abraham sat behind his desk looking not a bit perturbed.

The distribution plan was discussed for the next day. Byron was going to drive around in his own van, dropping off piles of newspapers everywhere. Ron had something to say about that, to which I only half-listened. What business did he have even being here anyway, let alone acting like the boss? I was starting to get seriously annoyed, and it didn't help that he and I were sitting only about three feet apart.

Then there was some talk about future plans for display ads. Byron was going to need another hand, which meant paying out more money, etc. etc. What did any of this have to do with me? I just wanted to get back to finishing up the layout.

Finally Abraham looked at me and asked, "Is the paper ready to go to the printer?"

"Not quite," I said. "We're almost there. It just needs a few more tweaks, and I still have to write that open letter to the community that you asked me for. But I can do that in less than an hour."

Ron startled the company by slamming his fist down on Abraham's desk. "Goddammit, is it ready to go or not?" he demanded. "We're supposed to bring this thing out tomorrow, and you're all draggin' your fucking feet! You --" he pointed at Byron, "haven't sold shit as far as ads, and you --" he pointed at me, "you're takin' forever to get the fucking paper together! Is it ready to go or not?"

Shocked silence in the room for a second. Ron's outburst took everyone by surprise. Why didn't Abraham say something? This was his enterprise after all, not Ron's. What the hell was Ron so wound up about? He might have had some money sunk in this, but it was Abraham's paper. How the hell did I get myself into this again? It was supposed to help get me out of the park. But right now the park didn't look so bad. And I was pissed. I wanted a drink.

"Hey, I want to put out a good product, okay?" I said to Ron. "You think you can do better, you go back there and be the editor. Who the hell ARE you, anyway? This is Abraham's paper, not yours. I'm sick of your shit."

It was the "I'm sick of your shit" that did it. Ron, his face nearly purple, jumped up and came at me. I wasn't about to let him attack me sitting down. I jumped up too. In a fraction of a second we had our fingers around each other's throats. Quite a scene, when I think about it now: two guys in their early sixties, one of them with bad knees (me) and one of them with a big belly (Ron) trying to choke each other.

I heard Abraham shout "Ron!" but that was all I heard him say. He didn't say another word that I remember.

The whole thing was over in seconds. I was taller than Ron, but he outweighed me by at least fifty pounds. He jumped on me and wrapped his legs around my waist. A bar-fight tactic, probably, using his bulk to his advantage. It worked: with all that hillbilly weight suddenly on top of me, I went down like a house of cards. My knees buckled and I went to the carpet. Ron jumped on top of me again. No punches were thrown; it was just a wrestling match, but Ron's fifty pounds of gut gave him the advantage. Before Abraham, Byron and Javon could pull him off me, my face had been ground into the carpet, and Abraham's office had one of those outdoor rugs that are intended for patios – it was of some kind of plastic and it was very rough. As I got up from the floor, in the wall-mirror over Abraham's desk I could see that my face was lacerated. There was some blood.

I said the only word I could think of. "Shit."

"Yer *outta here*," Ron growled. It wasn't his place to fire me, it was Abraham's. But for some reason Abraham didn't say a word. Maybe he was just too shocked by this sudden display of violence to speak. I didn't care. I wanted no more of this Three Stooges movie. Without a glance at any of them, I walked out the door, got in my van and drove back to the park. Abraham owed me money, but we could sort that out later.

Back at the park I had a drink all right. I had plenty. Before it had been a celebration, Frankie and me killing a little Jack to celebrate my newspaper venture. Now it was just rage. Rage and disappointment. Was anything ever going to work out for me? I went to Crown, got a liter of

Scoresby, a bottle of club soda and some cheese and crackers for later. I sat in the van for a long time, staring out the hatch at the trees and the sunshine, listening to Dexter Gordon and Charles Mingus on the radio, coffee mug in hand, watching the level in the Scoresby bottle go down while keeping it tucked into one of my milk crates between drinks so no passing cop or nosy neighbor would see it. I got pretty drunk, and then Cyrus came around and saw how drunk I was and, although my memory of that night is fuzzy, I do remember giving Cyrus a sloppy-drunk account of what happened.

"Ever try to stand up with 250 pounds of redneck on top of you?" I asked him.

"Once, in jail. Only with me it was 300 pounds of nigger."

I felt better. Cyrus had experienced a similar humiliation.

Only I didn't really feel better. I remember Cyrus telling me I should sleep it off. I was sleepy so I didn't argue. I remember getting into my cot in the van, and I remember Cyrus setting up my director's chair on the grass across the sidewalk from the van (the hatch was still open) and sitting for a while. He took the radio out there with him; he also liked jazz. Probably he was sticking around to make sure I was safely asleep before closing up the van and leaving. He was my friend and would have done that. Marianne must have come and joined him because I heard them talking.

Later I knew what a good thing it was that they had been there that night. Because I remember sitting up and telling Cyrus that I didn't feel well. "Whatsamatter with you?" "I don't know. I just don't feel well. Something's wrong." "You want me to call 911?" A pause. "Yeah. I think you probably should," I said. "Okay, I'm dialing."

The ambulance came and I remember Cyrus and Marianne helping me to get out of the van and reach the ambulance. Then the EMTs took over and I didn't see Cyrus, or Marianne or anyone else except doctors and nurses for quite a while. I was to learn later that both of them, and a few others as well, saw me, but I didn't see them. Or if I did, I certainly didn't remember.

28

I had been carted off, or had dragged myself, to the ER perhaps a dozen times in my adult life. Except for one attack of diverticulitis, all of those visits had been booze-related. I would drink myself sick and then go to the ER. (And you don't know what nausea *is* until you've inflamed your liver with too much cheap booze.)

These adventures never got me into trouble with the law, believe it or not. The hospitals didn't report drunks to the police, not even if they've fallen off their scooters with a .14 blood alcohol level and been whisked away in an ambulance before the cops arrived. My point is that my hospital stays were generally of a few hours only. They would sober me up, patch me up, give me a 72-hour supply of Librium to get me started on my next promised dry-out and send me on my way. They kept me overnight for observation that one time I got banged up falling off my scooter, but usually it was in by nine, out by three.

Not this time.

I threw up in triage. That wasn't unusual. When you're virtually living on beer you throw up a lot. My mornings often began with the dry heaves. The triage nurses had seen this kind of shit a million times. They gave me a plastic bag and a wastebasket to lean over and waited until I was finished, then got on with processing me in.

They wheeled me in back and put me into a bed. I was given a hospital gown. So far the drill was familiar. A nurse came and took my temperature and blood pressure again, and someone from hospital admin came around to make sure I had health insurance (I did, Medi-Cal Molina.)

They took me down to X-ray and took pictures of my chest. They gave me an EKG. They took me back to my bed. I lay for a long time, staring at the ceiling and listening to the pleasantly hypnotic, stereophonic beep-beeping that goes on in an ER. I asked for a drink of water but was told that would have to wait until the doctor had seen me. I expected that.

I was quickly found to be dehydrated, another "as usual." They ran an I.V. into my arm and started dripping saline solution into me.

Then they moved me from the ER to a regular hospital room. That was my first signal that something out-of-the-ordinary was going on. They intended to keep me overnight at least.

About an hour later a doctor, a cardiologist, walked up to my bedside and stood there talking to me for a long time. As I said, I'd been in and out of the hospital quite a few times, almost always for alcohol-related problems. The hospital had my records of course, and this doctor, whose name I didn't bother to get, had obviously looked at mine. He confirmed that my swollen ankles indicated congestive heart failure. I told him that my father had had CHF in his last years, and his ankles, too had gotten quite swollen.

"But my father was a heavy cigarette smoker for most of his life," I said. "I figured that had to have something to do with it. He couldn't go half an hour without a cigarette. I smoke a pipe once or twice a day, but nothing like he did."

"Heavy drinking can do it too," the doctor said.

"I didn't know that. We all know booze is bad for your liver, but I never knew it was bad for your heart."

"Anything in excess is bad," he replied. "How many years have you been drinking?"

"Count backward to college. That would make it about forty I guess."

He tapped on his clipboard with a ballpoint pen. "If you don't quit drinking," he said, "you're gonna be dead in two years."

This prediction didn't really shock or surprise me as much as you might think. On some level, surely, I had seen something like this coming. Perhaps not stated quite this bluntly, but let's face it, I had been going to seed since Melissa died, and before that too. Her getting killed in that traffic accident coming back from San Diego had only speeded up the process. With the one break in the clouds that had been my engagement to her, my life had been pretty much *Stark Bewölkt* since Valerie had divorced me and then I'd gotten laid off my job back east, returning to California to live with my dad and younger sister, each of whom promptly died on me. I hadn't done much to improve things. The truth is that I never had been very proactive, as they say now. My tendency had always been to "ride with the tide" as the cliché goes, wait for the next big thing. Or the next small thing. Or the next lousy thing if that's what came along. When it happens, deal with it. That hokey Victorian poem our parents and grandparents had to learn in grammar school, *Invictus,* the one that ends with "I am the master of my fate: I am the captain of my soul" had not aged well. Nobody was the master of their fate or the captain of their soul anymore. Certainly not I.

I remember the doctor going away and I pondered the death-sentence he'd just handed me.

I hadn't completely sobered up yet; don't forget that I'd been drinking Scoresby-soda all that afternoon and right into the evening. I was still slightly buzzed but a headache was coming on. They gave me some Tylenol when I complained of the headache and they gave me something else too. In the hospital I never asked what they were giving me, I figured they were professionals who knew what they were doing and swallowed whatever was in the paper cup. But I was still just drunk enough to feel a little defiance, a little bravado in face of all this mortality. I asked myself, as though I were merely choosing between two movies on Netflix, "So what's it going to be? Two more years, or a few more years?" It didn't seem to make much difference. Now that the *Zip* venture had suddenly gone bust, I didn't have much on the horizon other than getting that steak dinner bet settled with

Cyrus. Beyond that I didn't have any plans. Of any kind. What was the point of more than another two years or so? I was past sixty. It was pretty obvious (or so it seemed then) that whatever I was going to do in this life, I'd already done it.

Of course I knew that all of this was bullshit even as I was thinking it while waiting for the pills to kick in. But it didn't matter, because these were the last thoughts, or at any rate the last lucid thoughts of any kind that I was going to have that month, or for a considerable chunk of the following month. It was the 29th of May when I checked into the ER. The next time I had even the vaguest idea of where I was, it was the 19th of June. For most of what I know about the three weeks that followed I have to rely upon witnesses.

After I got out of the hospital I re-read Saul Bellow's last novel, *Ravelstein,* a thinly-disguised memoir about his long friendship with the late Allan Bloom, an influential professor of political philosophy at the University of Chicago who late in life published an international bestseller about the failures of American higher education which stirred up a hornet's nest of outrage in academia. Bloom died of complications from AIDS in 1992, and asked Bellow to write his biography. The author decided to make it a novel instead of a bio. Not hard to understand, really: by the time Bloom died, Bellow was already 77 himself; probably he didn't want to undertake as big a project as a fully-researched biography. I had read Bloom's book too, but for now it was Bellow's novel that I wanted to read again. Why? Because his first-person narrator, a writer known only to the reader as "Chick," goes through an experience while hospitalized that's very similar to the one I had. Chick becomes deathly ill after eating a toxic fish during a vacation trip to the Caribbean. Whisked back to Boston and placed in the hospital, he goes through much of what I did. The first time I read the book, I more-or-less skipped over that part. This time I gave it my closest attention.

Bellow's protagonist and I both experienced vivid hallucinations during our hospital stays. Hallucinations are not dreams. Dreams, as Chick points out, "have an escape hatch." Hallucinations don't. You honestly feel that the experience you're having is reality, even if, later on, you know that it could not possibly have been.

I spoke with my doctor afterward, when I woke up, discovered that I had a tube up my nose and couldn't remember how it got there. He told me that what I had experienced was Wernicke-Korsakoff syndrome, an amnesia-like disorder resulting from a thiamine deficiency in the brain (Vitamin B1) not unusual among heavy boozers who are also malnourished, which heavy boozers often are and I certainly was. The alcohol exacerbates the lack of thiamine and what you get is often memory loss and "confabulation," that is, invented memories which are taken by the patient to be true. Self-created memory gap-fillers.

Chick has his visions under the influence of a drug called Versed (the author spells it "Verset.")

I think Bellow made a small mistake here, and not only with the spelling. Versed is usually given to people who are undergoing surgery, which Chick does not. But it does "suspend mental activity," as the author says. So does Atavan if they give you enough of it, and they did me. I was being hugely uncooperative, (so I hear) kicking, thrashing, trying to get out of bed, punching the nurses ... They dosed me with Librium at the start to get me through the alcohol withdrawal (again), but later, when I was resisting their attempts to help me with all the fervor of a Turkish prisoner of war, they started pumping me full of Atavan as an alternative to putting me in restraints, restraint being something that hospitals are increasingly reluctant to do anymore, since physically restrained patients have been known to injure themselves. (Lawsuits.)

For the next two and a half weeks they kept giving me more and more Atavan to keep me quiet. I'm told they moved me to the ICU when I started having trouble breathing. Betty, one of the ICU nurses I got to know during this ordeal, told me later that she had tried to get them to stop giving me all that Atavan. "Will you quit knocking this man out?" she demanded. But they had their reasons for keeping me under I guess. And I can remember some of the alternative realities I visited while I was down there.

In one of those realities, I was not in the hospital, but rather in some sort of youth hostel. Sun streamed through the window behind the wooden bunk in which I was lying. There was no door on my room; I could see out into the hall. I was being taken care of by a bunch of what seemed to me to be college kids. They came and went as I lay there with absolutely no awareness of time. I lay in my bunk in this wide-open cabin that looked like it might be part of a summer camp somewhere. Periodically I was pissing and shitting myself. My only awareness of that was when the kids would come and clean me up. I remember that, and I remember that every time they did, I apologized for having made this mess which they now had to deal with, and they, of course, being hospital professionals and not the college kids I was seeing, assured me over and over that this was quite routine and I shouldn't worry about it. I wondered who all these collegians were and why they kept wandering in and out of the wooden room in which I lay in my wooden bunk. At one point they moved me to another wooden room with another wooden bunk, and yes, I learned later that I had indeed been moved to Intensive Care. I was vaguely aware that I was being cared for, but I was experiencing a schizophrenic disconnect between the "I" and the "not-I," including my own body. It was as if I were watching a movie about myself being made.

I had other, similar episodes during this sojourn in my own private Twilight Zone, some of them involving people I knew, whom I believed to be there but who couldn't possibly have been, people I had known for a long time who lived thousands of miles away. I don't remember being visited by any of my dead, and I suppose I should be grateful for that, having heard plenty of those stories about people encountering their dead loved ones during near-death experiences.

But since I brought up the subject, this brief tour of duty I served in the chemical underworld did change my perspective on death itself, at least somewhat. I did almost die in that hospital bed. I had no idea I was dying; they told me about it later. They went so far as to seriously consider pulling the plug on me and letting me go. I suppose if they had known that I had a sister in Oklahoma City they would have contacted her. If I hadn't gone under so quickly, I would certainly have made sure that they had that information. I no longer had any relatives in the L.A. area, but if Jessie had known what was going on she would have flown out immediately. But I didn't tell her and nobody else did either because they weren't aware of her existence and I had checked in thinking that this was just another ER visit and I'd be back on the street in no time.

But coming as close to death as I did, I must say that I came away, not unafraid of death, but at least a little more sanguine about it. None of us knows what's over that particular precipice, but I came pretty close to it, and it wasn't all that bad. How hard can death be, after all? Everyone does it. Edith did it with relative ease. My father did it, and I had never thought of him as being especially adept at much of anything. I've reached that stage of life where people you know are vanishing all the time, and of course the older you get the faster it goes. Our own nonexistence is the bitterest pill any of us ever has to swallow, but consider: before you were born you didn't exist either. (Okay, I'm Catholic; before you were *conceived* you didn't exist either.)

Or maybe you did. My mother believed in reincarnation. She had not had an especially happy life and wanted to believe she was going to get another shot at it. My father lacked the imagination to believe in much of anything beyond his retirement pension. But who knew? There are a thousand different versions of this story. I'm no more qualified to make a decisive call on the question than anyone else is, but believe me, anyone who thinks they know the ultimate answer, from the pope to Christopher Hitchens, from the Dalai Lama to that guy in Okeechobee, FL whom I sometimes hear on the shortwave late at night shouting about the Book of Revelation, is a liar, or at best, seriously deluded. I'm leaving it there. For the moment I have other things to worry about, to which I must give precedence.

Actually my sister Jessie did show up. Here's how that happened (apparently): Cyrus and Marianne came to see me while I was out of town, so to speak. They were standing right by my bed and I didn't know they were there. I had some other mystery visitors, too, but of that in a moment. Cyrus knew that I had a sister in Oklahoma; I had even told him that her married name was Lawton. he guessed that she would want to know what was going on, did a name-search at the library, found a Jessica D. Lawton in Oklahoma City and made the call. The hospital informed Jessie when she got there that I had been close to death for a while, and if they had been able to contact her, they would have asked her for instructions. Fortunately by this time I was more-or-less out of danger.

When they finally quit billyclubbing me with the Atavan and I came slowly around to discover myself with a plastic tube up my nose, I noticed that on the table next to my bed was a get-well card which turned out to be from Jessie and which had scribbled on it a note saying that she was in town and had given the hospital instructions to call her on her cellphone as soon as I was awake, if not alert. Ready to be yelled at, in other words.

She couldn't yell too loudly; after all it was a hospital. Besides, I was still not quite all there. I'd been doped-up for two weeks, my weight was down to 173 and I must have looked a pathetic sight with that tube up my nose.

"Well. Thank God you decided to come back," she said.

"What's today?"

"The nineteenth."

"The nineteenth of what?"

"June."

"That means, that means I've been here..." I tried to remember. What day – what night – had I been brought in?

"According to Dr. Bodiford, you've been here exactly three weeks."

"Who's Dr. Bodiford?"

"She's your cardiologist. You never met her?"

"Not that I remember. What are you doing here? I mean, I'm glad you're here and all, but how did you know I was in the hospital?"

"Your friend Cyrus called me," she said. "I flew out the next day. I thought someone from the family should be around, just in case you decided to buy the farm, which you almost did, by the way. I haven't heard from you since you left for Turkey. You didn't even let me know when you came back. Why did you stay out of touch for so long? We had no idea what had happened to you."

"I guess I didn't think my current circumstances were anything to call up and brag about. I've been living in the park since I got back from Istanbul."

"So you decided to be a bum?"

"I decided I didn't want to be anything."

"Other than a drunk."

That called for a "fuck you." But I'd been putting up with this kind of crap from my sister for over fifty years. The older-sibling syndrome. Bossy old broad. I was used to it. I decided to let it go this time.

I looked out the window. "What's the weather like outside?"

But she wasn't ready to quit yet. "Warm. Stop trying to change the subject. You know I saw this coming. You've been drinking too much for years. You and Dad were drinking buddies. Then, well, you were all discombobulated over that woman –"

"Don't call her 'that woman.' We were going to be married."

"I'm sorry. But you know when I heard about it I had my doubts about you marrying someone over twenty years younger than you."

"It wasn't any of your business. And it doesn't matter now anyway. Drop it." She could tell from the tone of my voice that I meant it.

"I apologize." There was a chair next to the bed. She sat down "Bad choice of words. I know you were in love with her. You've been terribly lonely ever since Edith died. But back to what brought you here. You know you *have* to quit drinking now. There's no more 'if' about it. I had a long talk with Dr. Bodiford. You have a weak heart. Your heart's getting enough blood, but it's not pumping enough out. Your blood pressure is dangerously low. If you tried to stand up now, you'd probably pass out."

"I wouldn't be surprised, after lying on my back for three weeks."

"You shouldn't be surprised after drinking like a fish for over thirty years. You've done some serious damage to yourself. I don't think you're safe living alone, especially not in that van. I want you to think about coming back to Oklahoma City and living with me and Ray."

"That would probably last about two days and you know it. You and I can't be under the same roof."

"I don't want you going back to that park. I know you, as soon as you're feeling better you're going to start drinking again. Remember Edith? I think it's in our genes. Somehow it just skipped me."

"Don't you think that dodging the grim reaper just might throw the fear of God into a guy?"

"It might. But I'm not sure about you. You've always had the luck of the Irish and I think sometimes you count on it. It was with you this time, but I wouldn't count on it too often."

We went back and forth like that for a while. Moving in with Jessie made a kind of sense, I'll admit. She was all the family I had left. But setting aside the fact that she and I had always tended to butt heads, there was the question of what the hell was I going to do in Oklahoma City? Sit and listen to the wind come sweepin' down the plain? Aside from my sister I didn't know anybody there. At least out here on the coast I knew my way around, and I knew a handful of people, such as they were, such as we were. Jessie was surely right that I shouldn't go back to the park, but I'd never planned to stay there forever, I just hadn't thought much about where to go next. Maybe if I could find part-time work doing something, even if it were stocking shelves at WalMart, combined with my Social Security it would enable me to rent a room somewhere. It was high time to start thinking about such things anyway. Too bad that business with Abraham's fledgling paper hadn't worked out.

I put off my sister for the moment by telling her I would think about her offer.

My head slowly cleared from the drugs and I began feeling a little better. I felt better still when they took that stupid tube out of my nose and let me go back to eating normal food.

They kept me a few more days. Jessie was right; my blood pressure was so low I couldn't stand up to go to the bathroom without having to sit down immediately. I used a urinal instead. They adjusted my medications. No more Atavan anyway. Folic acid and Vitamin B supplements; Digoxin for my heart, a few other things – I was taking a cocktail of pills twice a day. I slowly got to where I could walk up and down the corridors a bit under supervision. My blood pressure gradually came back up.

They also gave me back my wallet and cellphone, which they had stashed away for safekeeping while I was off in La-La Land. I wanted to go home, even if home still only meant my van. I had a lot of things to figure out.

My sister had insisted that I had the luck of the Irish. Maybe I did, after all. Here's what happened.

A couple of days before I was discharged from the hospital the cellphone rang, and when I picked up and said hello, the first thing I heard was a cheerful "Patrick, my Patrick!"

"Sam!"

"How are you feeling, old friend?"

"I've had better days. What's going on with you? How did you find out I was here?"

"I talked to Bill, who referred to me to your other friend … Cyrus?"

"Jesus, Cyrus is becoming my press secretary! I hope he doesn't expect me to pay him for this."

Sam told me the reason he had called. Abraham had liked the first issue of *Zip*, was pleased at how many copies had circulated after they'd had it printed and distributed, and wanted to continue with the project. He liked my work as editor and wanted me to come back.

"I'm not coming back if that knuckle-dragging ape Ron is anywhere within a thousand feet of me," I said. "I don't want him anywhere near me. I don't want to talk to him, I don't want to see him, I don't want to smell him."

"No problem. Abraham fired Ron."

"I thought Ron was his partner, not his employee," I said.

"Ron is his partner in the parking business, not the newspaper. Abraham told Ron that from now on he is to stay away from the newspaper venture. He's out of it. He has nothing to do with it. If you come back to *Zip,* you will be reporting to no one except Abraham. From now on Ron is only allowed to aggravate me, and he was already doing that." Sam laughed.

So the *Zip* thing wasn't quite dead after all. Although it might not last more than one more issue, Abraham still owed me for the one issue I had already worked on, and if we got out a second issue he would owe me for two. I began to think, what the hell? If this thing lasts a few issues, I might make enough money working on Abraham's little paper to rent myself a room. Or at least trade up to a better van than the one I was living in now.

I called Abraham directly after talking with Sam, and he confirmed that yes, he did want to get started on another issue of the paper as soon as I was feeling strong enough to drive over to his place and discuss it. "There's no hurry; wait 'til you feel better," he said. I assumed that Sam, having spoken to Cyrus, knew of and had filled his cousin in on the reasons behind my hospital stay, but Abraham didn't mention them.

"And Sam was telling the truth? I won't see that Ron again?"

"I promise you will not see Ron again," Abraham said. "I was so angry at him after that incident between you two that I didn't speak to him for two days. I've told him not to come near my house unless it's something very urgent, and he will have no connection in the future with *Zip.*"

"You know, I still hate that name," I said. "Like I said before, *Zip* is a brand of high-end bicycle tire."

Abraham laughed. "Well, we can talk about that. If you think you have a better idea for a name, I'm willing to hear it."

By the time I was discharged from the hospital I was feeling stronger still, at least strong enough to walk away under my own power once they had wheelchaired me to the main exit (they insisted on that – insurance I guess.) But I was still too weak to walk all the way back to the park, where I had to go if only because that was where I had left my van. I called for a taxi. I could have called Uber or Lyft I know, but as a former cabbie I felt some loyalty to my former colleagues, who after all included Sam Fasil, To whom I owed a lot.

I couldn't find the key to my van, though. What the hell had I done with it? The last time I was in the van was the night they took me to the hospital. I must have had the key then. Nothing panics me like losing my keys. During the cab ride I furiously dialed Cyrus' cell number, and thank God, he answered.

"Cyrus, do you have my truck keys?" I asked. "I was pretty wasted the night the paramedics picked me up. *Please* tell me you have them."

"No, I don't have them," was the answer.

"Oh, shit!" Waves of panic.

"Relax, relax, I'm just messing with you. Bill has your keys. I took them the night you left, but Bill offered to move your van around while you were gone, you know, like he did when you were in detox, so it wouldn't get ticketed or towed. He has them. He also says your van needs gas. Are you out of the hospital?"

"Yeah, I'm on my way back to the park now."

"Well, see you when you get here." He was as nonchalant as if I'd just gone down to Crown Liquor for a beer, something I reminded myself I could not do anymore.

I had the driver drop me off right next to my van on Davidson Street. It looked the same, same dents, same cracked driver's-side rearview mirror from that day when I'd hit a tree try to scrooch past a double-parked SUV around the corner near the liquor store. I don't know why I would have thought it might look any different. Now I had to go find Cyrus or Bill or both of them and get my keys back.

But before I had a chance to do that, I spied a figure, obviously female, lying face-down on the grass over near the tweaker tree. The tweaking crowd had pretty much scattered; they seldom gathered here anymore, and when they did, it was in smaller numbers. So who was this? Out of curiosity I walked over to the supine figure, whose face was turned away from me on the lawn. Whoever it was, she wore a pink tank-top, faded jeans and beat-up Nikes. I went around quietly just to see if it was anyone I knew.

It was Jennifer, Cage's mother, the feisty gal who had once told me she was going to kick my ass if she ever caught me climbing on my motor scooter drunk again. I hadn't seen her in at least a year. A tweaker herself, she had once been a familiar figure near this tree. But I'd heard she had gotten a Section 08 apartment. So what was she doing back here?

I squeezed the toe of her sneaker. "Well, hello, stranger," I said.

She stirred, sat up, shook her head, yawned, recognized me and smiled. "Oh, hi, Pat!"

"Look what the cat dragged in."

We shared a hug and a quick kiss.

"Where have you been?" I asked.

"I had a place. I lost it," she said.

"I heard you had a place. Why'd you lose it?"

"My son, of course. What have you been up to?"

"Well, I just got out of the hospital."

"What was the matter? How long were you there?"

I told her the story. Then she hugged me again and said, "You stupid asshole. I'm so glad you're not dead."

"Well, I am too, I guess."

Then she told me her story, which was that while she had been down in Temecula for a week staying at her sister's, Cage and his friends had gotten into her place and trashed it. They were there over a weekend, doing drugs of course. Making noise. She didn't say whether Chantal were among them, but someone called the cops. The result was that Jennifer had gotten kicked out, even though technically (if she were telling me the truth, anyway), she wasn't there.

"So...you're back on the street now?" I asked.

"Yeah. For now."

"Where are you staying?"

"No place."

That probably meant the alley. There was an alley just the other side of McKinley Avenue where homeless people often camped overnight because the buildings were businesses and apartments and they had rear awnings and parking lots. Good places to sleep if you stayed quiet and out of sight. The alley was where Yvonne had caught Chantal and Cage *in flagrante delicto* that one night that I'd heard about.

"Listen," I said. "If the alley is where you're where you're sleeping, you don't have to stay there. I got rid of the scooter – you remember my scooter – a long time ago. That van over there," – I pointed – "It's mine. There's room for two. Well, sort of. I mean, it'll be a tight squeeze, but you'll be sheltered if it rains, and I promise you won't be robbed, as you probably would be in the alley."

"I have been robbed in the alley," she said. "Who hasn't?"

"Well, there you go. And I promise you I'm too weak for any funny business."

She liked that. She demurred for a moment, then gave me another little kiss. She was being flirty now, and I liked it. Jennifer had once been beautiful. You could see it. She was kind of beat-up these days; apart from just aging like the rest of us, the tweaking and the hard times and the travails with her ne'er-do-well son had taken their toll. But for a woman the same age as I, she wasn't bad-looking. She still had pretty blue eyes, and even in my diminished post-hospital condition, I couldn't keep my own eyes from straying toward the freckled cleavage that her pink tank-top shared with the world.

I had to go find Cyrus, or Bill, or both of them, to get my keys back. Jennifer tagged along. I guessed she didn't have anything else to do. Cyrus and, when we tracked him down, Bill, were both very happy to see her again.

29

The doctors and nurses at the hospital were in agreement with my sister that I should not return to Aurora Park. It was the same message you hear in every rehab program in the world: "You have to stay away from all the people you used to hang out with. If you go back to your old haunts, you're just going to start using (or drinking) again," etc. etc.

Easy for them to say; they all had homes. Same with the members of the HOT team, who told me the same thing. It's easy to tell someone what to do or not do when you already enjoy an advantage they don't have. I've already mentioned that I was not keen on the idea of moving in with my sister in Oklahoma City. I had to decide what my next move was going to be, but for the moment my van and I were still parked on Davidson St.

Now that Jennifer had squeezed herself into my van at night (I offered her the cot, but she wouldn't hear of it because I was still convalescing) it was natural, once I was feeling stronger, to re-open Café Patrick in the mornings. We had to have coffee anyway. I would set up the Coleman stove on the sidewalk and she would go fill the coffeepot with water at the drinking fountain. Cyrus, Marianne, Larry, Bridget and sometimes even Frankie would come around to join us for morning coffee.

I had detoxed in the hospital, so I wasn't getting the shakes anymore. There was no need to go for a sunrise beer or two if I could just stay firm about not doing it. And that was actually easier than I might have thought, not surprising I suppose, considering my experiences of the past month and what I had learned about my own beat-up heart.

"So, you two have set up housekeeping?" Cyrus asked as he poured coffee for himself and Marianne, who promptly put five or six sugars in hers. "I saw Jennifer filling up the coffeepot."

"We got married last night," I said. "Ed performed the ceremony."

Jennifer gave me a playful whack on the side of the head with the palm of her hand. "Don't get any gossip started, Pat. That's all I need around here."

"I think you two would make a cute couple," Cyrus said.

"Shut up, Cyrus," said Jennifer. But she patted my shoulder as she said this, which was friendlier than whacking my head anyway.

"Where is Ed?" Marianne asked.

"Over there, sleeping it off in his car as usual," Cyrus said. "Well," he sat in the hatch of the van, "I got some news. They found a place for me and my girls. At least two of them anyway. The older ones. The small ones'll stay with their foster parents."

"So what will you do, Marianne?"

"Go back to Long Beach, for now, I guess."

"It's not a done deal yet," Cyrus said. "I haven't even seen the place. It's in Tujunga. But don't that let get around. I don't want everybody knowing where I am. But if it works out, you're gonna owe me that steak dinner, homie."

"Looks like it. I'm glad we agreed on Denny's instead of the Black Angus," I said. I paused, then I said, "I'll tell you what. If you accept this place, I'll move you and your stuff up there. I know you got some stuff in storage. My moving services are cheap, too. It'll only cost you one steak dinner at Denny's."

Cyrus sipped his coffee. "You asshole," he said. "I knew you'd figure out a way not to pay up."

"When it comes to figuring out ways not to pay up," I said, I had a good teacher."

I couldn't resist laughing. But then I said, "Oh, come on, I'm just kidding! I'll pay over the bet. But you know there's another way I could have weaseled out of it. Haul myself and my van, right now, up to Glendale, stake out a chunk of curb in front of Abraham's place, declare that my new home and escape on a technicality."

"Abraham –" Cyrus had either forgotten the name or I hadn't mentioned it to him.

"Abraham Negassi, the valet parking mogul starting his own newspaper."

"The place you got your ass kicked the day they took you to the hospital! I thought they fired you. That's why you was getting drunk that night."

"Yeah. Well, the firing – or quitting – was never formal. No words were exchanged that day, I just walked off and assumed it was over. But I talked to him from my hospital bed. He wants me to stay on as editor. I don't know if anything's going to come of it, it's a slender thread to make plans on, but it's a 'next thing' of some kind."

"It sure enough is," Cyrus said.

I had been joking about the change of venue, But the more I thought about it the more sense it made. My old gang in the park was dwindling now; there was less and less to keep me around. Not that there had been that much to begin with. Sandy had been at Bayview Towers for quite a while now. Cyrus was getting ready to leave. Marianne would go back to Long Beach. Yvonne had been gone for more than a year. Chantal wasn't around anymore. Larry was still there, sort of, but he drifted in and out the way Jennifer used to when she was following the drugs. Bill spent most of his time in the library reading the Bible. Ed had never been much company, in fact now that Chantal was no longer there for him to moon over, he wasn't even a source of amusement.

Jennifer and I had a serious discussion later that day, sitting on the same bench over near the library where I had met Sandy on my first day at the park.

I suggested to Jennifer that we might pool our resources and do something different from what we had both been doing up until that moment. She was on disability and I was on Social Security now. I got out a pencil and a piece of paper and figured out that between her SSI and my monthly check we would have about $2,200 a month coming in. Then there was whatever I might make working for *Zip* or *Zap* or *The Daily Planet* or whatever the hell else we might end up calling Abraham's weekly gazette. Of course that was tenuous and might end at any moment, but still, it was clear that Jennifer and I could manage better together than either of us could alone. And if Abraham's paper folded, as it probably would, I could find something else to do, even at my age. I'd already thought about stocking shelves at WalMart while I was lying in the hospital.

"Maybe we couldn't afford an apartment, but we might be able to share a room," I said.

"And what makes you think I'd want to share a room with with you?" Jennifer grinned.

Her options at this point weren't much broader than mine and we both knew it. But clearly she intended to make this a little game. She wanted to be persuaded. I was willing to play along.

"You're already sharing a van with me," I said. "Beats the alley, doesn't it?"

"You have me there. Still, I'm not sure."

"Not sure about what? Whether my intentions are honorable? Look, Jennifer, I'm sixty-two years old. I hardly think I'm going to jump your bones."

"You wouldn't even be tempted."

"At my age? Come on."

"Stop harping on your damn age."

"*Our* damn age."

She stood up and placed her fists on her hips. "You really know how to talk to a woman, don't you?" she said with an exasperated grin.

"Well, I'm out of practice."

"You're an attractive man, Pat."

"I am not. I'm an old drunk."

"So am I. You don't think two old drunks could end up in a relationship? It's happened before."

"I don't think that should be our main topic right now."

She sat back down. "So you don't find me attractive." She affected a pout, but I could see she was messing with me.

I was being flirted with again. Second time in two days. And yes, recently near-death or not, the old carcass was responding as best as it could. Aided by digoxin, my heart was still doing its job.

"I didn't say that. Look, can we stay on subject? I'm talking about getting us both out of this park. Now, we might be able to rent a room together, or with what Abraham's hopefully going to be paying me, I might be able to at least get a better van than that one. One with two bunks, maybe a kitchenette. You could have your own bed. We'd be the damndest pair of gypsies you ever saw."

"And you would promise to stay out of my bed, of course."

"Of course. Easily done. I promise."

I had a feeling that that wasn't exactly what she wanted to hear, so I added, "But you know the old saw about promises, how they were made to be broken."

"I don't want you to promise, you dumb shit." She leaned against me on the bench and put her head on my shoulder for a moment. "You'd better not promise."

I liked that.

I had finally had a chance to meet Dr. Jane Bodiford, the young cardiologist who looked after me during my long hiatus in the parallel universe, when I came out of the drugs and could sit up again. I liked her right away, and asked if I might make her my regular cardiologist. I had no regular doctor of any kind up until then. She was only at the hospital two afternoons a week, her regular office was at the South Bay Heart Health

Clinic, a three-story office building past which I had driven many times. It was only about half a mile west of the park.

Dr. Bodiford said she wanted to see me for a follow-up visit a week after my discharge. I had an appointment on Tuesday. I was continuing to feel a little stronger every day, and since the day of my appointment was a beautiful one anyway, I decided to take a chance, leave the van parked where it was and walk to the clinic. Or try to. The 704 bus went that way; if I started to feel too pooped I could always hop on the bus. Jennifer had gone off someplace, I hoped not to a drug connection. I had already spoken with Abraham again and had an appointment with him up in Glendale to discuss the next issue of whatever-we-ended-up-calling-it the next afternoon.

Now, the coincidence that follows is going to make the reader roll his or her eyeballs. "He made that up," he or she will be thinking. "That could not possibly have happened."

I swear it did. I wouldn't dare make something like this up.

About halfway between the park and the clinic, following the route of the 704, I started to feel a bit winded. Perhaps a half-mile walk was something I wasn't ready for yet. Maybe I should go to the CVS Pharmacy and invest in one of those aluminum canes. At least for temporary. For the moment, however, all I wanted was a place to sit down and catch my breath. I began looking for the next bus bench.

I spotted one about half a block ahead of me. A lone figure was seated there. As I drew nearer, the figure grew more familiar.

Yes, it was. Bob the Bum. I hadn't seen him since that morning when they hauled his sprinkler-soaked ass out of the bushes and took him away.

I stood in front of him. Beside him on the bench were a half-eaten tuna salad sandwich from 7-Eleven, still in its wrapper, and a 32 oz. Big Gulp.

"Well, hello, Robert," I said. "We haven't seen you in ages. Where have you been keeping yourself?"

It did not not surprise me that when he looked up and saw me, it took him two or three seconds to remember who I was. Actually I was surprised that he remembered me at all. But he did.

"Uh...uh...Pat, right?"

"That's right. How've you been? *Where* have you been?"

He stroked that dirty long beard of his for a moment, composing his answer.

"I was in a house," he said. "I was in a house with some other people."

"Where was it? Do you remember?"

More beard-stroking. "South Gate? Yeah, South Gate. But I got kicked out."

"What for?"

Another pause. "They...caught me pissin' on the wall. I had to take a piss and somebody was in the bathroom. So I went outside and pissed on the wall. They kicked me out for that!"

"It does seem a little extreme." I thought about how many times we in the park had, all of us, pissed on walls. And in bushes. And in the corners of parking garages. And behind Crown Liquor.

He warmed up to his tale of outrage. "It was nighttime! They kicked me out for pissing on the wall at night! Nobody could even see me except one guy who happened to be standing in the kitchen, looking out the window. That was bullshit. They just wanted me out of there."

"You're on Social Security now," I said. "By God, I should remember if anybody does, after what we went through to get you and your first check united with each other. Can't you pay for a room somewhere?"

"I...I don't remember where the bank is."

He was right where we'd left him last year. He had a little money now, but he couldn't remember where it was.

"Where are you going?" I asked him. "You're waiting for the bus, where are you on your way to?"

"HHSA. I gotta renew my EBT."

"Life on the street's just a big bowl of alphabet soup, isn't it?"

"What?"

"Nothing. Listen, you need to go to the Social Security office. They'll know where your bank is. We set up direct deposit, remember?"

"Social Security office."

"Yeah. Go to the SSA. Take the 704 bus and switch to the 929 at Grainger Ave. It's right behind a 7-Eleven at Grainger and Hayworth. Show 'em your card, and ask what bank your payments are going into and where it is."

I knew all of this was going to be too much for him to remember, and I didn't have anything to write it down with.

"Look, never mind all that," I said. "When you get to HHSA this morning, ask them for directions to the Social Security office. And make sure they write them down."

"Okay."

I looked at my watch. "Sorry, I gotta go. I have a medical appointment. Look, don't forget to ask at HHS, when you get there, how to get to the Social Security office. Got that?"

He gave me the old, familiar Bob-the-Bum-bewildered-squint. "Okay," he said again.

After sitting on that bench with Bob for a couple of minutes, I felt a little stronger and decided I probably could walk the rest of the way to the clinic. Besides, I didn't want to get on the bus with Bob and run the risk of having to continue sitting next to him. I walked a little farther down the street, then I heard the bus pull up behind me. I turned and watched Bob climb aboard. The door closed, the bus pulled away from the curb and passed me as it got underway again. Bob was still looking for a seat.

There's only so much anyone can do.

As I approached the next intersection I saw Terry, Frankie's dad. Not such a coincidence this time; we parkies often spotted each other on the street. There was no mistaking Terry, with that scarecrow gait of his, slightly stooped forward with his hands behind his back, that Wyatt

Earp mustache he always wore, his glasses and his perennial Dodgers cap. According to my watch it was almost straight-up eleven O'clock. I knew exactly where Terry was going: where he always went around 11 a.m. – to the Salvation Army for the free lunch. I had tagged along with him there once. I didn't care especially for the food or the singing and decided it wasn't worth going again. But with Terry it was a daily ritual.

He spied me at the same moment I saw him. We waved to each other, then he continued on his way south and I continued on my way west.

I would tell what was left of the gang back at the park that I had seen Bob the Bum at the bus stop. Jennifer probably wouldn't remember him, but Cyrus surely would. After all it was Cyrus who had nicknamed him "Bob the Bum" in the first place. I couldn't wait to tell him all about it. Kicked out of a safe house for pissing on an outside wall. Cyrus was going to love that.

2020

CPSIA information can be obtained
at www.ICGtesting.com
Printed in the USA
LVHW090346170720
660942LV00001B/59